ALSO BY RONI LOREN

The Ones Who Got Away
The Ones Who Got Away
The One You Can't Forget
The One You Fight For
The One for You

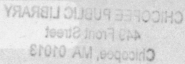
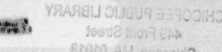

The One for You

RONI LOREN

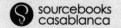
sourcebooks
casablanca

Published by Sourcebooks Casablanca, an imprint of Sourcebooks
P.O. Box 4410, Naperville, Illinois 60567-4410
(630) 961-3900
sourcebooks.com

Printed and bound in Canada.
MBP 10 9 8 7 6 5 4 3 2 1

prologue

2005

ASHTON ISAACS HAD A HARD-ON IN THE BACK ROW OF The Stuffed Shelf's children's section, and Kincaid Breslin had never been more delighted. Ash didn't see her standing there as she pressed her lips together to keep from laughing since he was currently reclined in a bright-green beanbag chair half inside the tent they'd set up as a reading nook for the kids. The main lights of the store had been turned off, but the two lamps in the children's area still threw off enough of a warm glow for Kincaid to figure out what was going on. Ash's face was hidden behind his floppy dark hair and the novel he was reading, but he was far from relaxed. Besides the obvious situation in his pants, his beat-up Chuck Taylors were bouncing like he was nervous—or anticipating something.

Kincaid grinned, enjoying the sight of her normally staid friend looking so undone. She tucked her hands into the back pockets of her jeans. "Got to the good part, huh?"

Ash jolted so hard that he thumped his head on the top of the tent and almost collapsed the whole thing. "What the—"

Kincaid watched with amusement as he scrambled to extract himself from the too-small-for-a-seventeen-year-old reading nook, all long limbs and jabbing elbows. Shelves rattled behind him.

"Dammit, KC," he said, getting to his feet and quickly turning his back to her as he pretended to check the state of the tent. "What the hell are you doing, sneaking up like that? You left, like, half an hour ago."

She rocked onto her toes, trying to get her eyes on the book he'd been reading. "I forgot my backpack. I thought I left it over here. I didn't mean to…interrupt."

"Well, damn, give a guy some warning. What if I'd thought you were an intruder? I could've hurt you." He shoved the book he'd been reading onto a shelf next to *Don't Let the Pigeon Drive the Bus*. The cartoon pigeon on the cover looked scandalized.

"How? By throwing a dirty book at me?" she teased, stepping closer.

"It's not a—"

Kincaid snagged the paperback from the shelf and flipped it over to get a closer look at the cover. She smiled at the sexy, open-shirted duke on the cover. "Wow, look at you. Mr. Thriller Reader is branching out. The cover got ya, huh? I don't blame you. Look at those abs. Ooh-la-la."

Ash grunted, keeping his back to her. "I didn't choose it for the abs. We're supposed to read as much stock as we can so that we can make accurate recommendations. These are popular. I'm being a diligent employee."

Kincaid nodded. "Of course. Ash Isaacs working overtime. Such a model employee. Reading naughty scenes and getting all hot and bothered in the kids' section. Someone give this boy a raise."

Ash groaned and finally turned around to face her, blue eyes wary behind his dark-rimmed glasses. "You're like a dog with a bone, Breslin. You know, a normal person would just politely ignore the situation and change the subject."

She smirked. "Good thing I'm not normal. And are you really going to throw the word *bone* out there right now? Also, did you just call your junk a situation? Because you're making this too easy." She eyed the edge of the book to see where the space between pages was obvious and opened to the part he'd been reading. "So what turns the book snob's crank?" She started reading. "'William ran his tongue along Isabella's sweet—'"

Ashton plucked the book from her hands before she could get to the scandalous part and tucked it under his arm. "You're not old enough for this one, KC." He grabbed the pigeon book and handed it to her. "This may be more your speed. That pigeon is nothing but trouble. You'll have a lot in common."

Kincaid laughed and put the children's book back on the shelf. Ash was only three months older than she was, and she'd bet every penny of her meager savings that she was more experienced. Ash hadn't had a girlfriend in the three years since they'd worked together at the bookstore, and before that, he'd only briefly dated Harmony Johnson freshman year. And *dating* seemed like a strong word for what that had involved—a few trips to the movies and the homecoming dance.

Since then, anytime a girl came in the store and flirted with him, Ash seemed damn oblivious. Kincaid knew that Ash was too focused on getting a scholarship and getting out of this town to get distracted with a relationship, but her boyfriend, Graham, had declared that a ridiculous tactic. *Why can't you study hard and have fun at the same time?* he'd say.

But Kincaid understood Ash's drive in a way Graham couldn't. Graham's parents owned the bookstore and had the money to send Graham to whatever school he wanted. Ash's parents had more than she and her mom had, which wasn't saying much, but his dad, the high school football coach, had too many strings attached to the money. Ash only got college money if he majored in something practical at the University of Texas, his dad's alma mater. Ash wasn't much for practical. He had big dreams of writing and travel and didn't want to get stuck here. So just like her, if he wanted something beyond a Long Acre High School diploma, he was going to have to figure a way out on his own.

"Come on, don't lie," she said with a smile. "You're just taking the book back because as soon as I leave, you're going to finish it. You're dying to know what William is going to do with his tongue." She reached for the book again. "Heck, I'm dying to know."

He batted her hand away. "Nope."

She caught sight of a number on the spine of the book. "Hold up. This is the *fifth* in a series?" Her grin went wider, delight filling her like fizzy soda. "Which means you've read four of these already because my buddy Ash would never dare read a book series out of order. Sacrilege. Have you taken good notes? Scribbled naughty marginalia? Highlighted? Tell me everything."

He groaned. "Why do I allow you to be my friend again?"

She laughed and batted her eyelashes dramatically. "Because you can't help but love me?"

"I can't escape you," he said with a snort, but she didn't miss the flash of friendly affection in his eyes. "But find your own smut. This is mine. And marginalia? Someone's been using that Word-A-Day calendar I gave her for Christmas."

She gave him a narrow-eyed look. "I know lots of big words. Like 'pretentious.' 'Judgmental.' 'Self-important.'"

He nodded. "Touché."

"You know, if you'd let me set you up with one of my friends, you could have the chance to experience your own smut." She frowned and shook her head. "Wait, that makes my friends sound like hookers. You know what I mean. You could get out of this bookstore and hang out with a *real, live girl*." She spread her hands out as if she could conjure him up a girl out of thin air. "Prom is coming up. You need a date. Groundwork needs to be laid!"

Ash's gaze met hers, his lips hitching at one corner. "Sounds like you're just trying to get *me* laid."

Kincaid made a you-said-it-I-didn't face. "Would that be so terrible?"

"Did I miss the part where you're actually a dude, and we're suddenly in a locker room?" He puffed out his chest and deepened his voice. "Bro, you need to find some hot chick and drain the snake."

She cringed. "Oh my God, gross, no one says 'drain the snake.'" She waved her hand between them, trying to clear that disgusting image from her mind.

"Hit that?" he suggested.

"This further proves that we need to get you out of this bookstore. You don't even know how to *speak*."

"Says the girl who pronounces the word 'fire' with one syllable and 'fair' with two," he said, overexaggerating the East Texas accent that had followed her from childhood.

"Shut up. And for the record, I would be an awesome dude who would never dare use the words 'bro' or 'hit that,' thank you very much." She nudged his shoulder. "I just want you to come to prom with me and Graham. Isn't there *someone* you want to go with? You've got to like somebody at school."

Ash's expression flattened, and his gaze slid away. "Not really."

"Not *really*?" A shimmer of excitement moved through her, her internal sensors going off. "That's not a no. Oh my God, you *do* have someone. Ash has a secret crush!" She stepped closer to catch his eye. "I must know. You must tell me right now. I promise I'll keep it a secret."

Ash let out a long-suffering sigh. "You are relentless."

She nodded. "Yep. It's one of my finest qualities."

He shook his head. "Too bad. It's not going to work. I'm not telling you because (a) you're physically unable to contain a secret. You would hurt yourself trying to do that, and I don't want that on my conscience. And (b) this person is unattainable, so it doesn't matter anyway."

"No one is unattainable," she said resolutely. "Have

you seen who I'm dating? Who would've ever thought *the* Graham Lowell would be dating the daughter of a woman whose best skill is getting her rent paid by a different guy every month?"

Ash frowned and adjusted his glasses. "Don't do that."

"Do what?"

"Don't talk like Graham's above you just because he's got money and parents who actually know how to be decent humans. No offense to him, but that's a life lottery situation, not an accomplishment. And you have no idea how badly he wanted to impress you when he was trying to get you to go out with him. You were out of his league, not the other way around."

Kincaid's chest squeezed at the fervor in his voice. "Aww, Ash, you do love me."

He rolled his eyes.

"But see, then maybe your secret crush isn't so unattainable either," she went on. "Maybe you should try Graham's method and write her some romantic letters. I think I was half in love with the guy before I even said yes to a date. After those notes he left me, how could I resist?"

Ash's expression soured at that. "I don't think love letters would work in this case."

"Why not?"

He put his hand on her shoulder, giving her the this-conversation-is-over look. "Because this girl is not an option. She's with someone else."

Kincaid's lips parted, the words hanging between them. Her mind started to scan girls who were in relationships at school, but before she could process all that, the door in the back creaked, and heavy footsteps sounded on the worn wooden floors of the shop. "What's taking so long, babe?"

Ash quickly removed his hand from her shoulder and took a big step back, almost stumbling backward over the top of the kiddie tent.

Kincaid turned her head as Graham's voice drifted over the shelves, and the floorboards squeaked with her boyfriend's approach. "In the kids' section," she called out. "Ash needed help getting some inappropriate material off the shelves."

Graham appeared at the end of the aisle, all blond hair and big, brown eyes, his smile going warm and wide at the sight of her. "There's my girl."

Kincaid's stomach did a little flip as Graham walked over and gathered her to his side, kissing the top of her head. She'd dated a lot of guys throughout high school, usually briefly and disastrously, but she'd never had a boyfriend like Graham. One who wasn't shy about giving affection or declaring sappy things about her. One who *loved* her. Like for real. Not just because she had big boobs and was on the dance team.

"Hey, baby," she said, leaning into his side. "Sorry. I was about to head back out. But—"

"You started rambling on and completely forgot that I was sitting out in the cold," he said knowingly. "And now we're going to be even later. Kincaiditis strikes again."

He delivered the words with a light tone, like he was teasing, but they still made her wince inwardly. Lately Graham had been on her about how flighty she could be. She was trying to be better, but…well, she really did have *Ooh, squirrel!* syndrome pretty badly. "I'm sorry. I didn't mean—"

"It was my fault," Ash said, cutting her off. "I needed her help. I didn't realize you were waiting outside."

"Haven't you spent enough time with my girl already today, Isaacs?" Graham teased. "If it were anyone but you, I think I'd have to be jealous."

Ash gave him a droll look. "Gee, thanks, man. Glad I'm so nonthreatening."

Graham chuckled and gently punched Ash's arm. "Aww, don't get all offended. You know what I mean."

Kincaid leaned into Graham, inhaling deeply. His hair smelled like the tea tree shampoo she'd bought for him. "Yeah, he's like the annoying brother I never had."

Ash made some sound she translated as sarcasm as he turned away to straighten the area he'd been reading in.

Graham glanced over at Kincaid. "So, did you find your purse?"

She wrinkled her nose. "Oops, I sort of forgot to keep looking when I ran into Ash."

Graham gave her an exasperated look, as though she were an adorable puppy that had peed on the carpet *again*. "Babe—"

She pushed up on her toes, kissing him and cutting him off. "Two seconds. I promise."

He tugged her ponytail. "You're lucky I love you so much that I think this is cute."

She grinned, his words moving over her like a summer breeze. For so long when guys looked at her, they saw only one thing—a party girl to get in bed. Like mother, like daughter, right? Graham didn't look at her that way. He didn't see where she came from or who her family was. He didn't see her as an easy score. Sure, he appreciated how she looked, but he saw so much deeper than that layer. He loved who she was and wanted to help make her even better.

The guy who'd once seemed so out of her league— student council vice president, son of a well-known family in town, guy on his way to big things—*loved* her. Loved her so much that he was trying to figure out a way to take her with him to college. Believed in their relationship so much that he was going to ask his family to help her out with costs to attend the community college near Graham so they could be together. Graham was the real deal. Somehow, some way, despite her mom's repeated declarations that all men were selfish scumbags who were only out for one thing, Kincaid had found herself in a real love story.

"Let's go find your purse." Graham stepped over and bumped fists with Ash. "And get out of here, man. I know my parents aren't paying you overtime."

"On my way," Ash said, tucking the book into the back waistband of his jeans.

Kincaid smiled his way. "And let me know what William decides to do with that tongue."

Ash kept a stoic expression, but his neck flushed bright red.

"Huh?" Graham asked.

"Nothing, baby," she said cheerfully. "Just messing with my annoying brother."

As soon as Graham's back was turned to head down the aisle, Ash flipped Kincaid the bird.

She smooched the air silently and whispered. "Love you, too."

When she was a few steps away, following Graham, Ash said something under his breath that sounded like *love you more*, but it was too low for her to hear it clearly. She turned, surprised. "What?"

Ash crossed his arms, and his gaze shifted away. "I said, see you tomorrow."

She frowned. "Oh."

She didn't like the weird look on his face and almost asked more questions, but Graham was already far ahead of her, and she didn't want to make him wait even longer. The guy was sweet as pie but had a pouty temper when he got annoyed. She didn't want to ruin the night with a bad mood.

So she turned and followed Graham.

She dismissed what she thought she'd heard and the odd feeling it had stirred within her.

She left Ash behind.

chapter
ONE

NOW

KINCAID BRESLIN WAS THE GIRL WHO WAS SUPPOSED TO DIE first in the horror movie. In high school, it had been a running joke among her friends during their annual Halloween marathon of scary movies that she'd be the first character topless, screaming, and running for her life.

She was the dance team captain. The girl with the superstar boyfriend. The nonvirgin. All those things spelled *dead* in those classic eighties horror movies. Her character probably wouldn't have been on-screen long enough to even get a name. In the credits, she'd be listed as Blond Cheerleader #1 or Hysterical Girl #2. But her friends had been wrong. When Kincaid's life had turned into an actual horror movie, she'd somehow managed to get out alive. Most of those friends hadn't. Real life didn't follow movie rules.

So you would think after actually surviving what she had, she'd be extra-vigilant about putting herself in any situation that resembled a scary movie ever again. But as she stared up at the rambling farmhouse that could star in the next teen slasher film, she fell head over heels in love.

"Holy shit," her friend Liv said from next to her, camera clutched in her hands. "Are we supposed to go inside that thing?"

Kincaid frowned. "Well, yeah. I need photos of the interior. There are none online yet, and Bethany wanted pictures ASAP. And what Bethany wants, she gets. I need this sale." Kincaid sent Liv a beseeching look. "Please make this place look gorgeous."

Liv's expression turned wary, as if she were already regretting offering her photography skills for Kincaid's demanding real-estate client. "Has it been opened and aired out recently? Maybe had some sage burned and a spirit guide cleanse the thing?"

Kincaid snorted, surprised at her normally unflappable friend's reaction. "Honey, I didn't take you for the superstitious sort. That's usually my job. It's just an old farmhouse."

Liv gave her a pointed look, dark eyes holding her gaze as she very deliberately made the sign of the cross and recited something in Spanish. "*Chica*, that thing for sure houses the angry spirits of serial killers or maybe vampires. I bet there are bones in the attic. Or portals to hell in the basement. I am not playing Willow to your Buffy the Vampire Slayer."

Kincaid laughed. "Vampire slaying would be awesome, but there are no basements here." She put her hands on her hips and looked at the house again. "I think it's…quaint."

Liv gave her a *girl, please* look. "Quaint? You're using your real-estate-agent words. 'Cozy' means small. 'Fixer-upper' means money pit. 'Quaint' means...portals-of-hell demons ready to eat your soul for the mere price of... What's this thing cost anyway?"

Kincaid checked her notes from her earlier chat with her fellow agent, Ferris. "Owner's asking five hundred."

"Wow," Liv said, lifting her camera and taking a shot of the wide, sagging porch. "Someone's proud of their creepy-ass haunted house."

"That price includes a decent chunk of land. Plus, the home was owned by one of the original families of Long Acre. It's historic," Kincaid countered, not sure why she was trying to defend the house. Maybe because if she didn't make a big sale soon, the agency was going to start questioning whether they needed four full-time agents.

"Ha. Another real-estate-agent word. 'Historic,' not 'old.'" Liv stepped to the left and aimed her camera at the second story and all its peeling-white-paint glory. "I have faith in you, though. You could sell hair products to a bald guy. I'm sure you'll find someone who finds it...quaint."

"I think Bethany will love it." Bethany Winterbourne was moving to the area from Austin and wanted the perfect fixer-upper to create her "superadorable, glam dream palace away from the city" after her divorce. The woman had watched too many home-design shows and thought small-town Texas would be chock-full of big houses that would be cheap and fall into her lap.

Kincaid had been on the hunt for Bethany for six months now with countless smaller houses in nearby

Wilder discarded out of hand. Now finally, she'd come across this prospect in Long Acre, which had the square footage Bethany wanted. Plus, it hadn't come onto the market officially, so no one had seen the house yet. Maybe she could get a good price for Bethany without competition.

Ferris had given her a heads-up because he knew Kincaid was more than ready to get Bethany out of her hair. Plus, after a particularly dry year where Kincaid had only made a few sales, Ferris knew she needed a win. This could be the answer.

However, now that Kincaid was looking at the old house, she got a spoiled-milk taste in her mouth at the thought of it being filled with Bethany's style, which, given the decor of Bethany's current condo, would be white lacquer furniture and pink-sequined pillows that had sayings like *Shine Bright* on them.

Kincaid could appreciate unique tastes. She was currently wearing underwear with purple llamas on them, so who was she to judge? *You do you, girl.* But this house had old, beautiful bones—hopefully not the attic kind like Liv was talking about—and was begging to be restored to its former glory. She could almost feel it shudder at the thought of a sequin passing its threshold.

Kincaid let her gaze travel over the facade, her mind smoothing over the peeling paint and the warped windows, imagining what the grand house must've looked like when it was first built right outside town. Nothing for miles around, the Texas wine country not yet rolling with grapevines and tourists, and the land rich with possibility. It was the kind of house where she'd dreamed of living when she'd walk home from school through the nicer neighborhoods on her way back to the broken-down rental house she'd shared with her mom. Houses with warmth and laughter and good smells coming from the kitchen. Houses that didn't have a dry-rotted hole in the floor of the bathroom, dingy tan walls, and nothing but boxed macaroni and cheese and Vienna sausage in the cabinets—food her mom knew a kid could cook for herself since she was rarely home at night.

Liv sidled up next to Kincaid, pushing a lock of hair that had escaped her loose bun away from her face. "Don't worry. I'm just giving you a hard time. I'll be able to make the place look really cool in my photos. It's all about the angles and lighting. Plus, worn and damaged can look beautiful to the right person. I mean, Finn sees what I look like in the morning and still wants to sleep with me."

Kincaid rolled her eyes at her friend, who even in jeans and a T-shirt looked like a goddess with her long lashes, light-brown skin, and thick black hair. "Oh, hush your mouth. You are neither worn nor damaged, and you know it."

Plus, even if Liv looked like a troll, Kincaid knew that Finn wouldn't look at her any differently. That guy was so in love that he practically glowed like a radioactive superhero when he was around his woman. Kincaid had only been looked at like that by one person long ago, but she remembered the all-encompassing high of that, of knowing you were loved so completely. Familiar sadness welled, but she pushed it down before it could make it to her expression. She pasted on a smile instead—a tactic she'd used so many times over the years that it was second nature now to smile when hurting.

"Please. We're all a little damaged," Liv said, bumping her shoulder into Kincaid's. "It's what makes us interesting, though, right? Like this house." She grabbed Kincaid's hand. "Come on, let's see what this old girl looks like on the inside." She peeked over her shoulder as she dragged Kincaid along. "But fair warning, if I see any spirits seeking a host or hell demons wanting to eat some souls, you're on your own, sister."

Kincaid's smile eased into a genuine one at that. "So nice to hear you have my back. Sweet as sugar, that Olivia Arias."

Liv laughed. "Hey, you're wearing heels you can't run in. Plus you know they always go after the busty blond first. You're doomed. I'm just being practical. I'll run for help. Promise."

Kincaid snorted.

Liv led her up the charmingly crooked front steps, and Kincaid got the key from the lockbox. She opened the front door, squeaky hinges announcing their arrival. She half expected the witch from Hansel and Gretel to pop out and toss her and Liv in a cauldron, but when they stepped inside the foyer, only dust motes and the stale smell of a closed-up house greeted them.

Still, despite the air of neglect overlaying everything, Kincaid could see the potential. Hardwood floors that could be refinished. High ceilings. Beautiful door casings and original moldings. A grand old house with soul baked in. Perfectly imperfect. She cringed. That'd be something else Bethany would put on a pillow. Probably in this very house if she got the chance.

Liv was looking around curiously and snapped a few

pictures of the foyer, which opened up to the main living area on the right, the soft click of her camera the only sound. She sent Kincaid a glance over her shoulder. "No sparkly vampires."

Kincaid ran her hand over the worn banister at the base of the stairs. "Bummer."

"But hey, no one in a hockey mask has attacked us either, so there's that." Liv gave her an exaggerated thumbs-up.

"Small victories." Kincaid put a hand on her hip, her eyes scanning the space as she tried to be objective. "Original details. Needs a lot of refurbishing. Inspection could be tricky." She pulled a printout from her purse. "The plumbing was replaced a few years ago. Wiring updated. That's good. Mostly needs cosmetic work."

"Cosmetic work?" Liv lifted a skeptical brow. "Girl, this is more than a hair fluff and a little blush and lipstick. This needs full-scale plastic surgery."

A gust of wind rattled the windows, and the front door slammed shut, sending a sonic boom through the foyer and adjoining living area. They both yelped.

"Son of a bitch," Liv said on a pant, her hand to her chest. "Totally unnecessary, House! Don't try to scare us away."

"Uh-oh, you've angered the poltergeists," Kincaid said with mock seriousness. "You shouldn't say mean things about the house." She placed a finger over her lips and glanced up the stairs with a deliberate look. Then, she called out, "You look so pretty, darlin'. Like a new flower on a spring morning. Just the sweetest, most beautiful house on the block. All the other houses are *so* jealous."

Liv nodded and announced, "The belle of the ball for sure!"

They both peeked upward as if they were expecting the lady of the house to descend the stairs and then laughed when they realized they'd actually waited for a response. Kincaid cocked her head to the right, and Liv followed her into the main living area. The floorboards creaked in protest beneath their feet. The living room was high-ceilinged and sun-dappled from the dusty light shining in through the tall windows, making it look like an Instagram filter had been applied.

"This place is big," Liv said, her head tilted back to take in the ceilings.

"Especially for a house this age. Must've been a really large family."

"And a wealthy one. I like this room." Liv traced her finger along one of the windowpanes, leaving a streak in the thick dust. "Gets good light. Even with the dirty windows."

"Yeah. This would be a fantastic family room. The house has six bedrooms upstairs and two down, so people with lots of kids or aging parents living with them could have all the space they wanted."

Not that Bethany would need that since she was single with no children, like Kincaid. Instead of focusing on family friendly, Kincaid would play up this room as an entertaining space. Extra bedrooms could be pitched as potential dressing rooms, hobby rooms, guest rooms.

Liv snapped a photo of the fireplace, which was surrounded by stone and had a simple but beautiful natural oak mantel above it. "Could you imagine growing up in a place like this? I mean, when it was in its prime. I think my family's entire place could fit in one third of this bottom floor."

"It's like something out of an old movie or TV show." Kincaid could imagine a bunch of kids thumping along the floorboards, tracking in mud from the outside field, maybe a dog nipping at their heels. The images made her smile. They were of the fantasy family she used to imagine lived in those houses she'd pass on her walks home from school. The loving couple. The happy kids. Dinners shared together at the table. Books read aloud to children at night. She'd used to think *one day*. One day she'd be one of those people framed in the warm glow of those windows, have her own kids tracking mud across her floor, a loving husband waiting for her to get home.

But she'd lost the guy who'd starred in those fantasies a long time ago, and at thirty-two, with a countless number of failed relationships in her wake, she'd accepted that you only got one shot at a soul mate. No one had ever compared since. She'd had to move on from that dream. She'd come to peace with that, but now a different kind of temptation pulled at her.

A vision of cushy furniture and people sitting around drinking coffee filled her mind's eye. Happy conversation echoing down the hallway. A woman reading a book near the fireplace. A couple planning their day in the Texas wine country. She could almost smell the cinnamon rolls she'd bake for those guests.

The dangerous image was rife with temptation, like that too-smooth guy at the bar who'd smile and say, *Come on, just one more drink. What could it hurt?* This was not what she was here to do. She needed to stop with the pretty fantasies. She wasn't that daydreaming little girl anymore. The one who could weave a fairy tale out of scraps of anything.

But as usual, her mouth opened before her brain got the shut-up message. "It could make an adorable bed-and-breakfast."

Liv lowered her camera and eyed Kincaid. "You think?"

"You can't see it?" Kincaid couldn't imagine *not* seeing it. The place looked made for it.

Liv glanced around again with a pensive expression, taking her time. "The photographer in me pictures a great set for Halloween portraits or maybe a location for one of those murder mystery weekends, but maybe you're right. If it had a major overhaul, it could work. It definitely has the space for that kind of thing." She looked back to Kincaid. "But it would take a crap ton of money to get it there, and would that really be a wise business move for someone? Long Acre isn't exactly a tourist destination. Except for those true-crime rubber-neckers, and for them, a room with a portal to hell would be just fine."

Kincaid blanched at the thought. Nothing irritated her more than the people who drove by her old high school and took photos like it was the set from some thriller movie instead of the place where actual people had died. *Her* people. It was one of the reasons the real estate market was so tough there. Who wanted to send their kids to a school known for a mass shooting?

"I don't know," she said. "I think it could be marketed as a tucked-away, quiet retreat that is only a fifteen-minute drive to Lake Wilder and a quick hour away from the bustle of Austin. There are wineries within easy driving distance. We're far off the road, so it has a sense of getting away from it all."

"Or being in a place where no one could hear you scream," Liv pointed out.

"Liv!"

Her friend lifted her hand with a grin. "Kidding. Mostly. But you're right. It could have potential. Maybe? Do you have someone looking for a B and B site?"

"Not exactly," Kincaid said more to herself than to Liv. She looked down at the asking price to remind herself why she couldn't gallop down this road. *Half a million dollars*. For something that needed a ton of work. She needed the rational side of her brain, which really was only on a part-time schedule to begin with, to step up and do its job. "Just thinking out loud."

Kincaid wandered past Liv toward a doorway at the back corner of the living area, gasping when she entered the next room. Liv hurried in behind her, camera swinging around her neck. "What? Werewolf? Evil clown?" She groaned when she stepped inside. "Oh. The pink. Wow. That's...*pink*."

But that wasn't what Kincaid was speechless about. The kitchen space was a dream. Larger than she'd expected for a house this age and so charming she could barely stand it. The whole thing would have to be gutted, of course—the pink cabinets and Formica countertops looked like Pepto-Bismol and bad wallpaper had gotten drunk together and made an ugly baby—but the bones of the room were beautiful. She could picture double ovens and a big island where she could prep for cooking.

"This room was clearly redone in the eighties," Liv

said, her opinion of the decor clear in her tone. "By someone with bad taste even by eighties standards."

Kincaid walked over and looked out the window above the kitchen sink to find an overgrown herb garden out back. Rosemary, thyme, and some kind of mint that looked like it'd taken over half the garden by force. "I—"

A door creaked loudly from somewhere, and both she and Liv startled, instinctively moving toward each other. Liv gripped Kincaid's arm with one hand and raised her camera with the other, poised to use it as a weapon. Kincaid's mind raced ahead to all the pictures Liv had painted—ghosts, serial killers, demons. And of course, the ever-present, always-right-near-the-surface image of boys with guns.

However, the voice that drifted down the hallway wasn't male and wasn't demonic in the supernatural way, just in the completely and utterly annoying way. "*Gorgeous* period detailing. Truly *historic*. I mean, this gem isn't going to stay on the market long. I barely was able to sneak in a preview today. But I have my secret ways. It's just so *quaint*, don't you think?"

Kincaid's stomach turned, wondering what she'd done to piss off the universe today. "Oh, Lord, give me strength and a shot of tequila."

"What's wrong?" Liv whispered. "Who's that?"

Kincaid hoped she was wrong, but she'd know that nasal, syrupy voice anywhere. "Valerie Van Arden, top seller over at Wilder Realty. I have no idea how she's here. It's Ferris's listing, and it's not even online yet."

"I take it we don't like Valerie Van Arden?"

Kincaid eyed the kitchen doorway, Valerie's too-high

voice echoing off the walls of the house like an off-key song. "We do not. She thinks the sun comes up just to hear her crow. Also, she hates me because I once dated a guy she had her eye on, claims I stole him. As if that's a thing. Like a person can be stolen."

"Fun," Liv said with a grim look as she and Kincaid headed out of the kitchen and returned to the living room.

Valerie stepped into the room from the foyer, clad in all violet—her self-designated signature color—and a well-dressed couple followed behind her. Val's blue eyes went wide, and she put a hand to her chest as she spotted Kincaid and Liv standing there. "Well, I'll be," she said dramatically. "Kincaid Breslin. I didn't know the house was being shown already. You gave me quite the scare."

Kincaid put on a beaming smile and whipped out her own version of southern-style hostility. "Well, honey, our car is parked right outside. I'm sure you saw it."

"Oh, is that yours?" she mused. "It looked so dusty, I thought it was abandoned."

Kincaid's teeth clenched as she held her smile. "You know how it is. I stay so busy, I just haven't had time to bring it in for a wash. Clients come first."

"Of course." Valerie's red lips twitched. "Well, we won't get in your way. I'm just going to show the Nicholsons around." She glanced at the couple. "Isn't this place so *special*?"

"I don't know. It's pretty run-down," Kincaid said with a dismissive shrug.

Valerie's lips pursed. "Oh, it's just the surface that needs a little polishing. Jason here is an architect. He could make this place into a showpiece, couldn't you, Jason?"

The man was scanning the space with analytical eyes. He nodded. "I could. The size is perfect." He glanced at his wife, who was snapping a photo with her phone. "Sweetheart, we could strip out everything and start fresh, maintain the look outside. Go modern minimalist on the inside. White walls. Black and gray furniture. It would be so open and airy."

Modern minimalist? Something died inside Kincaid. "You can't be serious," she blurted out.

The man's attention swung Kincaid's way, and he sent her an affronted look. "Excuse me?"

Liv made a choked sound next to her, but Kincaid couldn't hold her tongue. "I'm just saying, if you want modern, get a loft in Austin or go grab one of the lots in Wilder and build from scratch. Why would you want to turn this into something it's not?"

"Because we could turn it into something better." His chin lifted a fraction, like a little kid putting his little foot down.

"But this has character." Kincaid crossed her arms, ready to argue.

"Oh, Kincaid, you're too much," Valerie said with faux lightness, the tension showing in the lines around her eyes. "She's just messing with you, Jason. Better watch her, y'all. She's a wily one. She'll steal something from right under your nose. Just like that." Valerie snapped her fingers, the sharp sound echoing in the cavernous room.

"She probably has a client who wants it, and she's just trying to scare you off. But we don't scare easily."

She gave Jason a wink. "Let's continue the tour, shall we?" Valerie pretended like Kincaid and Liv weren't there as she passed them on her way to the kitchen. The Nicholsons and a cloud of Valerie's lavender perfume followed. "Eight bedrooms. A mudroom. Beautiful yard out back with a pond."

Kincaid stayed frozen to the spot. Something was beating at the walls of her brain, her heart pounding against her temples. She listened as the couple exclaimed over how great the kitchen would be if converted to an industrial look.

Industrial. Deep breaths.

"Kincaid." Liv put a hand on her arm. "Are you all right? Your cheeks are all flushed."

Kincaid pressed her lips together, her eyes still focused in the direction of the kitchen. She had trouble pinpointing the emotions coursing through her. Anger was one. But the other one felt like…loss. Like this was her house those people were tromping through. Her dreams they were traipsing upon.

"Are you worried you're going to lose the sale?" Liv asked. "Should you call your client? Maybe she can move fast if she loves it. I can send the pics to her as soon as I get to a laptop if she can't make it out here quickly enough."

"This house is not for them," Kincaid declared.

"I agree," Liv said with a nod. "I love modern, but this is not the house for that. Even if they had a good vision for it, I wouldn't want that horrible woman to make the commission. Call your client."

Kincaid shook her head. "It's not for my client either. She won't understand it."

Liv's brow wrinkled. "Understand what?"

Kincaid spread her arms out. "That it's already beautiful and just needs some help getting back to its glory, not to become something else entirely. Why is the world so obsessed with making things into what they're not?"

Liv frowned. "Well, does it really matter what someone does to it as long as you're the one getting the sale? That's the main point, right? Sell the house. Make the money."

That *should* be the main point. Kincaid needed this sale if she wanted to keep her gig at the agency.

"Oh, sweetheart. I think this is the one," the woman client said somewhere in the distance. "We should snatch this one up before anyone else can."

Valerie made a gleeful sound. "I think that is an excellent idea. You have brilliant taste. Let's talk offer."

Liv gave her a panicked look. "Oh shit. They're going to buy. Call your client, Kincaid."

Kincaid pulled her phone from her purse and dialed Ferris.

He answered on the first ring, the sounds of a keyboard clacking in the background. "Talk to me, gorgeous. Tell me you're going to make us both money."

Kincaid wet her lips. "I have an offer on the farmhouse."

"That's fantastic. You're an angel." The typing stopped. "Bethany's putting in an offer?"

"No," Kincaid said, her throat tightening. "I am. Full price if they take the offer without waiting for others."

"You?" he asked, concern filling his voice. "Oh, sweetie, I don't think that's a good idea. You know how dangerous it can be to get heart eyes for a new property. Believe me, I've been there. That's a lot of money you'd need to come up with. Maybe you should take some time—"

The suggestion that she didn't have enough, that she couldn't afford it pushed an old, sore button and launched her right over the railing of the already sinking ship.

"Put in the offer," she said, her voice brooking no argument. "This isn't about heart eyes."

Ferris paused for a long moment but then sighed. "Yes, ma'am. I'll do that right now."

"Thank you, Ferris."

She ended the call and turned to Liv, who had a horror-movie expression on her face. "Girl, *what* are you doing?" she whisper-shouted.

Kincaid swallowed, the phone call catching up with her and a hot panic rolling through her. "I think I just bought myself a bed-and-breakfast."

One she hadn't planned on.

One she couldn't afford.

One she simply could not walk away from.

chapter
TWO

ASHTON ISAACS HAD NEVER BEEN EVICTED BEFORE, WHICH
was surprising considering how little money he'd left his
hometown with all those years ago, but today he might
break that streak. If he didn't get his shit out the door
and his ass out of his Brooklyn apartment, he was going
to get booted to the curb in front of all his neighbors.

Former neighbors.

He checked his watch and then set a box of carefully
packed books in the hallway outside his apartment door.
A box of random items his now ex-fiancée had left behind
was sitting out there, too, hastily labeled *Melanie's Crap*.
He wasn't proud of scrawling that on the box, but last
night when he was packing up an entire apartment alone,
it'd made him feel better. Plus, it'd been safer than his
first instinct—to burn it. Not that it really mattered
anyway. Ash doubted Melanie would even come back
for it. Harlan from the Hamptons would probably replace
anything she was missing. Hell, she didn't need Harlan
from the Hamptons. She could replace it herself.

Mel's attorney income was the reason Ash had ended up with such a high-priced apartment in the first place. They'd been sharing his dingy flat outside London, where they'd met, while she was doing an internship in international law, but once they'd moved to New York, Melanie's standards had changed. She'd covered two-thirds of the rent, which he'd protested up front, but she'd insisted. *"I'm not living in New Jersey just so you can feel like we're even. You're a writer. It's just the way of the world that you make less. Not a sign of you being less."*

He didn't want to act like some chauvinist who was threatened by his girlfriend making more money. He *hadn't* been threatened by that. He'd just spent most of his time since graduating from high school living as frugally as possible because he hadn't walked out of Long Acre with anything to spare. Being careful had kept him afloat and traveling to all the places he'd wanted to see and write about. But he'd loved Melanie and had wanted to make her happy and comfortable. Now he realized why he should've fought harder against the uneven split. When you're the one making less, when things end, it's your butt on the curb without a place to live.

It didn't help that he'd spent such a big chunk of the money he'd made when he turned in his last book on her engagement ring—a ring she had conveniently forgotten to give back when she'd called off the engagement. And no way was he calling her to ask for it back. He couldn't stomach the thought of her looking at him with pity, like he *needed* the money. Fuck that. She could keep the damn thing.

But not having the ring to cash in left him here, stacking boxes in the hallway. Without that money, until he got a payment on another book contract—if he could *get* another book contract—he didn't even have enough to get a place in Jersey and last more than a few months without going under. He'd worked too hard to slide that far back into the hole now.

So after drinking too much the night Melanie left, he'd made a decision. He was going to have to do what he swore he would never do. The only way he could figure out how to save up money fast.

His phone buzzed in his back pocket. He set down another box, wiped the sweat from his forehead with his sleeve, and stepped back into the apartment. When he saw the number on the screen, he took a breath, not wanting his irritation with his situation to come through in his voice. He forced a smile, hoping she'd be able to hear it in his tone. "Hey there, Grace. How's my favorite lady?"

"Oh, just fine, sweetie," Grace said, her voice a soothing balm to his frazzled state. "Just wanted to check on you. How's the packing going?"

"Almost done, ma'am," he said, his Texas accent bubbling up despite him having spent the last decade trying to shake it. Grace did that to him. "With all the traveling, I don't keep much. I just have to get the last few boxes into the moving van, and I'll be on my way."

"That's great to hear. Do you know how long the drive's going to take?" she asked, the sound of water running in the background.

He could picture her outside by her and Charlie's pool, the little waterfall feature running while she sipped her coffee on the back porch, the air probably already heavy with humidity. His mood lightened a little at the comforting image. "I plan on doing the drive over two days, so I should be there Sunday afternoon if that works for y'all."

"Of course. We'll be looking forward to seeing you, though I'm sorry about the circumstances," she said. "You doing okay, hon?"

The genuine concern in her voice made his chest tighten, made him wish he'd had Grace in his corner from the very start, but he forced a bright tone. "Totally fine. They say everything happens for a reason, right?"

Lies. Total fucking lies. If he'd ever had any hope that the sentiment was true, he'd lost it after the Long Acre shooting. There was no reason good enough for all those people dying. But he wanted to reassure Grace.

Grace paused as though she knew exactly the amount of bullshit he was feeding her, but she didn't call him on it. "Good. And I'm not going to get involved, but I'll just say that if Melanie is going to be the type of woman to see another man behind your back, better she showed herself now and not after the wedding. I say, good riddance. She had terrible taste in books anyway."

Ash laughed, the sound surprising him. "Egregious taste."

"See? You've saved yourself a lot of future heartache. Now, Charlie is planning on fried chicken, coleslaw, and macaroni for when you get here," she said, making it clear he didn't need to discuss the demise of his relationship with her beyond that. "You have any special requests for dessert?"

His stomach rumbled at the thought of Charlie's food.

"Tell him not to go to any trouble. I already appreciate y'all letting me stay in the apartment above the store while I finish this book. You both have already done enough."

More than he'd ever in his life have time to thank them for.

"Nonsense," she said. "You're family. And with all your world traveling, we haven't seen you since last Christmas. That calls for a homecoming meal."

Homecoming. *Home*.

His gut twisted, the hunger turning into something more acidic. He looked forward to seeing Grace and Charlie. They were the kind of family he'd always wished he'd had, and they treated him like he was one of their own. But the thought of rolling back into his hometown with an unwritten book, no contract, and no good idea of when he could leave again made every inch of his skin itch. He'd sworn he'd never return for more than a holiday visit with the Lowells. That he'd never let the grass grow under his feet in that smothering small town again.

Since he'd left for college, he'd traveled and lived in so many interesting places. He'd become a writer. He'd formed a new identity, a new story. Back home, no matter what he'd accomplished, he'd just be Ashton Isaacs again. The disappointing, estranged son of Pete Isaacs, revered high-school football coach. Survivor of the Long Acre High tragedy. The guy who bailed on a town in mourning and didn't look back. *Couldn't* look back.

Ash tucked his phone into his back pocket after wrapping up the call and ran a hand over his face. Anxiety was welling up in him like an old friend. Part of him wanted to ditch the whole plan. Just suck it up, give up the writing gig, and go find a random job in some low-cost-of-living town. But even as he thought it, his shoulders sagged. He wasn't ready to give up yet. He'd lost his fiancée. He didn't want to lose his dream career, too.

Long Acre came with baggage. So much baggage. But right now, it also came with a rent-free apartment and the kind of quiet atmosphere that could lend itself to getting through this writer's block. As long as he stayed out of the way, he could avoid his parents and the trappings that came with going back to that town where people knew who you were before you were a grown-up.

This was not giving up. This was not running home with his tail between his legs. This was an economical writing retreat...*said Jack Torrance as he pulled up to the Overlook Hotel.*

Ugh. Images of typing *All work and no play makes Ash a dull boy* flitted through his head, but he pushed the thoughts away. At least in Long Acre there was no chance of getting snowed in.

But there were definitely ghosts.

With one last look at his now-former apartment building, Ash packed his things into the rental van, got behind the wheel, and cued up the longest and scariest audiobook he owned. Horror seemed appropriate right now. The road home was a long one.

Kincaid was aggressively frying eggs on Sunday morning. The sizzle, like white noise in her ears, was usually soothing, but her head was pulsing with steady panic. She flipped the eggs and accidentally broke the yolk on one.

"Dammit." She grabbed a whisk to turn this batch into scrambled instead of over-easy.

She never messed up eggs. This dish was one of the things she'd been perfecting since childhood—the perfect fried egg. But the signed contract sitting in her purse seemed to be emanating some kind of "Tell-Tale Heart" signal, asking silently—*What have you done, what have you done?* It was totally throwing off her cooking mojo.

At least she hadn't burned the biscuits.

"No, genius, just your life savings," she muttered to herself, "and your goddamned good sense. Ashes for both of them."

For so long, she'd prided herself on not being like her mother, on being responsible and saving each penny, on taking care of herself and never having to count on anyone to bail her out. She'd already learned what putting all of her hope on someone else could do to you. And in one fell swoop, she'd pulled a classic Judith Breslin. She'd taken money she'd spent so much time saving, dropped it on a random number, and spun the goddamned roulette wheel of her life.

She could end up back in the same situation she'd grown up in. Panic tried to choke off her breath, but a quick knock and then the sound of a key turning distracted her from the spiral. Her friends had arrived for their long-standing Bitching Brunch date. Kincaid took a few deep breaths and practiced her normal smile, her everything-is-just-peachy-keen smile, and transferred the eggs to a plate with a shaking hand. She rubbed her lips together, smoothing her lip gloss, and called out, "In the kitchen, y'all."

Footsteps sounded on the polished floorboards of her lake house, and her friend Rebecca stepped inside the kitchen first, her red hair pulled back into a loose braid and a cute gingham dress making her look more like a farm girl than the lawyer she was. Rebecca closed her eyes and inhaled. "Wow, it smells awesome in here. Please tell me those are your famous biscuits."

"As if I'd serve breakfast without homemade biscuits," Kincaid said. "What do I look like? An amateur?"

Rebecca grinned and put a hand on her cutely rounded belly. "And tell me that you made two trays because I need one just for myself. These other bitches can share."

Kincaid laughed, the arrival of her friends softening the sharp edges of her panic. "Sweetie pie, I made three trays *and* grabbed a big jar of fresh strawberry jam from the farmers market. I've got two pregnant ladies to feed. I'm not gonna mess around."

Kincaid's other friend, Taryn, smiled from behind Rebecca's shoulder. Her own baby bump was barely showing beneath her flowy maroon top, but her brown skin was glowing with those magic baby hormones—or maybe that was just happiness. Either way, Kincaid wished it could be bottled so she could slather some of that glow onto her own skin.

"Bec talks like she hasn't eaten in forever," Taryn said with an eye roll. "When I picked her up, Wes was cleaning up from making her chocolate muffins this morning."

"Hey, this kid in here loves its carbs. Plus"—Rebecca tipped up her chin like an aristocrat—"I can't help that my husband is a chef and has to test recipes. It'd be rude not to be his taste tester. I'm really doing it for him."

Taryn snorted. "Yep, totally self-sacrificing. But hey, if you need an extra taste tester, I'm always willing to come over." Taryn turned her brown eyes on Kincaid, her expression going comically serious. "Shaw keeps trying to make me smoothies. *Green* ones."

"Green smoothies?" Kincaid asked in horror, taking the pan off the heat and shaking her head. "Oh, bless his handsome little heart."

Taryn smirked as she stepped over to the island and poured herself a glass of orange juice. "That's what I get for falling for an athlete. Killer abs and a health streak. He's been researching all the best foods for pregnancy and trying to whip them up in the blender. It's really sweet, but word to the wise, garlic is no good in a smoothie."

"Ick." Rebecca blanched. "I'll send over some baked goods. Wes can throw in some whole grains and call them healthy."

"Bless you," Taryn said, handing Rebecca a glass of juice and then toasting her.

Despite Kincaid's I've-completely-blown-up-my-life internal freak-out, a wash of warmth went through her at the sight of her two friends, pregnant and happy. She'd never doubted that her friends would find their way, but it had only been two years since the four of them had rekindled their former friendship. They'd reconnected while filming a documentary about the Long Acre shooting. They'd all been pretty lost in their lives at the time, and now her three friends had found their happy place—and love.

Three couples...and Kincaid.

She probably should be jealous since she was in the middle of a crisis of her own making and didn't have a husband, boyfriend, or even a cute guy in town to call up for baked goods or a fun night. Okay, well, she did have a few guys she could call if she really wanted to. Just lately, she hadn't found herself wanting any of them. But truly, she was thrilled for her friends. One of her favorite hobbies was playing matchmaker, and she'd had a little part in each of her friends' romances. So she was totally taking credit for their big ol' smiles and growing bellies.

"Where's Liv?" Kincaid asked, donning oven mitts. She'd last talked to Liv when they'd left the farmhouse the other day. Liv had told her to go straight to the office and undo the rash mistake she'd made by putting in a verbal offer. Kincaid had nodded. Agreed.

Yep. Uh-huh. Of course.

Then she'd gone down to the office and signed the papers, guaranteeing the down payment.

"She was a few minutes behind us. She should be here any minute," Rebecca said, plucking a piece of watermelon from the fruit salad Kincaid had left on the counter. "She called me on the way and said you were going to have quite a story to tell. What's that about?"

Kincaid paused halfway to opening the oven. "What's that now?"

"Something about a snotty real-estate agent and some haunted house," Rebecca said, lifting a brow. "I sense a Kincaid story coming on."

Taryn adjusted the hairband she'd used to push back

her halo of curly black hair and smiled in delight. "Ooh, I love a Kincaid story."

A Kincaid story. Yeah, her friends were used to those. Weird things tended to happen to her—or, well, maybe *because* of her. Really, who was keeping track? But the stories often got her friends laughing. She had a feeling this time her story wouldn't go over quite like that. She pulled the last tray of biscuits from the oven and set them on a trivet. "Why don't we wait for Liv?"

The front door opened and closed as if on cue, echoing into the kitchen. Liv strode into the room, her floppy bun bouncing with her steps. "Hey, sorry I'm late. Did I hear my name?"

Taryn gave Liv a quick side hug in greeting. "Yeah, we were just gearing up for a Kincaid story."

Liv gave Kincaid a look, lips curving. "Is this the one where Kincaid almost accidentally bought a half-million-dollars-worth of haunted house to piss off a rival agent?"

Rebecca's lips parted, amusement lifting the corners of her blue eyes. "*Really?*"

Kincaid stared at the expectant faces of her friends. "Well, not exactly."

"What do you mean *not exactly*?" Liv asked, clearly sensing Kincaid's tone.

Kincaid looked down at her oven mitts, which had flying cartoon pigs all over them. "Well, this is more the story about when Kincaid actually *does* buy the half-million-dollar farmhouse, empties her savings to put a down payment on it, and now has to sell her cute little lake house because there's no way she can afford two mortgages."

Liv's eyes went wide. "*What?*"

Kincaid cringed. "Well, see, what happened was—"

"Kincaid!" Shock filled Liv's face. "You said you were going to the office to *undo it*."

Kincaid bit her lip, words bubbling up. "I was. I really was. But by the time I got there, that annoying, let's-turn-a-historic-home-into-a-minimalist-vortex couple had called to put in an offer, too. And Ferris needed me to make a decision and I just—" She looked to her other two friends, looking for support. "Y'all should see the house. It's this beautiful farmhouse that needs to be restored and would make the cutest bed-and-breakfast, and this couple that was there—they had horrible taste and had coordinated their outfits. Who does that?"

Taryn and Rebecca stared at her, clearly confused.

"Well, that doesn't matter." Kincaid waved a hand between them, her oven mitts still on. "But they were going to gut the poor house and make it modern and industrial and things it just shouldn't be. And it was, like, my *obligation*, you know, to good taste and…history and, I don't know…the *soul* of the house to save it from that. And—" She knew she was rambling, but she couldn't seem to stop now that she'd gotten started. "And it just reminded me of the house I always dreamed of when I was a little girl. A Hallmark Movie house. One with a big family and big dinners and big cushy furniture and board games and a fireplace. One filled with people who loved each other. You know, one completely different from my own."

The last words rang out between them, ones she hadn't meant to say, but the horror on her friends' faces softened.

"Oh, sweetie," Rebecca said, empathy filling her expression.

Kincaid felt something wet slide down her cheek. *Goddammit*. When had she started to cry?

"Kincaid," Taryn said gently, "is this about your letter?"

The letters. The ones their teenage selves had written to their future selves and buried in a time capsule. They'd opened them two years ago, spilling out all their teen dreams and reminding them of how much they hadn't accomplished.

"Buying an aging farmhouse and trying to open a bed-and-breakfast were most definitely not in my letter," Kincaid pointed out.

"No, but your letter talked about never having to live like your mom did," Rebecca said, obviously treading carefully. "You talked about having a great job and a beautiful home."

"I honestly wasn't thinking about my letter. I already *have* a nice home. And I have a job." She released a breath. "I don't know what happened. It just felt like the house was supposed to be mine." She swiped at her cheek, streaking mascara over the flying pigs. "I know it's really, really stupid. I'm completely aware of that. I have no idea how I'm going to make this work, but…"

"But what?" Liv asked, no censure in her voice.

Kincaid searched for the words. "But have you ever just looked at something and known that it had to be yours or you'd just die?"

Understanding lit Liv's face.

Rebecca got a soft look in her eyes and nodded. "That's how I feel about Wes."

Liv and Taryn nodded like they knew the *amen* to that same prayer. Taryn walked over and pulled Kincaid into a hug. "Girl, sounds like you fell in love. Hard."

Kincaid sniffed indelicately, the tears still sneaking out, but a smile touched her lips. "Of course. Leave it to me to fall in love with a haunted house and not some sexy guy who tries to feed me muffins or smoothies. This is a complete mess."

"Love usually is," Rebecca said, stepping closer as Taryn released Kincaid from the hug. "But I've learned that sometimes you have to trust your gut and figure out the rest later."

"Says the woman who actively uses three day planners," Kincaid pointed out. "And two planning apps."

"I know, I know. I do love a plan." Rebecca got a brief, nerdy sparkle in her eye. "But sometimes you have to just say, *Fuck the plan*. You know? If I hadn't done that, I wouldn't have Wes. Or this baby. I'd still be in my dad's law firm, working too many hours, helping people get as much as they can from their exes. Sometimes chasing a whim pays off." She reached out and gave Kincaid's arm a squeeze. "We'll help you figure this out."

"Of course we will," Taryn said before arching a brow. "As long as this place isn't actually haunted, because if that's the case, I'm *O-U-T* out."

Kincaid laughed, pulled off the oven mitts, and grabbed a napkin to dab her eyes. "Not you, too. I'm friends with a bunch of chickens. Y'all should've seen Liv going into the house. She was ready to sacrifice me to the demons if anything popped out."

Liv crossed her arms and shook her head, amusement there. "Have you seen *The Exorcist*? I'm not offering myself as host. My friendship only goes so far."

"Liar," Kincaid teased. "You know you'd host a demon for me."

Liv gave her a patient look and swiped one of the biscuits from the tray. "Only because you feed me biscuits."

Kincaid blew Liv a kiss. "You hear that, demons? Liv has offered herself as tribute."

Liv made the sign of the cross and then flipped Kincaid the middle finger before taking a bite of biscuit.

"So," Rebecca said, grabbing plates from the cabinet but already going into no-nonsense lawyer voice. "How long do you have with two mortgages before you're in trouble?"

Kincaid took a deep breath as she started bringing food to the table. "A few months. The down payment and getting the farmhouse livable are going to drain my savings. I don't doubt I can sell this place, because houses on the lake are in demand, but I'd have to get at least a corner of the farmhouse habitable first so I could move in."

"Yeah, it's not just about the mortgage. I saw the place. She's gonna need all the money she can get to fix it up," Liv said, her tone grim. "It needs a lot of work. Especially if she's going to turn it into a B and B."

"A B and B?" Taryn asked, looking up as she laid out napkins. "You want to leave real estate?"

Kincaid swallowed hard. Saying it out loud made it more real. "My real estate job pays the bills, but it's not what I set out to do forever. I've always had this dream of running my own business. I like to cook and entertain.

I love having people around and making them happy. A bed-and-breakfast could be a good fit."

"You'd be fantastic at that," Rebecca said without a trace of doubt. "But it will take a pretty big chunk of change. That's more than just remodeling a house for private use. You could apply for a small-business loan, though that will just add to the debt. Are you willing to take on partners or investors?"

Kincaid's first instinct was to say no. She wanted the house and business to be hers. Taking money or gifts from someone meant letting them have some amount of control over her. She'd seen that dynamic play out over and over again with her mother. "That's not my preference, but I don't see how I can finance all of it on my own. Not if I want to get it up and running anytime in the near future."

"Do you have anyone you can think of who'd be interested?" Rebecca continued. "Any connections to someone looking for a business investment? What about the Lowells?"

The Lowells. Graham's parents. They were her family in so many ways, but the thought of asking them for anything at all made bile burn in her stomach. She felt selfish enough accepting their kindness and love when it should've been Graham in that place instead. They'd already given her so much, helping her with school costs and being there for her after her mom left town. "I think the Lowells already have too much invested in their bookstore. I get the sense the store isn't doing as well as it used to. I have some business contacts I could call."

Taryn nodded. "All right, let's do some brainstorming. But let's do it over breakfast because I'm about to go all hot-dog-eating-contest with that tray of hot biscuits if we don't start eating soon."

"Amen, mama," Rebecca said, stepping past Kincaid and grabbing another biscuit. "Let's do this the right way—with *all* the calories."

Kincaid laughed, the image of her two pregnant friends shoving as many biscuits as they could into their mouths lifting her mood. "Well, I guess my first note for my new business should be 'Make sure to feed the guests biscuits.'"

"Oh, that's a given," Liv said, sliding into her spot at the table. "These things are gold, *chica.*"

Kincaid sighed as she joined her friends, sinking into her chair. "Too bad the bank doesn't take deposits in biscuits."

Taryn reached out and gave Kincaid's hand a pat. "You'll figure this out, girl. If anyone can pull it off, you can."

"And hey, if you can't sell the biscuits, you can sell your soul. I bet you can find the devil hiding in the basement of that farmhouse and make a deal," Liv said.

"How many times do I have to tell you? It doesn't have a basement," Kincaid declared, tossing her napkin at Liv.

Liv ducked and laughed.

"Notice she didn't say that it doesn't house the devil," Taryn pointed out between bites.

Kincaid narrowed her eyes at her friend. "I hate you all."

"We love you, too," Liv said.

Well, at least Kincaid had that. The love of her friends. Because after this contract went through, she might not have much else to her name.

chapter

THREE

ASH'S HEAD WAS POUNDING FROM LACK OF SLEEP AND absence of coffee as he stepped out of the tiny shower in the apartment above the bookstore. The hot water had helped wake him up some, but the headache was going to take something more drastic. Like a double shot of espresso from the coffee shop on the corner. Maybe a triple. It wouldn't taste like his usual from his favorite shop in Brooklyn, but he couldn't be choosy.

Not that many years ago, Long Acre didn't have a coffee shop at all. If you wanted coffee, you had to go to Toby's Diner and drink the weak, brown water they passed off as coffee. As a teen, he'd thought it was quality stuff. He and Kincaid used to stop there all the time after their evening shifts at the bookstore to meet Graham, order a pot of coffee, eat cheese toast—the cheapest thing on the menu—and get their homework done. Well, mostly it'd been Ash attempting to do his homework while Kincaid narrated everything about her day or the customers she'd helped in the store. He'd never met anyone who seemed to say every thought in her head even while doing a completely unrelated task. Some people worked to background music. He'd taken to working to the hum of her chatter. After a while, it'd become something he missed when he tried to work in silence.

He grimaced and dried his face on his towel, trying to wipe away the memory. *No thinking about the past.* Being back in Long Acre was bad enough. He didn't need to do the memory-lane thing. That road was populated with a whole bunch of sites he didn't want to visit ever again. That was one reason the little gourmet coffee shop was perfect. It was new, probably some transplant business owner from Austin looking for small-town life, and when Ash had stopped in the last two mornings, he hadn't recognized a soul and no one had recognized him.

Ash finished drying off and knotted the towel around his waist. He felt around the edge of the sink. *Dammit.* Where had he left his glasses? He squinted through the steam trapped in the small room and didn't see them. He sighed, wishing, not for the first time, that he was back in his New York apartment where he had defined places for everything.

He vaguely remembered pulling off his glasses when he'd gotten undressed by the bed, so he headed out of the bathroom, vision blurry but manageable. The apartment was just a studio with a small kitchen in the corner, a bed, and a table where he could eat and work at his laptop, but the layout was unfamiliar. Plus, the place was filled with boxes and dark, the curtains still drawn. He walked carefully, hoping not to stub a toe or knock something over. He finally located his glasses on the small bedside table and slipped them on. He reached for the lamp, but when he heard a sound off to his left, he only had time to register that someone was standing near the door before a woman's shriek tore through the small room.

He lifted his palms as if it were a holdup and jumped back in surprise. But before he could get a word out, something heavy and solid crashed into his shoulder.

Oof. Pain rocketed down his arm and up his neck. The sound of breaking glass exploded at his feet. "What the fu—"

"I have pepper spray and know self-defense!" the woman shouted. "Don't you move!"

"*Me?*" he asked incredulously. "*You* don't move. This is my apartment. And if you have pepper spray, why the hell didn't you use that instead?" He rubbed his throbbing shoulder and took a step toward the lamp to illuminate his unwelcome visitor, but sharp pain pinched the bottom of his foot. "*Fuck.*"

"*Your* apartment?" she said, affronted. "I don't think so, squatter. This place is on the market."

Ash's foot was on fire with pain. The glass had nicked him, and he was losing his patience and possibly blood. "Look, calm down. I think there's been a mix-up, but give me a sec. Let me turn on a light." He kept his feet where they were and reached for the lamp again. He clicked it on, soft light flooding the room. He was ready to yell at whoever this stranger was for attacking him, but when he saw the blond woman standing there, pepper spray aimed, familiar just-try-me expression on her face, all his breath left him. "*Kincaid?*"

Kincaid's face, which he hadn't seen since their last awkward shared Christmas at the Lowells—an annual tradition that always involved a lot of tense, fake smiling at each other—was the picture of shock. Eyes widening. Lips parting. Her gaze slid down his body, which he now remembered was bare except for his tattoos and the damp towel around his hips. He cleared his throat.

Her attention snapped back up to his face. "*Ash?* What the hell?"

He grabbed the knotted towel at his hip, not trusting the thing to hold up. Apparently the universe hated him, so full frontal nudity was imminent if he didn't take precautionary measures. "I could say the same to you. How'd you get in?"

"I have a key. I'm showing the place for the Lowells so they can rent it out." She lowered the pepper spray and swept her other hand in his direction. "I was bringing flowers by to brighten up the place. I have someone coming over later to see it."

Ash looked down at his feet where shards of glass glinted in the lamplight and a puddle of water had spread like some kind of abstract art, mixing with the blood from his cut and the scattered flowers. His foot was burning like hell. "Well, it's not for rent anymore. I'm…using it."

Her brow creased, and she glanced around, noticing the boxes for the first time. "Using it? You always stay at Grace and Charlie's when you visit."

God, he didn't want to get into this with Kincaid. He'd always made sure to bring a date home for Christmas, and he'd been extra thrilled the last two years to bring a serious girlfriend home to prove to everyone how well he was doing. Without this town. Without his parents. Without Kincaid. That he was just fine. Now here he was, right back where he'd started. "I needed a place for a little longer to get some writing done. Someplace quiet."

"Where's Melanie?"

In the Hamptons, fucking Harlan. "Can we focus? I'm kind of bleeding and stranded over here."

She blinked. "Oh, right. Bleeding. Naked. Don't move. You'll make it worse."

"Not much choice, KC."

Her attention flicked back to him, and he realized the mistake he'd made. The old nickname had tripped off his tongue unbidden. He didn't get to call her that anymore. He hadn't called her that since they were seventeen.

She looked down at her large purse and made a show of tucking away her pepper spray, thankfully ignoring his gaffe. "Is there a broom here? I can clear a path for you."

"Check the closet by the door. I think I saw some cleaning supplies in there."

Kincaid set her stuff down on the table and then made her way toward the front door, her black heels clicking along the floorboards with purpose. He couldn't help but watch her. Kincaid had always walked like she was inviting every eye in the room to follow—chin up, hips swaying, blond hair spilling down her back. Not seductive per se. More like she was issuing a challenge she didn't expect anyone to meet.

Today she was wearing some outfit that made Ash think of the pink ladies in *Grease*. Fitted black pants that stopped at her ankles and a pink suit jacket over a black top. It was business wear, but he had no doubt that her outfit had some of her male clients forgetting that they were supposed to be buying or selling a house.

Kincaid had always known she was beautiful and had leveraged that when she needed it. He couldn't blame her for that. Being pretty and bubbly was how she'd eventually risen above the scorn from others about where she came from and who her mother was. When she turned her charm on you, it was nearly impossible not to be drawn in. By the end of high school, no one was calling her white trash like they had in middle school. They were voting her prom queen.

Kincaid rummaged in the closet by the front door and came back with a hand broom and dustpan. She frowned at the mess at his feet and let out a heavy sigh. "What a waste. That was such a pretty bouquet."

Ash's lip curled. "Glad you're so concerned for the flowers, Breslin. Meanwhile, I'm bleeding out. Can I have the broom, please?"

She gave him a cocked brow and a head tilt. "Honey, you don't want to squat down right now. I saw quite enough of what's under there in sixth grade when your swim trunks got snagged on a branch at the lake. I'm still slightly traumatized. I don't need a repeat."

Heat crawled up the back of his neck, some remnant of the awkward boy he used to be trying to surface, but he shoved the feeling down. He wasn't that person anymore. Plus, they both knew that sixth grade wasn't the last time she'd seen him naked. She would never mention that other time, though. *Pretend, pretend, pretend*. That was the game they played. "Just leave me with the broom and go. I'll clean up when you're gone."

She waved him off. "Oh, don't be hardheaded. If you try to do it, you're going to get more glass in your feet." She pointed in the general direction of his crotch. "Or more delicate places."

"Kincaid," he warned.

"I'm just saying. I can help." She examined the mess on the floor. "Stay still. I promise I won't look up. I don't want Melanie coming after me for compromising your virtue."

He sniffed.

Kincaid crouched near his feet and started sweeping up the shards of glass. Ash watched for a second, but when he realized he could see straight down her shirt to the lacy black edges of her bra, he lifted his head and took a strong interest in a water spot on the ceiling. He didn't need to see Kincaid Breslin's anything.

"So what's the deal?" she asked, the sound of broken glass tinkling beneath him.

"The deal?"

"Yes. Why are you staying here? What are all these boxes? Where's your lady friend? Why aren't you traveling hither and yon like usual?" she asked in rapid fire. "And Ashton Isaacs, are you getting pedicures now? Because your toenails look buffed."

He groaned. "Can you just get this cleared up? I've got things to do."

She paused, and he was forced to look down. As expected, she was staring up at him with a perturbed look on her face. "I suggest you don't speak to me like I'm your maid. I'm trying to help. And I'm just asking some basic questions. Making conversation."

"We don't do that," he said, irritated.

"What?"

"Make conversation. Unless the Lowells are around. Or didn't you notice?"

A line appeared between her brows, and her lips thinned. She returned her attention to cleaning up. "Right."

He let out a tired breath, knowing he'd spoken the truth but feeling like a jerk for being so short with her. She *was* trying to help, even if she was the one who'd caused the mess in the first place. He relented. "Fine. I occasionally have gotten a pedicure."

He expected her to jump on that and tease him. The Kincaid he used to know would've eaten up that bit of information like candy. But of course she wasn't that Kincaid to him anymore. All he caught was the slight twitch of her lip as if she was fighting back a smile. "Fancy."

"Melanie used to like getting them done as a couple because she found it awkward to make conversation with the person handling her feet," he said, rambling just to fill the silence.

"Used to?" she asked. "Not a fan anymore?"

He cringed at his slip. He didn't want to get into this with Kincaid. She would find out through the Lowells at some point that he and Melanie were no more, but he didn't want to have that conversation. Didn't want to admit that some things never changed, that he was someone's second choice yet again. Ash Isaacs, professional runner-up. "I think I can make it out of the danger zone now. The path to the bathroom looks clear."

Kincaid rose and nodded. "Just go over to the bed and sit down. I can grab supplies if you have them so you don't get more blood all over the floor."

"Thank you." Ash hobbled to the side of the bed, his foot screaming at him, and cocked his head toward the bathroom door. "I have a travel bag under the sink. There should be a little first aid kid in there. And if you could grab my boxers off the top of my suitcase, that would be great."

"On it," she said a little too brightly. "I'll grab some bandages and some boy panties, and we'll get you fixed right up."

Fixed. Sure. If only he could slap a bandage on his life as easily as he could on his foot and say the same.

—⁂—

Kincaid rummaged around in Ash's bathroom cabinet, fishing for supplies and trying to gather her senses. Beyond the panic of walking into an apartment and thinking a stranger was about to attack her, the shock of Ash standing there half-naked in front of her had been a whole different kind of jolt.

Her first reaction had been one borne of pure female instinct. She hadn't been able to stop herself from staring and taking in the view. Growing up, Ash had been her best friend, and she'd always thought of him as cute in his unique, adorably bookish way, but she hadn't let herself think about his looks any further than that. They'd been best friends. There had been lines not to cross.

At least there were supposed to have been lines not to cross.

As an adult, she'd gotten to see him almost every Christmas at the Lowells, dressed in his skinny jeans and his buttoned-up shirts and his dark-rimmed glasses, always with a polished woman on his arm. So she knew he'd grown into a good-looking guy—even though she had to bite her tongue not to tease him about becoming some New York hipster writer. But she had *not* been prepared for Ash in all his shirtless, tattooed glory. Her body had tingled with something very not okay considering (a) he had a fiancée, and (b) he was the boy who'd broken her goddamned heart like no one in her life before or since.

No way in hell. Look. Away.

Kincaid repeated those words in her head as she gathered what she needed from the bathroom and grabbed a pair of boxer briefs from the top of his suitcase. She would not let herself be distracted by the fact that Ash was gorgeous. Hot guys were a dime a dozen. She could go find one to spend time with if needed. Ash was off-limits in so many ways, he might as well have been wrapped in caution tape and surrounded by a moat. She needed to get him bandaged up and then get the hell out of there.

She handed Ash his underwear and promptly turned her back. She flicked her wrist where he could see it. "Go ahead. Get decent."

She could hear rustling behind her, and she was absolutely not thinking about the fact that he was naked. Nope. Not even a little bit. She caught a brief reflection of his bare ass in the window off to her left, and a tight sound escaped the back of her throat. She squeezed her eyes shut.

"What?" he asked.

She took a breath and then glued her attention onto the blank wall in front of her. "Didn't say anything."

"You looked, didn't you?"

She snorted. "Don't flatter yourself."

"Pervert," he said with no ire in it. "All right, I'm good." The bedsprings squeaked as he sat. "Except for the fact that my foot hurts like hell."

She turned around, not comforted at all by the sight of Ash in his underwear. The boxer briefs hid even fewer secrets than the towel. He crossed his ankle over his knee to get a look at his foot, and her face got hot at the unencumbered view of the bulge between his legs. *Eyes up, woman.* Good Lord, what was *wrong* with her? This was *Ash.*

This was a clear sign that she'd gone too long without a date. Her brain was separating past Ash from current Ash, pretending as if this man in front of her was simply some hot stranger. She could not be thinking these thoughts about Ashton Isaacs.

"How bad is it?" she asked, shoving a packet of disinfectant wipes and a box of bandages at him.

He eyed the cut, which had made a mess on the bottom of his foot, and took the wipes from her. "The glass got me pretty good, but I don't see any shards stuck in there. I won't need stitches, so there's that."

"Excellent."

He looked up and smirked. "Next time just use the pepper spray, Breslin. The recovery time will be quicker."

"I'll keep that in mind next time I'm in a dark room and startled by a naked stranger," she said wryly.

Ash hissed in pain when he cleaned the cut and then quickly bandaged it. "I guess I should be happy you aimed for my shoulder."

"Oh, that's not where I was aiming, sunshine," she said, taking the box of bandages from him and setting them on the side table. "Just be thankful I wasn't on the softball team."

He chuckled under his breath, and the simple act changed his whole face, making him look more like the boy she used to know, the one who used to make her days at the bookstore fun with his sneaky, dry sense of humor. "No possibility of that. You were the worst at softball. Remember that time you accidentally let go of the bat and almost took Coach Orion's head off?"

She crossed her arms as Ash got up and hobbled over to his suitcase to fish out a pair of jeans. "I'm not sure that was an accident. I think that was my subconscious getting him back for that time he made me run laps in the boys' gym for being late while the girls went outside and played four square."

Ash tugged on his jeans and turned around as he buttoned them. "That gym class became the stuff of legend—at least among the middle-school male population."

"Ugh. I remember. Bouncy Breslin. God, I hated that name." By that time, she'd already been self-conscious that she'd developed early. Plus, she hadn't discovered the wonders of the supportive sports bra yet. A bunch of hormonal twelve-year-old boys gawking at her as she ran had made it so much worse.

"Kids are jerks," he said with a shake of his head. "If I remember correctly, I was Assface Ashton at the time because my skin had broken out so badly. At least it was a break from the teasing about my glasses." He made a disgusted sound in the back of his throat. "I don't know how anyone walks out of middle school alive." As soon as the words were out, he cringed and ran a hand over the back of his dark hair. "Sorry. You know what I mean."

And there it was. The shared history that they could never shake. Both tied to it like a ball and chain around their collective ankles. A lot of those kids who'd teased them *hadn't* made it out of school alive. It'd just taken until high school to be handed that death sentence.

"Yeah, I know." She wet her lips and glanced at the door. "Well, I better get going. I need to call the client and let them know the apartment is taken for…how long exactly?"

Ash's expression shuttered, and he looked away. "Not entirely sure. A couple of months, maybe. This book is going to take a while."

She glanced at the boxes that littered the area near the kitchen. "Is Melanie staying in New York to work?"

His eyes met hers briefly. "Yeah."

"So the wedding next summer?"

He turned to his suitcase again and dug around, pulling a shirt out. "On hold."

Kincaid felt her brows lifting, but she held her tongue and didn't ask more questions—a Herculean feat for her. She mentally gave herself a gold star. "Oh. Well, okay. Guess I'll hold onto that bread maker I was planning on giving y'all."

He peeked over his shoulder, his nose wrinkled. "A bread maker?"

She smiled. "What? Everyone loves bread."

"Melanie's gluten-free."

"Oh," Kincaid said, all wide-eyed innocence. "Is she? I didn't realize that. Poor thing. No bread? Bless her heart."

Ash shook his head, biting his lip and turning away. "You're a bad liar. *Bless her heart?* I haven't been away so long that I forgot what that means in Kincaid-speak."

She watched him as he tugged on a long-sleeved T-shirt, covering up all that beautifully inked skin. "It's been fourteen years. I'd say that's plenty long."

"Not long enough," he muttered.

"What?"

He turned suddenly, demeanor stiffening. "Look, I don't want to be rude, but I need to get some work done."

"Of course." She smoothed her hair and straightened her jacket. "I'll get out of your way. I would say sorry about the whole throwing-a-vase-at-your-head thing, but really, that wasn't my fault. A woman has to protect herself."

"Speaking of which," he said with a pointed look, "leave the key behind. I don't want to worry I'm going to get maced in the night."

She couldn't help but smile at that. "Well, you don't have to worry about that now. You're not a stranger."

He made a dismissive sound. "Aren't I?"

Her smile fell. "What?"

"Let's not pretend." He crossed his arms, a grim look on his face. "That's exactly what we are to each other now."

"Ash."

"Goodbye, Kincaid."

She stared at him for a long moment but knew there was no point in arguing about it. What was done was done. She turned with a swish of her hair, tossing the key on the table as she passed it, and walked out the door.

He was right. He was a stranger.

And she needed to keep it that way.

chapter
FOUR

KINCAID HEADED DOWN THE BACK STAIRWELL OF THE bookstore building, the boards creaking beneath her as she tried to shake off her run-in with Ash. She'd already had a bad start to the morning, and a half-naked ghost from her past had only made it worse. Why did *he* have to be here, his very presence reminding her of the worst time in her life? And he was planning to stay for a while, based on those boxes. Her stomach turned.

Things were so much easier when Ash was traveling the world or living far away in New York. Then, she only had to hear about him through Grace and Charlie or see him on the back of his books and at the annual Christmas dinner. That made the pain easier to ignore. She could forget for a while that she was someone a person could walk away from without looking back, that she wasn't worth staying and fighting for.

She and Ash had been among the few who'd survived the Long Acre shooting, but she'd lost him anyhow. Her best friend since grade school. Her person. Still alive but gone in all the important ways. Seeing him, especially the glimpses of the boy he used to be, made grief cut through her like a jagged knife. In one swift tragedy, she'd been left without the two people who were most important to her, Graham and Ash. Two boys she'd loved more than anything, in different ways and for different reasons.

Old memories tried to surface, but she forced them to the back of her mind. Maybe she should skip the stop at the coffee shop she'd planned and head straight to the wine store instead. Her phone buzzed in her purse. She perked up. Maybe that was the universe sending an *I'm sorry* for her shitty morning.

She lifted the phone, saw the number, and took a deep breath. *Please, please, PLEASE say yes.* "Hi, Alexis," she said brightly. "Tell me the good news."

Kincaid braced herself. This couldn't go worse than the last one at least. Alexis, her former boss from her first real estate job, wasn't going to take the tactic of the last business associate she'd contacted about the B and B. Billy Weathers, who owned a grocery store in town and who liked to invest in other local businesses, had said he'd consider investing if Kincaid joined him on his upcoming vacation to Vail so they could discuss it—in their shared suite. It'd taken everything she had not to pick up the computer monitor in his office and throw it at his big, ugly head. Her mother had moved out of town a decade ago, but still, the specter of her reputation haunted Kincaid.

"Alexis?" she asked again when her phone companion didn't respond.

Alexis sighed. "I'm sorry, hon. I appreciate you

thinking of me, and this has nothing to do with you. I know you're a savvy businesswoman. But this isn't the right opportunity for me. I've been burned by investments in Long Acre before. The location is too much of a challenge. I hate to say it, I really do, but that town will always be associated with one thing."

The words fell like icicles into an already chilly river. "That's not true. It's been over a decade and—"

"I know it's hard to see when you're living there," Alexis said, cutting her off with gentle firmness. "I know you love your town, but look hard. You're in that market. You know what the real estate numbers look like. Tourist-based businesses are going to be even worse. It's not a destination town. It may not be fair, but it is what it is."

Kincaid's fingers curled into the palm of her free hand. "No, it doesn't have to be that way. There are other towns that have changed their image. Waco used to only be associated with a crazy cult and an infernal government screwup, but now it's a popular city for people who want to refurbish old houses with shiplap."

"Yes, but you don't have a national TV show helping you out with the image. All you have is a documentary reminding people about the terrible thing that happened there," Alexis said, pulling no punches.

Kincaid grumbled, suddenly regretting being part of that documentary—even if it had been for charity. "Let me change your mind. Come out and see the place."

She could hear Alexis shift on the other end of the phone. "I'm sorry, Kincaid. I really am. Good luck with the project, and if you decide to expand out to Wilder, give me a call."

Kincaid closed her eyes, pausing on the stairs to

gather herself. "Thanks, Alexis. I appreciate you considering it in the first place."

Alexis wished her luck again and ended the call.

Kincaid tipped her head back, giving the universe the evil eye for her no good, very bad day continuing, and dropped her phone into her purse. Alexis had been her last hope as an investor. She was going to have to back out of the deal, lose the house and the earnest money she put down, and risk the seller suing her to recoup the lost sale. She'd called a number of her business contacts over the last few days to see if any of them would be interested. A few had seemed mildly intrigued, but most had said no outright. The reasons had been the same. Long Acre was not a destination spot. It was a bad memory for the country. A scar.

She understood, but it also pissed her off. How could everyone write off a whole town because of what two damaged teenagers had done over a decade ago? Real people still lived here. Good people. Long Acre had tragedy, but it also had big blue skies, quaint little shops, and beautiful hills and vineyards nearby.

When she'd first moved here from Houston in the fourth grade, Long Acre had seemed like a place right out of a storybook. Little shops downtown that didn't have brand names on them. Friendly people who didn't mind talking to an overly chatty little girl. Streets that weren't packed with traffic. It was a place that wasn't dangerous to wander around even after the sun went down. At the time, she hadn't cared that the rental house she and her mom had moved into was run-down. She hadn't cared that she was going to have to start at a whole new school. She hadn't even cared that her father had decided he no longer wanted to be a part of her life. She'd hated those once-a-month visits with her dad and his "real" family anyway. Long Acre had seemed like a fresh start.

She hadn't known then that her mom had moved there to escape all kinds of trouble and gambling debt in Houston, that she'd squandered the child support Kincaid's dad had been paying her, that things would only get worse. All Kincaid knew was that after being dragged around from place to place in the city, Long Acre seemed magical. She'd fallen in love with the town from day one. And one of the places she'd fallen hardest for was the adorable store at the bottom of this staircase—The Stuffed Shelf.

When Kincaid reached the ground floor, she looked over at the door that led to the back rooms of the bookstore. She could remember the very first time she'd walked by The Stuffed Shelf. Her mother had brought her along as she applied for waitressing jobs, but having a little girl in tow wasn't the best for interviews, so her mom had told her to go keep herself busy in the bookstore. There'd been a colorful Harry Potter display in the window, and when Kincaid had walked in, she'd been enamored with the cozy, quirky comfort of The Stuffed Shelf. She'd felt as if she'd stepped into the actual pages of a book.

Grace Lowell had been manning the main desk and had given her a warm smile, her auburn hair in an elegant twist that seemed more appropriate for a fancy ball than a small-town bookstore. She'd stepped around the counter and crouched to Kincaid's level. "What can I help you with, cutie pie?"

Kincaid, not shy even back then, had told Grace that

she needed a big book to keep her busy because her mom was looking for a job but not to give her anything boring. Grace hadn't blinked at the idea of a child being dropped off in her care. Instead, she'd set Kincaid up with a pile of books and parked her in a bright-blue chair in the children's section. When Kincaid's mom had shown up two hours later with a sway in her step and whiskey on her breath, Grace had sent her along to the diner to sober up and told her she'd walk Kincaid over later. Grace had given Kincaid the books she'd been reading for free and had made sure her mother was safe to drive before releasing Kincaid to her care. Her mom had promptly forbidden Kincaid to return to the bookstore because *"That woman thinks she's better than us."*

That, of course, had made the bookstore Kincaid's favorite place from that point on. Forbidding her to do something was a surefire way to make her want to do it more than anything. She'd spent many an afternoon there in the years following, getting to know Grace and Charlie, and it'd been the first place she'd applied for a job when she'd been old enough. So many of her best early memories had happened within its walls. She'd gotten Ash a job there. She'd also fallen in love with Graham, Grace and Charlie's son, there. Graham had hidden love letters in different books for her to find so he could win her over. Her own romantic scavenger hunt. He'd given her a fairy tale in the magical bookstore.

Kincaid's stomach tightened. Good memories tainted by bad ones. Now she avoided the place like it had a disease. When she needed books, she put in an order with Grace and picked up the books when she stopped by their house for her regular dinners with them.

Kincaid stared at the door that led to The Stuffed Shelf. She could almost smell its familiar scent—old paper and the cinnamon potpourri Grace had always favored. Kincaid had the overwhelming urge just to peek inside, but she resisted, knowing no good would come of it. The store didn't open until ten anyway.

She turned toward the steel door that would lead out to the parking lot, but before she could push it open, a crashing noise came from somewhere behind her. She spun around, cocking her head to listen. Another sound, one she couldn't identify, drifted from beneath the closed door of the bookstore. Already on edge from earlier, she pulled her pepper spray out of her purse again. The noise had probably just been a worker dropping something while getting shelves stocked. She could see that a light was on under the door, but she wanted to be sure every-thing was okay. She stepped closer and put her ear to the door. She heard a low, pained moan, and her heart jumped into her throat.

She grabbed the door handle, thankful it wasn't locked, and charged inside. The door opened into a narrow carpeted hallway that led to a small office, the storage room, and then the main store. The moan sounded again. Louder this time.

"Hello?" she called out.

"In here," a familiar male voice croaked out. "Help."

"Charlie!" She'd recognize his deep, scratchy voice anywhere. Kincaid dropped the pepper spray into her purse and hurried toward the front of the store. The main lights weren't on yet, but the morning sun shining through the front windows gave off enough light for her to get her bearings. The store hadn't changed much since she'd last been in it—maybe more cluttered and dustier than Grace usually liked—but the familiarity took Kincaid's breath away for a second. Her head swam, the past and present ramming together, but she grabbed the edge of a shelf in the horror section and fought back the sensation. "Charlie, it's Kincaid. Where are you?"

"Science fiction," he ground out, pain in his voice.

Kincaid hurried through the cluttered store, dodging displays, and found Charlie on the floor, clutching the front of his shirt, a pile of books spilled next to him and a look of anguish on his face.

Kincaid dropped to her knees, panic filling her. "Charlie."

"Chest. Can't—"

Shit. Adrenaline zipped through her, making her tremble. Kincaid yanked her phone out of her purse and dialed for help as quickly as her fingers would allow her. "Okay, hang on, Charlie. Just breathe."

The 911 operator answered immediately, and Kincaid reported everything she was seeing. She grabbed Charlie's hand, finding his fingers clammy. "He's cold. And pale." *Hang on, Charlie.*

"Stay on the line, ma'am." The operator said an ambulance was being dispatched.

Kincaid murmured words of encouragement to Charlie, her heart like thunder in her throat. She didn't know what to do. She wanted to help, but she didn't want to move him or make anything worse. "It's going to be okay, Charlie. I'm here."

Heavy footsteps thumped behind her. "What's going on? I heard a crash."

Kincaid turned, phone still on her ear, and found Ash

staring down at the two of them in wide-eyed horror. The dispatcher asked her more questions, and she answered as if she were on autopilot. "Yes, chest pains. I don't know for how long. I found him on the floor. Yes, he's still conscious. No, I don't know CPR. Ash?"

Ash was taking all of it in as she spoke. He shook his head and dropped down next to Kincaid, his eyes on Charlie. "I don't. I'm sorry. Mr. Lowell, can you hear me? Help is on the way."

Charlie squeezed his eyes shut. "Stop calling me that, boy."

Ash smiled, though Kincaid could see the fear in his eyes. "Sorry, sir."

Charlie looked like he was going to protest the *sir,* too, but then he said something else instead. "Tell Grace I love her."

"Oh, hell no," Kincaid said, squeezing his hand. "You listen to me, Charlie. You're not going anywhere. You're going to tell her yourself."

He had to. Grace had lost enough in her life already. Kincaid had seen her face when she'd found out about Graham. That woman wouldn't survive another blow.

Ash met Kincaid's gaze and saw her own fear reflected there. Without warning, she was yanked back to *that* night. Images flashing in her vision. Blood all over her, not her own. Her head pounding. Shock turning her cold and stiff. Her thoughts scrambled from the concussion. Graham nowhere to be found. Ash holding her, refusing to let her run back inside.

The pieces were always the same. The aftermath but never the event itself. Big swaths of blankness in her brain. Some said her memory loss was a blessing, but scary things hid in that darkness and changed faces all the time.

"You're staying here with us," Ash said, his voice blending with the nightmare in her mind. "Don't try to get out of it."

Charlie's grip on her hand went limp, and her mind sank deeper into the memories. "Ash…we need to help him. Graham's inside…"

The sirens screamed in the distance, and tears welled in her eyes, panic like a living monster inside her, breathing its hot breath into all the scary places in her mind.

Ash looked her way and scooted closer. He took her face in his hands with a firm grip, catching her gaze. He gave her a determined look. "No. *Not* Graham. Charlie. Stay with me, KC. *Charlie* is going to be fine. It's going to be okay. You're here in the bookstore. You're with me. Me and Charlie. Feel my hands. Look at me."

She stared into Ash's eyes, the clear blue offering some kind of safe harbor from the memories. *Charlie.* The name rang like a bell in her head, jolting her from the flashback and making the present rush back to her in full force. A whispered plea escaped her. "Charlie."

Ash nodded, still cradling her face. "That's it," he said, voice gentle and soothing. "Stay with me. Don't go back there. Please. I need you here."

She closed her eyes, tears escaping silently. "Ash, we can't lose him, too."

He nodded and released his hold on her. "We won't." He looked away and focused on Charlie again. "I won't let you lose anyone else."

The sadness that washed through her at the thought threatened to drown her, but she didn't have time to lose it because the paramedics arrived a few seconds later. Ash let them in and they quickly surrounded Charlie. When she heard them say they had a heartbeat, she sagged against a nearby bookshelf and sobbed.

Not this time. Not today.

Thank you, universe.

Maybe it had been looking out for her today after all.

Ash stepped into the busy hallway at the hospital with two cups of steaming coffee. He could see Kincaid through the window of the waiting room. She'd pulled her knees up to her chest in the chair and was resting her chin atop them, her eyes closed. She looked incredibly young in that moment. Small and fragile and so unlike the brash, fearless woman she was on a normal day. Charlie's heart attack had terrified them both, but it'd triggered some kind of flashback for Kincaid. He'd recognized the dazed, lost quality of her voice instantly. Then she'd said Graham's name, and his stomach had hollowed out. He never wanted the memory of that night to come back to her. Just the thought sent dread rolling through him. He remembered enough for them both.

But she hadn't reacted any differently toward him after the flashback, so he knew she'd only seen what she already remembered—not that those memories were a walk in the park either.

Ash had been triggered a few times over the years and knew what those vivid images could do to a person, that descent back to the past. That kind of intense emotion left him feeling like his insides had been scooped out with a rusty spoon. Raw. Jittery. And he was probably the last person Kincaid wanted to deal with right now, but Grace was with Charlie, and he wasn't going to leave Kincaid sitting there alone.

With a steadying breath, he stepped forward and pushed open the door to the waiting room with his hip. Kincaid looked up at the sound, her eyes red-rimmed from crying. When she saw it was him, she frowned. "Oh. Hey."

He lifted the two paper cups in his hands. "I thought you might want a coffee. I also have a candy bar in my back pocket."

"Thanks. I'm not hungry." But she did accept the coffee from him.

"Even if you aren't, the sugar might help. All that adrenaline and...everything can leave you feeling shaky." He set an Almond Joy on the seat next to her. "I'm not sure if that's still your favorite but—"

She nodded, face expressionless. "Still is."

He released a tired breath and sank into the chair across from her. "Did the nurse come in with any other news?"

"They're prepping him for surgery but seem optimistic." She sipped the coffee and blanched a little. "I just can't shake that feeling that I almost walked out. If you hadn't cut your foot, if I hadn't gotten held up for a few extra minutes... If I'd known ahead of time that the apartment was taken. The tiniest change and he wouldn't have..."

Ash felt queasy at the thought. "But you were, and he's going to be okay. Don't do that to yourself. It's a shitty game that will make you insane. The what-if game is only good for writing books. In real life, it will drive you to drinking."

Something heavy hovered in her eyes. "You speaking from experience?"

He looked down at his coffee. "Not about the drinking. But the driving myself crazy thing? For sure."

"Right," she said, almost absently. He thought she wasn't going to say anything else to him, but then she asked, "How'd you make that stop?"

His attention flicked up. "What? Stop from driving myself crazy?"

"Yeah."

He ran a hand over the back of his neck, wary. "I did whatever I had to do."

"Meaning?"

"Meaning, I kept moving forward. I closed the door on the past." He stared down at his coffee. "I took on the pen name and started introducing myself with it. I stopped telling people where I was from so I didn't have to tell the story anymore or see those looks on their faces. I worked and traveled so much that I didn't have time to think about anything except writing and working odd jobs to make sure I had money to pay rent until I could get published."

"You became someone else." She said it like an accusation, not an observation. "How nice for you."

He bristled. "Being who I was hadn't worked out so well for me up until that point. It wasn't much of a loss to leave that guy behind."

A chilly expression filled her face, lips pressed together, eyes steely. "Right. Who cares who else you left behind with him?"

Ash's shoulders tightened, his defenses fully activated now. "Don't. Let's not pretend I didn't have your two hands on my back, pushing me out the door. What happened with us—that was a two-person job."

She looked away, a sag to her shoulders. "I just don't think it's fair that you get to walk away and not have to think about Long Acre anymore."

He scoffed. "You honestly think I don't think about it? Come on, Kincaid. Moving on with my life doesn't mean I'm heartless. What happened here is burned into me, always there. There's no forgetting. Even if I wanted to."

She gave him a skeptical look. "So what was your big what-if?"

"My what?"

"Your what-if. About prom night. We all have them."

"Kincaid," he warned.

"No, I want to know," she said, determination in her gaze. "If you think about it so much, you must have a few."

His throat felt dry even after swallowing a big gulp of coffee. He didn't know if he could answer that question. There were too many what-ifs he'd gone through over the years. But as he sat there, one floated up to the top. *What if I'd never fallen in love with you?*

"What if I'd skipped prom?" he said instead. Even though that wasn't his main one, it was a valid one. He'd wondered countless times what would've happened if he'd stuck with his original plan and hadn't gone that night. If he hadn't seen what he'd seen. If he hadn't made the decision he had.

Would Graham still be alive? Would Kincaid now be married to him with a house full of kids? Would she be happy?

Ash would never know those answers.

She gave him an unimpressed look. "Not a very original one, writer boy."

"I didn't know we were being graded on creativity."

She set aside her coffee and grabbed the candy bar, picking absently at the wrapper. "I don't ask that one. I never would've skipped prom. That wasn't a what-if for me."

"What's yours then?" he asked, unable to stop himself. "No, let me guess. *What if Ash would've taken the bullet instead of Graham?*"

Her gasp was audible in the quiet hum of the empty waiting room. "Jesus, Ash."

His jaw flexed. "What? You're saying you never had that thought? It's one of my what-ifs."

Hurt flashed over her face. "Is that really what you believe I'd wish for? You think I could ever hate you that much?"

He turned his head, unable to keep looking at her. She could, *would*, if she remembered how that night had really gone. "I don't know what to think."

She let out a heavy sigh, and after a long pause, she placed a segment of Almond Joy on top of his jean-clad thigh, sharing like she used to do when they were kids. Halfsies were always the deal with candy bars. "Well, you're an idiot. I hate how things went down with us. I hate how things are now. And of course I wish Graham were still here. But I would never, ever wish it were you instead. What you're forgetting is that I loved you *both*. You were my best friend, Ash. I wanted a world with both of you in it. Turns out, I ended up with one that has neither."

Ash stared at the small piece of chocolate, a heaviness settling on him.

"So my what-if," she went on, "is what if I hadn't been so concerned about winning the popularity prize of prom queen, and we had all left early to go to the after-party instead of staying until the crowning. Then I'd still have you both. My soul mate *and* my best friend. Or who knows, maybe I wouldn't have you. You always couldn't wait to leave. I just never thought that you'd be able to do it and not look back."

Nausea welled up in him, the words cutting little scars into his already ravaged psyche. "Let's not play this game anymore, okay? It's useless. We can't go back."

"No," she said, resignation coming into her voice. "We can't."

She set her half of the candy bar down on the table, stood, and walked away without another word.

chapter
FIVE

"So how exactly does this best-friend-is-a-girl thing work?" Graham asked without preamble as he leaned a shoulder against the locker next to Ash's and watched him load books into his backpack. "Like, how much does Kincaid tell you?"

Ash glanced over at Graham, who had that intense look he sometimes got when he was overly focused on something, the look that caused a vertical line in his forehead. Ash hedged. "What do you mean?"

Graham frowned. "You know, does she talk to you like she'd talk to another girl?"

Ash snorted. "If you're worried that she's telling me the private details of your relationship or whatever, don't. I don't need to know what kind of kisser you are. Believe me, that's a line neither of us is interested in crossing."

"No, not about me and her," Graham said. "I mean

before we were together. Did she confide in you about stuff?"

Ash shoved his PE uniform in his locker and made room for Trevor Lockwood, who had the locker to the left of Ash's. He nodded at Trevor in a silent *what's up* acknowledgment. The kid never said much, but that was an improvement over last year when Ash's locker was next to Vivian Lansing's. She was always making out with her boyfriend and blocking the way to Ash's locker with their PDAs.

Trevor nodded back at Ash, gave Graham the side-eye, and then turned to his locker, acting as if Ash and Graham weren't there. Ash refocused on his friend. "She's your girlfriend, man. You know how she talks. She talks about everything. Quickly. Constantly. Sometimes I listen, sometimes it all blends together. Why?"

That wasn't entirely true. Ash listened more than he should. Filed away more details about Kincaid these days than he had any right to. But he knew Graham well enough to know he wouldn't appreciate that tidbit of trivia.

"Hey, dude, you almost done?" Graham asked, eyeing Trevor. "Personal shit to discuss."

Trevor ignored him but slammed his locker shut with extra force a few seconds later and loped off down the hallway.

"That kid's weird," Graham said before crossing his arms and looking back to Ash. "So I know Kincaid talks a lot and she trusts you."

"Right," Ash said, still not following.

"So you must know who's on her list."

The final bell for bus riders sounded as a few

freshmen hurried by. Ash's dad's bulldog voice came over the intercom, announcing football practice would start fifteen minutes late. The requisite shudder at hearing his father's voice went through him. Ash closed his locker and turned to Graham. "Her list?"

"Yeah." He shrugged a shoulder. "You know, of guys she's slept with."

Ash stiffened. "What?"

"Come on," Graham said, tone light but brown eyes serious. "You two have been friends forever. You know who she's dated."

Ash scowled as he hitched his backpack onto his shoulders, and the two of them started to walk down the hall. "So do you."

"Yeah, but a lot of those guys were just casual things. I'm talking about the ones who were more than that. I mean, I'm assuming that asshole Nick Lightman because she wouldn't have pulled that stunt last year when he cheated on her if he hadn't meant something to her."

Ash smirked. He'd helped Kincaid buy the discounted dog food at the Feed and Farm for that big show. It'd taken the two of them a full hour to load Nick's convertible with all that kibble. But when Nick had walked outside and seen the word *Dawg* scrawled across his windshield and his precious Mustang filled with dog food, Ash had almost given himself away because he couldn't wipe the grin off his face. That prick had had it coming.

But Ash didn't like the direction this conversation was going. Graham was a good friend to him, a good guy in general. But lately, the way he'd been talking and acting about Kincaid was giving Ash a queasy feeling. "If you want to know, why don't you ask her?"

"Because she made me promise early on that we wouldn't discuss past relationships." Graham peeked over his shoulder as if to verify Kincaid wasn't behind him. "I think she worries that I'm going to think she's a slut or something."

The word was like a record scratch in Ash's ears. Of all the things someone could call Kincaid, that word would cut her the deepest. "You can't blame her for being worried. It's been thrown at her before."

"It's not her fault who her mother is," Graham said with a frown. "You know I don't judge her for that."

Ash adjusted his backpack on his shoulders, the weight feeling somehow heavier all of a sudden. "But would you if you found out she'd slept with ten guys before you?"

His head turned Ash's way, his jaw hardening. "There were *ten*?"

Ash's frown deepened at Graham's reaction. The guy looked ready to crack someone's skull. "Dude, calm down. I have no idea what her number is or who's on her list. She doesn't tell me about *that* stuff. But why does it matter? As long as she's not sleeping with other people while she's with you, it's the past. You have a list, too."

Graham hooked his thumbs in the straps of his backpack. "Yeah, but those girls didn't mean anything to me. I mean, I cared about them at the time, but it wasn't, like, love or whatever."

Ash shrugged. "I'm sure hers weren't either. I can tell you that she's never said she loved a guy before—at least not to me. You were the first guy she ever used that word about."

"She says she loves you all the time," he pointed out.

Ash shook his head. "You know that's different." Totally, completely, *painfully* different. "But all I'm saying is I wouldn't worry about the guys from her past. You're just going to drive yourself nuts."

"It *does* drive me nuts. That guy Justin she used to date has been hanging around her a lot lately, making jokes and being nice to her. I see how he looks at her when she walks away. And she just rolls her eyes when I bring it up. She's too nice to him. It encourages him. She doesn't see what he's trying to do."

"Kincaid's friendly to everybody, man," Ash said. "That's just how she is. Let it go. She loves *you*. It's obvious to anyone who's around the two of you. You guys are sickening. You've got nothing to worry about."

Graham let out a breath, and finally, the corners of his lips turned up a little. "You're right. I'm overreacting. I just can't stand when other guys look at her like that, especially the ones who've already touched her. And she's, like, oblivious, being all friendly back. Guys take that shit like an invitation, especially ones like Justin. It makes me want to ruin my perfect school record and punch the dude in the face just to remind him that she's mine."

"That who's yours?" a lilting voice asked.

Ash and Graham looked ahead to find Kincaid smiling at them from a few steps away. She was already in her dance-team workout clothes, ready for after-school practice. Ash dutifully ignored the short shorts and her long, tanned legs, tried to remember her as a fifth grader with dirty, bony knees instead. Failed.

Graham grinned and stepped forward to wrap an arm around her waist. "That you're all mine, baby. I was just telling Ash that I can't wait to get to college so we can get our own little apartment, and I can have you all to myself."

All to himself. A muscle in Ash's jaw twitched, and something like dread rolled through him. He hated even having that feeling about his friend, but lately he couldn't shake that uncomfortable itch. He rolled his shoulders, trying to shrug it off. His own crap was clouding things. He was probably seeing stuff that wasn't really there. "Y'all are getting an apartment together? I thought you were going to be in a dorm, Graham."

Kincaid hugged Graham and sent Ash a smile from over Graham's shoulder. "He's supposed to be. No way are the Lowells going to let me shack up with him. He's dreaming."

Graham leaned back, looking down at her. "They will see logic. I just have to pitch it the right way. They love you. And it's more economical than paying for separate housing for both of us. The community college is only a few miles from TCU. It makes sense to get one place in between."

Ash shifted on his feet. Part of him was thrilled for Kincaid. He knew better than anyone how distant a dream college had been for her until the Lowells and Graham had come into her life. When Graham's family had offered to help her go to a community college near the university Graham had chosen, it was as if Kincaid had been given a golden ticket. But the thought of Graham and Kincaid being on their own in another town, sharing an apartment next year? Kincaid being uprooted from everyone she knew and depending on Graham and his family entirely? It left a bad taste in Ash's mouth.

Maybe Ash needed to face that this was probably straight-up jealousy. For so long, it'd been him and Kincaid. Way before more complicated feelings had gotten involved, she'd been his closest friend. Now he had to share her with Graham and would soon be going to school in a completely different state from her while Graham got to be with her. He'd dreamt of getting out of this claustrophobic small town and away from his family for as long as he could remember. He could go somewhere else and not be the famous Coach Isaacs letdown of a son. He could be whoever he wanted to be. Start fresh. He still wanted that so much, his muscles ached. He'd worked so damn hard for his scholarship, worked all those long hours at the store in order to say *Fuck you, I don't need your money or your approval* to his dad. But he'd never considered that leaving Long Acre also meant leaving Kincaid on her own with Graham.

"You okay, Ash?" Kincaid asked, eyeing him. "You look weird."

Ash choked down the feeling of dread and forced a wry look onto his face. "Your girlfriend is way too obsessed with me, man. I mean, I feel outright objectified."

Graham snorted and Kincaid rolled her eyes.

"And maybe I'm just weird," Ash said, cocking a brow.

"Hell yes, you are," Kincaid declared. She strode over and patted his cheek, almost dislodging his glasses. "That's why I love you. Weirdo."

Ash felt like a world-class dick for the image that floated through his mind, a fantasy where he looped his

fingers around Kincaid's wrist, dragged her against a
locker, and kissed that watermelon-flavored gloss off
her lips while Graham watched. Showed her that she had
options beyond hitching a ride on Graham's coattails.
Ash curled his fingers into his palm. If he needed any
more confirmation that all these bad feelings were
rooted in jealousy, that was all he needed.

He was a horrible friend. To Graham. And to Kincaid.
She'd never trust him again or be so at ease around
him if she knew the things that went through his mind
anytime she was around. He'd broken a promise they'd
made to each other long ago when yet another boy had
called her Bouncy Breslin and made lewd comments.
Ash had promised that he'd never look at her that way,
that they'd always be friends and not let the boy-girl
stuff get in the way. His boy stuff was in serious breach
of contract.

"You're the weird one," he managed to croak out.

"Thanks, pumpkin." She smiled that mischievous
Kincaid smile and then grabbed Graham's hand. "Come
and watch practice for a little while. I get to do a solo
part this time." She waggled her eyebrows at him. "The
splits are involved."

Graham groaned and sent a what-can-you-do look to
Ash. "Can you cover for me a little while at the store?"

Ash nodded. "I got it."

It wasn't like Grace and Charlie were going to fire
their own son.

Graham smiled. "You're the best, Isaacs."

No, he was the worst, but he managed to keep his
expression neutral. "You know it."

And as they turned and walked away, Kincaid

leaning her head on Graham's shoulder and broadcasting her happiness with every bit of her body language, Ash made a promise to himself to stop acting like this. Kincaid was his best friend. She had never shown one inkling of romantic interest in him. She was happy. Graham was happy. And the Lowells were going to help Kincaid escape this town and her shitty mother.

Ash was not going to get in the way of that.

He pushed down the nagging feelings that had surfaced earlier with Graham and made a decision. He wasn't going to torture himself with thinking about what couldn't be anymore. He needed to move on. The first order of business would be finding a prom date so Kincaid would stop asking him about it and making him want things he couldn't have.

He needed to show her and himself that he was capable of doing more than reading books. He pulled out his cell phone and dialed his lab partner, Evie, from chemistry. She accepted without hesitation.

There. Done. He would go to prom. Be normal. Have fun. Maybe even kiss someone. He was done pining for Kincaid Breslin.

chapter

SIX

ASH OPENED THE FRONT DOOR OF THE LOWELLS' HOUSE TO find Kincaid standing on the porch with food containers stacked three high in her arms. She peeked around the tower of food and her eyebrows arched. "Oh, hey. What are you doing here?"

It'd been a few days since Charlie had returned home after an angioplasty and stenting, and Ash had managed to avoid Kincaid during the visits he'd made. He should've known his luck would run out sooner or later. He reached out to take the load from her. "I brought over some groceries. Grace didn't feel comfortable leaving Charlie alone and asked if I could stop by the store for her."

"Oh," Kincaid said with a frown. "Well, I could've done that. She called me earlier, and I told her I'd be bringing some food by."

"I didn't mind." The bottom casserole dish was warm against his arms. "What is all this?"

"A few dinners for the freezer. Two kinds of muffins."

Her nose wrinkled. "The muffins are an experiment. I'm not used to cooking with all the whole-grain stuff so hopefully they don't taste like baked dirt."

"Oh, I'm sure they'll be delicious," Grace said, stepping into the foyer, her eyes tired but her smile bright and her auburn hair in her signature twist. She pressed her hands together, giving Kincaid a warm look. "Everything you make is amazing, sweetheart. You've surpassed Charlie in the kitchen, which isn't an easy thing to do." She shook her head. "To think when we met you, your idea of gourmet was a cream cheese and Froot Loop sandwich."

Ash grimaced. "Ugh. She served me that once when we were kids. It was very…crunchy. And moist."

Kincaid laughed. "Says the guy who thought mayo and mustard sandwiches were a valid life choice."

"Hey, I stand by that sandwich," Ash said. "Poor man's egg-salad sandwich."

Kincaid snorted. "Well, thankfully I'm past the Froot Loop phase, and you were never that poor, so that was no excuse."

Ash winced. "I didn't mean—"

She rolled her eyes. "It was a joke. Don't be so sensitive, Ash."

Still, he felt like a dick. His solidly middle-class upbringing looked lavish compared to how Kincaid had grown up.

"Plus," she went on, oblivious to the sour feeling in Ash's stomach, "once I had Charlie's homemade mac and cheese, I knew I could never go back to living on boxed stuff. I had to learn how to cook."

Enticing smells wafted up from the containers Ash

was holding. It was hard to imagine Kincaid as some master cook. She'd grown up having to fend for herself with frozen and boxed meals because her mom worked nights, but he remembered her cookbook-obsession phase at the bookstore. She used to read recipe descriptions aloud to him in a sex-operator voice. She'd done it as a joke, but more than once, he'd had to take a strategic position behind the main desk to hide how she was affecting him. He'd learned quickly that seventeen-year-old penises *could not* be trusted.

But along the way, Kincaid had apparently started doing more than reading the recipes. He'd tasted some of her offerings at Christmases over the years. The woman cooked like she had a seasoned southern grandma who'd handed down her generations-old recipe box. Maybe that was what she told people who didn't know her real story.

"I'll just put these in the kitchen," Ash said, wanting to escape the old familiarity that was trying to leach in.

"Thanks, hon," Grace said as he passed by. "After you get all that put away, can you meet us in the living room? Charlie and I want to speak to both of you about something."

Ash glanced over his shoulder and caught Kincaid's confused look. It probably mirrored his own. "Everything okay?" he asked.

Grace nodded. "Yes, of course. Look at the two of you, both with the worried faces. It's nothing bad."

Ash let out a breath he didn't realize he'd been holding. "Okay, good. Just give me a minute."

"And bring some of those muffins with you," Charlie called out from the living room.

Kincaid's lips curved. "His heart may have some

issues, but his hearing's as good as a bat's. The muffins have flax," she called out to him. "You've been warned."

"*Flax*?" Charlie said as if the word were from a foreign language. "I don't know what that is, but bring some butter with them."

"No butter," Grace announced to Charlie and then poked Ash in the shoulder. "No butter for him, you hear?"

"Yes, ma'am." Ash couldn't help but laugh as he carried the food into the kitchen. Charlie had scared the hell out of him the other day. It was good to hear the guy demanding baked goods.

After Ash had put away the food that needed to be refrigerated, he brought out a plate of molasses brown muffins, the smell of warm spices making his stomach rumble. The living room was big, with high-beamed ceilings and tall windows that looked out onto the rolling green of the backyard and the pool. Yet Grace had made the place cozy with cushy, dark leather furniture and soft lamplight. Charlie was propped up in a recliner, still looking worn and pale, but the glint in his eyes was back. Grace was in a nearby chair, staying within arm's length of her husband. Kincaid had taken the couch, her legs crossed, her knee-high boot bouncing with nervous energy.

Ash set the muffins on the coffee table, his skin prickling with a weird electric awareness. Something was off about the way the Lowells were looking at him and Kincaid.

"Thank you," Grace said and motioned toward the couch. "Sit. We'll eat in a minute. We wanted to talk to you both first."

Ash took the spot next to Kincaid. She smelled like the muffins mixed with her own familiar scent, a vanilla lotion she'd been using for as long as he'd known her. Part of him wanted to take a deeper inhale—the stupid, totally driven-by-instinct part of him. He resisted leaning any closer, and she gave him a do-you-know-what-this-is-about look. He shrugged.

Grace glanced back and forth between the two of them, expression pensive. "First, I want you both to know that what we're going to discuss is not a decision we made lightly. It's something we've been thinking about for a while. Charlie's heart scare has just…made the decision easier."

Ash's jaw tightened, her tone making him nervous. It was a tone similar to the one Melanie had used when she'd sat him down and said, *We need to talk about the wedding*. "What decision?"

"Well," Grace said, folding her hands in her lap, her voice as calm as ever. "As you know, the bookstore has been a treasure to us for a very long time. It has been our livelihood, yes, but also our passion. Running the store has given us so much joy and has supported us through good and very bad times. It also brought the two of you into our lives. Into our son's life."

Ash's muscles tensed.

"It will always be special to us. But," Grace contin-ued, "we can no longer fool ourselves into thinking we're as young and spry as we used to be. Running a business is a huge responsibility and a heck of a lot of work, especially when the market has changed and the store's not bringing in as much as it once was. We've had to change a lot of our offerings, cut back staff, and do a lot of work ourselves."

Ash frowned. So that was why Charlie had been

lifting boxes and stocking books the other day instead of some high-school kid.

"But we've realized that we can't and don't want to keep doing that," Charlie interjected. "My body reminded me of that this week."

"Right," Grace continued. "We want to be able to savor our retirement years, to slow down and go on vacations, to reap the rewards of all that we've worked for. We can't do that if we run ourselves into the ground before we ever get a chance."

"Can you hire a general manager?" Kincaid asked. "Just be the owners?"

"General managers are expensive, and there's still a lot involved in ownership," Grace explained. "And I feel like it's just…time. I think we've held onto it more for nostalgia than for anything else these last few years. I can still picture Graham toddling through the aisles and pulling all the books off the shelves when we first stocked the store." Her eyes misted even though a tender smile stayed in place.

"I also remember you, Kincaid, walking in there that first day and demanding a big book to read, your little blond ponytail sitting on top of your head like an exclamation point. And you, Ash, so sweet and hardworking, determined to read a pile of books each week so you could make good recommendations. It's a scrapbook of our lives in a lot of ways."

Ash swallowed hard, his throat burning.

"But memories are in our heads and in our hearts. I don't need the physical place to hold them. I have them all in here." Grace pressed a hand to her chest. "Which is why we've decided to sell the business."

Ash's heart dropped into his stomach and a hundred protests jumped to his lips, but Kincaid was the first to voice what was in his head.

"*Sell?*" she said, a hairline fracture of panic in her voice. "You can't sell the store. It's...who you are. It's...memories. Not just yours. So many people's. It's part of this town."

Ash glanced her way, seeing the earnestness on her face, the heartbreak. Another loss handed to her. He knew Kincaid had grown up in that store. He hadn't fallen in love with it until he was around twelve, when she'd dragged him from his usual spot at the library and introduced him to the wonders of The Stuffed Shelf. Before that, he'd figured why bother since his parents would never have given him money to buy books.

His father wouldn't want to encourage his son's "weird, loner habit." Boys should play outside. Boys should be involved in sports. Boys should be the star on their father's football team. But even with Ash's later start with The Stuffed Shelf, the store occupied a special spot in his memory bank, too—both happy and sad memories resided there. It was the first place he'd ever felt like he truly belonged.

"Are you sure that's the only way?" Ash asked. "There's got to be some other option."

"I know this may be upsetting," Grace went on. "It warms my heart to know that you both feel an attachment to it. That does more for me than you realize." She pressed her lips together for a moment, gathering herself. "It was always our intention to pass the store along to Graham when we got to this age, to make it a family legacy."

Charlie reached out and grabbed Grace's hand when her voice caught.

"But that wasn't meant to be," she said softly. "And who knows? Maybe Graham would've wanted to make his own path. We'll never know. Lord knows I could never make him a bookworm. He had a stubborn streak a mile long. But seeing you both here today, how you're reacting, makes me feel at peace with what we're going to ask of you."

"I don't understand," Ash said.

Grace sat up straighter, her elegant demeanor making her look ten years younger. "We're going to sell the business, and we need both of you to help us do that."

"What do you mean?" Kincaid asked.

Charlie cleared his throat, a great rumble of a noise. "I hate to say it, but the store isn't what it used to be. We haven't been able to keep it up as well as we would like. We've only been opening four days a week lately, and sales haven't been great. But that's our fault, not the store's. We need to sell it, but it breaks my heart—no pun intended," he said with a wink and a gentle tap to his chest, "to think of it becoming another type of business and the town losing its only bookstore. I want to sell it to someone who wants to keep it as a bookstore."

"Charlie, that's…" Kincaid started but let her words trail off.

Ash could fill in for her. *Difficult. Challenging. Nearly impossible.*

"It needs to be attractive to buyers to get top dollar," Charlie continued. "Cleaned out. Modernized a little. It needs some of its charm back."

"Right," Grace said. "And you two know that store almost as well as we do, which is where you come in. We know you're both busy and it's a lot to ask, but it seems serendipitous to have Ash in town for a while, like this was how it was supposed to be. Even though I'm sorry it was a breakup that brought you back here, Ash."

Kincaid turned her head his way, and he cringed inwardly.

"But we would love it if you two could help us get it looking as pretty as a picture again," Grace continued. "Then once it's ready, Kincaid, if you could use your real-estate skills to get us a good sale, that would be a tremendous help."

"Of course," Kincaid said, still looking taken aback. "I'll do whatever you need me to do. I don't want the town to lose the store."

"Ash?" Grace's gaze flicked to him.

"Absolutely," Ash said without hesitation, even though it felt as though he was stumbling drunk along the edge of some cliff. "Whatever you need."

Grace smiled, eyes sparkling with unshed tears. "Thank you. You are both a gift to us. I don't know what we would've done without you two after everything happened. I feel deep in my heart that Graham sent you both to us, knowing the two of you would keep us from losing ourselves in all that grief."

Ash looked down, his ribs cinching tight, guilt like a black beastly thing inside him. He could see Kincaid's knuckles whiten as she gripped the edge of the couch cushion and took a deep breath.

"So here's the second part of our news," Grace went on. "When we sell it, we're sharing the profit with the

two of you. A third to each of you. The last third will be
used to start a foundation in Graham's name."

Ash's head snapped up. "What? Grace, Charlie, no,
you don't need to do that. This is your retirement money."

"Your go-to-the-Bahamas money," Kincaid agreed.
"We could never accept something like that. You've
earned that money. It's yours to burn."

"No," Charlie said gruffly. "It's ours to share with
our family. We have enough savings to see us through
retirement. We want to give this to you both."

Ash's throat was burning, an overwhelming sensation
welling up in him and cutting off his breath. *Family*. He
wanted so much for that to be true. He wanted to claim
Grace and Charlie as his own, forget the people who'd
raised him and cut him from their lives. But he couldn't
accept the gift of the Lowells' family legacy, of their
love. He didn't deserve it.

"We couldn't," Ash said finally.

"You will," said Grace. "I wasn't giving you an
option, young man."

Kincaid scooted closer, presumably to plead with
Grace, but her knee ended up bumping against Ash's,
she was so close. "Give it all to Graham's foundation,"
she said. "It was supposed to be his store. Let all of it
go to his name."

Grace arched a brow. "Missy, didn't I hear at my
lady's business luncheon this week that a certain local
real-estate agent bought that old farmhouse off Millcreek
Road and was looking for investors for her new B and
B? Didn't I hear that she needed a significant amount
of money to get the project off the ground, or she was
going to be in trouble?"

Ash turned his head in surprise. "You bought a farmhouse?"

Kincaid bit her lip but then straightened her shoulders. "You know how gossipy those ladies can be. I wouldn't believe a word of it."

"Lying ain't nice," Charlie chided.

Kincaid closed her eyes briefly. "Yes, sir. I may have made an impulsive purchase."

Grace nodded. "Well, stop being so hardheaded then. My boy loved you and wanted to give you the world. He'd sure as heck want you to use this money for something you're passionate about. I'm sure he's smiling up there right now at the thought."

Kincaid let out a shaky breath, obviously trying not to cry.

"If you can get a good price for the store, we can help you with what you need," Grace continued. "Be warned. It's not going to be easy. The last appraisal we got on it was not promising. But I have faith in the two of you."

Ash grimaced. If Graham was up in heaven, he'd sure as hell *not* want Ash taking his money. Ash should probably watch out for stray lightning bolts or swarms of locusts. "I don't know anything about real estate, Grace."

"No, hon, but you know books," she replied. "You know what's hot now and what's selling. You've probably seen hundreds of modern bookshops in New York and around the world that you could draw inspiration from. Just make the place somewhere you'd want to hang out."

"I already want to hang out there," he answered.

"Aside from nostalgia, is that really true?" she

pressed. "Would Ashton Stone, thriller writer extraordinaire, want to host a book signing there?"

Ash thought about the current dusty, cramped state of the store. The too-dim lights. The worn furniture. "Maybe?"

Grace lifted a brow, making her point. The woman had missed her calling as a lawyer. "Then it's settled. We're putting you two in charge. You can close the shop while you evaluate things. The sooner we get moving on this, the better. Now"—she slapped her hands on her thighs and pushed herself up from her seat—"who's ready for muffins?"

Ash looked over to Kincaid as Grace busied herself with the muffins. Kincaid gave him a wary look and then touched his knee. "Hey, I could go for some coffee. Ash, why don't you help me in the kitchen? I can't carry four mugs at once."

Ash blinked at her bright tone, but Kincaid gave him a tight, don't-you-dare-question-me smile. He nodded. "Yeah, sure."

He stood and Kincaid hurried into the kitchen, her boots *click-click-clicking* on the hardwood. When they both reached the kitchen, she whirled around, blond hair swinging like a curtain around her. "What in *the hell* are we doing?"

chapter
SEVEN

ASH RAKED A HAND THROUGH HIS HAIR AT KINCAID'S exasperated tone. What in the hell *were* they doing? "I don't know. How are we supposed to say no?"

"How can we say *yes*?"

"They need our help," he replied, determination hardening his words. "I know this isn't…an ideal situation, but I would literally do anything for Grace and Charlie. I'm not going to say no."

"Listen to what you're saying. You really want to spend the next month cleaning up The Stuffed Shelf with me? Think about that, Ash."

He scowled.

"Besides the fact that we…are what we are these days, I can't even go in there anymore without"—she looked away, jaw flexing—"without remembering…"

Graham. She didn't say it but she didn't have to. They both had so many memories tied up in that little shop. Ash's were of her. Hers were of Graham. His defensiveness deflated. "I understand. Look, if it's too hard for you, I can handle getting the store ready. I can do it alone. I'm stuck in writer's block with my book anyway. It will give me thinking time. You can just focus on selling the place."

She looked to the ceiling and blew out a long breath. "I can't trust you to do that by yourself."

"What?" he asked, affronted. "You think I would mess up things for Grace and Charlie? You—"

"You don't live here anymore. You said it yourself. You're a different person now. You don't know what this town needs." She gave him a petulant look as she grabbed the full coffee carafe and started pouring the coffee into mugs. "Even if you're trying to be helpful, you're going to make it into some weird hipster, man-cave bookstore."

Ash huffed and crossed his arms. "Did you just call me a hipster?"

She set down the carafe and pointed her finger at him, indicating his general person. "Darlin', your photo could be in Wikipedia describing your hipster species. You just need to grow out the I'm-a-writer-who-stayed-up-too-late-and-forgot-to-shave stubble into a full beard."

He glanced down at his outfit, a plaid shirt thrown over a T-shirt and jeans. "Hey, I could also be a lumber-jack. Or a cowboy."

"Lumberjacks and cowboys don't wear skinny jeans and dark-rimmed glasses," she said, grabbing sweetener packets. "Not that I'm surprised you've gone down this road. You were always a little froufrou. Even when you didn't put egg on those mayo and mustard sandwiches, you'd cut the crusts off."

He flipped her off, but the gesture didn't have any

ire behind it. It'd been a reflex, something he used to do when they were teens and she'd tease him. He dropped his arm to his side. "Maybe I'm just not as comfortable being a small-town bumpkin, like some people, *darlin'*."

"*Bumpkin?*" She blinked in shock and then threw a packet of Sweet'N Low at him. "You take that back, Ashton Isaacs. I am a lot of things, but I am no bumpkin. Just because I stayed here and didn't run away like *some people* doesn't make me backward. It makes me loyal."

His jaw flexed. "Stop saying I ran. I was always planning on getting out of this town. You knew that."

"Yeah, well, you sure did it fast," she said. "Right after you got what you wanted from me."

He stared at her in disbelief. "What I *wanted?* Right, because what I wanted was to lose my virginity to someone who called me by another guy's name and then kicked me out like I'd taken advantage of her. That was real high on my bucket list, let me tell you."

She sucked in a breath, her eyes going wide. "Wait, your *what* now?"

He raked a hand through his hair. "Forget it. It doesn't matter."

But Kincaid wasn't one to let things go. He knew that. He couldn't believe he'd let the virginity comment slip. She stared at him, coffee forgotten. "That was your *first time?*" She sounded horrified. "Ash. *God.* Why would you let that... Why would you...with me?"

He shook his head and stared at a scratch on the counter. "Who knows? We were both so emotionally fucked up that night that I don't even remember how it happened." One truth and a lie. "There wasn't a lot of thinking involved. I think we both just wanted to stop hurting for a few minutes."

She looked well and truly disturbed. "You should've said something. You should've—"

"I should've never touched you," he said simply, cutting her off with a firm look. "You were his. Even after he was gone. Even now."

She frowned.

"You were never going to forgive me for that night. Our friendship went up in flames the moment we crossed that line. The trust was gone. There was no point in sticking around to watch it burn."

She gave him a disbelieving look. "Just like that. You got to decide that with no input from me? I was freaking out that night, Ash. What we did... I earned that freak-out. When I kicked you out, I expected we would fight about it the next day. I didn't expect you to drop our friendship like it was a piece of trash, to drop *me* like I was a piece of trash. Real friends don't bail like that. You were my *person*. I had no one when you left. You wouldn't even take my calls."

He looked down, shame welling in him. "I couldn't be around you. It was all...too much. I needed to block everything out, pretend Long Acre didn't happen for a while."

She sucked in a breath. "*Pretend it didn't happen?* How could you—"

"It was the only way I could handle it, all right?" he said, his words sharper than he intended. "I'm not saying it was a good way or a noble way, but it was the only way I knew how to survive." To not feel. To cut off all that empty, bottomless grief. The black guilt. The broken heart. To block out that he'd lost everyone important to him in one fell swoop. He refused to drown himself in a bottle like he'd wanted to, but he'd disappeared in another way. He'd jumped right into a summer program at college. He'd buried himself in his first attempt at a novel, living in the head of his character instead of residing in his own.

"You can't just pretend something like that away, Ash," she said, hurt simmering there. "You pretended *me* away."

"And you pretended I was someone else."

She winced, confirming that her calling him Graham back then hadn't been a slip of the tongue.

"How's that coffee coming?" Grace called from the living room. "Do you need any help?"

"No, we got it. Be there in a minute," Kincaid called out, voice pinched. She paused for a long moment and then let out a defeated breath. "I hate this."

"What?" he asked, voice quiet.

"This. It's exhausting." She rubbed the spot between her eyes. "This is not how I live my life. You had your way of surviving. Well, mine has been that I refuse to let the past drag me down. I don't want that tragedy's fingerprints all over my life. And this—this ugly thing between us—it absolutely sucks my life force."

His shoulders sagged. "I don't want to do that to you."

She gave him a pleading look. "So why do we do this to each other? What good does it do? It's not going to bring Graham or anyone else back. It's not going to erase the fact that you left me behind or that I apparently *took your virginity*, that we used each other in a way we shouldn't have because we were young and grieving and stupid. All it does is make me freaking miserable anytime I'm around you. What's the point?"

His mouth lifted at one corner. "Because Kincaid Breslin loves a grudge?"

She made a choked sound, almost a laugh. "Well, okay, I'll give you that. I am pretty good at them. High horses are my favorite to get up on."

He gave her a tentative smile.

"God." She tilted her head back and stared at the ceiling. "I can't believe you were a virgin."

He rubbed a hand over the back of his neck. "I can't believe you couldn't tell."

She groaned and faced him, some light coming back into her eyes. "And the name thing. You must've demanded every woman you've slept with since call out your name."

He couldn't help but snort. Only Kincaid would think it was okay to ask him what women called him in bed. "Actually, I prefer they call me *sir*. When they're not gagged, that is."

Her eyebrows shot up, and then she burst out laughing when she realized he was kidding.

"But with all the panting and moaning, they really can't form words anyway," he added, deadpan.

She bit her lips together, quelling the laugh, and cocked her head to the side, evaluating him. "You *have* changed. The Ash I knew would've never been able to make that joke without blushing."

He braced his hands on the counter, leaning forward and lowering his voice to a conspiratorial whisper. "Don't tell anyone, but I'm not a seventeen-year-old virgin anymore."

He straightened and something unreadable flickered in her eyes. "No, I guess you're not." A little line appeared between her brows, but then she smoothed it with a smile. "I was never a seventeen-year-old virgin. I finally beat the overachiever at something."

He smirked. "Yeah, because dog food guy was an excellent choice for that honor."

"Lord, don't remind me." She got a wistful look. "But do you remember his abs?"

"I remember you *talking* about his abs. A lot. I tried to block out those conversations."

"You never had a proper appreciation for girl talk," she griped.

"Yes. I was a failure as a best friend."

She huffed.

"No, really," he said, dropping the playful tone. "I was. I'm not sorry I left. I wouldn't have survived here. But I'm sorry I abandoned our friendship. I should've let you fight it out with me."

She nodded and wet her lips. "We both made mistakes. I think all this time in my head, I imagined you seduced me, convinced me in my mixed-up state that it would make things better. I felt so sick that it had happened, that I had betrayed Graham so soon after his death. But you didn't seduce me. You came over to comfort me, and I showed you how I wanted to be comforted."

"I still should've said no," he said. "I could've stopped it."

"Why didn't you?" she asked softly.

Because I'd wanted you so long. Because I'd loved you even longer. Because I thought you were finally seeing me like I saw you. "Because I needed to forget what was going on for a little while, too. I wasn't thinking beyond the next moment back then."

She wrinkled her nose. "I still seem to have a problem with that. The not-thinking-ahead part."

"Like when you automatically agreed to refurb and sell a bookstore with your sworn enemy?"

Kincaid stepped closer and put her hand on his arm. "How about I take you off the sworn enemies list? There's a loophole in the must-hate-you contract."

"A loophole?"

"Yeah, the I-took-your-virginity-and-called-you-by-my-boyfriend's-name loophole. There's also the we-were-seventeen-and-completely-annihilated-by-grief clause."

He couldn't help but notice she said *boyfriend* and not *ex*. What did you call someone who you never got to break up with? "Those are very specific loopholes."

"So I am willing to agree that we were both kids and that we've both made mistakes. You've made more. Let's be clear on that," she said, poking him in the shoulder. "You abandoned a girl with abandonment issues."

He smirked at the glimpse of normal Kincaid surfacing. "Noted."

"But it's been fourteen years of letting those assholes who brought guns to prom demolish our friendship," she said, irritation coming into her voice. "If they never showed up, we don't end up traumatized. Graham never dies. You and I never sleep together. We never hurt each other like we did. That's my new what-if."

Something twisted deep in his chest, painful and wistful at the same time.

"What-ifs still don't change anything," he said quietly.

"Yes, but we can," she said, resolve in her voice.

"Grace and Charlie need us. We're not going to let them down because of the past. This"—she indicated the space between them with her hand—"is day one of Ash and Kincaid's friendship 2.0."

Ash stared at her, taken aback. "Friendship."

"Yes. Now if it gets screwed up, we can only blame ourselves. No one else gets a hand in that, especially cowards with guns." She nodded as if she was stamping approval on her own declaration. "Our fresh start begins now."

"You assume I'm going to agree to this."

She rolled her eyes. "Oh please, you know you want me around. I am an amazing friend. I could give classes on how to be an awesome friend."

"Superhumble, too," he teased. "As always."

"Plus," she said, her tone turning chipper. "Grudges give people bad wrinkles. When I'm an old lady, my wrinkles damn well better be smile lines."

Ash laughed under his breath, taking the olive branch she was offering him with both hands. "Hashtag LifeGoals."

She reached out and touched the spot between his brows. "You better start working on that goal more. You've already got the frowny face started. Serious writer looks very serious. Maybe some moisturizer."

"Hey," he said, batting her hand away and grinning. "Writing takes some hard thinking. These are thinking lines. It makes me distinguished."

She patted his cheek. "Keep telling yourself that, sugar. Now let's bring these lovely people some coffee before they send out a search party."

Ash grabbed the cream from the fridge, his head

spinning with the sudden shift in events, in his world, really. He and Kincaid were going to try to be friends again. He didn't know what to do with that.

"So," she said, "in honor of our new friendship, are you going to tell me why you're here in the first place? I'm assuming the fiancée is no more, based on what Grace said?"

He groaned in resignation. "I forgot that with Kincaid friendship comes Kincaid nosiness. Can't we skip this part?"

She gave him a satisfied smirk. "Take it or leave it, Isaacs. Spill."

"Fine," he said, knowing resistance was futile. "I'm here to save money. I've sent in a proposal to my publisher about a thriller set in Mexico and they're dragging their feet, so I'm not under a book contract right now. The Lowells are letting me use the apartment for free because I'm no longer with Melanie."

Her brow knit as she poured the cream. "I'm sorry."

"Don't be," he said, meaning it. "I'm glad she's gone. Though where were you when I needed a wingman for dumping dog food?"

She pursed her lips, her eyes flaring with irritation. "She cheated on you?"

"Spectacularly. Though instead of dog food, maybe caviar would've been appropriate. She's with some asshole in the Hamptons. They're in love apparently."

Kincaid made a sound of disgust. "Gross. Though I'm not surprised."

He frowned at that. "Gee, thanks."

She flicked her hand at him dismissively. "Not because of you. Because of her. I got that wants-her-man-to-be-fancy vibe off her the first Christmas you brought her home. She kept talking to me about how huge your next book was going to be, how acclaimed, and about some publisher party y'all had gone to. She never actually said anything nice about *you*."

He took a deep breath and let it out slowly, not shocked, but it still stung to hear that once his social stock went down, Melanie bailed. "She hated you."

Kincaid nodded. "Oh, I have no doubt. People like her don't like when other people see through their bull. And that chick had my bullshit meter pinging in the red." She shrugged. "But for what it's worth, I'm sorry. Being cheated on sucks. Did you love her?"

He shifted uncomfortably at the jumbled feelings that surfaced. "I wouldn't have proposed if I didn't."

She gave him a genuine look of sympathy. "Well, then I'm real sorry, Ash. Honestly."

"Thanks," he said, off-balance from the shift between them. It'd been so long since he'd seen the Kincaid he remembered, the one without that ten-foot-tall electrified fence between them. It took his breath for a second. He needed to be careful. He couldn't let his guard down too much. That was how he'd gotten in trouble the last time.

He could be friends with her again. Nothing more. He was done falling for people who loved someone else. And there was no doubt in his mind that Kincaid still loved Graham as much as she had when he was alive. It was no accident that she was still single after all these years. Her heart was already taken.

Well, so was his. He wasn't giving his out anymore. He was never going to be that pathetic, lovesick teen again, and he wasn't going to be the blind idiot who thought when a woman said yes to a marriage proposal that she actually meant she wanted to be with him and him alone. He'd left a lot of the old Ashton behind when he'd moved away from Long Acre. But when he left New York, he'd let the final thread of that kid go. He used to pride himself on not being like other guys who were phobic about commitment, but now he saw that they'd had it right all along. Take the fun parts — the flirting, the laughs, the sex — and leave the rest — the self-doubt, the humiliation, the heartbreak — for the suckers.

Kincaid finished up with the coffee and gave him a beauty-queen smile. "Your forehead wrinkle is showing again, Ashton Isaacs."

"I'm full of deep thoughts, Kincaid Breslin."

She handed him two mugs. "Call me KC."

"KC," he said, trying to prove to himself that he could say the old nickname without a wave of nostalgia, of feeling. He mostly succeeded.

But the glimmer of a memory was a clear warning that he needed to tread carefully. Thank God he was only going to be here for a little while. The sooner he could get out of here, the better.

He couldn't let Kincaid or this town in again, not even a little. That woman and this place were dangerous. Memories were dangerous.

He would not get swallowed up. Once upon a time, he had truly been just her friend. He could do it again. Because she was right about one thing. She was an amazing friend.

And of all the things he needed right now, he could use that more than anything.

Maybe she could, too.

chapter
EIGHT

THEN—2002

KINCAID TRIPPED OVER AN EXPOSED ROOT IN HER FRONT YARD and nearly fell as she tried to get to the door without anyone seeing her. Two buttons on her shirt had been ripped off, and she held it closed with trembling fingers, fighting to keep her tears at bay. Her heart was still pounding hard against her ribs. She just needed to get inside without her mom seeing her, take a hot shower, and get under her covers so she could forget this stupid night had ever happened.

She pulled her foot free of the root and made her way to the cracked sidewalk in front of her house. But in her rush to get to the door, she hadn't noticed there was a vehicle on the other side of her mom's banged-up Toyota. A shiny, black expensive car. She didn't know the makes of cars enough to know the brand, but she knew what it meant. Her mother had brought home another guy—probably married. The rent was probably due. Her mom could always get some guy to help out "just a little" once she took him home.

Kincaid's stomach turned over when she got close to the front door and heard her mom laughing that laugh that was meant to entice, not because anything was funny. *No way*. Kincaid could not face that shit tonight. She wanted to sit down on the porch and cry. In frustration. In anger. In embarrassment.

But that wouldn't do her any good. She'd still be able to hear her mom and her date. And if she snuck in the back door, it would only be worse. If her mom didn't realize she was there, Kincaid would end up hearing more than laughing. The walls in the house were thin. She glanced down at the haggard state of her outfit. She was in no shape to go traipsing through the neighborhood, especially at this hour, but suddenly she knew exactly where she needed to be, the one place she could go.

With one last look at the front windows, she hitched her purse on her shoulder and slipped in between her house and the neighbor's to get to the narrow path that ran along the ditch behind the houses, traveling a well-worn route along the chain-link fences of people's yards. After a few turns and a standoff with a territorial stray cat, she made it to the edge of the Grandview neighborhood, so close to where she lived but worlds away at the same time. This was the kind of neighborhood that had a well-lit entrance sign and houses with neat lawns and driveways with basketball hoops. She made sure to steer clear of people's yards so she wouldn't set off motion lights and headed to the street she wanted.

When she saw the single-story brick house with the

Long Acre High flag hanging from the porch, her breathing eased a little. She hurried to the side yard, knowing
there were no security lights on this house, and snuck
around the back. *Please be up. Please be up.* The mantra
became a prayer.

The weight of the night lifted a fraction when she saw
the glow of Ash's lamp in his window. That kid stayed
up too late. Tonight, she was thankful. She carefully
picked her way through the prickly rosebushes lining the
back of the house, cursing the makeshift burglar deter-
rent, and tapped on the window.

She held her breath. She'd never snuck over like this
before. They rarely hung out at his house because even
though his dad was almost always at football practice,
his mom was home, and she didn't believe in letting girls
like Kincaid in her son's bedroom. His mom didn't say
that to Kincaid's face, but she'd overheard her talking
to one of her church friends one day, gossiping about
Kincaid's mother and how apples don't fall far from the
tree. Like she was some temptress. For Ash. *Please.*

Kincaid's was the empty house, so they'd made that
their hangout spot if they wanted a change from the
diner or the bookstore. But tonight she was desperate
and willing to risk it. She just hoped his parents didn't
hear and think she was trying to rob the place. She had
no doubt Mr. Isaacs had a gun somewhere in the house.

The first taps on the glass didn't work, so Kincaid had
to knock louder. She cringed, expecting to be discovered by his parents, but finally, she saw movement. Ash
peeked through the blinds and then startled when he saw
her staring back.

She could hear his curse through the window.

"Let me in," she said, trying to keep her voice down and hoping he could read her lips.

Ash frowned but quickly yanked the blinds up and opened the window, a rush of frosty air-conditioning coming with him. "What the hell, KC? What are you doing out here? It's midnight."

"I know. I'm sorry. Just let me in," she said, using all the energy she could muster to put command in her voice. "I just... I need to come in. Please."

Ash glanced down at the hand clutching her shirt closed, and concern filled his eyes. "Shit." He reached out a hand. "Yeah. Okay. Come on. But be quiet."

Ash helped her climb through the window none too gracefully, and she lost a shoe on the way in but didn't care. The warm light of his bedroom and his calm presence made something knotted inside her loosen. She straightened and took the first deep breath she'd taken in the last two hours. "Hey."

Ash was standing there in his plaid boxer shorts and a Long Acre High gym shirt, staring at her disheveled state in horror. "KC, what happened? You look... Are you okay?"

"I'm not wanted for murder," she declared, anger finally flooding in to replace the fear. "But I almost was."

His brow knit. "What?"

"Xavier Capello is an absolute, douchebag asshole," she declared.

"Wait." Fury flashed in Ash's eyes, dark and hot. "He did something to you?"

Kincaid's heart picked up speed, the panic trying to come back. She hugged her shirt to her. "He tried.

Handsy scumbag." She stared at a small ink spot on the otherwise pristine tan carpet, too embarrassed to look Ash in the eye. "We went out tonight. I thought he liked me. You know, like wanted to go out to get to know me. Well, apparently, 'get to know me' means sticking his hand up my shirt and trying to get my bra off."

"He *forced* you? I will fucking kill him," Ash said, surprising Kincaid with the intensity of his anger.

She shook her head and finally met his gaze. "No need to get jail time, Isaacs. I stopped him. He listened to no. Eventually." *Thank God*. She shivered. "But he said horrible things afterward. About what he'd heard about me. About the things he knew I knew how to do with boys. He said if I wanted to be with a senior, I'd better start acting like I wasn't a little girl." Tears finally fell. "I haven't done any of those things he said. I've only kissed a few boys. I thought he liked me…"

Ash was still looking murderous. "What you'd have to do to be with a senior? What a prick."

"He was. *Is*. God, I just feel stupid and…gross. And then I went home and Mom…has someone over, and I just couldn't handle that crap right now. I'm sorry. I know it's late. I don't want to get you in trouble. I just didn't know where to go."

Ash stepped closer and put his arm around her shoulders, giving her a friendly squeeze. "Yeah, you did. You can always come find me if you need me, okay? You know *I'm* not on a date."

She snorted.

"And don't worry," he continued. "My parents won't be checking to see if I've snuck a girl into my room. I heard Mom tell Dad that she thinks I'm gay. That's her latest worry. There must've been a sermon at church this week. Signs your teen son is really a ho-mo-sexual," he said, sounding out the words with the full twang and fervor of his reverend.

She lifted her brows, surprised by that. "Are you?"

"Not gay."

"Ugh. It'd be easier if you were," she said, leaning in to him. He smelled like Irish Spring soap and whatever deodorant he used. Familiar. It was beyond comforting. "Then it wouldn't be as weird if I asked to sleep here."

He stepped back and ran a hand through his mop of dark hair. "It doesn't have to be weird. Best friends have sleepovers all the time."

"You know it's not the same. You're a boy. There's one bed. I can sleep on the floor, if you have extra blankets or something."

He laughed and held his hands out to his sides. "What? You think I'm going to make some move on you, Breslin?"

She made a face. "Eww, gross, shut up."

He rolled his eyes. "Get over yourself. You're not sleeping on the floor. Come on. You can borrow some of my clothes. We'll sleep back-to-back if that makes you feel better. And my door stays locked, so my parents won't find you."

Feeling better just being there with her Ash, she grinned. "Why you locking your door, Ash? I hope I wasn't interrupting special time with internet porn or something."

"Nope." He walked over to his dresser and opened a drawer. "Porn time is eight thirty to nine on weeknights, ten to eleven on Saturdays. You've missed that window."

She rolled her eyes. "You're disgusting."

"Porn is disgusting actually. I've looked. It's not worth getting a virus on your computer. You can find better stuff in books. A good story plus some imagination is much more effective."

She made a sour face. "I really do not want to know about your pornographic imagination, Isaacs."

He snorted. "You're the one who brought up porn, not me." He tossed her a pair of his boxer shorts and a T-shirt. She clutched them to her chest, and his face softened. "You sure you're okay, KC? Like, for real?"

She nodded. "Yeah. I feel better now that I'm here."

The smile he gave her lit up a dark place inside her. "Good."

He left her alone for a few minutes to change, made sure the coast was clear for her to make a trip to the bathroom, and then she crawled under the covers with her best friend. Ash's body heat was radiating against her even though they were facing each other and not touching. He laid his head on his arm, studying her face. "You gonna be able to sleep?"

"I hope so. My mind is racing still." Kincaid rubbed her lips together, the taste of Xavier's aggressive kisses lingering even though she'd finger-brushed her teeth with Ash's toothpaste. "Tonight sucked. I want to believe it was just Xavier. That he's a jerk, and it was a one-time thing. But he's not the only one who's said stuff to me like that before."

Ash's forehead wrinkled.

"Don't look surprised. You've heard what they say. Guys only see me as one thing, you know? I feel...I don't know. Like no one will ever see *me*. Like the actual me. They may think I'm pretty or whatever, but they really just want me 'cause I've got boobs and some bogus reputation."

He frowned.

She reached out and took his hand. "Except you, of course. Thanks for thinking I'm ugly and disgusting and just liking me for my personality."

He laughed and used their joined hands to tap her on the forehead. "I never said you were ugly and disgusting. But the thought of kissing you does make me want to gag a little."

"Gee, thanks," she said, letting go of his hand. "You're so sweet I can barely stand it."

He rolled onto his back. "I know. But you eat Froot Loop sandwiches. I want no part of that flavor in my mouth."

She sniffed but that response gave her what she needed to know. Ash was safe. He didn't see her like other boys did. And tonight, she really didn't want to lie on the other side of the bed alone with her thoughts. The incident with Xavier had shaken her more than she was admitting. She needed to be hugged, to be comforted. She scooted closer and laid her head in the crook of his shoulder, tense because she was worried he was going to freak out. But after an initial stiffening of his muscles, she felt him release a breath and he adjusted his arm to put it around her.

"Is this okay?" she asked.

"Get some sleep, KC," he said, voice gruff. "And don't snore."

She huffed in indignation. "As if a delicate flower such as myself would make such awful noises."

"You're about as delicate as a leather shoe. I can already feel you plotting your revenge against Xavier." He shifted, pulling the covers over them.

She smiled in the dark. "I'm thinking a little sugar in the gas tank of his precious pickup truck."

"See? Evil," Ash said, his voice sleepy.

Kincaid closed her eyes, listened to Ash's breathing slow, inhaled his familiar scent, and let the horrible night drift away as sleep finally came for her. She was with Ash now. She was safe.

But the peace didn't last long. An hour later, she heard the shout. The sudden noise ripped her out of sleep. Her eyes blinked open. She was disoriented in the dark, none of the shapes and shadows familiar. Her heart jumped into her throat, but then she felt an arm tighten around her. *Ash*. She was with Ash. She let out a breath.

But the noise from outside the door came again. Something loud crashing against the floor or a wall. Coach Isaacs's voice boomed from somewhere in the front of the small house. "*You lying bitch!*"

Ash turned to stone next to her.

His dad's voice rattled the wall again. "*Where the fuck have you been?*"

There was a higher-pitched response, Ash's mother, but it was unintelligible.

"Ash," Kincaid said with concern.

"Shh, it's okay," he said in an urgent whisper. "Just be quiet."

He got up quickly and turned on the oscillating fan that sat on his desk, the whirring sound coming to life. He climbed back into bed, sitting next to her.

"What's happening?" she asked, her heart beating fast.

"They're fighting," he said, voice dull and flat. "Dad must've had a bad practice with the team. Mom must've gotten home late again."

The sound of something breaking cut through the air, clear even over the drone of the fan. His mother cried out. His dad yelled again.

"Ash," Kincaid said again, lifting her head to look at him. "Is your mom okay? Should we…"

His eyes were staring straight ahead at the wall, his expression hollow. "No. We shouldn't."

"But—"

"There's nothing we can do, KC," he said, voice hard. "Nothing I haven't tried before."

Kincaid pushed up higher on her elbow, concern filling her. "He hurts her? Like this is a regular thing?"

She'd been around Coach Isaacs at school. He was a wide-shouldered, gruff guy, and she knew Ash had a tense relationship with him, but the football players seemed to love him. She'd seen him joking around with the guys in the hall. Plus, he was a hero in town for winning two championships in the last two years.

That guy hurt his wife?

Ash wouldn't look at her. "Not all the time. But if Dad has a bad day at school or practice and starts drinking, he gets mean and paranoid. He'll check on when her shifts end at the hospital. If she's later than he thinks she should be, he gets like this. He convinces himself she's having an affair with a doctor or something. Sometimes he implies that I'm not his."

Kincaid gripped the blanket in her fists. "Jesus."

"Before you ask, no, she won't leave. I've tried to talk to her." He stared toward the door. "It's been like this a long time. She said she loves him too much to do that, that she made a commitment to him in front of God, that it's only the stressful job and the alcohol talking, not him."

The sound of a slap made Kincaid's stomach turn over with dread.

Ash winced ever so slightly, as if he was simply enduring, shutting some part of himself down.

"If that's what it means to love someone that much, I don't want any part of it," Kincaid said.

"No shit," Ash said gravely. "Whatever they have isn't love. It's…fucked up."

Kincaid suddenly understood why he always wanted to come to her house instead of the other way around. She'd thought it was because of his mom's restrictions, but now she realized that despite the nicer house on the nicer block, there was a whole lot of ugly in his house, too.

She wet her lips, treading carefully. "Ash, I'm sorry. Does your dad hurt you?"

He shifted next to her. "Physically? No. He's too protective of his job. He knows if he left a mark on me, I'd show it to every damn person I could find. So he just yells at me or ignores me. Fucking coward. He only hits the person he knows would never tell." He glanced over at her, eyes unreadable. "Can we not talk about this? Can we just pretend it's not happening right now?"

"Okay," she said softly, her heart breaking for her friend. She reached out and cupped his shoulder, guiding him to lie back down next to her. He moved like he was going to turn his back to her, but instead she wrapped her arm around his neck. He went willingly when she eased him down to lie in the crook of her shoulder like he had done for her. When another noise made its way through the door, she could feel Ash recoil. She pulled the blanket up over them and pressed her hand over his ear.

He closed his eyes. "KC."

"Shh, no more talking," she said, sadness filling her. She wasn't the only one who couldn't count on her parents. Ash always seemed so self-contained, so in control, but he was scared and hurting, too. She wanted to go out there and scream at his dad, tell him to go to hell and never come back. But she was just a fifteen-year-old kid. So was Ash.

They couldn't fix their parents. They couldn't even share the burden with siblings because they were only children.

But they had each other.

"I promise I won't bring this up again. But you can always talk to me, okay?" she whispered next to his ear. "Whatever it is. I'm here. I'm always going to be here. I promise."

Ash took a deep breath against her. "Back at you, KC. And I'll help you put sugar in Xavier's tank. No one's going to hurt you and get away with it. I've got your back. Always."

Something unlocked inside her, and she held Ash close. "Best friends forever."

She could feel his sardonic smile even in the dark. "We should get matching BFF necklaces from Claire's."

"Shut up, Isaacs. Go to sleep."

They both lay quietly in the dark for the rest of the night. Neither slept.

chapter
NINE

KINCAID TUCKED A SET OF EARBUDS IN HER PURSE BEFORE getting out of the car and carrying two cups of coffee into The Stuffed Shelf. Day one. She could do this. She'd strongly considered Irishing her coffee, but whiskey at seven in the morning seemed a little too close to her mother's style for comfort. The earbuds would have to do. If things felt weird being inside the store again or brought up hard memories, she would tuck those puppies in her ears, blast her music, and avoid reality while she and Ash cleaned up the store.

She was going to have to get used to cleaning anyhow. She'd picked up the keys to the farmhouse last night and had done a more thorough tour. She didn't want to think about how many families of spiders she was going to need to evict. She shuddered at the thought as she used the key Grace had given her to let herself into the store through the back door. She took a deep breath, the old book smell as familiar as ever, and then headed down the hallway. The lights were already on in the front, and a movie score was playing a bit too loud over the store's speakers.

She found Ash sitting behind the checkout counter, feet propped up and a stack of papers in his hand. He was wearing a snug, dark-blue T-shirt that had *Go Local Sports Team!* across the front and broken-in jeans. His dark hair was slicked back, shorn short on the sides but still long on the top, and his glasses had migrated a little down his nose as he read. The tattoos on his arm flexed as he turned a page. Kincaid shouldn't be staring, but goddamn, the guy had gotten unfairly hot.

How was she supposed to deal with that? Her brain was all *No, girl*. Her brain knew why Ash was not that kind of option. Sex was what had messed up things the first time. And *God*, he'd been a virgin. She felt like such an idiot for not knowing that back then. He'd said he was surprised she hadn't realized it, but she couldn't even remember if the sex had felt good or not. The whole thing was a haze of grief. When she'd realized what they'd done, the guilt she'd felt, the anger at Ash...both had exploded inside her and obliterated most of the other memories from that horrible night.

That was what crossing lines in friendship did. So if they had any shot at having any kind of workable friendship now, she needed to keep the boundaries crystal clear. No ogling people you had real history with. Her brain knew that. But every other part of her was all *Heyyyy, history smishtory*. She set a cup of coffee on the counter, jolting Ash from his concentrated state and forcing herself off her dangerous line of thought.

"Looks like someone decided to get a head start," she observed.

Ash glanced up from the papers, obviously surprised to see her standing there. "Oh, hey. I didn't hear you come in."

"I'm a ninja on the side." She pulled a bag of pastries from her purse. "Plus, this music is loud. I feel like I should be preparing to storm the castle or something."

He reached out, turned a dial on the old system that controlled the store's speakers, and the movie music softened. "Sorry. The quiet, empty store was creeping me out a little."

She knew the feeling. Ghosts were everywhere in this place. She could almost feel their past selves whispering to each other between the aisles somewhere. "Aren't writers supposed to sleep 'til noon and then stumble to work half-drunk?"

"I'm not so good with the sleeping or the drinking. Plus, the commute from upstairs is short. I figured I'd come down and take a look at some of the numbers." His gaze drifted to the coffee and greasy paper bag, brows lifting. "You come bearing gifts?"

Kincaid shrugged. "It was buy one, get one free at the new coffee place. You can have the tall one. It's cold brew something or other. I figured your hipster self would prefer something fancy. There are kolaches in the bag, too. I got those from the Czech gas station because I'm not trusting the fancy coffee shop with my pastries."

His smile was slow, eyes sparking with mischief. "Cold brew, huh? But is it from coffee beans harvested by baby foxes at the stroke of midnight on the summer solstice from atop a mountain in Costa Rica? Because I have standards."

She gave a dramatic sigh. "Baby-fox coffee is *so*

over. We're using armadillos to harvest beans now. We're calling it grumpy cowboy coffee."

He chuckled and motioned as if he was tipping an invisible cowboy hat her way and then lowered his feet to the floor. "Well, thank you kindly, ma'am. I appreciate the hospitality. And for the record, I do actually prefer cold brew. Don't judge me."

"Judging," she said, pulling a lemon kolache out of the bag and taking a big bite. "So, find…interesting in…umbers?"

Ash gave her a bemused look and set the papers down. "I'm assuming you're asking me about the sales numbers. I don't translate kolache dialect well."

She rolled her eyes and kept chewing but waved her hand in a *gimme* motion.

"Right. Well, top headline is that the sales on *my* books are *dismal*," he said with faux dramatic gravitas. "A book about manure sold more than mine."

"That's shitty."

He paused, gave her a look. "Really?"

She shrugged. "You walked right into that one. Or stepped into it, as the case may be. Not my fault."

"*Anyway*, my local author status is clearly not moving any extra books—even with the prime cover-facing-out shelf space the Lowells have given me up front. My self-esteem has taken quite the hit."

Kincaid licked a bit of lemon curd off her fingers. "First of all, are you really a local author? You use a pen name, and you don't advertise where you're from."

"True."

"Also, maybe you should write some stories where everyone doesn't die at the end, and they'll move more copies," she said, pointing her kolache at him. "You're probably bumming people out."

Ash's gaze, which had drifted to her mouth—probably because she had lemon curd somewhere it shouldn't be—flicked up to hers, surprise there. "You've read my books?"

"Uh… I…" *Shit*. Things she didn't want him to know. That she had still paid attention to what he was doing even after everything had happened between them. "I read the first one. The Lowells gave me an early copy, and I knew they'd want to discuss it. I've seen some of the reviews of the others."

He smiled between sips of his coffee. "So you hated it."

The writing had been fantastic. A page-turner of a thriller. Great characters. And the setting had brought Madrid to life on the page. But… "I didn't…*hate* it per se."

He laughed. "Per se?"

She tried to think of a polite way to phrase it, but that wasn't her strong suit. Her real opinion jumped out of her mouth before she could edit it. "Ash, you killed off the love interest. And the *pet bird*. What is wrong with you? Are you trying to make people throw your book against the wall?"

He lifted a finger as though he were in debate class. "Okay, I'll give it to you on the love interest, but the bird was old. Like ancient. And it made the hero come to terms with the loss of his brother."

"Old? Percy was a *pet*, Ash," she said, giving him a disbelieving look. "You don't kill the pet. Damn." She put a hand over her heart. "RIP Percy." That freaking bird death had made her cry in the waiting room of her ob-gyn's office. She caught Ash's expression. "Why are you smiling?"

He bit his lip as if he was trying to hide the smile, but he couldn't. He looked too damned pleased. "Because you clearly feel passionate about my book. I'll take that over someone feeling indifferent."

"Anger is better than indifference?" she asked skeptically.

"Sometimes." He held her gaze long enough to make her look away.

She grabbed the papers. "Anything interesting besides your sluggish sales?"

He blew out a sigh. "Yeah, the bestselling books for the store make my books look like riding-on-a-unicorn-through-the-clouds uplifting."

"What do you mean?" She tried to scan the pages but didn't quite understand the format of the report.

He pointed to a column on the paper. "True crime is the bestseller," he said flatly. "Particularly books about Long Acre High."

Her stomach turned. "Are you kidding me?"

"I know." He shook his head. "I'm surprised Grace and Charlie even stock the stuff, but I guess they were giving the tourists what they wanted."

Kincaid dropped the papers on the desk, her face getting hot. "I can't even. Imagine how horrible that has to be for Grace and Charlie. Some rando out-of-towner coming in here, the place where their son grew up, looking for a splashy tell-all about Long Acre High?"

Ash rubbed a hand over the back of his head, his expression weary. "It's what the town's known for. I don't know if that will ever change."

"Ugh, I'm so done with people saying that. It's bullshit." Kincaid felt her anger bubbling up from a much deeper place than the true-crime section of the bookstore. "I get that those books have the right to be written. I get that documentaries are made. I know that some of them are handled with care and respect. The world needs to learn from what happened here. People's stories should be told. But I am so *freaking* sick of everything being about that one night. This town deserves better than that." Her fist curled at her side. "We deserve better than that. We shouldn't have to stock books in here that tell our horror story. Let people buy that somewhere else."

Tears of frustration burned her eyes. *Dammit*. She didn't want to cry.

Ash frowned, setting down his coffee, and stepped around the desk. "Hey, it's all right. If this is too hard…"

Kincaid shook her head. "These aren't sad tears. These are pissed-off ones." She pressed her fingers beneath her eyes so her mascara wouldn't raccoon on her. "I just… It's been a long week. I haven't slept much. And the whole reason I couldn't get investors for my bed-and-breakfast was because of how outsiders perceive Long Acre. No one believes that people would come here for a vacation. That horrible night finds new ways to haunt me each year. Don't we ever get to *move on*?"

Ash looked like he was going to reach out to her, but then he paused and shoved his hands in his pockets. "You *have* moved on. Look at what you're doing. We're going to sell this store, and you're going to take the money and open your B and B anyway. And it's going to be great because…" He shrugged. "Because you're you, and everything you put your mind to, you're a success at."

She scoffed and gave him a disbelieving look. "Oh my God, are you kidding me? That's your logic? That is so opposite the truth. Do you remember me, Ash? Let me refresh that memory bank of yours. I'm impulsive and regularly get myself into trouble. It's kind of my thing. I'm just upping the ante now, like buying a half-million-dollar farmhouse I can't afford in a place where no one wants to visit a B and B. It's no better than my mother throwing her month's salary down on a blackjack table."

"Now who's talking bullshit?" He pulled his hands from his pockets and crossed his arms. "Kincaid, you came from *nothing*. Less than nothing. You had no help from the start, and then you got slammed in the face with a national tragedy. Most people would be destroyed by that. Yet somehow, you've built up a real estate business, you run a blog, you have a home, and now you're going to start a new business."

"Wait, you read my blog?"

He groaned. "Missing the point. I'm saying, look at what you've built. You're killing it. And if you decide you're going to open a B and B, you're going to figure out a way to get it done and get people there because that's what you do. You bulldoze your own path where there isn't one. *That's* your thing. You say *screw you* with a smile to the people who tell you that you can't."

Something warm and fuzzy moved through her, and her lips curved. "That *is* kind of my thing, isn't it?"

"Bulldoze and steamroll?" he teased. "Most definitely."

She playfully punched him in the shoulder. "Oh, Isaacs, you say the sweetest things. You should be a writer."

He smirked. "I'll think about it."

"But you're right—"

He held up a hand. "Wait. Give me a second. Let me absorb those words fully. *I'm right. I'm right…*"

"Shut up. No one likes a bragger," she declared, a little wary of how easily they were slipping back into their old banter. She needed to watch herself. "But you're right that I shouldn't stand by and let other people define this town for me. The rebranding of Long Acre starts now. Right here in this bookstore." She jabbed a thumb behind her. "The true-crime section gets moved to the back. Books about the Long Acre shooting are by mail order only. I don't care if they're the bestsellers. Locals should be able to come in here and not be hit with in-your-face reminders. A trigger-free space."

"Agreed," Ash said.

"In fact, maybe we take the opposite direction. Maybe there's a way to celebrate the good things about the town in here. Change the vibe."

"The good things about the town?" he asked, clearly skeptical. "Like what? The brand-new stoplight down the street? Or the movie theater that only shows dollar movies? The near-religious obsession with high school football?"

"Shut up, snob." She gave him a petulant look. "There are good things."

He didn't look convinced, but he nodded in a *go on* motion.

"I'm just saying that there has to be some way to show people who come in here that this place isn't one thing. That it's a great little town with friendly, interesting people. That it's worth visiting. Maybe staying."

Ash tucked his hands in his back pockets and looked around at the store. "Right now, this store says it's a dusty, sad town that's seen better days."

Kincaid followed his gaze, watched the dust motes dance in the early-morning sunshine coming through the windows. "Then I guess we better get to work. Ready to bulldoze?"

Ash's blue eyes sparkled, a genuine smile touching his lips. "Let's do this."

She put a hand to her hip. "You sure you remember how to get your hands dirty, city boy?"

He reached out and grabbed her hand. An electric awareness zipped through her body at the warm, roughened touch of his fingers. For a second, as he lifted her hand higher, she thought he was going to kiss the top of it. But then he stopped, her hand halfway to his mouth, and he looked down at her fingers. "Sure you're not afraid to mess up your manicure, bumpkin?"

Her teeth clicked together, and she yanked her hand back. "Just for that, you're assigned the bathrooms."

"You can't assign," he said, amusement on his face.

"Oh, you're cute. You think this is a democracy." Then she turned on her heel, grabbed her coffee, and headed to the front of the store.

She thought he would continue to protest, but when she went to throw away her coffee cup a little while later, she found Ash scrubbing the sink of the small bathroom. A glimmer of guilt went through her. She was teasing Ash about being too posh and a city boy, but she knew better than anyone where he came from. Ash's family had always had more money than hers but just as many problems. She knew he'd been estranged from his family since he'd left town, that they'd cut him off in every way. Anything Ash had now, he'd gotten through hard work and determination—all on his own. She shouldn't tease him for a little fanciness. He'd earned it.

Kincaid leaned against the doorway of the bathroom. Ash looked over, hair falling into his face. "Everything okay?"

She smiled and stepped inside the small space. "Give me that bottle of cleaner. I've got the toilet."

He waved her off. "It's fine. I don't mind doing the dirty stuff."

She reached past him, her arm brushing his as she grabbed the spray bottle. "Stop oversharing, Isaacs. I didn't ask you about your bedroom habits."

He laughed under his breath and then met her eyes, his gaze flickering with something more serious. "Hey."

"Yeah?" she asked, somehow frozen in that gaze of his.

"Thanks."

"For the toilet?" she asked.

"No. For just, I don't know, being how you are…" He looked back to the sink and started scrubbing again. "A lot of people say 'fresh start' and don't mean it. You do. It's…nice to be able to joke around with you again."

She stared at him, her words leaving her for a moment and something twisting in her chest. The wounds between them would always be there, but in the deepest, darkest tangled part of her, something loosened a little.

Their friendship had helped forge her personality. For better or worse, Ash was a part of her. Her world just felt more aligned having him there, not having to hate him.

She swallowed past the lump in her throat. "You're easy to be friends with, Ash. Always were."

Ash glanced over as if checking if she was telling the truth or messing with him. Whatever he saw in her face must've pleased him because the genuine smile he gave her broke her a little.

"Except when you went through that pine-scented cologne phase," she said, wrinkling her nose. "You weren't easy to be friends with then."

He laughed. "I was trying to be rustic and manly."

"You smelled like one of those Christmas-tree car deodorizers people hang from their mirrors." She leaned over and sniffed, catching his scent beneath the astringent layer of the cleaners they were using. "You smell better now."

He laughed. "Did you just smell me? I think I feel violated."

"My apologies."

"So what do I smell like?" he asked, leaning against the sink, curiosity on his face.

She shrugged. "Like a writer. A mix of coffee and angst."

He snorted.

In truth, he smelled like Ash. Irish Spring soap and something earthier beneath it. It was a scent imprinted on her brain from all the nights they'd hung out, the nights they'd slept in the same bed. For a long time, she'd associated that scent with safety. Comfort.

Now it just scrambled her brain, sending her thoughts down paths where they shouldn't go.

She dropped the toilet brush into the holder. "I'm going to sort some books."

She walked out without waiting for a response.

chapter
TEN

ASH WAS COVERED WITH A FINE LAYER OF GRIME BY THE TIME
the orange rays of late-afternoon sun slanted across the
store shelves. He'd cleaned the rest of the bathroom,
which hadn't been in bad shape, and then had set about
helping Kincaid to box up any books that weren't on
shelves. Charlie and Grace had taken to stacking books
they didn't have shelf space for and stuffing those stacks
into every nook and cranny of the store, including on top
of the bookshelves. The layer of dust atop those stacks
told him exactly how effective a selling technique a
teetering tower of books was. Customers were probably
terrified they'd pull one book and set off a Jenga-like
avalanche through the whole store.

Having the tops of the bookshelves cleared and the
crevices of the store emptied out helped. They still had
a lot of work to do, but it was progress. Kincaid had
spent most of the day sorting the books into boxes and
rearranging shelves. When he found her in the children's
section of the store, she somehow looked ten times

fresher than he did. She had her back to him as she rearranged one set of shelves, but her blond hair was in a big, floppy bun on top of her head, her tank top had managed to stay clean, and her jeans only had a little dust on them. He knew she'd been working hard, too, so she must've cleaned herself up at some point.

Ash opened his mouth to let her know it was quitting time, but the words got caught in his throat as she bent down to put something on a lower shelf. Her tank top rode up a little at her waist, giving him a delicious glimpse of her smooth, creamy skin and the dip of her spine. God help him. Attraction, white-hot and electric, hummed through him as if he'd been plugged into a socket.

His fingers itched for him to step forward, grab her by the waist, spin her around, and push her up against one of these bookshelves. He'd pin her hands above her head, knocking books to the floor, and kiss her. He could almost taste the lip gloss she'd been reapplying all day. It smelled like peaches and probably tasted like pie. He could imagine how soft she'd be in his hands.

And it was completely *not okay* to be having those fantasies. He tried to ignore the heat building behind the fly of his jeans. He'd thought he was over this kind of physical reaction to Kincaid. When he'd brought Melanie home for the holidays, he hadn't been affected by Kincaid like this. He and Kincaid had tension between them because of their past, but not this kind of tension. He'd locked that door firmly shut. Apparently, the old attraction had just been lying in wait while he was busy in another relationship.

Shut it down, man.

If he was going to shift from a committed relationship into casual hookups, Kincaid was *not* a candidate. There was nothing casual about their relationship. He adjusted the front of his jeans and then cleared his throat to let Kincaid know he was behind her. She stood quickly and turned around. She pushed an errant lock of hair away from her face, her cheek smudged with dust. "Oh, hey."

"You ready to wrap up? I think we've put in a solid day. I may need to shower twice, though." He pulled his T-shirt away from his chest and let it go, laughing when a puff of dust released into the air.

She smiled. "You and me both. I can't believe how much stuff they have crammed in here. The sorting alone is going to take forever."

He gazed around. "I don't know. A few more days like this and we'll be okay. We made a lot of progress." He leaned forward and reached out his hand. "You have a—" He swiped at her cheek. "A little something."

She lifted her hand, accidentally bumping his arm as she tried to wipe her face herself. "Oh, thanks. I got it."

Ash dropped his hand to his side, berating himself for reaching out and touching her like that. He had no right.

"So," she said, peeking at the clock on the wall. "You get any writing inspiration with all this thinking time?"

He frowned. The only thing he'd been thinking about the last two hours was how to avoid Kincaid. "Not really. My brain was probably clogged with dust."

"So you're not going to write tonight?" she asked, head tilted, something unreadable in her eyes.

The thought made him want to groan. He hadn't written a word in weeks. He feared he had no good ones left. He was fucking empty. Usually he pulled inspiration from wherever he was setting up shop at the time. His settings were as much a part of the story as the characters. An old bookshop in the town he hated didn't make for inspiring thriller writing. "Don't think so. Just going to order a pizza and watch some TV."

"All by yourself?" She wrinkled her nose.

Kincaid had never quite understood anyone's need for solitude. Frankly, he was shocked that she was living alone these days. He'd have expected her to be married with a house full of kids by now. Or at least have a few roommates. She'd always craved people, activity, lots of energy around her. Being an only child with her mother gone most of the time had been like sticking a flowering plant in a dark closet without a chance for sun. But he suspected her solo state had a lot less to do with her personality and a lot more to do with her past.

"It's fine," he said.

"Nope." She put her hands on her hips, her on-a-mission face making her chin tip upward. "You should come out with me and my friends. We're going for drinks and listening to my friend Taryn perform at a little bar."

He fought back a wince. "Uh, no, that's okay. I really am exhausted."

"Ash Isaacs." She stepped forward, a sparkle in her eye. "You're still a party pooper after all these years?"

"It's called introverted, Kincaid. In-tro-ver-ted," he said patiently. "I like to be alone."

"This is not about wanting alone time, and you know it. This, what you're doing"—she waved a hand in front of him—"is called brooding, cupcake. You're post-breakup. Brooding does no one any good. You're like half a second away from getting a gallon of ice cream and watching Nora Ephron movies."

He lifted a brow. "You do realize I'm a guy, right?"

"Fine. A bucket of wings and a Star Wars marathon? A large pizza and porn?"

"Still not into porn. But those wings might—"

"Nope. You only get wings if you come out with us. Alone wings are sad wings," she said seriously. "Come on, you haven't been out since you got back into town. You've been alone enough. If you're going to be here for a while to work on the book, you might as well have some people you can go out and have a beer with. And don't writers need inspiration? Don't you have to, like, actually live in the world a little bit?"

Ash shifted uncomfortably. "You don't have to take the fresh start this far, Kincaid. I'm okay."

"I wouldn't ask if I didn't want you to come," she said. "Is it that hard to believe I don't want to see you sad over a breakup? I've been cheated on. I know what that feels like, and wallowing doesn't fix it. Come out, be distracted."

He stared at her, surprised by the genuine invitation but not surprised that Kincaid couldn't turn off that part of her personality. She'd never liked to see anyone down. "I'm not sure your friends would want some guy you knew from high school tagging along."

She rolled her eyes. "My friends *are* people from high school. Small town, remember?"

"But…" He couldn't finish the sentence. He'd known Kincaid's friends from high school. He'd been one of them. None of the others she'd hung out with regularly had survived.

"We weren't close back then, but we are now," she said as if reading his mind. "You'll know who they are. Didn't you used to have honors classes with Rebecca Lindt and Taryn Landry? And Finn Dorsey played on the team for your dad. He's married to Liv Arias now."

"When did you become friends with them?" he asked, confused by the motley crew of names.

"We became friends after…everything," she said, the pep in her voice mellowing. "Liv, Taryn, Rebecca, and I were in a support group together. Those three kept me from completely losing it back then."

Something hollowed out in his stomach. That should've been him. He and Kincaid had been each other's support system since they were kids. But he'd ruined it. He'd been alone after that night. He was relieved to hear she hadn't been. "I'm glad you had somebody," he said quietly.

Her eyes met his briefly, and he could tell she caught his meaning. She wet her lips. "I lost touch with them for years after the support group disbanded, but we reconnected when they filmed that Long Acre documentary here. They're good people. The best, actually. You'll like them. And their husbands."

Ash felt itchy in his own skin. He recognized the names she'd listed, but he felt so *other* from all those people now. He'd left. He hadn't gone through the town's collective grieving process. He'd refused to participate in the documentary. He felt like a stranger to this town and the people in it. "Kincaid, I don't think—"

She reached out and gave his upper arm a squeeze, the simple touch making him lose his words. Her hazel eyes were beseeching. "Come on, Ash. I know it'll feel weird at first, but holing yourself up in that apartment isn't good for you. Plus, don't be such a snob, fancy writer boy. Hang out with us backwoods bumpkins."

She'd amped up her already strong accent to damn near unintelligible with the affected twang. He couldn't help but smile. "You're going to goad me into going?"

She gave him a pointed look. "If that's what it takes. I'm a wee bit relentless."

"You don't say."

"Look, you've just been cheated on. You're in writer's block. You had to leave New York. Being Broody McBroody Pants helps none of that. To change your situation, change what you're doing. And if nothing else, have a damn drink and eat some cheese fries. That makes everything better."

"The prescription from Dr. Breslin. Liquor and cheese fries."

"Hey, don't knock it 'til you try it. Play nice, and I'll even throw some wings into the deal." She waggled her eyebrows.

He sighed. "You're not going to let me say no."

"Nope," she said happily and patted his shoulder. "Now go and get showered because you look disgusting and smell like stale books. I'll swing by and pick you up in an hour."

He shook his head, too tired to argue. "Why are you doing this? The only thing you agreed to was getting along while we worked here. You don't have to bring me into the rest of your world."

"I know." She shrugged. "But you have a bit of my kryptonite going, I'm afraid. And I can't stand by and ignore it."

"Your kryptonite?"

She nodded. "Yep. A broken heart in need."

"I'm not in need."

"Yes, you are. You're in need of cheese fries. Wings. And possibly a one-night stand to cleanse that been-cheated-on fog," she declared.

He blinked, a record scratch sounding in his head. "What?"

She patted his chest. "But we'll worry about that one later. First, freshen up. Next, fries. Then…"

He stared at her, almost expecting her to list a third *f*-word after the other two.

"Oh, don't look so scandalized," she said with a laugh, "like I'm offering to provide a hooker for you. I'm just saying. If we go somewhere with single women, don't rule it out. You know what they say about the best way to get over someone."

Get under someone else. He'd heard that, of course, but he'd never been one to follow that advice. He'd always been a monogamous dater. *How's that working for you?* a snarky voice in his head asked.

He gave Kincaid a nod. Maybe she was right. He didn't need help forgetting Melanie. He'd already burned that memory to ashes. But he *could* use a distraction from a certain someone else. "I'll be ready in forty-five minutes."

A pleased look filled her eyes. "There you go. Now was that so difficult?"

"You're hard to resist, Breslin." His tone was sarcastic but truer words have never been spoken.

She gave him a cheeky grin. "I know, right? It's my superpower."

And Ash's long-standing curse.

Kincaid breezed past him, leaving him standing there in the self-help section, wondering what he'd gotten himself into. The cover of one of the books stared back at him, an eager-eyed self-help guru named Emma smiling from the cover, the tagline *Girl, Get Your Life Together!* emblazoned under her face in bold print.

He grabbed the book and flipped it backward on the shelf. *Go fuck yourself, Emma.*

chapter

ELEVEN

Ash was leaning against the brick wall outside the bookstore, his face lit by his phone as he waited for Kincaid. She'd had to park a little ways down the street, and Ash hadn't noticed her yet. He'd chosen a simple black T-shirt, a pair of what had to be designer jeans, and some motorcycle boots. Under the glow of the old-fashioned streetlights on Main Street, he looked like some kind of erotic hallucination.

Kincaid wished Ash were a stranger she'd happened upon. Wanted to saunter up to him, send him a suggestive smile, and ask him to buy her a drink somewhere. She wanted it to be simple. Her dealings with guys were always that way now. Impulsive. Short-lived. Low drama.

After she'd lost Graham, she'd had to let go of the idea that she'd end up with her soul mate. Her soul mate was gone. She'd lost her chance at that fairy-tale ending. But as she'd gotten older and accepted the fact that no guy was living up to what she once had, she'd learned to embrace the freedom of it. There was no pressure to find The One. She liked men. Flirting was fun. Kissing was exciting. Sex was a good time.

She never wanted to be like her mother, but her mom had been right on one account. Men couldn't be trusted. But if it was just a date or two, what did that matter? They got tired of her just as quickly as she got tired of them. She was *too much, best in small doses*. That was the common theme. Fun and exciting for a good time, not so much for the long term. That was how she'd known Graham was her soul mate. He'd loved that she was too much. He'd loved her so much that he'd wanted to marry her and make sure no other guy laid a finger on her. An echo of familiar grief moved through her, part of her DNA now.

No focusing on negative stuff tonight. Tonight was about getting Ash out of his apartment and having fun with her friends. That was it.

Ash reached up and tunneled his fingers absently through his hair. Kincaid bit her lip, and her belly tightened. *Gah. Stop.* Her attraction to him was damn inconvenient. Why did he have to be so freaking man-pretty? All soulful eyes and long lashes and brooding looks. And he was hurting. He'd admitted that he'd loved that Melanie woman. Kincaid believed him. Despite the complicated past between her and Ash, she hated to see him moping. She wanted to help him get past that. But she *could not* be the one to do that. At least not in *that* way. Hell no. Land mines everywhere in that scenario.

She needed to remember him as a teen when they were friends and only friends, when she could literally sleep in his bed next to him and not have one thought about kissing him.

Ash looked up as if hearing her thoughts and caught

sight of her. He smiled that half smile of his, the one that said he was in on some long-running joke the rest of the world hadn't caught onto yet, and lifted a hand in greeting. His gaze skimmed down over the casual blue dress she'd thrown on and then down to her cowboy boots. His eyes met hers again, something sharp there. A hard kick of desire hit her, making her cheeks instantly hot.

She could hear Whoopi Goldberg's voice from *Ghost* in her head. *You in danger, girl.*

Ash pushed off the wall to walk toward her, but she held up a finger. "One sec. I need to make a quick call. A private one."

His brows lowered in confusion, and he stepped back. "Yeah, sure."

She slipped into the narrow alley between the stores, her heart beating too fast, and hit a name on her phone screen. Liv answered on the first ring, the hum of a car engine in the background. "Hey," she said. "You on your way? We're heading out now."

"Liv," Kincaid said, keeping her voice low but urgent. "I need a favor."

"Sure, what's up?"

She cupped her hand over the mouthpiece. "I'm bringing Ashton Isaacs with me tonight. Do you remember him?"

"Ashton." There was a pause. "Ash Isaacs from high school? The coach's son?"

"That's the one. I'm not sure if you know, but we used to be best friends."

"Okay. Used to be," Liv said carefully.

"He's back in town for a little while and it's complicated—like, really complicated—but…"

"What is it?" Liv asked, concern slipping into her voice.

"I just need you to make sure that I don't drink too much or get too overly friendly, you know, too *me* with him. Keep me…corralled."

Liv snorted. "Like a horse? I think you just insulted yourself."

"You'll see why I'm asking when we get there. Just promise me," Kincaid pleaded, feeling a little ridiculous. She was a grown woman who should be able to control her impulses, but she also knew how she could get with a few drinks in her and a lot of people around. All that energy dialed her personality up to eleven. Usually, that was fun. Making friends with strangers in the bar and harmlessly flirting. But with Ash, it could be disastrous.

"Yeah sure, *chica*. I've got you," Liv said.

"Everything okay?" a voice asked in the background—Finn, Liv's husband.

"Yeah," Liv said, amusement in her voice. "We have to keep Kincaid from being herself tonight apparently."

Kincaid could hear Finn scoff. "Good luck with that."

"I heard that, Dorsey," Kincaid said.

Liv laughed. "He's just teasing. Everything will be fine. It's not like Taryn and Bec will be drinking anyway. You can join the pregnant ladies for the sober squad."

"Oh, pumpkin, I said don't let me get drunk. I didn't say I was abstaining. Let's not talk crazy now."

Liv laughed, said she understood, and Kincaid ended the call. After a quick, steeling breath, she stepped out of the alley and walked toward Ash, giving him a beaming, welcome-committee smile. "Ready for your big night out?"

"No," he said, a hint of teasing in his eyes, "but I fear you'll take me hostage if I don't agree."

"Truth." She gave him a once-over, schooling her expression into neutrality. "You clean up nice, Isaacs. You may get yourself a date tonight without even trying."

He made a derisive sound and stepped up next to her. "This isn't about finding a date. I was told there would be wings."

She cocked her head in the direction her car was parked. "And wings there shall be. Come on."

He fell into step beside her. "So where are we going? Tell me the bar options have gotten better in Long Acre since I left. The ones we had weren't even worth sneaking into when we were underage."

That was the damn truth, especially since the main bar everyone frequented back then had her mom behind the counter pouring drinks. "Sadly, no. But we're not staying here. We're going to Austin."

His steps stuttered. "Wait, what? That's an hour away."

"Afraid you'll be out past your bedtime?" she teased.

"No." He glanced back over his shoulder, looking a bit like a trapped animal. "It's just…well, I figured if I wanted to leave early, it wouldn't be a big deal."

She lifted a brow and hit her key fob to unlock her doors. "Oh, look at you. I'm no amateur at this taking-hostages thing. Like I'd take you to a place that was easy to escape."

He groaned as he stepped over to the driver's side to open her door for her. "Don't look so evilly pleased. I know how to summon an Uber, you know?"

She slipped into her seat and looked up at him. "Guess I'll just have to make sure you stay so entertained that you won't want to leave."

She realized how flirty her words had come out when she caught the guarded look on Ash's face. *Shit*. She cleared her throat and changed her tone to a flat one. "Come on, Isaacs. Stop whining and get in. I don't want to be late for my friend's performance."

Ash sighed, shut her door, and then got into the passenger side. She pulled out of the parking spot, and he reached for the dial on her radio. She slapped his hand away.

"Hey," he said, affronted.

"Driver gets to choose. Them's the rules."

He gave her a look. "Does this mean I'm going to be subjected to country music and your loud, off-key singing for the next hour?"

She grinned. She and Ash used to ride with Graham to school sometimes, and Graham would let her listen to whatever she wanted. And when good music was on, well, it was kind of an obligation to sing along, enthusiastically. Why do a half-assed performance? "You know you miss it."

He gave her a pleading look. "I really, really don't like country music."

"No problem." She plugged in her phone. "Post-country Taylor Swift it is then!"

Ash made a sound of pain and tipped his head back against the headrest. It was so comically dramatic, so vintage Ash, that a wave of fondness flooded Kincaid. The song "22" came on, and she sang the opening lyrics straight at him. When she got to the line about dressing up like hipsters, his head snapped her way.

He gave her an accusatory look, but then they both burst out laughing. She hadn't planned the song. It just happened to be the first alphabetically on her Swift playlist. But the words were so perfect that the heavy worry she'd been feeling before they got in the car lifted a little. This was Ash. Just Ash.

She sang louder and rolled the windows down just enough to let a breeze in as they pulled onto the interstate. By the second verse, she caught him in the act. He was singing along. Accurately.

She peeked over at him with faux shock. "Well, as I live and breathe. Ashton Isaacs, you're a Swiftie!"

He sat up taller in his seat and gave her a quelling look. "I am no such thing. Her songs are just...catchy. They're laced with earworms. It's a conspiracy."

Kincaid laughed and sang the line about him looking like bad news. But then she realized she'd trapped herself into singing "I gotta have you" straight to his face. She quickly turned her attention back to the road and hit the button on her steering wheel to skip to the next song.

Maybe she should've played "Bad Blood" instead. That was where she needed to keep her head at. This was Ashton Isaacs. This was a fresh start, but that didn't make the past disappear. This was the guy who had broken her heart and left her without looking back.

He would leave again.

She had enough going on in her life not to add that to the mix.

—~~~—

The Tipsy Hound was filling up by the time she and Ash arrived. She looked around at the place in all its divey glory. The bar was small but not claustrophobic, the dim lighting making it seem like some secret hideaway. The black floor had a vague stickiness beneath her feet, but the wooden tables were always sparkling clean.

Kincaid smirked. "I know it doesn't look like much, but it grows on you. The drinks are cheap and usually the entertainment is good—well, on karaoke night, 'good' isn't exactly the right word, but 'entertaining' still applies. Tonight will definitely be great because Taryn is performing."

Ash looked uncomfortable as hell—hands in the pockets of his jeans, gaze shifting around the place—but he sent her a quick smile. "It's cool."

The statement seemed genuine despite his obvious discomfort. She bumped her shoulder into his. "Come on, you didn't do the club or bar scene in all your travels?"

He shrugged. "Not much. I'm more of a coffee-shop guy. Once I moved back to New York, Melanie and I went out for drinks occasionally, but she liked upscale places where we could meet up with her friends. No karaoke for sure. She'd be horrified."

"Yeah," Kincaid agreed. "She didn't strike me as the karaoke type. So this is good. You're guaranteed not to meet someone like her here."

He gave her a patient look. "Kincaid, watch my lips." He circled his mouth with his finger, and she was trans-fixed for a moment. "I'm. Not. Here. To. Meet. Anyone. I don't want to be your project. I know how you can get when you're focused on something."

"Helpful?" she suggested.

He put his hands on her shoulders. "Other words. I was thinking *other words*."

She sighed. "Fine. You just fired the best wing woman ever." She nodded toward a table at the back of the bar. "You see that beautifully happy crew over there? See how they're all nicely paired off? Those are my friends. Guess who made all those relationships happen?"

"Fate," he said with mock seriousness as he lowered his hands to his sides. "Probably some alcohol. And maybe a little hormonal magic."

She pointed to her chest. "Nope. This girl. I'm great at matchmaking. It's my third best skill."

He lifted a brow. "And what are the first two?"

"Wouldn't you like to know." She grabbed his hand. "Come on."

Kincaid led Ash through the crowd, her heart beating a little faster when Ash tightened his grip on her hand. She could tell he was nervous about meeting her friends. She tried to imagine what it'd be like to walk into an already established group, especially with people you sort of knew from the past. For her, that wouldn't be a big deal. She loved meeting new people, but Ash had always been more reserved. He had been able to do customer service at the bookstore, but Kincaid knew that was only surface Ash, not the real him. He only let his guard down with a choice few.

Her friends looked up when she approached. They'd gotten a big table in the back. Finn was standing behind Liv's chair, his hands on her shoulders, his normally serious FBI agent face soft with amusement over something someone had said. Rebecca was laughing and leaning into her husband, Wes, who must've come straight from work since he still had on a T-shirt with the name of his food truck. And Shaw, Taryn's husband, was flying solo while Taryn was probably getting ready to sing, his thickly muscled arm thrown over the back of an empty seat.

Kincaid's chest warmed at the sight of all of them together. These were her people. She was never as happy as she was when she was with them. "Hey, y'all," she said, dragging Ash with her. "What'd I miss?"

Shaw smiled her way. "Nothing really. Just telling them about a guy who came into the gym way too confident and didn't listen to the safety instructions. He fell off an obstacle and got his too-loose pants hooked on the equipment in the process. Ended up in the foam pit naked as a jaybird."

Kincaid laughed. "Hope you had surveillance video. You could win money on *America's Funniest Home Videos*."

"Oh, there was video," Shaw said with a grin. "Not sure he'll sign a release waiver for that one, though." He nodded toward her. "So, who's your friend?"

Ash released her hand and stepped up next to her.

"Guys," Kincaid said, "this is Ashton Isaacs. Old friend. Long Acre alum. Writer extraordinaire. And currently a New Yorker visiting our fair city for a few months for inspiration."

Rebecca's eyes lit with recognition. "Hey, Ash. I remember you. AP English. You beat me out for the lit award."

Ash smirked. "Good memory. Hi, Rebecca."

"Bec never forgets someone who beat her out for an academic award," Liv teased.

Rebecca stuck out her tongue at her.

Liv pointed to her chest. "Liv." She pointed upward. "Finn."

Finn reached out his hand. "You're Coach Isaacs's son, right? I played for your dad."

Ash shook his hand, his expression revealing nothing. "Yeah, I remember. Nice to see you."

"How's your dad doing?" Finn asked. "I haven't seen him around lately."

Ash gave a tight smile. "I wouldn't know. I've been traveling a lot."

Finn, ever observant, nodded in understanding. "Gotcha."

Ash made his way through the rest of the introductions and shook hands, but Kincaid didn't miss Liv's evaluating look. As soon as Ash turned his back to Kincaid to grab another chair, Liv looked at her with knowing eyes and mouthed *holy shit*.

"Girl, preach," Kincaid said, keeping her voice low and sliding into her seat. "Hence the emergency call."

Rebecca bit her lip, apparently previously informed of the situation, and looked as though she was trying not to laugh.

Ash tucked in a chair next to Kincaid at the table but didn't sit down. "So, what's everyone drinking? I can grab the next round." The others replied with their orders. Wes and Rebecca had soda, everyone else beer. Ash leaned down close to Kincaid. "What's your poison, KC?"

KC. She'd given him a death glare the first time he'd used that nickname, but only because it hurt to remember. This time, it hit her in a place that made her want to close her eyes and transport back to a time when things had been so much simpler in her life, when Ash was just the best friend she'd ever had and the world was waiting for them. She swallowed past the dryness in her throat. "Margarita on the rocks, please."

"You sure about that?" Liv asked, giving her a look. "You know the margaritas here are...not the best."

That was a lie. They were strong and delicious. Liv was trying to do her job. But Kincaid needed a little something to take the edge off this night. Too many things were whirling around her head. "Yeah, I'm craving one."

"On it," Ash said and headed toward the bar.

As soon as he was out of earshot, Liv leaned forward, elbows on the table. "One margarita. That's all I'm giving you."

"Noted." Kincaid's gaze followed Ash to the bar.

"So," Liv continued, drawing Kincaid's attention back to her. "How complicated is complicated? Because, whoa...*hot*."

"Hey," Finn said with mock offense as he dropped into the seat next to his wife. "Literally right here."

Liv snorted. "Shut up, gorgeous. But seriously, how complicated?"

"Astrophysics complicated," Kincaid replied.

"Married?" Rebecca asked.

"God, no." If he were, this wouldn't be a conversation. She wasn't her mother. "He just broke off an engagement, though. Also, once upon a time, he broke my heart into a million pieces, and we never even dated."

"Ouch." Rebecca winced.

Wes looked to the other two men at the table. "Guys, do you get the feeling they're having a conversation in code right now?"

"Yep," Finn said with a nod. "We've got no shot. So...how 'bout them Cowboys?"

Liv rolled her eyes and then zeroed back in on Kincaid. "I say sleep with him."

Shaw choked on his beer.

"*What?*" Kincaid asked, feeling the shock twist her expression. Her friends were supposed to give her *rational* advice. She depended on that. She was the one who needed to be reeled in. "That's not what you're supposed to say."

Liv shrugged and took a sip of her beer. "It's the advice you would give me if the situations were reversed. He's only here for a little while, right?"

"A couple of months at most," Kincaid confirmed.

"See, built-in safety net," Liv said, as if it were the most practical perspective in the world. "I love you, but you're bad at taking your own advice. How many times have you told us all work and no play is no good for us? You've got way too much on your plate."

"I—"

"She's right about that. We've all noticed it lately," Rebecca said, interrupting her. "You've lost some spark, girlie. You've been downright serious."

Kincaid frowned.

"And a serious Kincaid is not a happy Kincaid. Plus, you're going to need a little fun to get through that haunted house renovation," Liv said. "Why not have it with him?"

She stared at her friends as if they'd been taken over by pod people. Where were her reasonable, cautious counterbalances?

"Because...reasons," Kincaid said, slapping the table lightly.

Rebecca smiled as she set down her glass. "Reasons?"

Kincaid threw up her hands. "Yes. We were best friends since we were kids. We worked at the bookstore together. He was close friends with…Graham."

Rebecca and Liv both frowned. Kincaid had confided in them about what Graham had meant to her.

Ash stepped back to the table, hands full of drinks. He set them each down in front of the right person. Kincaid smiled as her margarita appeared in front of her. "You carried those like a pro."

Ash's lips kicked up at the corner. "You don't become a published writer out of the gate. I waited more than my fair share of tables in college."

The information was simply conversational, the story of so many college students, but it hit her in a weird place that she didn't know about that time in his life. After high school, there was just a big blank space where Ash was concerned. As if he'd been surgically removed from her life. She picked up her drink and took a long sip.

Ash slipped into the spot next to her and sipped the craft beer he'd selected for himself. "So when's Taryn go on?"

"Any minute now," Shaw said, glancing toward the stage with a proud look in his eyes. "She's trying out a few original songs tonight."

Ash turned his chair so that he could see the stage better, and his arm brushed against Kincaid's. He glanced over at her. "How's the drink?"

The tart strength of it made her lips pucker. "Effective."

He chuckled. "Am I going to be choosing the music on the way home?"

"Hey, I can control myself."

He gave her an amused look. "Of course. I'm sure you've progressed since the time you snagged that bottle of peach schnapps from your mom's stash and ended up wearing your Halloween costume to the grocery store because you thought you really *were* Buffy the Vampire Slayer."

She groaned. "Man, I paid for that the next morning. I've never been so sick. But hey, I got us free cookies. That cashier thought I was adorable."

"I don't think 'adorable' would be the word he would've used. You melted his brain with that outfit. Those boots and that skirt... He had no shot." Ash shook his head ruefully. "No one did."

She turned her head to look at him, but he was focused on the stage. A muscle in his jaw twitched.

She frowned, sensing the shift. "Ash..."

But before she could finish her question, a heavy hand landed on her shoulder. "Well, I'll be damned if it isn't Kincaid Breslin. Fancy meeting you here."

Kincaid tensed at the unwelcome touch and turned in her seat. She could feel all her friends' attention swing the same way. A broad-shouldered guy with a cowboy hat grinned down at her. Sam Caldone. A few months ago, she'd sold him a nearby ranch. He'd bought her expensive whiskey as a thank-you gift, and after they'd shared a bit too much, they'd ended up in bed.

Kincaid gave Sam a tight smile and casually shrugged his hand off his shoulder. "Well, hi there, Sam. Come out to see the show?"

"Came out for a drink." His grin went lopsided in a way that said he'd already had a few of them. "Didn't expect to get a nice surprise like this, though. It's been a while. You didn't return my messages."

Hell. "Things have been busy. You know how it is. Everything okay with the ranch?"

"It's just fine. Main house could use a feminine touch, though, if you know what I mean. You should stop by. Share some of your expertise and whatnot. Like last time."

She winced inwardly, his thinly veiled innuendo not lost on her friends. "I'll email you the name of my favorite interior decorator. She'll be able to help you out," she said with false brightness. "Hope you have a good night. Enjoy the music."

"Tryin' to get rid of me, huh?" He braced a hand on the back of her chair, and his smile flattened into something less flattering.

Kincaid's smile became a strain to hold. "Just trying to catch up with my friends before the show starts."

"Sure," he said, tone snide. "But the polite thing would be to invite me to sit down with y'all. Maybe you just don't want your nice friends to know we fucked."

Kincaid sucked in a breath and shot to her feet, but before she could say anything, Ash was there next to her.

"Hey," Ash said, half stepping in front of her. "I don't know who the hell you are, but I would suggest you shut your damn mouth and go back to the bar."

Sam's lip curled. "Oh, are you the new guy? Fair warning, friend. Enjoy the ride while you can. It's a good one. A dirty one. But she'll be looking for the next dude after two dates. Sluts like her don't stick around. They always need new dick to make them feel special."

Ash raised his fist, but Kincaid beat him to it. She slapped Sam hard across the face, her palm wrenching his head sideways. Sam's gaze jumped back to her, fury there, and he raised his hand as if to return the favor. That was all it took for Ash to rush the guy like a linebacker. He shoved his shoulder into Sam's chest and took him down, knocking a chair to the floor along with him. People in the bar stopped to stare. Kincaid hurried to them, planning to kick the asshole in the ribs with her pointy boot if necessary, but Ash kept her behind him.

Sam was broader and bigger than Ash and quickly scrambled to get to his feet, but by the time he got his footing, Wes, Shaw, and Finn had sidled up behind Ash. Liv was looking scrappy, too. Sam was dumb with drunkenness, but he wasn't stupid. Shaw was a beast with all his muscles, Finn was an FBI agent who could probably kill a person in ten different ways, Wes looked ready for anything, and Ash, bookish or not, was strong and riding high on outrage.

Sam sneered. "What? She screwing all of you?"

Welp. Maybe he was stupid. Ash swung and landed a punch solidly on Sam's square jaw.

Finn quickly got behind Sam and grabbed him, getting him in a hold and neutralizing any counterattack. The other guys stayed in front of him like a menacing band of brothers.

Rebecca and Liv joined Kincaid. Rebecca gave Kincaid's arm a squeeze. "It'll be all right. Finn's got him."

"Listen to me very carefully, you dumb shit," Finn said. "When I let you go, you're going to call a cab and go the hell home. If you make one move toward any of

us or open your mouth again, I'm arresting you." Finn
sounded utterly calm, almost bored. "Or maybe I'll just
turn my head and let these guys and the ladies have a
go at you."

Sam looked ready to fight some more, but when he
took in the expressions on Kincaid's friends' faces, he
stopped struggling in Finn's hold. "Fine. Let me go."

Finn kept his word, and the other guys watched Sam,
making sure he wasn't going to make another move. Sam,
apparently not wanting to get arrested for a witty comeback,
flipped them the bird and then spun around to head for the
door, bumping into other people along the way.

Kincaid let out the breath she'd been holding and tried
to ignore the tremble that was working its way through
her body. "Show's over, everyone," she announced,
trying to feign a smile. "Drunken asshole has exited the
building."

A few people clapped half-heartedly, probably disappointed that the entertainment was over, and her friends
made their way back to the table. When Ash turned
around, there was anger simmering hot in his eyes.
Kincaid reached out as he got close, taking him by the
arm and steering him toward the back of the bar and into
the hallway near the bathrooms. "Hey, are you okay?
Let me see your hand."

"I'm fine," he said stonily. "Prick."

"Yeah, his momma must be so proud," she said,
taking Ash's hand and examining his knuckles under the
bluish light in the hallway. His hand was already starting
to swell a little. "Well, damn, you're going to feel that in
the morning. You shouldn't have risked your precious
typing hands on a jerk like that. I could've handled him."

Ash's gaze flicked up to hers, an argument there. "He was going to *hit* you."

She looked down, a ripple of unease going through her again. "Yeah, well, hurt egos and alcohol make men do stupid things."

"Don't," Ash warned. "Don't give him an excuse. There's no excuse for the things he said to you. And there's damn well no excuse for him even thinking about hitting a woman."

She nodded and let out a breath. "I know. I'm not trying to give him a pass, believe me. I think I'm just a little shaken up. And a lot embarrassed."

"Embarrassed?" he said, confused.

She shrugged and focused on his hand, flexing each of his fingers as she went, her stomach tying in knots. "Yeah. For sleeping with that idiot in the first place. For having my sex life announced to all my friends and everyone else in the bar." Her cheeks burned. "Even though he has no right to call me anything at all, it still rattles me to be called a slut. Feels like middle school all over again. Makes me wonder if I'm more like my mother than I think."

"Hey." Ash slipped his hand out of her grasp and cupped her chin with his good hand to force her to look at him. "Don't even go there. You're not your mother. You could walk naked down Main Street and fuck a whole county of single guys and you wouldn't be her."

"Hashtag life goals," she whispered, trying to make a joke, but the words got caught and her eyes stung with tears.

"Ah, hell, KC," he said, pulling her in for a hug and setting his chin atop her head. "Don't cry. That idiot doesn't deserve your tears. He should be thanking God that he got to touch you once because he's never going to be near anything that good again."

She sniffed indelicately against his shirt collar. "I don't want to be crying. I hate crying. Especially over some stupid guy. And he wasn't even good in bed, so it was a total waste."

Ash snorted. "I really don't want to know about the guy's bedroom skills."

"He hung his cowboy hat on his dick like I should be impressed," she said, her voice muffled against his shirt.

Ash groaned but she could hear the laughter in it. "I'm officially traumatized. Please stop."

"And he refused to take off his boots," she said, smiling into his shoulder, some weird delirium replacing the tears. "Like for the whole time."

"The visuals are literally killing me, KC. Please, no more," he begged, making the plea overdramatic.

She lifted her head. "When he came—"

Ash pressed his fingers over her lips, shaking his head, biting back a grin. "Nope. Not gonna listen. Can't—"

"He said 'yeehaw,'" she finished from behind his fingers.

Ash's eyes widened, and then he burst out laughing, tipping his head back against the wall and his own tears appearing. "Holy shit. You're making this up."

She snort-laughed. "Sadly no. It was really that bad. So, so bad."

Ash swiped at the corners of his eyes with his knuckle. "Good God. Part of me is glad some guys are that terrible in bed. It must make the rest of us look like rock stars by default."

She rolled her eyes. "I'm sure you're better than good by default. I mean, look at you."

Ash stilled, and she realized too late what she'd said. And that they were still standing way too close. She stepped out of his space.

"I mean—" she hedged, but better, more appropriate words didn't appear.

"Why don't we get back to the table?" he suggested, filling the awkward silence. "I'm sure your friend is about to go on."

Kincaid swallowed past the dryness in her throat. "Right. Yes. We should do that."

They both headed back toward the table, a healthy distance apart. As soon as they took their seats, the lights went down and Taryn stepped onto the stage.

Ash didn't look at Kincaid again the whole time. She ordered another drink.

When it was dropped in front of her, she ignored Liv's silent protests and downed it in a few sips.

chapter

TWELVE

"Sweet baby Jesus, this is the worst music I've ever heard in my entire life," Kincaid declared from the passenger seat. She reached for the dial to change the old-school punk station he'd put on, and Ash batted her hand away.

"Nope," Ash said happily. "I'm driving now. Someone shouldn't have had so many margaritas if she wanted to be radio queen."

Kincaid grumbled dramatically and raked her fingers through her hair. "You're the worst."

"I know," he said, taking the exit to get them to Long Acre. "Which way do I need to go to get to your place?"

"Hmm?" she said, distracted.

"Your house, Breslin?"

"You can't go to my house. How are you going to get back?" she asked. "Just bring me to the coffee shop by your place. A cup of coffee, and I'll be fine to drive after. I'm not that far gone. I can hold my liquor."

He eyed her. She wasn't sloppy drunk. He'd seen her

that way before and knew what that looked like. She got overly handsy and silly. But he also wasn't going to risk letting her get behind the wheel, especially this late at night. "I'll drop you off at your house and take your car to my place. I can swing by and get you in the morning," he said. "I'd say I'd take an Uber back tonight, but I'm thinking pickings might be slim in Long Acre."

She lolled her head toward him with a sardonic look. "You'd have better luck calling for a horse and buggy." She pressed a button on the dash. "Directions to home, please."

The GPS pulled up the location, and Ash headed toward Lake Wilder. Kincaid closed her eyes, giving him the chance to look at her without her noticing. Even a little tipsy and undone from the night out, she still looked beautiful in a way that only she could. She was more than pretty. Lots of women were pretty. But add that inner spark that seemed to light every part of her, and she became like a tractor beam, pulling people in without effort. That was what made her a straight-up knockout. She never tried to be anyone but herself, and that take-it-or-leave-it bravado never failed to make him want to *take, take, take*.

He'd let his guard slip at the bar. He'd been so goddamned angry when that dumb cowboy had insulted her, and he'd seen red when the guy had dared raise his hand to her. Ash hadn't felt that kind of primal rage in a long damn time. Rage and something else he didn't want to acknowledge but couldn't deny—jealousy. The emotion had burned bright and hot that some idiot like the cowboy had been with Kincaid.

He didn't want to feel that. He had no right to feel

anything about who she did or didn't sleep with. But he'd felt it nonetheless. He'd also wanted to question her about the choice—another thing that was none of his business—since he couldn't help wondering why someone like Kincaid would even give a guy like that a second of her time. Was it because he had money? She had her own now, so Ash didn't see how that could be a factor.

Ash flexed his hand, his knuckles stiff from the punch, and turned onto a darkened road. Kincaid dozed as he made his way through Long Acre and into Wilder. The houses became more upscale rustic and spaced out. The black lake came into view, the moonlight shimmering off the surface. This was prime property in this part of the world. Open space. Gorgeous views. Privacy. In high school, everyone had wanted invites to the parties hosted at the lake. Well, everyone except him. Others saw the tangle of trees as a perfect place to sneak off and hook up, the lake a perfect place to skinny-dip. His writer mind had always thought the area looked like the perfect setting for a horror movie. A guy in a hockey mask would fit right in. No way was he getting naked out there. Not that he would've had anyone back then to get naked with.

He glanced over at Kincaid, wondering if she and Graham had carved out a secret place at the lake. He dismissed the thought almost as quickly as it came, though. Kincaid was a romantic, but she was also terrified of bugs. Outdoor sex would probably be a comedy of errors for her.

Annnnd…he should not be thinking about Kincaid and sex in the same thought. He'd already come close to saying something he shouldn't have when she'd made a comment about how he looked. He didn't need to know that Kincaid liked how he looked. That would lead his mind down a dangerous path. He turned the radio up a little louder, forced himself to focus on the song.

When the GPS indicated that he'd arrived at their destination, he turned into the curved driveway and blinked at the beautiful home that came into view. The well-manicured lawn was lit with soft lighting, highlighting a bed of flowers, and the tall windows reflected back the night. The house, made mostly of natural wood and stone, was like a picture out of a vacation magazine. Not too big but elegant and welcoming.

Ash's heart clenched. *This* was where Kincaid lived now? Kincaid who'd grown up in a broken-down, almost always empty house that literally had holes in the floor. Emotions welled in him. He glanced over at her. *God, KC, look what you've done for yourself.* It made him ache inside and feel so fucking proud of her, but he shoved the feelings down. Not the time or place to get sentimental.

He pressed the button to shut off the engine and reached out to give Kincaid's arm a squeeze. "KC, you're home."

She blinked her eyes open as if she'd just been resting and not sleeping, glanced up at her house, and then sent him a half smile. "Right. My home. Yay."

Her tone gave him pause. "Why do you say it like that?"

She shook her head and unbuckled her seat belt. "Nothing. Sorry. Ignore me."

"No," he said. "Tell me. What's up?"

She sighed and brushed her fingers through her hair, an old nervous habit. "Nothing. It's just that this home won't be mine for much longer. I can't afford both this and the farmhouse. I have six months here, tops." She gave him a tight smile. "Because I make stupid decisions before I think. Like sleeping with dumb-asses and buying things I can't afford. That Kincaid, she's so flighty, you know. Can't trust her to act like an adult."

He frowned. "Don't say that. You're chasing a dream. Sometimes that requires rash decisions."

"Yeah, well, I'm good at being rash. I get an A-plus on that one." She reached for the door handle and gave him a terse smile. "Thanks for the ride. And for punching out a cowboy for me. You can add bodyguard to your résumé now." She leaned over and pecked his cheek. "Drive safe, okay?"

She started to open the door.

"KC."

She glanced back. "Yeah."

"You're going to want to punch me for this, so be prepared to swing, but...you know you deserve better, right?"

Her expression first went confused and then morphed into a full frown. "Ash, don't."

But he was unable to stop himself. "You can't tell me that you looked at that guy and thought, yep, he's totally a candidate for a relationship. He has future husband and father of my children written all over him. He totally deserves my time."

"You think *that's* what I thought about him?" she gave him a horrified look. "Lord, Ash, give me more credit than that. He was a hookup. A brief, clearly misguided distraction. I'm not looking for a husband. Or father for future children. Or any of that stuff." She shrugged. "Simple men mean simple fun. Uncomplicated and no one gets hurt. Well, in this case, he got punched, but that was his own fault."

He heard the words and knew that she had every right not to be seeking those things. But he couldn't shut up anyway. Maybe her impulsiveness was contagious.

"But that was never your style. In high school, you wanted…" He let the words trail off, but she had to know what he was talking about. She'd dated a number of guys, but she'd always been set on not being her mother, on seeing each relationship as something with real potential. She'd been an utter romantic determined to break free of her lonely childhood and find real love, create her own family one day. Back then, he would've called it her obsession.

She looked down, bitterness entering her expression. "In high school, I had Graham. I had hope then that things could be different." She lifted her lashes, meeting his eyes. "Nothing has felt like that since. I've tried. Developed some feelings for a few guys along the way. I just ended up getting hurt over and over again. I was miserable."

"But—"

"And you know why I'm not miserable now? Why I can be so happy and upbeat and everyone else's cheerleader?" she challenged.

He shook his head.

"Because I stopped hoping for things that weren't meant to be. Hope is the thing that hurts the most," she said, a tired edge to her voice. "It's the thing that makes people make plans even though we have almost no control over whether that plan comes true. I *had* a plan. Well, turns out, so did Joseph and Trevor, and guns at prom trumped my plan to marry the guy I loved and live happily ever after. So why bother planning ahead? Someone could show up with their own agenda at any moment and just wipe you out or take someone from you, take everything from you."

Her words made his chest hurt. "KC—"

"So I decided a long time ago that I wasn't going to waste my time trying to find some guy who kinda sorta fit the mold of who I thought I'd be with forever. I don't want a facsimile of Graham."

Graham. Always Graham. Frustration rippled through Ash. "Isn't that letting Joseph and Trevor win, though? You just gave up because no guy can compete with a ghost."

She flinched. "Don't call Graham that."

"I'm not trying to be mean. But that's what he is, KC. Graham died at eighteen. He's got a perfect record in your head only because he didn't get to grow up and make mistakes or piss you off or break your heart."

"He wouldn't have…" she said, looking away.

"That's bullshit and you know it. The guy was human. He had flaws." *Big ones.* "You don't know how things would've turned out."

A muscle in her jaw flexed. "It doesn't matter. I don't need a guy in my life to be happy. I'm fine on my own—great, in fact. It's been a big relief not to worry about it anymore. I don't have to waste time watching men let me down again and again. I want to live each day like it's my last, you know? Because it could be.

Have fun. Have great friends. Be a great friend. Don't take things too seriously. And don't count on anyone to stick around."

That last blow landed solid.

"And certainly stop looking for some guy to give me a fairy tale. Even if I wanted to cling to that illusion, I'm not the kind of woman guys marry. I've been informed of that over and over again." Her lip curled in derision. "I'm like high-end liquor. Best in small doses. Or so I'm told. I think the guy who said that to me thought he was being romantic."

Ash's fist clenched in his lap. "Another guy who sounds like he needs to be punched."

"Yeah, well. He was the only one who said it. The other guys just demonstrated it." She reached for her purse, which she'd stashed on the floorboard. "Even you, right?"

Ash leaned back, the words slapping him in the face. "Kincaid—"

She lifted a hand. "Sorry. I didn't mean to say that. My filter setting is on low. Three margaritas. I need to get inside."

Before he could say anything else, she climbed out of the car, tossed her key fob on the passenger seat, and shut the door.

Kincaid had always loved having the last word, but he couldn't let her have this one tonight. He grabbed the key and climbed out. She was already halfway to the door. "KC, wait."

She ignored him.

He braced his arms on top of the car and called out louder, "You're baby-fox coffee."

The words boomed in the quiet around them, only the crickets filling the space in between. Her quick steps stuttered and then she paused. She turned her head to look back at him, confused. "What?"

He breathed past the tightness in his throat and stepped around the car. "You're baby-fox coffee, not fine liquor. You're rare and full of energy and straight-up addictive. Only those with a very refined palate can appreciate you. But those people are out there, and once they get a sip, they won't know how they got through the days without you before that."

She blinked rapidly, and her eyes glistened in the garden lights. "Ash."

He ran a hand over the back of his head, uncomfortable all of a sudden. "I didn't leave because I was tired of you or because you were too much. I had to leave because I was too messed up to stay," he said, needing her to know that. "You were the best friend I'd ever had. My world was a much darker place without you in it, and it was one of the hardest things I've ever had to do—go out in the world without having you in my corner."

She stared at him.

"So don't let any guy sell you some line of bullshit that you're too much to handle. If you don't want the marriage-and-kids thing, that's your prerogative. I get it. I'm not so fond of the idea these days either. But don't let some asshole or a gaggle of them decide that for you. If they don't want to be with you because you're 'too much,' that just means they're not enough."

A tear escaped down her cheek, and she walked toward him. His heart was beating fast by the time she stopped in front of him. She reached out and took his hand in hers, giving it a squeeze. "You always had a way with words, Ashton Isaacs. No wonder people pay you for them now."

He gave her a small smile. "I just want to make sure you hear these."

To his surprise, she stepped into his space and wrapped her arms around him. She put her cheek against his shoulder and hugged him tight. Stunned for a moment, he stood there, arms hanging at his sides, but then his brain finally kicked into gear, and he hugged her back.

"I missed you," she said, the words almost a whisper.

He closed his eyes and inhaled the scent of her—that sweet vanilla—and his body relaxed into the hug. "I missed you back."

She leaned back in his arms, her face just inches from his as she looked up at him. "Don't drive all the way back to Long Acre. You can stay here."

A bolt of unadulterated *wanting* went through him both at her nearness and the words, but that bolt was quickly followed by warning bells. "KC—"

"I have a nice guest room with extra toiletries. It will save you the trip now and the drive back in the morning. It'll be like old times but without the sneaking around or the questionable scent of a teenage boy's bedroom."

"Hey," he said, "my bedroom did not stink. I washed my sheets at least every three-ish months."

She laughed and put her hands on his shoulders. "Come on. I'll make my kickass pancakes in the morning. You can give me a trial run on my bed-and-breakfast skills."

He knew the offer was completely innocent. This was at the heart of Kincaid's DNA—she did for her friends. She didn't want him to drive this late and make him go out of the way in the morning. She wanted to cook for him because she liked feeding people. But part of him wished right now that they were two other people in a different set of circumstances because he wanted to pull her back to him, cup her face, and kiss her. He wanted her to invite him inside for more than pancakes. But he'd stupidly messed up their friendship once before with those kinds of feelings. No way was he making that mistake again, not when they were finally mending some things between them.

"So?" She looked up expectantly.

He sighed. "You got me with pancakes."

"Yay!" she said with a little bounce on her toes as she stepped back. "A sleepover."

He groaned. "People in their thirties can't have sleepovers. And you can't paint my toes or curl my hair."

She smirked. "What about curling your toes?"

The words hit him like a hot gust of wind. "What?"

She laughed. "Oh, don't look so scandalized, Isaacs. I'm teasing. If I were inviting you in for that, you'd know it, honey. Now come on. The mosquitoes are going to eat us alive if we don't get inside."

She turned and left him there, staring after her.

chapter

THIRTEEN

KINCAID SPRINKLED MINI CHOCOLATE CHIPS INTO THE pancake batter, popped a few in her mouth, and then stirred, trying to get the batter to the perfect texture. The coffeepot sputtered along, filling the kitchen with its comforting scent, and her mind was drawn back to Ash's comment last night. *You're baby-fox coffee.*

She smiled to herself, a warm feeling spreading through her. She'd been called a lot of things in her life, but that definitely was one of the weirdest...and sweetest. Ash had changed since they'd last been friends. He'd hardened in a lot of ways, but some things had remained the same. The guy still knew how to say the perfect thing to make her feel better. His words had made her cry. They'd also made her want to kiss him, but she'd actively ignored that dangerous impulse. After having a night filled with one of her hookups coming back to haunt her, she definitely didn't need to make that kind of mistake with Ash. She'd just gotten him back as a friend. She wasn't going to ruin it just because he said sweet things and looked aggressively hot in a T-shirt.

Kincaid set the batter aside to let it rest for a minute and checked the time. Ash had told her he had trouble sleeping late, but maybe that was because he was sleeping on a thin, old mattress at the apartment. When she'd passed by the guest room at seven, she'd heard the steady sounds of his sleep-heavy breathing still going strong. She'd left him to it, made a few work calls, and returned a slew of emails. She'd also set up some appointments with contractors to come out and take a look at the farmhouse. But now it was almost nine, and she was getting hungry. She'd give him a few more minutes, and then she would start cooking without him. But first, more coffee.

She was reaching for the pot to make herself a fresh cup when a buzzing sounded behind her. She turned. Ash had left his cell phone plugged into her charging station on the counter next to her keys, and the screen had lit up. She set the coffeepot down, walked over to silence the phone, and grimaced when she saw Melanie's face on the screen. The picture Ash had saved for her number had her blowing a kiss to the camera, the Eiffel Tower rising up behind her. *Ugh.* Kincaid had never liked the woman, but knowing that Melanie had cheated on Ash made her outright despise her. She knew there were two sides to every breakup, but she drew a hard line at cheating. There were no excuses for that bullshit, especially when you had someone's ring on your finger.

She hit the button to silence the phone, but before she could walk away, the screen lit with a text. She was too nosy not to look.

> Don't be a jerk. I know u have ur phone. I
> need to talk to u.

Kincaid rolled her eyes. The screen lit again.

> This is just like u. U don't want to deal w/
> something so u just avoid it. Coward.

Coward? Kincaid gritted her teeth and flipped the phone the middle finger even though Melanie obviously couldn't see the gesture. "Your ex carried me out of a mass shooting and saved my life. Maybe cool it on the coward talk, cheater girl."

The phone started buzzing again. Kincaid hit the decline button. Three seconds later, it vibrated again.

"Oh for the love of God, woman." Kincaid was about to turn the damn thing off completely so she could make her pancakes in peace, but then she got an idea. She lifted the phone, pulling the charger out, and slid her thumb across the screen. "Hello, this is Ash's phone, how may I help you?"

"You stubborn—" But then Melanie's voice cut off. "Wait, who is this?"

"Oh, sugar, I could ask you the same thing. Calling a man's phone so many times in the morning really is a nuisance. Maybe leaving a message would suffice."

"Where's Ash?" Melanie bit out through what sounded like clenched teeth. "I need to speak with him."

"Oh, well, he's still in bed, not quite ready for talking," Kincaid said with her best and brightest voice, the one she used when she'd cover the reception desk at the real estate agency. "Want to leave a message? I'll be sure to get it to him."

"Look, I don't know who this is, and I don't care. I just need him on the phone now. It's important," she said, voice clipped. "This is his fiancée."

Kincaid sniffed derisively. *Fiancée? Nice try.* That was stooping pretty low, trying to get the ex *she* cheated on in trouble with a new woman. Kincaid let out a heavy sigh, making sure Melanie heard it. "Well, even though we both know he no longer has a fiancée, if it's an emergency, I'll go get him."

And make you pay for being so damn rude. Kincaid walked to the guest room and put the phone on mute before she knocked.

A sleepy voice came through the door. "Come in."

Kincaid opened the door and found Ash shifting to sit up in bed, shirtless, tattooed, and with full-on bedhead. Every womanly cell in her body gave a cheer of appreciation, and she had the sudden annoying urge to tilt her head and twirl her hair like a smitten schoolgirl. Luckily, she stopped herself from that embarrassment. She wasn't there to ogle.

"Everything all right?" Ash asked, swiping a hand across his face and trying to wake up.

Kincaid lifted the phone. "Your ex has been burning up your phone. I got aggravated and answered. Sorry. She's still calling herself your fiancée, and I believe she wants to yell at you about something."

Ash groaned. "Hell no. I'm not starting my day off with that. Tell her I'll call her later or just hang up."

"I could. *Or*," Kincaid said conspiratorially, "we could have a little fun and piss her off in the process. You game?"

His eyebrows lifted, mischief in the tilt of his lips. "I could possibly be game."

Kincaid grinned and unmuted the phone so they could be heard. "Hey there, sleepyhead," she said in a flirty voice to Ash. "Rise and shine."

Ash cocked his head in confusion, but when he saw the look on her face, he caught on fast. "Morning, gorgeous."

Kincaid put a knee on the bed, knowing the guest bed squeaked and that Melanie would be able to hear and draw her own conclusions. "I know you wanted to sleep in after last night, but that Melanie woman has some sort of emergency and just couldn't wait."

Ash smirked, a deliciously evil look on his face. "Baby, you know you shouldn't be answering my phone this early. We have better things to do right now." Ash grabbed Kincaid's wrist and tugged her forward, making her tumble onto the bed and inadvertently laugh. She landed next to him, and he lifted her arm to his mouth, kissing the tender skin of her wrist with an audible sound. On the phone, that kiss could be imagined anywhere.

Kincaid's skin heated despite the fact that this was a farce. "You probably should take it or she'll keep calling. I don't want to be interrupted in the middle of anything, you know?"

Ash chuckled softly, this deep, private laugh, a lover's laugh. It sent hot shivers through Kincaid, waking up sensations that had been dormant as of late. "Of course not. Wouldn't want that. Give me just a minute." He took the phone, the smile dropping from his face. "Melanie."

Kincaid could hear the rapid-fire voice through the line and remained next to Ash on the bed. Melanie was saying something about him leaving the apartment messy when he moved out. About the landlord keeping the deposit.

Ash grunted, his tone and entire demeanor bored. "I wasn't paying for a cleaning service to clean up after you. Just because you moved out first doesn't mean it was my mess. You made this mess."

More yelling on her end, the volume notching up.

"Melanie," Ash said patiently, "clearly you feel passionately about this. I can't say I give a shit, so that puts us at an impasse. How about you send me back your ring, and I'll consider sending you half the deposit? Otherwise, I've got better things to do right now."

Melanie's next words were clear as a bell. "Right. You probably can't even afford the deposit. Are you back to the living-on-ramen plan, Ash? Don't have your woman's money to use up now? Or did you just find a new one to pay the rent?"

Ash's teeth clenched, his skin flushing red from the neck up—the words a match to a fuse. Kincaid saw what was happening, the fire racing up through him. She'd been there. That moment when an ex or a bully gets the best of you, and you stoop to their level. You lose your shit and end up looking like the dumb one or the hysterical one or the one who still cares too much. No way was she letting Melanie win this round. Without thinking, she scrambled to sit up and then swung her leg over Ash's middle, straddling him.

Ash's lips, which had been parted to yell, froze in almost comic silence. His shocked gaze jumped up to Kincaid's, her ambush plan working to stop him in his tracks. She took the phone from him and put it to her ear. "Hey, sugar, time's up. And I can promise you, neither of us are here for each other's money. Don't call again. Bye now."

Melanie gasped. "*Kincaid*."

Kincaid bit her lip, not sure if it was good for Melanie to know her identity and to think she and Ash were together, but that cat was already bolting away from the bag, too far to catch.

"Ugh," Melanie said into the phone. "I should've known. He always had a taste for the cheap stuff."

Kincaid smiled, almost entertained. *Oh, sweet, misguided Melanie*. If Melanie were here, she'd pat her on the hand and shake her head at the lame attempt. The woman was going to have to do better than that to get under her skin. "Oh, bless your heart. It's so cute when women try to throw other women under the bus just because a guy's involved—or in your case, two guys. Really moves that feminist needle forward, don't you think? You should burn a bra."

"You—"

"Enjoy your new relationship, sugar," Kincaid said, cutting her off. "I hope you two are made for each other in every way."

Melanie was silent, and Kincaid took the opportunity to hang up.

She tossed the phone to the side and braced her hands on either side of Ash on the bed. "Well, if you needed a sign that things aren't going so well with her new guy, that was a clear one. If she were happy, she wouldn't give a damn about a couple hundred dollars of a deposit, especially when she has money. And she certainly wouldn't care if you were sleeping with me—"

"Kincaid."

"And I know I probably shouldn't have answered. But she wouldn't let up, and I just couldn't help it and—"

"*Kincaid*—" Ash said more urgently.

"What?"

"You need to—" He grabbed her by the waist, shifting to hoist her off him, but before he could, she sucked in a breath as she became all too aware of the distinct firmness beneath her.

"Oh shit," she said, rolling herself off him as if he'd caught fire.

Ash made a pained sound and fell back against the pillow. "Yeah, that."

"I...uh." Her cheeks burned as she sat up.

Ash pulled the covers higher and shifted onto his side so the blanket wouldn't reveal his current condition. He gave her a droll look as he propped his head on his hand. "I really appreciate the effort to irritate my ex, I do. But maybe don't straddle a guy first thing in the morning. Little hard to control things."

Kincaid couldn't stop a snort from escaping. "Did you just say a little hard?"

Ash gave her a you've-got-to-be-kidding-me look and then hit her with a pillow.

She laughed as she defended herself from the blow and then couldn't stop, the laughter bubbling up from deep in her belly. "A little hard," she said between laughs. "Maybe more than a little. I mean, give yourself some credit."

Ash sat up, laughing now, and smacked her with the pillow a few more times. "What the hell were you trying to do? She can't see you on top of me."

She playfully fended off the swats and tried to grab

his pillow in retaliation. "I was trying to *help*. You were about to stoop to her level and lose your cool. She would've won. Getting on top of you was the only thing I thought might shut you up."

"Well, it worked!" The pillow hit her and she grabbed hold of it, yanking. But instead of him releasing it, she pulled him down with her.

Kincaid landed on her back with a squeak of the bedsprings, and Ash quickly let go of the pillow, bracing himself on his forearm so he wouldn't collapse onto her. His body heat wafted against her. Their shared laughter cut off almost immediately, and the playful mood burned up like dew on a hot day. His face was only inches from hers, both of them out of breath and flushed. His gaze searched hers.

She wet her lips. His nearness, the way he was looking at her, and his bare chest all making her thoughts scramble. "I'm sorry. I didn't think," she said. "I didn't realize…"

"That being straddled by a beautiful woman and feeling her soft and hot against me wouldn't make me hard," he answered, voice low, the words like warm honey against her. "Wouldn't make me want to touch her and see just how much hotter she could get."

Kincaid's breath left her in a rush, the words and the look on his face so out of character for Ash that she almost couldn't process it. "Ash."

He pushed a stray hair away from her face, his gaze never leaving hers. "Thank you for trying to help, but you need to hear this. We can't play around like that anymore. We're not fourteen. My body doesn't give a damn about our history or that we're supposed to be friends. All it knows in moments like this is that it wants you."

"Ash," she repeated. Her heartbeat was pounding in three different places, every nerve hyperaware. Even his finger brushing over her forehead felt erotic. Unable to resist, she reached up, letting her hand slide up his chest, the smooth feel of him setting off responses in her like gasoline on an already burning fire. Her nipples tightened against her tank top. His eyes moved downward, the telltale signal not escaping his notice. Guys weren't the only ones who had bodies that betrayed them.

His brow furrowed, and his gaze returned to her face. "You want me, too."

He said it as if surprised. She let her hand grip the back of his neck and gave him a half smile. "Don't roll on top of a woman first thing in the morning, half-naked and looking gorgeous, and not expect her to react."

The arm holding him up flexed as though he was barely resisting lowering all the way down and kissing her, but then a wary look darkened his features. He gently grabbed her wrist and eased her hand away from his neck. He pressed his lips to the inside of her wrist with a chaste kiss before lowering her arm back to the bed above her head. "You're tempting the hell out of me, Breslin, but this would be a really, really bad idea." His fingers trailed down the inside of her arm, making her shiver. "You know we can't."

"We can't?" She'd meant it as a statement, but it'd come out a question. Frankly, she was having trouble concentrating with his fingers moving along her skin and that look he kept giving her, the one that said he was three seconds away from ripping the tank top and yoga pants off her body.

He trailed his fingertip along her collarbone, his brow still furrowed as if he were having a stern conversation with himself instead of her. "We've made this mistake before. We destroyed a friendship over it."

She chilled, the words like a bucket of ice water on her desire. "Right."

He moved his hand away from her and met her gaze. "A lot of things are different now, but some are still very much the same. I'm only in town for a little while, and then I'm leaving again. I won't stay here."

"I'm not asking you to."

He frowned. "I know, but it's playing with fire, and I refuse to risk us again. Your friendship is more important to me than anything. Even more important than really"—he sighed heavily as his gaze raked over her body—"*really, really* hot sex."

She laughed at that, some of the tension breaking. "Three *really*s? Wow. Pretty sure of yourself there, huh? You just know it'd be that hot?"

He gave her a smug, confident look. "I do. Because you know what happens when a guy's first time results in the girl crying, yelling, and kicking him out?"

Her nose scrunched. She hated that she'd been that girl. "What?"

He leaned close to her ear. "He makes sure that going forward, he's so good at it that the girl will never, *ever* want him to leave her bed."

Hot goose bumps prickled her skin at the utter promise of his words. This wasn't a version of Ash she knew. This was the man, not the insecure boy. This was confidence and edge and sex appeal in spades. This Ash pushed buttons she didn't know she had. She tried not to sound breathless when she spoke again. "Now you're just being a tease, Isaacs."

He glanced down at her tank top, her arousal still glaringly obvious. "Said the pot to the kettle."

She smiled at the gruffness in his voice. This wasn't easy for him either, which made her feel better. At least they were suffering together. She dragged her nails lightly down his arm, scraping over his tattoos and channeling a little of her own confidence. "Oh, cupcake, you haven't seen me in tease mode. I promise, you wouldn't survive it."

The heat that flashed in his eyes nearly undid her, melting every bit of her resolve to do the smart thing, but she was not going to be her impulsive self this time. They both knew this was a bad idea. So, forcing back all the naughty thoughts dancing through her mind, she lifted her head and planted a lightning-fast peck on his lips. Before it could turn into anything more, she rolled from beneath him and then to her feet on the side of the bed.

Ash collapsed onto the bed and made a guttural sound. "Do they make gold stars for grown-ups? I think we each just earned one."

She laughed. "We should get a whole sheet of them."

"Also, I hope you have a lot of hot water in your tank because I'm going need a long shower." He turned his head to give her a disarming smirk. "A really long one."

She lifted a brow and put a hand on her hip. "You and me both, honey."

He closed his eyes as if in pain. "Not helping, KC. Writer. Vivid imagination."

"Not trying to. I shouldn't suffer alone." She walked to the door, forcing herself to get away from the temptation. "Breakfast is in twenty minutes. Enjoy your shower."

She walked out and shut the door behind her, leaning against it and catching her breath. *Holy shit.* Her body was pulsing just about everywhere, and the ache inside her was one she'd never felt so intensely before. She had a healthy sex drive and found herself attracted to men on a relatively regular basis. She wasn't inexperienced at what it felt like to be turned on. But she wasn't sure she'd ever felt this kind of desperate, almost clawing need before. Like she might jump out of her skin if Ash didn't touch her.

No way was she going back in there, though. They had made the right decision. Rational thinking instead of impulsive behavior. Gold stars for sure. Attraction wasn't anything special. Sex was just a fun physical release. Neither of those things compared to having one of her best friends back in her life. The risk wasn't worth the cost.

Probably.

With that in mind and ignoring the mental image of Ash shirtless, turned on, and sprawled on the bed, she pushed away from the door and went straight to her own bathroom. She hadn't been lying about the shower.

Defensive measures were definitely in order. Hell, right now, they were her only hope.

chapter
FOURTEEN

ASH COULDN'T CONCENTRATE AS HE REARRANGED THE health section of The Stuffed Shelf. It had been a week since the near disaster at Kincaid's house, and they'd worked together at the bookstore almost every day since without any more close calls, but he still couldn't shake how easy it had been to almost cross that line again. The first time they'd slept together, they'd been lost teens, and the act had been born out of grief, confusion, and almost a survival instinct to feel something other than despair for a few minutes. They'd been seeking a kind of mutual emotional numbness that first time. This time, the urge had been nothing of the sort.

This time, straight-up lust was to blame. He hadn't wanted her because they used to be best friends or because he used to be in love with her. The desire hadn't been nuanced or complicated. Kincaid was beautiful, made him laugh, and was sexy as hell. He'd wanted her naked in that bed. Right. That. Second. But that was where the simplicity of the pairing stopped, because he knew what would chase them down afterward if they gave in to that urge. The past was like a rabid dog. You could only throw it off your scent for a little while before it was hunting you down again, ready and eager to tear everything apart with its sharp teeth.

They'd made the right call. He knew that, but it didn't make it easier to be around her every day. Today she'd walked in with still-damp hair, obviously fresh from the shower, which, of course had reminded him of the other morning. Kincaid had walked into the kitchen after her shower that day to make him pancakes. There had been a high, bright flush on her cheeks that he'd known wasn't from the hot water. She'd done exactly the same thing he had in the shower after their tussle on the bed.

Now every time he thought of that moment, his vivid imagination went into overdrive—images of Kincaid naked under the shower spray, soaped up, her hands touching where he craved to touch. Had she done the same thing this morning? Had she pretended her hands were his? Had she imagined the things he'd do to her? Because, man, he wanted to do some things to her. *Ugh*. All of it was too much to process, and if he didn't reel it in, he was going to get hard *again*.

And out-of-control erections were *not cool*. He was a grown-ass man. He thought he'd gotten past that embarrassing phase during puberty, but being around Kincaid was turning out to be a hazard. He picked up a medical dictionary from the shelf and opened it to a random page. Photos of frostbite. *Yep, that'll do it*. He stared at the disgusting picture until his body cooled off. Maybe he should just carry around gross medical books as a precaution while he was working here.

Kincaid's cell phone rang from two aisles over, startling him and making him slam the dictionary shut with a snap, dust dancing in the air at the sudden movement. Ash set the book down and pulled his phone from his pocket to lower the music he'd rigged to play throughout the store with a new Bluetooth system he'd installed.

"Hello?" Kincaid answered.

Ash tucked his phone into his pocket and picked up a rag to wipe down the shelf he'd just cleared.

"Wait. What now?" Her voice had sharpened. "What do you mean *goats*?"

That caught Ash's full attention, and he stepped out of the aisle he was working on and headed her way. He found her with her hand braced on a shelf and a vaguely horrified expression on her face. Her gaze flicked up, catching Ash's briefly.

"Ferris, how was this not in the notes? Are you sure?" She pinched the bridge of her nose as Ferris apparently responded, and then she closed her eyes. "Yeah, all right. I guess I'll head over and take care of it. Not that I know how to take care of it. My goat experience is limited to enjoying their cheese. Are they okay?"

Ash crossed his arms, openly eavesdropping, his writer mind already filling in all kinds of possible pictures of what could be going on.

"Yeah, well, that's good at least." She gave Ash a look that said *Can you believe this guy?* "And what? Ferris, do you not know me at all? Of course I'll send you pictures. But if I didn't love you, I'd hate you right now." She ended the call, tucked her phone in her back pocket, and gave Ash an exasperated look. "I've got to go."

He frowned. "What's wrong?"

She pushed a stack of books she'd put on the floor aside with her foot and dusted off the front of her jeans. "Well, apparently, when I purchased the farmhouse, I also purchased a pair of goats."

"*Goats?*"

"Yes, because of course I did," she said with a welcome-to-my-life sweep of her arms. "And apparently Barry and Beula are escape artists who trashed the neighbor's vegetable garden. The neighbors chased them away, but now they're wandering the property and could indulge in more goatish hijinks, and it's my responsibility to prevent that."

"They're just on their own?" Ash asked, irritated on her behalf and the goats'. "Who leaves animals to fend for themselves without telling the new owners? That's cruel."

"The owner was senile and apparently forgot she had them. When the house was sold, the guy who took care of the property and goats was let go." Kincaid tilted her head back, looking at the ceiling, clearly exhausted by it all. "So now I have to go round up goats because I totally know how to do that."

Ash stepped forward, hooking his thumbs in his pockets. "I can go with you. I also have zero goat experience, but I'm dressed for the farm, like small furry animals, and could possibly help."

She glanced down at his plaid flannel shirt and jeans. "I don't think your wardrobe is going to help, but I'll take an extra set of hands."

"What do we do when we catch them? Is there a pen or something?"

"Yes." She huffed. "One that is apparently broken. Damn. I hadn't thought that far. Maybe we can—" Her face lit up. "Ooh, wait, I know someone who could help with this."

He lifted his brows. "You have someone skilled at goat wrangling? Your networking skills know no bounds."

"It's one of my magical powers." She grabbed her phone from her pocket. "Wes's brother is a vet and a really nice guy. If he's available, he'll help. Let me give him a call, and maybe he can meet us there."

"You do that, and I'll meet you out front. I'll get everything locked up."

She gave him a grateful look and then headed toward the back of the store, putting her phone to her ear.

After Ash finished securing the store, he stepped out into the late-morning sunlight, the air scented with coffee from the open-doored café a few yards down. Kincaid was leaning against her car, texting. When she looked up and saw him, she lifted her keys and jangled them. "You mind driving? I need to run into the convenience store on the way. Marco, my vet friend, is going to meet us there, but he said to get some animal crackers. We can use them to lure the goats if they won't come to us."

Ash opened his hand for the keys as she tossed them to him. "Animal crackers?" He walked over and she stepped away from the car, letting him open the door for her. "That seems kind of messed up. Do they come goat-shaped?"

She laughed as she lowered herself into the seat. "We eat gingerbread men, so I think we're all a little cannibalistic in our cookie choices."

After the quick stop at the gas station for cookies, Ash followed Kincaid's directions to the farmhouse. Soon they were on a winding road that curled through thick tangles of trees, leaving the populated part of Long Acre behind them. He'd grown up in this town, and he'd passed the entrance to this road a thousand times, but he'd never taken the turn. After a stretch of woods, a few crooked mailboxes appeared along the side of the road, and the edges of dirt and gravel driveways peeked out every hundred yards or so. Finally, right before the road dead-ended, Kincaid told him to take a left. He turned onto a blacktop road, and the large farmhouse came into view.

Ash leaned forward over the steering wheel to get a better view as he slowed and bumped over the uneven drive. The farmhouse looked as if it could be part of a movie set, something straight out of another era. Pale, cream-colored boards with peeling paint, lots of windows, crooked steps, and a long porch. Even one of those rooster weather-vane things sat atop the highest point on the roof.

People who went by *Ma* and *Pa* had definitely lived here once upon a time. But despite its obvious state of disrepair, he instantly understood why Kincaid had fallen in love with the farmhouse. There was something magical about the old home sitting beneath the bright-blue sky with nothing but trees around. There was a timeless quality, as if the place had a bubble around it and was safe from the high-speed life going on a few miles away in the rest of the world. An escape.

"What do you think?" Kincaid's fingers curled around her purse, her voice tentative.

"Wow," he said, pulling to a stop in front of the house.

She glanced over at him. "Like wow, I can't believe you spent your money on a haunted house?"

He laughed. "No, like wow, it's kind of amazing."

Her eyes lit, and she bit her lip. "Yeah?"

She looked so unsure of herself that he almost reached out and hugged her. Kincaid was nothing if not confident. He hated that she was questioning her gut decision, that everyone had convinced her that her feelings couldn't be trusted. He reached out and gave her shoulder a squeeze instead. "Yeah, really. I can see why you couldn't let this house get away. It's a find."

She put her hand over her heart and then leaned over to give him a quick kiss on the cheek. "Thank you." She sat back in her seat. "You're the first person to say that. I think I needed to hear that."

He smiled. "I haven't seen the inside yet. I may change my mind."

"Ha." She grabbed the door handle. "Did I mention it comes with its very own goats?"

"Bonus."

They both got out of the car, and Kincaid put her hands on her hips as if she were ready to go to battle or call forth superpowers. They scanned the immediate area, searching for rogue goats. Unlike the tangle of trees they'd driven through to get there, the land in front of the house was mostly cleared with only a few trees breaking the sight line. In the distance, there was some type of small shed that leaned too far to the left, and a fenced area was next to it. Kincaid pointed to the fencing. "That's probably where the goats are supposed to be. We can start looking around while we wait for Marco. Grab the animal crackers."

Ash leaned back into the car to snag the cookies and then shut the door. "Maybe we should start near the shed." But before Kincaid could respond, a thumping sound came from his left and then the sharp sound of a baby's cry. He spun to face the direction of the noise. "What the hell?"

Kincaid turned on her heel toward the house, and an oh-shit look crossed her face. "Oh. No."

The crying sound came again, and dread filled him. That wasn't a baby. "Is that..."

She looked over at him. "It is. And it's coming from inside the house."

The words were like a line from a horror movie. *The call's coming from inside the house!* But he didn't think mentioning that would be helpful since Kincaid already looked horrified. He cleared his throat. "I'm guessing that's bad. I'm guessing goats in the house are never good."

She closed her eyes and inhaled deeply. "They are not. I've already started moving some things over."

Ash cringed. He'd once had a raccoon sneak into his parents' garage. The destruction had been impressive. He couldn't imagine what two hungry goats could do. "Well, at least it will be easier to get them cornered."

Kincaid made a sound of resignation and pulled a key from her pocket. "Might as well see what the damage is."

Ash followed her up the front steps and onto the porch. The wooden slats beneath their feet creaked in protest. After one more deep breath, Kincaid unlocked the door and swung it open. The bleating sounds got louder, and the stench of farm animal was unmistakable in the air.

Kincaid wrinkled her nose. "Fantastic."

"Here. Let me go first," Ash said, stepping in front of her. "Just in case they're attack goats. I'm the one with the treats."

She arched a brow. "Attack goats?"

"You never know. I once had a swan go on a murderous rampage at a park and try to kill me." He gave her a pointed look. "Life tip: Don't run out of bread at the swan pond."

She was smiling now. "Noted."

Ash stepped inside the high-ceilinged foyer and looked toward the big living room on the right. Clothes and other detritus were strewn all over the floor. It looked as if someone had taken the boxes Kincaid had stacked in there, ripped them up Hulk-style, and then thrown the contents around the room in a rage. Pieces of chewed-up cardboard box littered every bit of the floor.

"How bad is it?" she asked from the porch.

"Um, I guess goats like cardboard," he said, sending her an apologetic look over his shoulder. "And possibly clothes."

She stepped inside and gasped. "Oh my God. You have got to be kidding me. How can two little goats do all that?"

"Barry and Beula appear to be the industrious sort."

The thumping and bleating hadn't ceased. The sounds were coming from somewhere deeper in the house. Kincaid grabbed the box of animal crackers from Ash and stomped forward. "All right, you little clothes-eating bastards, time to get evicted."

Ash followed as Kincaid maneuvered her way around the mess and the goat poop in the living room.

She cursed under her breath the whole way, muttering threats against the animals. The door in the back corner of the room opened into the kitchen, but she halted so suddenly in the doorway that he almost bumped into her. He grasped the doorjamb to keep from knocking her over and then took in the sight before them.

"Oh my word," Kincaid breathed.

The kitchen was a disaster, too. One goat, a small one with a black body and white ears, was standing atop the kitchen counter, happily tugging at the dingy curtains hanging from the window. A larger goat, also black but with a white diamond-shaped patch on his head, was standing near the back open doorway like a lookout. He had a piece of chewed-up wallpaper in front of him, a telltale blank spot on the wall nearby. He bleated at them in warning, the obnoxious sound thoroughly conveying how annoyed he was that they had dared enter his space. The female goat, presumably Beula, spared them a glance, gave a small bleat, and then went back to the curtain as though Ash and Kincaid weren't there.

"You have been very, very bad goats," Ash said. "The lady of the house is not happy."

Kincaid stepped forward, and he expected her to try to shoo them out. These two had caused an impressive amount of mess, and Kincaid already had enough on her plate with this house. She didn't need more repairs on the list.

He followed behind her, ready to provide backup herding. "Be careful. They can bite. Maybe we can try to lure them out with cookies first."

She turned around, a look of joyful surprise on her face. Absolutely not what he'd expected. She clutched the box of cookies to her chest. "Are they not the cutest things you've ever seen in your whole entire life?"

"I—"

"Ash, I have goats!"

He stared at her for a moment and then laughed at the childlike glee on her face. "Yes, on your kitchen counter, eating your curtains and wallpaper."

"They were hungry. Someone abandoned them. Of course they ate everything in sight." She turned back to them, focusing on the one on the counter, and opened the box of crackers. "You poor thing. You're probably starved. Here, Beula, let me help, sweetheart. I'm your new mama." She held out a cookie and the goat, surprisingly quick, swung her head toward Kincaid and nipped at her fingers, getting cookie and a little of Kincaid in the process. Kincaid snatched back her hand. "Ouch."

"Maybe we should wait to make friends after we get them back outside," Ash suggested. "Cute can still bite."

She looked down at her finger where a little drop of blood was forming. "Good idea. Plus, I don't want to scare them. Beula could get hurt falling off that counter."

"What time—"

As if on cue, a loud knock sounded from the front of the house, cutting off Ash's question. The vet. Thank God. They headed back into the living room, and Kincaid hurried to the door to open it.

"Marco," she said, delight in her voice. "Thank you so much for getting out here so fast."

A broad, linebacker-sized guy with light-brown skin, thick dark hair, and an easy smile stepped inside. "Of course," he said, his voice full of affection as he embraced her. "I wouldn't leave you dealing with a goat emergency alone. Plus, you lucked out that I happened to be nearby. I'm looking at a site for a new clinic in Wilder."

"A new site?" She slapped him lightly on the arm as she stepped back from the embrace. "You should've called me. You know I've got the real estate hookup out here."

Marco cocked his head. "I didn't realize you handled commercial property."

Kincaid put a hand on her hip and tipped up her chin. "I'm a woman of many talents."

"Of that I have no doubt," he said warmly. "And I'll take you up on that. The building I saw today isn't going to work."

Ash watched from a few steps away, the obvious ease between these two annoying him for some reason. Marco glanced over and noticed Ash for the first time. The guy sent him a genial smile and strode forward with his hand out. "Hey. I'm Marco."

Ash shook the guy's hand. "Ash."

"Oh," Kincaid said as if she'd forgotten she and Marco weren't alone. "Sorry. Dr. Marco Garrett, this is my friend, Ash Isaacs, also known as writer Ashton Stone. He's visiting from New York. Ash, this is Wes's brother."

"Ashton Stone?" Marco released his hand. "I've read one of your books."

Kincaid beamed like a mom getting a compliment about her kid.

"Oh really?" Ash asked.

Marco nodded. "Yeah, a while back. Great book."

"Thanks," Ash said, choking down his grumpiness.

"Except for that part where the bird died," Marco went on. "There's a treatment for that condition, you know? They wouldn't have had to put him down. He could've been saved."

The grumpiness came back like a chicken bone in Ash's throat.

Kincaid laughed and sent Ash an I-told-you-so look. "Believe me, I've lectured him about not killing any more fictional birds. We have an agreement now."

Marco chuckled. "Sorry. Didn't meant to reignite a debate. I really did enjoy the book."

Ash nodded, figuring he was better off keeping his mouth shut.

"So—" Marco turned to Kincaid. "I hear the goats." He peered into the living room past Ash. "And I see the destruction they've left behind. Where are our culprits?"

"In there, feasting on the curtains." She pointed toward the kitchen. "Just be prepared for the cutest things you've seen today. It's hard to be mad at them."

Marco gave her a dimpled smile. "I guarantee they won't be the cutest thing I've seen today."

Ash stiffened at Marco's obvious flirting. Ash looked to Kincaid to see her reaction.

She was all charm and aw-shucks smiles. She hooked her arm with Marco's. "Well, let me prove you wrong. They're this way."

The two left Ash in their wake, and he tried not to let the snap of jealousy nip at his heels as he followed. He didn't *do* jealousy. Especially not over someone he wasn't even dating.

Marco barked a big, full laugh when he stepped into the kitchen, and Kincaid released his arm. Both goats bleated loudly as if sensing a worthy opponent in their midst. "All right, you two," Marco said with a firm yet amused voice. "Buffet is closing for the day. You're coming with me."

The male goat made a louder, protesting bleat. Ash assumed it was goat-speak for *Go fuck yourself, doc*.

Kincaid frowned and put her hand on Marco's bicep. "What are you going to do with them? I want to bring them back to the property once it's up and running."

Marco gave her a reassuring look and patted her hand. "Nothing bad. I need to check them over, make sure they don't have any obvious health problems. I called a friend on the way. He has space to pen and take care of them while you're renovating. If you want to keep them, you'll just have to pay a small fee for the care and feeding until you can move them back onto the property. Then, if you want, I can teach you how to care for them."

Kincaid smiled. "Ooh, Goat Parenting 101 with Dr. Marco. Sounds perfect. Thank you."

"No problem. They can be great to have around," Marco said, eyeing the two interlopers. "But also cause a lot of havoc."

"You don't say?" Ash said wryly. "Maybe you should think that through, KC. You're already going to have a lot going on starting a B and B."

Kincaid frowned. "That's true."

Marco turned his back to the goats and spared Ash a glance. "She'll be fine. I'll teach her what she needs to know, and they'll have a good home. Plus, she'll have a vet on speed dial if anything comes up."

Kincaid's smile returned.

Ash's teeth clenched. "Right."

"I'll make sure they're happy here," Kincaid said, oblivious to the silent pissing contest. "But how do we get them out of the kitchen?"

Marco opened his mouth to reply, but Beula the counter-climbing goat had other plans. She put her cloven hooves on Marco's shoulders, bleated in victory, and then chomped down on a mouthful of Marco's hair.

"Hey!" Marco ducked and cursed.

Ash burst out laughing as the goat refused to let go and tugged harder.

Beula was his new spirit animal.

Kincaid cried out and tried to shoo the goat off Marco. But the goat only turned to go for her ponytail instead.

"Oh no you don't, sister," Kincaid said, dodging. "We can't be best friends if you mess with my hair."

Taking advantage of the goat being distracted by Kincaid's swinging ponytail, Marco turned and grabbed for Beula, deftly getting an arm around the goat and then hoisting her off the counter. The goat screamed like she was being murdered and then almost instantly calmed when Marco held her against his chest.

"There you go," Marco said with the calm voice of a guy who spent his days with skittish animals. "You don't want to fight. It's good to know when you're outmatched, my friend."

"Aww," Kincaid said, making goo-goo eyes at the animal. "You like Dr. Marco?" She carefully patted the goat on the head. "Of course you do. You have excellent taste."

"For curtains," Ash said before he could stop himself. *Ugh*. What was wrong with him? He was *not* this guy.

Marco sent him an oh-are-you-still-here look and then smiled at Kincaid as if she were the only one in the room. "Let me get our new friends outside before they do any more damage. I can give them a quick checkup, make sure they don't need anything immediate, and then load them into the trailer I brought over."

"You're the best," Kincaid said, still sending an adoring glance toward the goat. "Thanks for doing this."

"Not a problem," Marco said, heading toward the back door. "You might want to get a new lock on this one. Looks like the wind or someone knocked it open. You don't want something worse getting inside."

Ash took a deep breath, trying to center himself and get the proverbial stick out of his ass. "I'll board up the door."

About an hour later, the goats were fed, checked over, and loaded up. Ash had busied himself with boarding the door and then cleaning up the living room. He was carrying out a box of trash when he heard Kincaid laugh, the sound dancing on the breeze. He turned, spotting her at the bottom of the driveway near Marco's truck. She was standing close to Marco, her back to Ash, and had her head thrown back with the laughter. Ash couldn't hear what was being said, but he couldn't miss the way the veterinarian was looking at Kincaid. The guy wouldn't be good at poker. Even from this distance, Ash could see how spellbound he was. The dude had it bad. Ash knew that look because he'd worn it himself too many times.

Ash knew he should look away. It wasn't his business. But he couldn't seem to move from the spot where he was standing. So he watched as Marco reached out and gave Kincaid's hand a squeeze. He watched as the guy bent to kiss her on the cheek and then lingered there, saying something against her ear that made her dip her head.

Jealousy burned deep in Ash's gut, but that just made him angry at himself. What the hell was wrong with him? A guy was flirting with Kincaid. She apparently liked it. So what? Marco seemed like a decent guy. Why shouldn't she like it?

Ash tossed the box of trash behind the house with unnecessary force, letting it make a loud crash. He would not do this again. He'd spent way too much time feeling that burn in his gut while he'd watched Kincaid fall for Graham. That warring feeling of being happy that she was happy but wishing *he* was the one making her that way. He would not fall into that bottomless trap. When he turned back around, Kincaid was headed his way and Marco lifted a hand in goodbye. Ash raised his hand in response and tried to shake off the dangerous feelings that were stalking him.

Kincaid strode over to him, a spring in her step. "Barry and Beula are officially off to the spa. I got to feed them cookies." She pretended to fluff her hair and preen. "And not to toot my own horn, but they already have a crush on me."

Ash smirked. "I don't think the goats are the only ones."

The words were out before he could snatch them back. Kincaid tucked her hands in her back pockets, curiosity on her face. "What do you mean?"

"Nothing. Never mind." He stepped around her. "I got most of the living room cleared out and cleaned up.

And I secured the back door with some boards. You'll want to get a locksmith out here as soon as you can, though."

Kincaid was following right behind him and grabbed his arm. "Hey, what's wrong?"

He released a breath, letting her halt his step, and turned to face her. "Nothing. I'm just hungry and want to head back."

She frowned. "Wait…is this about him asking me out? That's who you think has a crush on me?"

"He asked you out?" Those weren't the words he was supposed to say. *No*. That was what he was supposed to say. His brain was refusing to follow the script.

A secret smile tugged at her lips. "Yeah, he did. He's asked before, and I've turned him down. But…"

Ash crossed his arms. "But what?"

She shrugged. "But this time, I said yes."

"Why?"

"Because you got me thinking. That talk we had the night we went out to the bar has been running through my head. I've always said no because Marco is Wes's brother and a really nice guy. I know he's someone who wants to settle down eventually. So even though I always thought he was cute, I said no because I didn't want things to get weird when I bailed after a few dates, you know?"

Ash just blinked at her.

"But what you said after the bar that night? That I deserve better. That I'm letting Joseph and Trevor win?" She looked down and nudged a small rock with the toe of her shoe. "Well, it got me wondering if maybe you're right. Maybe I should give someone like Marco a chance, not write the ending before I even go on the first date. Be open to the possibility of something good."

A pang went through Ash, one so lined with conflicting emotions that he couldn't tease out a specific one. "I'm...glad. You deserve good things. You deserve all the things."

She looked up, meeting his gaze, questions there.

He cleared his throat, trying to keep his expression blank. "Well, if you like this vet guy, then I'm glad you said yes."

"Yeah?"

He forced a smile. "Of course. I want you to be happy, KC."

She stepped closer to him and wrapped her arms around him, embracing him and pressing her cheek to his chest. "Thanks, Ash. I want that for you, too."

He closed his eyes and hugged her back, kissing the top of her head and inhaling the scent of her hair. He wasn't even sure what happy felt like anymore. "I'm good, KC. I'm all good."

And a liar.

chapter

FIFTEEN

KINCAID HAD MANAGED TO HAVE THE PERFECT DATE. In the world of dating, it'd win the blue ribbon, the shiny trophy, the sparkly tiara. People would throw flowers at this date. Marco was even more charming than she'd expected, so smart, and seemed genuinely interested in her. Not because he liked how she looked, though he'd definitely let her know that he did. Not because he was trying to get her in bed, though she doubted he'd turn her down if she offered. But because he honestly seemed to enjoy her company. He laughed at her jokes, had been nothing but a gentleman, and had treated her to a lovely dinner with good conversation. Now they were wrapping up a nighttime trip to the zoo where he had a special behind-the-scenes pass.

As they rounded a winding path, Marco reached out and took her hand. "Here, this way," he whispered. "Let's see if we get lucky."

Kincaid lifted a brow. "That's what she said."

His lips hitched up in a wry smile as he led her off

the path. They stopped in front of an enclosure marked *Special Exhibit*. In the near darkness, it was hard to tell what was inside beyond a few trees, but Marco pressed his finger over his lips and then pointed. She followed his signal and searched high in one of the trees. In the moonlight, she caught a flash of white. A large owl settled onto a branch and screeched, the sound like a needle scraping across an old record.

She sucked in a breath in awe and whispered, "He's beautiful."

Marco squeezed her hand and leaned close to her ear. "One of the benefits of coming here at night. The nocturnal animals are out." He pointed to a spot near the back corner of the enclosure. "His mate's back there. You can see her feathers. She's got more brown mixed in with the white."

Kincaid craned her neck to see. "What type of owl are they?"

"Barn owl," he said, keeping his voice low. "Really fascinating animal."

"How so?"

"For one, they mate for life," he said. "They even show affection and cuddle like people would."

She glanced over at him. "Aww, that's sweet."

He smiled. "Sweet but intense." He looked back toward the owls. "They take that mating-for-life thing seriously. I had a friend in vet school who did a paper on the bond. He told me that if one of the partners dies, the other owl goes into a depression and basically wills itself to die."

She frowned. "Seriously?"

"Yep." His tone had gone grim. "The owl goes into an almost catatonic state, and it often ends up dying as well."

Kincaid gasped and turned back to the owls. The female had flown to meet up with the bigger male in the tree. "Wow, that's romantic but terribly sad."

"Yeah." He frowned at the pair of owls. "The Romeo and Juliet of the bird world."

She watched as the bigger bird nuzzled the smaller one. They really were cute together, but she couldn't help thinking of their inevitable end. "The smart owls might want to stick to the singles scene. Save themselves the dramatic ending."

"I don't know," Marco said, tone pensive. "You could make the opposite argument. Wouldn't it be better to have known that kind of love before you go instead of never having experienced it at all? Even if it's intense and short-lived."

Intense and short-lived. Something heavy and sharp lodged in Kincaid's chest, making it hard to breathe for a moment.

Marco glanced over at her and cocked his head. "Sorry. That was a bleak note to end on. Come on. It's time to leave the zoo when I start getting philosophical." He gave her an apologetic smile. "I can be insufferable if you get me started on the wonders of animal behavior and how humans can learn from it."

Kincaid forced a smile even though her fingers and toes felt tingly and her body had gone cold, some sort of silent panic attack waging a war inside her. "Good idea. I need to get back anyway. I have an early morning."

They headed toward the parking lot and got into his truck. The trip to Long Acre was filled with Marco's easy chatter. Usually it was her job with people to fill the silence, to entertain and keep the stories going. But to her relief, Marco took the reins tonight and guided the conversation, making it easy for her to coast. The bad feeling that had overtaken her at the zoo was like a cloud of smoke in her brain. She couldn't pay attention to much else no matter how much she tried.

Once they arrived in Long Acre, Marco turned onto the street where The Stuffed Shelf was located. She'd had him pick her up from the store this afternoon because she'd still been working. Plus, picking her up there guaranteed that she wouldn't let this date take the typical Kincaid course. This date with Marco was supposed to be different, not just a prelude to a hookup. She wanted to take things slow. This was going to be New Kincaid. Patient Kincaid.

But now she was happy she didn't have to do the should we/shouldn't we dance. Her mind was too locked up to think sexy thoughts, no matter how adorable the veterinarian was.

Marco pulled into an open spot in front of the store. "So, more bookstore renovating tomorrow?"

She nodded, her brain humming like a live wire but her small talk system going on autopilot. "Yes, and taking care of some work stuff. I have to squeeze the bookstore in between my job and lining up things for the B and B."

"Sounds like a lot."

She shrugged. "I don't mind being busy."

Marco turned off the truck and climbed out. He opened her door and offered his hand to help her out, ever the gentleman. She took it and gave him a brief smile.

"Well," he said, still holding her hand. "I know

you're really busy, but if you can find time in that crazy schedule, I'd like to do this again. I had a really great time tonight."

The smile he was giving her was genuine and sexy, and he was just so *nice*. A solidly great guy. She knew women who dismissed *nice* or used the term as an insult because they wanted a bad boy or a guy with an edge. But Kincaid had never thought of nice as a bad thing. She'd been with her share of bad boys, and they were often just a big pain in the butt or, worse, outright assholes. Marco was the kind of guy who would treat her with respect, who loved animals, who would be a great dad one day. He was smart and handsome and kind. If she wanted to give a guy a chance beyond a hookup, Marco would be the perfect candidate.

She let honesty slip past her lips. "I had a really great time tonight, too."

He lifted his other hand and cupped the side of her face. When she didn't protest, he leaned down and kissed her gently.

The kiss was warm and soft, a sweet I-like-you kiss. She let it linger for a second and then put her hand to his chest, giving him the silent signal not to take it further. He eased back instantly and gave her a look filled with promise. "I'll give you a call."

She nodded as he stepped back. "Do that. Drive safe."

"Good night, Kincaid."

She stepped onto the curb and watched him climb into the truck. He gave her a little wave and then drove off down the empty street. Once his taillights were out of sight, the last hour and all the things she'd been feeling came crashing down on her. Her knees wobbled, and she sank to the ground, sitting on the curb and putting her head in her hands.

The sob that burst out of her couldn't be stopped. The well of emotion came out in a gasp and made her shoulders shake. She couldn't even articulate what she was feeling. She was just feeling all of it at once. As if her mental piñata had been whacked, and now all the contents were spilling out all over the place.

She let the wave of sadness take over and drag her under, knowing there was no way she could drive home until she got it out. Grief was like a fever. When it came on, you had to sweat it out and break it before you could feel better. Tears fell warm and wet down her cheeks and splashed onto the pavement. One. Two. Three. She watched them bleed into larger spots beneath her on the ground.

She didn't know how long she'd been sitting there when a hand touched her shoulder. "Hey."

She startled and looked up. Ash stood there on the sidewalk in black sweats and a gray T-shirt. When he saw her face, his expression creased in concern, and he dropped down to squat next to her.

"KC, what's wrong?" He scanned her face. "Did something happen?" He looked down the road, his jaw clenching. "Did Marco do something?"

She shook her head, trying to get her hysterical self under control. What the hell was wrong with her? *Stop crying. Stop crying.* The internal chant did nothing but make the sobbing worse. "No, Marco was…great. He's great. So great!"

Ash frowned as if she'd spoken in another language. "Then what are you doing out here bawling your eyes out?"

"I don't know." The answer came out as a cross between a sob and a hiccup.

"KC," he said, voice gentle. "Tell me what's going on."

She shook her head again, embarrassment welling up in her, but words started spilling out anyway. "There were barn owls. And he was just…so nice. And the owls *die*—and then I just felt—" More choked tears came. "I'm sorry. I can't." She swiped at her cheeks. "Maybe it's PMS. I need to go home. I'll be fine. Just leave me be."

He looked unmoved. "Don't try to scare me away with hormonal excuses. You're not driving home like this. Come upstairs. I'll make you tea or something."

She sniffed loudly, the sound coming out like a goose's honk, but there was no helping it. "You have tea?"

He stood and put his hand out to help her. "Of course I do. Green tea. Remember, I'm fancy?"

Despite the weird grief attack she was having, that made her smile a little. She took his hand and let him pull her to her feet. "I need a tissue."

"You're not kidding. You look like you've been in a fight with a bottle of mascara, and your nose is running."

"Hey." She swatted his arm with her purse. "A gentleman would pretend I was a pretty crier."

He gave her a solemn look. "It's not nice to lie to your friends."

She huffed. "Some friend you are—"

But before she could finish, he reached back and pulled his T-shirt over his head. He handed it to her. "Use this."

She took the warm cotton from him, too taken aback by his now half-naked state not to stare a little. How the hell did a guy who spent his days writing books get so fit? She hoped he really worked for it and wasn't one of those horrible people who could just eat and do whatever and look great. Those people unbalanced the universe. "Aren't you being a little too literal? Giving your friend the shirt off your back."

Ash smirked. "Maybe I'm just distracting you from your problems. You're an ogler. You can't cry when you're ogling." He stretched out his arms. "Take your fill, Breslin."

She gave him a droll look and soundly blew her nose into his T-shirt. "I'm not giving you the satisfaction of an ogle."

"Liar. Made you look." He tugged her hand. "Come on. It's getting chilly out here. Someone stole my shirt."

She followed him to the back door and up the stairs to the apartment. She hated to admit that he'd been right. She had ogled. And he *had* distracted her. She should not find Ash that distracting. She made a mental note to buy him a new T-shirt and tried to shrug off that disconcerting sensation she got every time she looked at him lately.

When they got upstairs, she found the apartment much more organized than the last time she'd seen it. The boxes had been put away. A few personal items were out. And his laptop was on the table, the screen saver on, and a mug of something sitting next to it. The window was open next to the laptop. He'd probably had quite a view of her losing her shit on the sidewalk.

She sent him a look. "Were you spying on me, Ashton Isaacs?"

Ash walked over to his dresser and pulled out another

T-shirt, a blue one this time. He tugged it over his head and turned around. "I wasn't spying. I went for a walk to try to clear my head and figure out this scene I'm trying to write. I happened to see you and Marco drive up as I was making my way back."

"How much did you see?" she asked, shutting his front door behind her and setting her purse on the counter.

He went into the small kitchen and filled an electric kettle with water, keeping his back to her. "I hung back because I didn't want to interrupt. But I saw a little. Sorry."

"Stalker." But she couldn't work up any ire behind the insult.

He turned after plugging in the kettle and leaned against the counter, crossing his arms. "So, care to tell me why this 'great' guy who took you on a date and kissed you good night ended up making you cry?"

Kincaid let out a weary sigh as she walked over and sat in one of the chairs at the table. "He didn't make me cry. It was the barn owls."

Ash's expression didn't change, as if he was used to Kincaid saying things that made no sense. "Barn owls."

"Yes. Did you know they mate for life?" she asked, running her finger along a small gash in the wooden table that had gone smooth with time.

"I didn't."

"Me neither." She looked over at him. "And apparently if one of them dies, the other basically goes into a depression and just gives up, like literally making itself die, too."

"Damn." Ash grimaced. "That's harsh."

Tears burned at the corners of her eyes again, and she could feel her lip start to quiver like a little kid's. *Gah. Stop.* But the internal commands were useless. Tears leaked out. "*Dammit.*"

"KC." Worry filled his face as hers crumpled. "What is it? Are you sad for the owls? I mean, maybe it is PMS then, because even though you're an animal lover, you—"

"No. What if *I'm* a barn owl?" The words came out sharp, scratching against her throat and cutting Ash off.

Ash's brows scrunched together, his arms lowering to his sides. "What?"

Her fingers pressed hard against the table. "What if I'm a barn owl? I mated for life, and my partner died, and now no matter what, I'm destined to be alone until I die from the heartbreak."

The dark fear she'd been afraid to speak aloud launched out of her and hung in the air between them like a fog.

"Jesus, KC. Don't do that." Ash grabbed a kitchen towel off the counter and came closer. He crouched in front of her and lifted the towel, wiping away her tears with gentle strokes. "What are you trying to do to yourself, thinking tragic shit like that?"

"I don't know," she said miserably.

He set the towel aside and looked up at her, waiting.

She tried to find the words. "I guess because tonight I had this great date with this great guy, and I have no doubt that he'd make an amazing boyfriend or husband. He'd be loving and loyal and sweet. He's handsome and smart. He has fantastic hair. I mean, really good and thick. Our kids would be adorable. He owns his own business. Hell, his sister-in-law is one of my best friends. He's, like, the definition of perfect. I couldn't draw him up any better."

Ash's mouth flattened, but he didn't say anything.

"But I just couldn't...feel it," she said in defeat. "I tried to imagine myself with him, imagined giving it a real chance beyond just a hookup, and I just felt...hollow. Like I was acting out some role in a play. Like no matter what I do, no matter how great the guy is, I'll never actually be able to touch that thing called 'being in love' again. Graham took it with him. It's like I've lost the receptor for it. Like that part of me is dead." Her eyes burned from the hard crying. "So maybe I'm a barn owl."

Ash stared at her, empathy there in his eyes, and then put his hands on her knees. "You *are not* a barn owl."

She looked away. "You don't know that."

He was quiet for a moment and then said, "Have you ever considered that maybe you didn't get that feeling tonight because Marco just isn't the right guy for you?"

"But—"

"I don't care what he looks like on paper. Or that he has great hair. Or that he's a damn doctor. Whatever it is that makes him supposedly ideal in your head is just a list. If you made a list of Melanie's qualities, she would've looked perfect for me, but you know how that worked out," he said. "You aren't a barn owl. None of us are. The soul-mate thing is bullshit, Kincaid. It's a tale of romanticism that movies and writers sell us. There's not *one* person in the world for you. How fucked up would it be that you only get one shot? There are all kinds of possibilities and people who could make you happy. But if you convince yourself that no one will ever be as good as Graham, you'll create that destiny. *Of course* you could fall in love again."

She looked down at her lap, shaking her head. He didn't understand.

"Hey." He reached up and put two fingers under her chin to get her to look at him. His blue-eyed gaze was fierce. "I've never met anyone with a bigger heart than yours. If we were talking about me, then yeah, maybe. I don't let a lot of people in, and I've gotten burned when I do. But you, you're not like that. You take in friends and let them into your life with an openness that very few people have." He lowered his hand from her face and pressed it against his chest, sitting back on his heels. "Look at how you've welcomed me back into your life, even after all the shit that happened between us. I didn't deserve that from you, and yet you gave me that chance anyway. Your heart is big and beautiful and resilient. You're the opposite of a barn owl. Your capacity to love is boundless, KC."

She blinked, the words stealing her breath for a moment.

"So the vet didn't flip your switch. So what?" he said with a shrug. "Chemistry is chemistry. It's either there or it isn't. Sometimes it's with a person who makes sense." His gaze drifted to her mouth before meeting her eyes again. "Sometimes it's with the last person you need it to be with and inconvenient as hell."

She wet her lips. "Ash."

His throat worked as he swallowed, and his eyes didn't leave her face. Her heartbeat picked up speed. The kettle switch flicked off, letting them know the water was ready, and they both startled.

As if snapped out of a spell, Ash shifted up from his crouched position, but Kincaid's hand shot out, grabbing the hem of his T-shirt before he could walk away. He paused, giving her a wary look. "Kincaid…"

Her grip tightened. "I think I'm done trying to make things make sense tonight."

A muscle in Ash's jaw twitched, but he didn't move away.

"I'm lonely, Ash." The confession bubbled out, and she swallowed past the anxiety that welled in her at the admission. "I'm really lonely. In a way that my other friends can't fix."

"KC…" A plea.

"And you're right. I'm tired of hooking up with guys who just see the surface, who don't really know me. But I'm also scared to think about big things like relationships and love and the future. I thought I was ready to consider those things, but I'm not. Tonight proved that." She took a deep breath. "I just want to feel close to someone, someone who knows me, someone who doesn't expect anything serious but also isn't going to treat me like I'm disposable." She stood, her hand still holding his shirt. "Someone who I feel so much chemistry with that I'm burning up inside with it every time I'm near him."

Ash inhaled a slow breath and closed his eyes like he was praying for strength.

But Kincaid didn't want him to find it. Not tonight. "Ash, tell me you don't want me."

He opened his eyes, heat and something akin to anguish simmering there behind his glasses. "I can't do that."

She released a breath—one she felt like she'd been holding since Ash had arrived back in town. "I keep trying to ignore it. I mean, you're *Ash*. I'm not supposed to think those kinds of things about you. You're the friend I used to confide in when I had crushes on boys, not the boy I crushed on."

His eyes creased at the corner in a barely there wince.

"But here we are, and those thoughts are there, and I don't know how to get rid of this feeling." She met his stare. "This *wanting*."

He shook his head but seemed to be having an argument more with himself than her. "We're going to fuck this up," he said, voice hoarse. "We're going to mess it up, and I don't want to destroy our friendship again. I can't go through that a second time."

She stepped closer, her heart beating so fast it hurt, and slid her palms beneath his shirt and onto his waist. His skin was hot against her palms, and a tremor of desire went through her. She wanted Ash. It felt both completely foreign and oddly familiar at the same time. "What if we give each other our word?"

His Adam's apple bobbed. "On what?"

"We won't let sex mess this up," she said. "I know you're leaving. I know this will just be rebound sex for you. We both understand this is temporary." She let her arms loop around his hips. "I'm good with temporary. When you leave, this part ends, but we'll wish each other well and stay friends. I'm one hundred percent capable of that if you are. This won't be like the last time. We're not kids anymore."

Ash reached up and cupped the side of her jaw, his gaze serious. "You're selling yourself short again."

She couldn't concentrate with his nearness and the heat of his hand pressing so close to her throat. "What do you mean?"

"Don't give me that kind of pass. You're not rebound sex to me," he said, voice firm. "If we do this, I need you to hear that. Yes, it'll be temporary, but this isn't random, KC. This attraction." He ran his thumb over her bottom lip, making heat pool low and fast in her belly. "It's very, very specific. You're driving me fucking mad I want you so much."

Her body pulsed with need at the fervor in his words.

"I'm not craving sex." His hand slid to the back of her neck and squeezed. "I'm craving *you*. Only you."

She closed her eyes, an electric shiver working its way through her. "I hear you."

"Good." The word was only a whisper against her ear, but she felt the change in Ash's body, the shift in the air around them. They'd both said yes. She was free to touch and be touched by him.

But fingers of panic gripped her muscles, freezing her in place. Usually with guys, she was completely comfortable taking the lead, being the one in charge in the bedroom. She did the flirting. She led the game. At this point with any other guy, she'd already be tugging off his shirt or starting a striptease of her own. But right now, she felt no motivation to be coy or play games. This was Ash. He'd see right through all that silly playacting. She'd lost the script for how to do this with someone who knew her as well as Ash did.

And one sensation overwhelmed her more than any other. Vulnerability.

"Ash…" she whispered.

He must've heard the unease in her voice because his hold on her neck softened. "Hey," he said, the word a gentle caress. "We don't have to. If you've changed—"

She opened her eyes, a dart of panic going through her at the thought of him backing out. "I haven't changed my mind. That's not it."

Something like relief flickered over his face. "Then what's wrong?"

She focused on his shoulder, too afraid he'd read everything she was feeling in her eyes. "I can't be that woman I usually am in these situations, so I feel a little lost."

"That woman?"

"It's going to sound ridiculous." She rubbed her lips together. "But I'm usually good at this part, being the bold and brassy seductress. I'm usually the one who knows just what to say and do in the bedroom. I can't be that right now."

He searched her face. "Why not?"

She reached for a way to explain it but then shook her head and gave him the simple truth. "Because that's not who I am with you."

He pushed a lock of hair away from her face, his lips close enough for her to feel his breath on her cheek. "Who are you then?"

Her heartbeat thumped against her ribs. "I don't know. I guess just me. Your friend who really, really wants to see you naked and do dirty things with you."

He smiled a sinfully sexy smile, one that said she didn't need her confidence right now because he had enough for both of them. "Good, because that's exactly who I want. And I'll tell you a secret." His lips brushed her ear, making goose bumps break out on her skin. "You've got nothing to worry about because you know what makes me hotter than anything in bed?"

The words rolled over her like a heat wave. She barely was able to form a response. "What?"

"Having the control." He slid his lips over the shell of her ear. "I don't need you to seduce me, KC. I just need you to surrender."

And then he kissed her.

chapter
SIXTEEN

KINCAID LET OUT A SOFT GASP AT ASH'S WORDS, A SECRET thrill rushing through her, and then his lips were on hers. His mouth was warm and commanding and felt like a deep drink of water after being in a hot, dry desert all day. All the things she hadn't been feeling when Marco kissed her flooded her body like a tidal wave—desire, need, and absolute urgency to have *more more more*.

As if hearing her silent plea, he tilted her head and deepened the kiss, swallowing the whimper that escaped her as their tongues collided. His fingers tunneled through the hair at the nape of her neck, angling her head just how he wanted, and his teeth nipped her bottom lip, his tongue following with a soothing swipe.

She wanted that tongue everywhere. Every cell in her body reverberated with oh-yes-please at his hungry exploration. Her muscles melted, her body going liquid as his grip tightened on her hip and pulled her fully against him. This was not the tentative boy she remembered from high school, the one who preferred to hang in the background. This was a man who had come into his own, one full of confidence and command.

Ash backed her up until she bumped the edge of the table and was forced to sit atop it. He stepped between her spread knees and cradled her jaw as he kissed her harder and deeper. The black tights she'd worn beneath her sweater dress offered no defense against the erotic feel of Ash's growing erection. The hard length of him pressed against where she'd now grown achy and hot. She couldn't help her reaction. She tilted her head back, a needy sound escaping her.

Ash kissed down her throat, his hand mapping her thigh and then sliding beneath the knit fabric of her dress. "Fuck, KC, you're going to kill me with those sounds you're making."

She looped her arms around his neck and looked at him, basking in the desire burning behind his glasses. To be that wanted was a heady high, and some of her confidence bubbled back up. "I'm not quiet in bed. I know you're shocked."

He smirked and slid his hand higher, tracing a thumb along her upper inner thigh and making her skin go tingly with awareness. She let out another desperate sound, and his smirk turned into Cheshire wickedness. "Good. I don't want you quiet. I want to figure out all the things I can do to hear every sexy sound you're capable of." His thumb whispered along the crease where her leg met her pelvis. "Want to do all the things I've been fantasizing about when I was supposed to be shelving books. Want to touch and kiss and…taste all of you."

Kincaid's mouth had gone dry. "You've been fantasizing."

"So much," he said, squeezing her thigh.

She tugged down the collar of his T-shirt, considered ripping the damn thing. "I'm game as long as I'm afforded the same privilege. You're not the only one who's been having dirty thoughts in the bookstore."

He groaned and pulled off his shirt, revealing all that lean, tattooed muscle. "You have a full access pass."

She let herself take her fill of the view and traced her fingertips over his shoulders and down his pecs. "What have you imagined, Ash?"

"So many things." He took her hand and kissed her palm. "You should've probably slapped me daily. My thoughts have been exceptionally indecent."

She lifted a brow. "Care to share with the class?"

He stepped back with a sly smile. "How about I show you instead?"

She wasn't going to say no to that.

Without waiting for her answer, he grabbed his laptop and the mug, clearing the table, and then closed the window and pulled the curtains shut. When he came back to her, he took off his glasses without breaking eye contact and set them on the windowsill.

He slid his hands behind her knees. "This is what I've imagined happening on top of the checkout counter."

She bit her lip, feeling so very present in her skin, as though every wire she had was plugged in. "We've had fantasy sex on the counter?"

"Not quite." He turned her, swinging her legs in front of her, and then he was carefully unzipping her knee-high boots. The movements were so patient and deliberate that they only revved her up more. His hands on her calves as he pulled off each boot, the soft leather brushing against her skin through the thin fabric of her tights. She was short of breath by the time his hands slipped beneath her dress. His fingers climbed higher and higher until they reached the waistband of her tights. Her belly dipped as he pulled them down and off, leaving her bare beneath the dress.

He inhaled deeply as if he was trying to gather himself. Or maybe he was just taking in the scent of her, the level of her desire no longer secret. That thought made her skin flush but not in embarrassment. She realized with sudden acuity that she wanted Ash to know exactly how much he was turning her on. The first time they were together, she'd taken something precious from him and hadn't given him anything in return. She'd never shown him that she wanted *him* that night, not just that she wanted someone to make her feel better. Now there would be no doubt.

"Touch me, Ash," she whispered. "Please."

Ash didn't obey or even lift her dress. Instead, he balled her tights in his hand and then braced a hand next to her on the table, leaning in to kiss her slowly and deeply again. When she was breathless, he wrapped an arm around her and guided her to lie back, only breaking the kiss when she was flat against the table. She panted as he released her, wanting, needing more of him. "Ash."

"You're not in charge, KC," he said, voice gentle but inviting no argument. He stepped to the end of the table where her head was and guided her arms above her. "I told you. I relieve you of your duties as seductress." He wrapped her tights loosely around her wrists. "Your only job right now is to feel. And to tell me to stop if I do anything you don't like."

The pressure on her wrists wasn't tight, but it was enough to ratchet up her vulnerability...and desire. He was giving her the gift of not having to perform or play the right role. *Just feel.* She closed her eyes. Breathed. She wasn't sure how to let go, but she was going to try. She and Ash had their history, but she trusted him wholeheartedly with her safety. He would never do anything she didn't want. She flexed her wrists in the bindings. "This is what you imagined on the checkout counter?"

She could hear his footsteps as he walked around to the other side of the table. "Yep. Only instead of tying you with stockings, I made you balance books in each hand. If you dropped one, I would stop touching you until you read a dirty passage from the book and then put it back in your hand."

She sucked in a breath at the image and opened her eyes to find him with a devious glint in his eyes. She laughed. "Ashton Isaacs, you kinky bastard. I should've known. It's always the quiet ones."

"Not card-carrying kinky. Just creative," he said without apology. "I read a lot. Makes for a diverse imagination."

"Bookish kink," she mused. "I'm finding this new side of you quite enlightening."

She was about to throw out another teasing comment, but he stepped between her knees and tugged her to the edge of the table, making her dress slide up her thighs and baring her. It should've been awkward. Her former best friend was staring down at her naked form, but the way he was looking down at her made any awkwardness dissolve. There was nothing friendly about that look.

Ash caressed the backs of her calves, sending lightning straight up to the aching spot between her legs, making her tremble with need.

He lifted one hand and gently traced his knuckle along the place she needed it most, her body slick and ready for him. "So fucking sexy, KC. I love that you're trembling for me. I'm hard as hell just thinking about what you're going to feel like around me."

She let out a soft moan, her wrists pressing against the bindings and her body arching with need. "Why doesn't this feel weird, Ash? This should feel weird. Right?"

"Why? Because we're old friends?" His voice was soft, his attention on where he was touching her as if mesmerized by how her body responded to him. He slipped a finger inside her, making every muscle in her body clench with want.

"Yes," she whispered, suddenly having trouble concentrating on conversation.

"Maybe that's what makes this better. We know each other through and through. The good stuff and the embarrassing stuff. We don't have to play any role right now. We don't have to impress each other." He lowered himself to his knees. "Instead, we can just admit that we turn each other on, indulge in it, and make sure we savor every delicious moment."

The last words were whispered against her tender skin with promise. He guided her legs over his shoulders, pressed a kiss to her inner thigh, and then his mouth was on her, tasting her in a place he'd only touched in the dark. All worries of weirdness flew out of her head. There was no room for that when everything felt so damn good.

Ash savored her, those full lips of his even more

devastating when unleashed upon her most sensitive flesh. His stubble tickled her thighs as he took his time, exploring, kissing, licking, and making her lose her ability for coherent thought. The man seemed intent on making this a seven-course meal, and she was so there for the reservation. She writhed beneath him, murmuring unintelligible sounds, and he slipped a second finger inside her, finding the perfect spot with his fingertips. He dragged his tongue along the center of her, and then kissed her there before drawing the little bud between his lips and rocking his fingers inside her. Her back arched up from the table, and his name fell from her mouth.

He moaned against her, the sound filthy and animalistic in the best way, and his blissful assault continued, his tongue working her like a talented musician playing an instrument. She melted into the table, fully at his mercy, and lost herself in the sensation of it all. Ash was in no rush, bringing her to the brink and then back down again. And that was the hottest thing of all. The patience. This was more than making her feel good. This whole thing was doing it for him, too. She loved that he loved it.

He pressed the flat of his tongue against her, his fingers hitting just the right spot inside, and her orgasm rocketed through her. She dug her heels into his back and her neck arched, a sharp cry escaping her. But he didn't relent. He kept going, making his own sounds, and bringing her higher and higher until she was panting and gasping.

When she thought she might pass out from lack of air, Ash eased back and kissed her inner thigh, dragging his stubble against her hypersensitive skin. She glanced down, finding him breathing hard, his eyes closed as if he was in pain. "Fuck, KC. That was…"

"Untie me," she said between pants. "Untie me and take me to bed, Ash. I need you."

Ash peered up at her, gaze nearly feral, and got to his feet. He stepped beside the table to untie her hands, but Kincaid couldn't concentrate on anything except the thick, obvious outline in his sweats. When her hands were free, she rolled to her side and immediately grabbed for his waistband, dragging him closer.

"KC..."

She slipped her hand inside his pants and wrapped her fingers around him. He was so hot and hard against her palm that her body clenched again.

Ash cursed and gripped the edge of the table. "Careful. I don't trust my control right now."

"My turn." She tugged the waistband just a little, revealing enough to make her shiver with anticipation. She wanted to make him feel as good as he'd made her feel. She leaned over and licked across the head of his cock, tasting how much he wanted her and relishing the sound of anguish he made.

He loomed over her, naked desire in his eyes, and grabbed her wrist. "I need to be inside you. Now."

The command in his voice made her quiver. She released him and let him help her sit up. Before she could stand, he lifted her off the table. He carried her the few steps to the bed and then put her on her feet. He didn't waste any time. In every jerky, hurried movement, she could tell she'd pushed him past his edge. He yanked her dress over her head and divested her of her bra in record time. He stared down at her naked breasts with open appreciation. He cupped her and ran a thumb over her nipple. "So goddamned beautiful."

The simple touch made her feel as frantic as he was feeling. She tracked her fingers down over his chest, taking advantage of having her hands free and able to roam. "Back at ya."

He stopped her hands before they could dip below his waistband again. "Condoms," he said on a ragged breath. "Tell me you have some because I'm not prepared for this."

She nodded to where she'd dropped her purse on the counter when she'd walked in. "The inside pocket of my purse. I put some in there earlier."

"One thing I can thank that vet for." He strode over and got what he needed quickly. Then he was pushing his sweats down and off, no underwear beneath. Kincaid stared, wanting to touch and taste him everywhere. The one time they'd been together had been under the covers in the dark. She'd never actually seen him like this. He was so beautifully made, so goddamned sexy.

She took the condom from him. "Let me."

Taking her time, she rolled on the condom, enjoying how his belly went tight and tense at her touch. She stepped closer and kissed him. He drew her against him skin to skin and kissed her back deeply, letting her taste herself on his lips and running his hands over her backside. When he pulled back, he brushed his thumb over her mouth. "This was such a brilliant idea. We are geniuses."

She smiled, and he lowered her to the bed, kissing her again and stretching out over her. She ran her hands through his hair, taking in the sight of him above her. "We are exceptionally smart people."

He grabbed her behind the knee, opening her body to

him. "I'm going to last about six point two seconds, but I promise the next time, I'll make you proud."

She lifted a brow. "Already planning the next time, huh?"

He eased himself inside her, stretching her and making her gasp with pleasure. "You're not leaving this bed until the sun comes up, Breslin. I hope you brought snacks."

She laughed, but the sound cut off quickly as he buried deep, filling her up and making her moan. She closed her eyes, fully joined with him, and dug her fingers into his backside to hold him there for a moment, feeling every bit of him inside her. Feeling Ash.

Ashton Isaacs. She was having sex with Ashton Isaacs.

A small flag of panic tried to rise in her at that, but she wasn't going to let it ruin this moment. She reached up to pull Ash down to her and kissed him.

Kissed him until she couldn't think straight. Until they were moving together in perfect rhythm.

Just feel. That was all they needed to do right now.

So she did. And a while later, when Ash came and called her KC and kissed away the tears that fell from her eyes, she convinced herself that she was only crying because it felt so good.

Not because it felt so different from any sex she'd ever had.

Ash couldn't sleep. He moved around in the dark of the bookstore in his bare feet, the motion of shelving books somehow soothing. He'd carried all the true crime books to the back corner of the store to replace the former cookbook section with the books Kincaid didn't want up front.

He hadn't turned on the lights in the store because he didn't want anyone to know he was there at this hour. The street outside was quiet and dark through the front windows. The stack of books about the Long Acre shooting loomed high on the floor next to him. How many books could they write about the same event? He picked up one and flipped through the pages. He saw familiar faces flash by—yearbook photos, teacher photos, photos of the aftermath.

He was about to shut the book when Kincaid and Graham's prom picture filled a page. The picture was captioned *The prom queen and the boy who saved her*. Kincaid was in her white dress looking like a movie star, no tiara on her head yet, the ceremony still to come. Graham was smiling like he owned the world, his arms wrapped firmly around Kincaid from behind. During this photo, Ash had been standing on the side watching and waiting for them to be done. He could almost see movement in the picture, the way Kincaid kept self-consciously touching her hair to make sure it was right for the picture. Graham reassuring her that she looked perfect.

Ash's stomach did a flip. He shut the book with a snap, but something fell out of the pages. He set the book aside and squatted down to grab the paper that had fallen out. There was a folded loose-leaf page. He opened it and stopped breathing for a moment.

Dear Kincaid,

You are the most beautiful girl I've ever seen. When you're in a room, it's like there's no one else there because you're all I can focus on. I wish I could tell

you all the things I think and feel about you to your
face, but I'm not sure I'm the guy you'd want to hear
them from. Even so, I want you to know that there's
someone in the world who realizes how special you
are. Not because you're pretty. Not because you're
funny. Not because you're smart. Though you are all
those things. But because you are full of a light that
outshines everyone else I've ever met. You, Kincaid
Breslin, are singular. You are everything.

> *Always,*
> *Your secret admirer*

Ash rocked back, sitting down hard on the floor,
his hands trembling. This couldn't be. The letter was
in pristine condition. And the book it'd fallen out of
hadn't been written when this letter had been hidden in
the bookstore. There was no way…

"That one was always my favorite."

The familiar voice sent a chill deep into Ash's skin
and made his breath freeze in his chest. *Not happening.*
Not happening. Don't look. But he couldn't help it. He
lifted his head.

Graham was leaning against the shelf across from
Ash in his prom tux, arms folded, expression smug.
"She loved that one."

Ash swallowed, but it felt like choking down glass.
"You're not here," he whispered.

Graham smirked and squatted in front of Ash, his
blond hair falling across his forehead. "Aren't I?" He
reached out and flicked the letter with his finger, making
Ash jolt and scoot back against the shelf.

"You hid that one in that cookbook she loved. The one with the cherry pie on the front," Graham said, tone wistful. "I watched her find it. She cried when she read it and pressed it to her chest like she wanted to absorb it. That was the one that did it. I knew it was time to finally get up the nerve and ask her out."

Ash stayed very still, his gaze on his former friend. His *dead* friend. "You didn't have to wait as long as you did," he said hoarsely. "From the very first letter, she wanted it to be you. You could've asked her at any time."

"Yeah, but then I would've been just another guy panting after her. She needed wooing. That's what you told me, right?" His smile turned cutting. "Always with the friendly advice and the helping hand. My good ol' buddy Ash."

Ash closed his eyes, wishing the vision would go away.

"But you were secretly hoping she'd think it was you, weren't you?" he asked. "That was why you agreed to help me. I should've known when the letters were so good that you had a thing for her. No one could write the stuff you wrote without feeling some of it. But stupid me, I just thought you were doing a really great job using your writing skills to help your friend win the girl."

Ash opened his eyes again, his jaw clenching. "What are you doing here?"

Graham got to his feet, his gaze hard, and slowly clapped his hands. "To congratulate you of course. You finally got what you wanted. You slept with her, and she called out your name and not mine this time. Feel like a man now?"

Ash stood then. "Shut up. You're not real."

Graham stepped closer, looming over him even though he was only an inch taller. His handsome face twisted into a sneer. "You think she'd be in your bed right now if I was still here? You think she'd still be there if she knew *I'm* not here because of *you*?"

The words were like bullets to Ash's anger and bravado. He flinched and looked away.

Graham chuckled and put a heavy hand on Ash's shoulder. His low voice rumbled against Ash's ear. "Enjoy your time with her, Isaacs. Just know that I'm always there. She'll never really be yours. I live in a place in her heart and mind that you will never get to no matter how hard you try. She was meant for me. You're just another guy warming her bed. Not the first and not the last."

Ash turned back to say something but recoiled. Graham's expression had morphed into fear, and then he jerked backward and was on the floor at Ash's feet, two bullet holes in his chest.

Ash screamed and dropped to his knees, pressing his hands over the wounds, trying to help, but blood just kept rushing out. *No. No. Not again*.

"I thought you were my friend, man," Graham said, eyes sad.

"Please. No." Ash started sobbing. "I didn't want this. I am your friend. Please."

"Ash!"

Ash startled awake, clenching the sheets and sweating. Kincaid was leaning over him, hand on his chest and a concerned look on her face. He looked around wildly, disoriented, taking in the surroundings. Not the

bookstore. The apartment. His bed. Kincaid. The room
was still dark. He looked at his palms. No blood.

He closed his eyes and let his head sag back onto the
pillow, his heart hammering and head pounding. "Jesus.
Sorry."

"You okay?" she asked, worry tingeing her voice.
"You were making noises like you were being hurt."

He let out a long breath, trying to calm himself, trying
not to see the images from the nightmare. He opened
his eyes and gave her an apologetic look. "Yeah, I'm all
right. I'm sorry I woke you. Bad dream."

She frowned. "Wanna talk about it?"

Images of the nightmare danced in the front of his
mind, and he shook his head, trying to shove them away.
"No, it's fine. Just a dumb dream."

She reached out, pushing his sweaty hair off his
forehead, and gave him a light kiss. "Want me to help
you forget about it?"

The saucy smile she gave him was a lifeline he
grabbed onto with both hands. He didn't want to think
about the nightmare. Couldn't. He needed to purge the
images, the words Graham had whispered, the dread
he'd felt. None of them were real. There were no such
things as ghosts.

He reached up and pulled Kincaid down to him.
"Yeah, make me forget, KC."

She leaned down to kiss him and chased away the
demons for another night.

chapter
SEVENTEEN

Aʜ ɢʀᴜɴᴛᴇᴅ ᴀꜱ ᴛʜᴇ ʙᴇᴅ ʙᴏᴜɴᴄᴇᴅ ᴀɴᴅ ᴊᴏʟᴛᴇᴅ ʜɪᴍ ᴀᴡᴀᴋᴇ. He cracked an eye open and found Kincaid kneeling next to him on the bed, a sunshine smile on her face. She slipped his glasses onto his face. "Wake up, writer boy."

His vision cleared. Kincaid's hair was pulled into a sleek ponytail, and her makeup was fully done. She looked fresh and rested and not at all like they'd spent half the night sweaty and rolling around in bed. The only clue that proved he hadn't dreamt the whole damn thing was that she smelled like his soap and was wearing the same sweater dress from last night. No tights.

Which meant… His gaze slid down. No panties.

His body stirred, seemingly never sated when it came to her. "You are wearing entirely too many clothes for this early in the morning."

She lifted his blanket and peeked beneath at his growing state of interest. "You are not, my friend. And good morning to you, too."

"There she goes again. Always ogling." Ash pulled the covers over himself. "What time is it?"

"Time to get up and get dressed. I have to make a quick run to meet a family and give them the keys to their new house, but I'm taking you to breakfast first. You don't have anything good to eat here, and I need to replenish all the calories I burned last night."

He propped his head up on his arm and reached for her. "Or we could just stay in and I'll get doughnuts delivered."

She smacked his hand lightly, fending off his advance. "No, sir. No touching and stop looking so hot and sleep-rumpled. It's distracting. Some of us have to work around here. Plus, hungry trumps horny for me. You can make a note of that in your Kincaid file."

He laughed and sat up. "Noted. Feed the lady first. Stock snacks."

She bent down, giving him a quick kiss. "Go shower and make yourself pretty for me. Then I'll buy you breakfast."

"I feel so objectified." He collapsed back onto his pillow with an exaggerated huff.

She smirked and climbed over him to get off the bed, giving him just enough of a peek beneath her dress to drive him wild.

"Vicious tease."

She looked over her shoulder and winked. "I have a name tag with that on it."

An hour later, they'd filled their bellies at the diner and were driving into familiar territory. Ash glanced around the neighborhood he used to call home, his stomach knotting with old anxiety. His parents didn't live here anymore. A couple of years after the shooting, they had gotten a big piece of a settlement in a class-action suit against local law enforcement, a suit that claimed many more lives could've been saved if they'd handled the crisis differently. His parents had used some of that money to buy a nicer house on the other side of town. He'd never been to that house, wasn't welcome there, but his mom had emailed him photos of the place. That was the only way they communicated these days. In secret. Online.

"The neighborhood hasn't changed much," he said, breaking the silence and shutting down his dark thoughts. "The trees are a lot bigger."

Kincaid glanced over from the driver's seat. "It's still a good place to live. A lot of the houses have been remodeled, and it's a quiet neighborhood. Plus, because the houses are older, first-time home buyers have a shot at getting a deal out here." She turned onto his old street. "The Gomezes, the family I'm bringing the keys to, are buying that blue house a few doors down from your old place."

"The Brownfields' house?"

"Yep. It's been fully redone and is going to make a great first house for this family. I'm really excited for them." She slowed in front of Ash's childhood home, letting him take a look. The paint color had changed and the garden had statues in it, but other than that, it looked the same.

Goose bumps prickled his arms, some sort of nostalgia mixing in with bad memories. He stared out the window. "It's like looking back in time."

"Same here." She reached out and gave his hand a squeeze. "It used to hurt a little every time I passed it."

He turned his head to look at her. "Why?"

She stared past him toward the house. "It's going to sound weird because I know your memories there aren't the happiest, but *my* memories of that house aren't all bad. That's the house where I snuck in and slept next to you all those nights. You made the world feel not as scary or lonely. It was my safe place."

His chest constricted.

She met his gaze. "So all these years, not talking to you and being so angry, well, this house just reminded me of how things used to be and the best friend I'd lost."

He tightened his grip on her hand. "KC."

She smiled self-consciously. "But let's not go down Depression Road. You're here now. We're friends again. And you're back to sharing a bed with me. Guess that's what they call a full-circle moment."

"This is past full circle," he said, trying to lighten the mood. "I think we passed it at nudity. Last night was a little different than those nights we shared a bed here."

She let out a quiet laugh and nodded. "It sure was. But either way, I'm glad I don't have to be sad driving past this house anymore."

He lifted her hand to his mouth and kissed her knuckles. "Me too."

Her phone buzzed in the cup holder, and she slipped her hand from his to check the text. She sighed. "Looks like I'm going to need to go into the office this afternoon. My broker—my boss—wants to see me."

"Everything okay?"

She frowned down at the text, distracted. "I'm sure it's fine. But you may be on bookstore duty without me."

"No worries. As long as you come by later, I'll be able to make it through the day."

She reached out and pinched his thigh playfully. "Can't get enough of me, can you?"

"I cannot."

"I know." She gave a put-upon sigh. "You're going to be ruined for all other women now. I apologize for being so awesome."

He laughed, but the dip in his stomach made him wonder if there was more truth to her statement than he cared to admit.

Kincaid parked in front of the house a few doors down from his old place. An older model Ford Explorer was already in the driveway, and the moment Kincaid turned off her engine, two dark-haired kids, a boy and a girl, came rushing out of the back seat of the SUV.

He and Kincaid got out of her car and the little girl, who looked to be about seven or so, threw her arms around Kincaid's waist. "Ms. Breslin! Ms. Breslin! Do you have them?"

Kincaid hugged the little girl and then bent down to get eye to eye with her. She pulled a set of keys out of her purse and held them out. "Oh, Daniela, you couldn't possibly mean these, could you?"

The little girl snatched the keys from her with a squeal of delight and shook them at her younger brother. "Tomás! We have a house!"

The two kids raced up the sidewalk to the door as their parents headed over to Kincaid with pleased smiles on their faces. The mom, a tall Hispanic woman with long, wavy hair, embraced Kincaid warmly, and the dad, a few inches shorter than his wife but solidly built, shook Kincaid's hand.

Kincaid touched Ash's arm. "Mr. and Mrs. Gomez, this is my friend, Ash. He's tagging along with me today."

The couple greeted him, their excitement about the day clear on their faces, and then turned back to Kincaid. "Thank you so much for getting out here early. I think Daniela would've burst if she'd had to wait until the afternoon. She's so excited about having her own room."

"Mama, I can't open the door!" Daniela shouted from the porch. "The key's too hard."

Kincaid swept her arm forward. "Let's not make her wait another second."

Mr. Gomez reached the door first and retrieved the key from Daniela. "Ready, little ones?"

The two kids bounced on their feet, and Ash couldn't help but get swept up in their enthusiasm. Mr. Gomez opened the door, and the kids barreled in, all stomping feet and shouting voices as the adults followed behind. Ash entered last, trying not to get in the way. The house smelled of fresh paint and cleaning products, but everything was bright and airy inside. The wooden floors looked new, the windows were sparkling, and the baseboards were freshly painted white. A clean slate.

Mrs. Gomez put her hand to her chest as she looked around, and her eyes went shiny. She grabbed her husband's hand, taking in the view. "It's all ours, my love. Finally."

The way he smiled at her, with such affection and appreciation, took Ash's breath for a second. Mr. Gomez leaned over and kissed his wife. "Yes it is, *mi alma*."

Ash caught Kincaid watching the couple, a tender expression on her face. She glanced at Ash and smiled before turning back to her clients. "Congratulations, you two. I hope you'll make many happy memories here."

The couple turned, smiling and thanking Kincaid

for helping them find the perfect house, but before they could finish, Daniela was back and grabbing Kincaid's hand.

"Ms. Breslin," she said, tugging on Kincaid's arm. "Come see my room." She glanced at Ash. "You can bring your boyfriend."

"He's not—" Kincaid started, but she was helpless in the face of the little girl's determination. Daniela was already pulling Kincaid down the hall. She sent Ash an apologetic look.

Ash chuckled and followed.

They stopped in front of a small room with a big window that looked out into the backyard. The walls were painted pale yellow. Daniela released Kincaid's hand and then spun around in the middle of the room with her arms out. "Isn't it soooo pretty?"

Kincaid beamed, clearly enchanted by Daniela. "It's the prettiest room I've ever seen. How are you going to decorate it?"

Daniela stopped and considered, her little mouth pursing. "Like a princess castle? Or a unicorn cloud? Or, or, maybe a superhero lair!" She frowned. "Can I do all three?"

"A lair for a superhero unicorn princess," Ash said. "That's a winner."

Daniela clapped and then went back to Kincaid to give her another tight hug. "Thank you for my room."

Kincaid stroked her hand over the little girl's silky hair. "I'm not the one to thank. Your mommy and daddy got this room for you. I just helped them find the perfect one."

The Gomezes stepped up behind them, and Mr. Gomez put a hand on Kincaid's shoulder. "You did more than that. You found the perfect house and got the price we could afford. We're grateful for all the time you took with us."

Kincaid patted his hand. "It was truly my pleasure. This is why I do this job." She tipped her head toward Daniela. "Moments like this. Every little girl and boy deserves a room they can feel at home in."

Emotion pinged through Ash at her words. *Every little girl deserves a room they can feel at home in.* Kincaid had never been given that growing up. Her room at her mother's house had been one to survive in, not feel at home in. Now she made sure other kids had a different experience. Ash wanted to take her in his arms and kiss her right there, but that urge felt far too dangerous because it had nothing to do with sex or wanting her. He just wanted to kiss her for being the person she was.

A few more minutes of signing papers and taking care of a few things, and then she and Ash were leaving the Gomezes so the family could start living in their new house. Kincaid was quiet, her expression pensive, as they pulled away. Without thinking, he reached out and took her hand. "You okay?"

She didn't look his way. "I'm fine. They're great, aren't they?"

"They are." He rubbed his thumb over the top of her hand. "I'm sorry no one ever gave you a room like that."

Her shoulders stiffened a little, but eventually she glanced over with a soft half smile. "I told you, Ash. I had that room. It was just at someone else's house."

The words hit him in a place that made his chest burn. He was happy to know that he'd given her that place for a little while, but it only made it hurt worse to

know how important his presence in her life had been
to her. Because he'd left her. He'd taken himself and
that room away, only thinking of himself and his own
grief. "I'm sorry, KC. I'm sorry I wasn't here for you
after...everything."

She frowned his way and gripped his hand tighter.
"None of that, okay? We're not looking back, remember? The past is in the past."

He nodded and shut up, but his brain didn't stop
going in that direction. The past was in the past. Maybe.
But based on his nightmare last night, maybe not.

She turned out of the neighborhood. "Mind if I drop
you off at the bookstore? I need to go home and change
before I meet with my broker. I can't face him in the
same dress I was wearing yesterday."

Ash smiled, but anxiety was still pinging inside him.
"Yeah, no problem. I'll get some work done."

When she pulled up in front of The Stuffed Shelf, she
leaned over and kissed him. "See you later?"

"Of course." He touched his forehead to hers. "I'll
bring snacks."

She laughed and nipped at his lip. "Smart man."

Kincaid pulled into the parking lot of Postman Realty,
and her phone rang before she could shut off her car.
She groaned when Bethany's name lit the screen. Ever
since she'd bought the farmhouse before Bethany could
put in a bid, Kincaid had been feeling like a terrible
agent. She'd told Bethany the farmhouse wasn't a good
fit. A flat-out lie. Even if she didn't like the woman very
much, she'd always taken pride in being good at her job.

Her role was to find the best home for her clients, not to jump in and snatch a house up before her client had a chance. She now was doubly determined to find Bethany the perfect home, but that didn't mean she wanted to talk to the woman right this moment.

Still, she had a job to do. "Hello?"

"Oh my God, Kincaid," Bethany said, talking fast and sounding oddly cheery. "You are such a sneaky bitch!"

"Uh…" *Crap on a cracker*. How the hell had Bethany found out about the farmhouse? "Pardon?"

"Don't pretend you don't know what I'm talking about. I called the office this morning and just happened to get that cutie pie Ferris on the phone. He told me that you had been holding back the *juiciest* information," she said as if she were gossiping with her best girlfriend. *"Girl.* Why didn't you tell me? Your lake house is going to be *perfect*! It is exactly what I'm looking for. Those windows and that view." She made a sound that was the verbal equivalent of a swoon. "And oh my God, the kitchen! I will give you whatever you're asking for it. *Do not* put that thing on the open market."

Kincaid leaned back in her seat, stunned. "My lake house? Ferris told you about *my* house."

"He is the sweetest," Bethany said, her saccharine tone more over the top than usual. "When were you going to tell me about it?"

"Well, I, uh…" *Damn, damn, damn*. "It's not on the market yet because I can't move out for at least six months. The house I'm moving into needs to be renovated, so my current one is not ready to sell. And you need to be out of your place in two months. The timing doesn't work."

"Girlfriend," Bethany said with a huff. "Get yourself a temporary apartment or a rental house or something. I need this house. Now that I've seen pictures, I'm not going to get it out of my head. You know I can give you the money you want for it. I'll even pay a little extra to get you to move quick. Plus, if you sell it directly to me, you won't have to go through that aggravation of having buyers tromp all over your house. It's the perfect solution."

Kincaid pinched the bridge of her nose. What in the hell was Ferris thinking? And how did he even get pictures? Did he use personal ones from when he'd come to her house for dinner parties? He knew she wasn't ready to sell it yet. She needed a place to live. "Bethany, I'm so sorry, but I'm late for a meeting with my broker, and I'm going to have to call you back on this. My timeline is six months so I'm not sure we can make that work and—"

"Call me back," Bethany said, cutting her off. "I'm not taking no for an answer."

The line went dead, and Kincaid stared at her phone in disbelief. After her meeting with Roger, she was going to have a come-to-Jesus talk with Ferris about sharing her private information with clients.

She headed into the office, which was quiet except for the chatter of Millicent, the office receptionist, who was answering calls. Two agents were there, bent over paperwork at their desks. Ferris's desk was empty but his screen saver was still on, which meant he was coming back. Kincaid gave a little wave to her fellow agents and then headed to the back to her broker's office.

Roger Postman had been the head of Postman Realty since his father had stepped down fifteen years ago. The agency had always been the most successful in town, but Roger had taken it over after the Long Acre shooting, and he'd had his work cut out for him when the market shifted. He worked hard to keep the business thriving and had exacting standards, but Kincaid had always found him to be a smart broker and a good manager. As long as they were bringing in steady commissions, he let the agents do their jobs without too much interference. When she knocked on his doorjamb, he looked up from his computer and frowned at her, making him look older than his fiftysomething years.

"You wanted to see me?" she reminded him.

He glanced past her into the main office and then waved her in. "Yes. Come on in and shut the door behind you, please."

Uh-oh. She stepped inside and clicked the door shut, a pang of dread going through her. Roger rarely had closed-door meetings. This probably meant she was going to get a talk about her dip in sales. Postman Realty only wanted top-selling agents on the team. The last few months, she'd tumbled down that list. But she had talking points prepared to discuss the reasons and a plan to improve. She'd been anticipating this talk. All of them got it at one time or another. It was a feast-or-famine kind of job.

Kincaid took a seat in the chair across from his desk. Roger turned away from his computer to face her and tugged at his striped tie as if it'd suddenly tightened on him. She laced her fingers in her lap. "Is everything okay, Roger?"

He stared at her for a moment and then sighed. "No, unfortunately, it's not."

Her laced fingers clenched. "If it's about my numbers, I have a plan—"

"It's not about your numbers," he said, cutting her off. "Those haven't been great lately, but that's not why I've called you in here."

Her brow scrunched. "Oh. Okay. Then what's going on?"

He flattened his palms on his desk calendar and looked to be steeling himself for the conversation. Foreboding filled her. He took a measured breath. "Kincaid, it's been brought to my attention that you have violated our ethics policy."

The words didn't compute at first. She blinked, trying to process. "Wait, what?"

He cleared his throat, and his gaze shifted away.

"Is this about me buying that farmhouse before showing it to clients? Because I paid full price. I didn't even negotiate. The seller got what they wanted."

"No, it's not that." He sat back in his chair and twisted his wedding band around his finger, round and round and round. "Sam Caldone came in here yesterday afternoon and informed me of, uh, certain improprieties that happened during his home-buying process."

A cold feeling crept through her. "Sam Caldone."

"Yes." Roger grabbed a yellow legal pad and flipped through a few pages. "He informed me that during the purchase of his ranch, you were acting as the seller's agent. Is that correct?"

Kincaid could already feel the train coming, felt the rumble in the tracks. "I was."

Roger shifted in his seat, still staring at his notes. "He also informed me that during this sale, you offered

to get him a bigger discount on the price if he would,
uh..." Roger flushed red from his collar up to his wide
forehead. "If he would"—he cleared his throat again—
"I'm quoting here. If he would 'rock your world in
bed.'"

Kincaid wished a trapdoor would open up in the
floor so she could fall through it. Shame burned through
her—shame and ugly, livid *anger*. Her hands trembled
with the rush of emotion. She flexed her fingers, trying
to center herself and stay calm. "Roger," she said, voice
steadier than she was feeling. "I'm sorry you had to deal
with him, but I can assure you that nothing happened
during the sale. I would never compromise my client's
needs for something personal like that. And I absolutely
did not offer a discount or anything else in exchange for
sex. That's ludicrous."

Roger's gaze flicked upward, a hint of relief there.
"So you're saying you didn't sleep with him?"

She swallowed past the lump in her throat. "I'm
saying I didn't sleep with him until after all papers had
been signed and the sale had gone through. I got the
sellers the best price and acted in their best interest. The
incident with Sam was after all was said and done. And I
regret that it happened, but the only reason he's coming
in here now is because I saw him out at a bar recently
and turned him down for a date. I hurt his ego. This is a
revenge thing."

Roger frowned, his shoulders dipping. "Do you
have any proof that the incident happened after and not
during?"

"Proof?" She made a sound of disbelief. "What
exactly would that look like? We were at his house. No

one else was there when it happened. But I'm telling you, hand to God, it was after the sale."

"I appreciate what you're saying," he said, looking weary. "But there's no way to prove that, especially if someone well known in town like Sam starts spouting off about it to others. People will believe him."

Outrage made her face burn. "So that must make it true? Because some asshole with money said it happened that way?"

Roger sighed. "For what it's worth, I believe you. But even if the incident *was* after the fact, your behavior was highly unprofessional. What if the sellers had seen you two out together? Don't you think they would've felt duped? Do you think they would've told others that our agents can't be trusted to be ethical? Sleeping with a client from either side of the table is not acceptable behavior at this agency. If there was an attraction there, you should've had someone else take over the sale."

Kincaid gripped the arms of the chair. "I'm sorry, Roger. It was a mistake. On a number of levels. But I promise I've never done anything like that before or since. I will never cross that line again."

"You're right," he said, tone resigned. "Because I have to let you go."

A loud buzzing started up in her ears as he went on.

"There are certain company policies I don't flex on, and this is one of them. This is a small town, and our professional reputation is everything. You compromised that."

"You want me to leave the brokerage?" The words came out flat, shell-shocked.

"I'm sorry. You've left me with no choice. And

frankly, if I don't take action, I bet Sam will file a complaint with the Real Estate Commission. He could get your license suspended, and then you won't be able to sell anywhere." He set the legal pad down and truly did look regretful. "Please pack up your desk by the end of the day. All your current listings will be transferred to other agents. We'll inform those clients for you."

Kincaid sat there, too stunned to move. She'd lost her job. Sam fucking Caldone had gotten her fired. *No.* Fucking Sam Caldone had gotten her fired. She closed her eyes. Inhaled. Exhaled.

When she opened her eyes again, she kept her face expressionless. She would walk out of this damn office with dignity. "I understand. I'm sorry that things have turned out like this."

"As am I," Roger said.

Kincaid stood on shaky legs. "I'll have my stuff out within the hour."

She turned to go.

"Kincaid."

She looked back. Roger's expression was pensive. "I heard you're looking to turn that farmhouse you bought into a bed-and-breakfast."

Great. He was going to dig into another way she'd acted unprofessionally. "I am."

He nodded. "You have a good eye. That's a great property."

"Thanks." A property she now had no job to support.

He turned back to his computer. "Let me know when it's taking reservations. I'll be first in line. The wife loves a good B and B."

The request caught her off guard, and her lips parted.

Roger clearly didn't want to talk anymore. However, the simple statement had done more than he probably imagined. In his own way, he was telling her that he believed she could pull it off. Yes, he'd just let her go from the agency, but he believed the bed-and-breakfast could happen. For some reason, that made her want to cry more than getting let go. She sucked back the tears that wanted to escape and walked out.

As soon as she stepped into the main office, she caught Ferris watching her from his desk, a crestfallen look on his face. The earlier phone call from Bethany came into focus, all the questions it'd raised now having answers. *This* was why Ferris had given Bethany all that information. He knew this was going to happen. He was trying to help.

She took a steadying breath and headed his way. *Do. Not. Cry.* She gave him a pained smile. "Well, that sucked."

"Oh, sweetie," he said, getting up from his chair and giving her a hug. "I'm so sorry. I couldn't say anything, but I heard that big cowboy through the door yesterday. What a jerk-off."

She gave her friend a squeeze before stepping back. "He's the worst."

Ferris leaned forward conspiratorially, his floppy brown hair falling into his eyes. "So it's true?" He lifted a palm. "I mean, I don't blame you if you did. The rich hick is hot, but why would he come in now?"

Kincaid glanced over her shoulder to make sure no one else was listening, not that word wouldn't get out when she left. The office was full of gossips. She should know since she used to be one of them. "He lied about

how it went down. We got together after the business
part was over and done. But he's coming in now because
he got his boxers in a knot when I turned him down at
a bar recently. He got real nasty with me after I said no.
One of my friends ended up punching him."

Ferris's eyebrows shot up. "Someone punched the
cowboy on your behalf? Who?"

"Ash. You don't know him. He's an old friend from
high school who's staying in town."

Ferris's mouth curved. "Oh, sweetie, you've got
yourself a brave knight. Is he cute?"

She gave a little shrug. "If you like that sexy, bookish,
skinny jeans type."

"Girl." Ferris lifted his palm for a quiet high five. "I
see you."

She laughed, thankful to her friend for making her
feel a shade better. "And guess I'll have lots of time to
spend with him now that I'm unemployed and facing
two mortgages."

Ferris frowned and reached out to take her hand
between his palms. He gave her a serious look. "I know
it's not what you want to hear right now, but you need to
sell the lake house, babe. You know Bethany will give
you top dollar."

She grimaced. "But I have nowhere to live. The
farmhouse isn't ready, and I don't have the money to
make it that way yet."

He gave her a look that said she didn't have a choice.
"Stay with a friend. Get a cheap apartment while you
renovate enough rooms to get by at the farmhouse.
Don't pass up a sale and money in your pocket."

The truth of his words settled over her, and now she

really wanted to cry. Her lake house. Gone. To Bethany Winters.

She gave Ferris another quick hug and went to her desk to clean out her stuff. The whole process seemed surreal. She wouldn't be back here. All her current clients were no longer hers. She had no job. Soon, she'd have no place to live.

How the hell had she gotten here? Shades of her past loomed over her like dark specters. She'd promised herself to never end up like anything resembling her mother. Yet somehow, she was now unemployed and, soon, without a place to live because of sleeping with the wrong man.

This was not happening.

It only took a few minutes to pack up her things, but before she carried her stuff out, she fished her phone out of her purse and dialed.

Bethany answered on the second ring. "Talk to me, Kincaid. Tell me what I want to hear."

Kincaid looked up at the ceiling, her throat tight. "Ten thousand over appraisal price for a quick sale. You can move into the house in a month."

Bethany squealed on the phone. "Sold! Yay, best day ever."

Kincaid ended the call, tightened her ponytail, and carried her box of stuff out the door.

Officially homeless.

chapter

EIGHTEEN

Ash loaded the last of the groceries into the small fridge in the apartment and put a bottle of Chardonnay inside to chill. A knock on the door had his lips curving. He'd expected Kincaid earlier, but she'd texted him that she had a few things to take care of before coming over.

He crossed the kitchen and opened the front door. "Hey, I—" But his words cut off when he saw Kincaid standing there looking like a stranger. Her ponytail was crooked, her eye makeup smudged, and the flat expression on her face made it seem as if some pod person had overtaken his normally perky friend.

"Hey." She stepped past him and dropped a duffel bag near the door. "Sorry I'm late."

"No problem. Is everything all right?" He shut the door and turned to face her. She was already unbuttoning her blouse.

"It's fine." She slid the silky navy-blue top off her shoulders. "Can we just not talk right now? It's been a long day."

Ash blinked. Kincaid didn't want to *talk?* That was a sign of the apocalypse. He opened his mouth to point that out, but her shirt fell to the floor, revealing a lacy black bra. His gaze traced over the plump curves of her breasts, his blood going hot, and his former thought got lost before it made its way to words. "KC…" She unzipped her skirt and wiggled it down over her hips. A barely there pair of black panties had his eye drawing downward. His brain short-circuited. "Uh…"

She smiled at his lack of language and let the skirt drop. "Sounds like you're not up for talking either."

She stepped out of the puddle of fabric, keeping her heels on as she bent to move the clothes out of the way. The back of her panties had even less material than the front—a thong. *Fucking hell.* Every male cell in his body was high-fiving the others at the fantasy on display. He'd seen women in lingerie, but he'd never seen a more erotic sight than *Kincaid* in lingerie. Seeing his high school crush like this made his mind go hazy. Maybe he'd knocked his head on the fridge earlier and was currently passed out on the floor. His mind was going to a happy, dirty place while the paramedics got him into the ambulance.

She stepped forward, a sway in her hips, and slid her hands onto his shoulders. Her gaze was steady, almost hard. "Missed me, cupcake?"

"Yes," he said, the vanilla scent of her like a drug. "So much. But—"

She smiled, the pink gloss on her lips reflecting the light. "Good."

She tracked her fingers down over his chest and then lowered her body, slowly going to her knees in front of

him. His cock was hard as steel already, and his skin
felt so hot he feared he'd melt before he got to enjoy
this. She reached for the button on his jeans. This was
a scene out of some forbidden fantasy he'd had when
he was seventeen. Kincaid Breslin wrapped in lace
and wanting to pleasure him. He wanted to stand there
and let the moment happen in all its glory, but some
warring faction inside him was sending a flare into his
sex-addled thoughts. A warning.

He tried to push the thought away. Any thought other
than *Let's enjoy this beautiful woman giving me a blow
job* seemed ludicrous. But when Kincaid dragged her
nails lightly over his fabric-clad erection and wet her
lips while looking at him with vixen eyes, the quiet
warning turned into a blaring alarm.

Fuck.

No. No. No.

But he couldn't deny the rush of awareness. His vision
had cleared, and now he saw the scene in a much less
favorable light. The woman at his feet was not Kincaid,
not the real Kincaid. This was the woman she was for
other men. The femme fatale. The southern seductress.
Butter won't melt in my mouth, but your body sure will.

And goddamn, he had no issues with being seduced.
Bring that shit on if it was all in good fun. But he knew
that, for Kincaid, this was an act. A role. She'd admitted
as much the night before. She was turning him into just
another guy. She wasn't really there with him.

She hooked her fingers in the band of his jeans and
boxers, tugging, but he grabbed her wrists before she
could pull them down. "Hey," he said softly. "Hold on."

Kincaid's gaze flicked upward, her brow arching.

"Getting shy on me, gorgeous? Or do you just need that control?" Her lips curved. "You can hold my hair if you want, show me how you like it."

Even her voice sounded different to his ear. Too smooth. He wrangled in his libido, which had formed a cheering squad chanting *Blow job! Blow job!* in the background. He kept hold of her wrists and lowered himself to his knees in front of her. He gave a small shake of his head. "Not like this."

A line formed between her brows, and her lips pressed together. "Not like what? On my knees?"

He searched her face and lifted her hand to kiss her knuckles. "I'm not sure I've ever seen anything sexier than you on your knees in front of me. But talk to me, KC. Something's off. This isn't you. Not the you I know."

"What? Too slutty? Maybe you don't know me as well as you think," she said, challenge in her eyes.

He didn't flinch. "You know that's not what I'm saying. This isn't about the sex. As dirty as you want to get, I'm here for it. Believe me. But it's about the rest of you. Your makeup is smudged like you've been crying, your whole body is stiff like you're trying to hold yourself together, and most importantly, you haven't eaten yet."

Her lips parted in surprise.

"Hungry trumps horny, right?" he asked with a small smile. "My Kincaid file is thick, detailed, and up-to-date. And though I realize I'm enormously irresistible and no woman can look at me long without dropping to her knees and offering sexual favors, I get the strong sense you're doing this because you want to avoid talking about something."

She rolled her lips together, her gaze sliding away.

"So talk to me," he said gently. "Then afterward, if you want to worship at the altar of Ashton, you're more than welcome to suck me off as long as your pretty little self desires."

She snorted at that. "The altar of Ashton? Please tell me you've never said that aloud to a woman."

He smiled, relieved to see some of her real self peeking through. "Of course not. Their mouths are always too full."

She rolled her eyes, and he let go of her wrists. She let out a sigh and sat back on her calves, her shoulders dipping. "You know, you suck at letting a woman distract you. I brought my A game."

He gave her a grim look. "Don't be fooled. You're enormously distracting. I'm about to pass out from the restraint this is requiring. You're wearing a thong, for Christ's sake," he said, breathless from the sight. "The teenage Ashton that still lives somewhere inside me just had a heart attack and died."

She tilted her head, eyes narrowing. "Teenage Ashton wanted to see me in a thong?"

Shit. "Teenage Ashton wanted to see any woman in a thong, but he's not our concern right now. He's dead. You've killed him. Tell me what's up with you."

She groaned and tipped her face toward the ceiling. "Ugh, fine." She closed her eyes. "In the short time span since I've seen you, I've managed to lose my job and my house. It's been a superfun day."

Ash sat down hard on the floor. "*What?*"

"Yeah," she said, a bitter edge to her voice. "Mr. Yeehaw Cowboy from the bar went to my broker and told him that I offered him a better deal on a house in exchange for sex."

The words were like a thunderclap in Ash's head. "He did *what?*"

"Yep. As if I would have to trade favors for sex with *him*. Are you kidding me? *He* pursued *me*, was like a damn dog on the hunt. And he told my broker we hooked up during the transaction, which is a lie. Not that I can prove that. A fact my broker had to point out."

Ash ran a hand through his hair, trying to process all that. "But he can't fire you for that. You didn't do anything wrong."

"Well, apparently sex with a client even after the transaction is over is still an ethical violation of the agency. Roger made the point that if the sellers had seen Sam and me out together, it would've made them question my integrity as their agent and the agency by default." She sighed. "I get that. Even though I don't think I should've gotten let go for it. I made a dumb mistake. One mistake." She held her arms out at her sides. "But that's all it takes I guess. One rash decision. My specialty."

Ash's jaw was clenched so tight his teeth hurt. "That's bullshit. This isn't your fault. Two consenting adults slept together after a business deal was over. Then the guy got his dick in a twist because you didn't want to do it again. This small-town, someone-might-see-you reasoning is crap. This kind of thing is why I hated living here so much. This wouldn't even be a blink on the radar in a big city. But because this guy has a couple of bucks in his pocket and people know him in town, he can get away with whatever he wants."

That kind of thing was the same reason Ash's dad

could parade around town like a hero even though his wife was always hiding bruises. No one wanted to think badly of or upset the winning football coach.

"Crap or not, the result is the same." Kincaid smoothed back a hair that had come free of her ponytail. "And if Roger had kept me, Sam could've gone to the real estate board and threatened my license."

Anger thumped through Ash. "We should've beat the shit out of the guy when we had the chance. Who the hell gets someone fired just because he got turned down for a second date?"

"Well." She tipped her chin up. "I am really great in bed. It makes men a little crazy."

Ash smirked and let his gaze travel over her lace-clad form. "This I won't dispute. But I promise not to come after your job when you leave me."

She gave him a wry look. "That won't be a problem since you're the one who will be leaving me."

The words landed on him like cold water. "Right."

"But now I'm out of a job, and I was already going to be fighting to keep two houses afloat. I know the bookstore sale will bring in money eventually, but it won't be soon enough. I can't risk going under on the mortgages. I had to make a deal with one of my clients. She's buying my lake house and needs me out within a month."

He blinked. "A month? But the farmhouse isn't ready."

"Tell me things I don't know." She shook her head. "I'll figure it out. If push comes to shove, I can stay with one of my friends while I renovate. I just can't believe I'll be couch surfing in my thirties. That's freaking depressing."

"Hey, you can have this apartment," he said. "I can find another place."

"No, it's fine. I know you're saving up money while you write. I'll be okay." She put her palms on the floor and leaned forward, giving him an unencumbered view of her cleavage. "But now can we do naughty things to each other and forget that my life is falling apart?" She kissed the side of his jaw. "You know, after we eat."

He laughed. "There she is. And yes, we definitely can."

Kincaid put on a pair of jeans and a T-shirt from the bag she'd brought while Ash put together sandwiches. Part of him, mostly the lower part, was sad she was covering up, but the other part knew he would've never made it through a meal otherwise.

They ate and chatted about her options for places to live and ways for her to make money until she could get the B and B open. If they could sell the bookstore, that would take care of a big part of the budget for renovations, so focusing on that was priority one.

Kincaid polished off her sandwich and took a long sip of the wine. She looked at him over the rim of the glass before setting the wine down. "You only drank half your glass."

He shrugged and looked at his mostly untouched wine. "I'm thinking I should stay clear-headed enough to drive."

She sat back in her chair and crossed her legs. "Drive? We going somewhere?"

He leaned forward on his forearms. An idea had been niggling at him all through dinner, and he couldn't shake it. That Sam guy had insulted Kincaid in public, called her the name that would hurt her the most, and then

topped it off with robbing her of her job and income.
All because he thought he had some right to her. That it
shouldn't be her decision whether or not to sleep with
him again. And what did he get for all that bad behavior? Just a punch to the face in a bar. It wasn't nearly
enough. He'd used his power to abuse her. Ash hated
a lot of things in this world, but a man who bullied a
woman was right there at the top. "I might be. You sold
the asshole cowboy his place, right?"

She gave him a wary look. "I did."

"So you know where he lives."

"I do," she said. "But Ash, don't get that look on your
face. He's not worth it. I don't want to have to bail you
out of jail for getting in a fight with the guy. Or worse, see
you get shot because you threatened him on his property."

Ash frowned. "He shouldn't get off scot-free. He
took your livelihood from you. It's way, way over the
line. And no one's saying boo about it."

She sighed. "Believe me, I know. I had to stop myself
from going over there. I was thinking a Taser to his
crotch would be appropriate, but I didn't feel like spending the night at county lockup. Plus, I'll just look like the
crazy woman, and he'll look like the poor guy who got
mixed up with me."

Ash pondered, briefly enjoying the image of Kincaid
shooting electric shocks straight at the guy's manhood.
"Maybe looking a little crazy isn't all that bad. But
you're right, bodily harm could get us in more trouble
than we want." He drummed his fingers on the table.
Maybe they could… He lifted his head, an idea sparking. "You know what kind of vehicle he drives?"

She ran her fingertip around the rim of her wineglass,

watching him carefully. "A truck, of course. One he's very proud of. He made me throw out a soda because he doesn't allow food or drinks inside."

"A truck he loves." Ash smiled a slow and deliberate smile and rested his chin in his hand. "Is that right?"

Kincaid's eyes widened. "Ash."

"KC."

She sat up straighter. "We couldn't."

He cocked his head. "Couldn't we, though?"

"Ash," she repeated, but a sparkle had entered her eyes.

"It's not like we don't have prior experience. Or the means. Charlie's truck is parked out back. He said I could use it whenever I needed it." He checked his watch. "I'm thinking the Feed and Farm is still open. I bet they have some dog food for sale."

Kincaid bit her lip, a smile forming. "We can't. We're not sixteen anymore. We're more mature and past the petty-revenge phase."

He tilted his head. "But are we? Are we *really?* The dude sabotaged your job and your house. I think he needs a little lesson in how to treat a woman."

Her grin went wide, and she drained the rest of her wine. "You are a bad, bad beautiful genius of a man."

He stood and grabbed her hand. "I learned from the best."

Fifteen minutes later, they were in the aisles of the Feed and Farm, staring at the meager dog-food offerings. All the large bags had been sold during a buy-one, get-one-free sale according to Carl, the guy running the register. Ash crossed his arms. "Damn. This isn't enough to even make a point. And cat food doesn't have the same symbolic effect."

Kincaid was frowning along with him, seemingly deep in thought. "There's got to be something else." After a moment, she lifted her head and got a devilish look on her face. "Hold on."

She left the aisle and went through the door that led to the outdoor shopping area in search of her new idea. A few seconds later, she called out for him. "Ash, out here."

Ash headed out to the fenced-in area that held the gardening supplies to find Kincaid grinning a sexy, evil grin. She clapped her hands together. "So. How committed to this revenge project are you?"

She looked so damn cute and excited that he wanted to pull her into his arms and kiss her. "What do you mean?"

She cocked her thumb to the left, indicating a large stack of bags. That was when the smell registered. "I'm saying we graduate to the next level. This won't be pretty, but it will certainly make a very obvious point. And will be an absolute bitch to clean up."

Ash eyed the bags with the picture of a happy cow on them, a laugh tumbling out of him. "*Manure?* You are truly diabolical. We are going to need the longest and most thorough shower after this."

"We are." She stepped forward, grabbed the front of his shirt, and kissed him, making his heart pick up speed and his body remind him of what he'd turned down earlier. She touched her finger to his throat and let it trail down his chest. "I have a shower big enough for two at my place. Afterward, we can get as clean as we want. You game for this, city boy?"

Ash wrapped his arms around her waist and lifted her off her feet. "You're on, Breslin. Go big or go home, right?"

She hooked her legs around his hips and looped her arms around his neck, pure glee on her face. "Always. Why do it any other way?"

Why, indeed. It'd always been one of the things he'd loved about Kincaid. When she was in, she was one hundred percent in. She'd never been one to waffle.

And right now, he was basking in the high of her being one hundred percent in with *him*.

A dangerous drug. But right now, he wasn't going to worry about that. They had sweet and stinky revenge to mete out.

—◦◦—

The lights inside the main house at Sam Caldone's ranch were off when Ash flipped off the headlights of Charlie's truck and quietly rolled into the long driveway. The tailgate of Sam's shiny Ford pickup was gleaming in the moonlight. He'd parked it in a small barn that had been converted into a garage. The barn sat about a hundred yards from the main house, and the large barn doors were wide open. An older, beat-up truck was parked in front of the main house.

"Even though I'm not walking up to the porch to punch his face in," Ash said as he backed in Charlie's truck to get tailgate to tailgate with the other truck, "we still need to be on the lookout for getting shot. We're on his property."

"Yeah, we need to be careful, but he won't hear us this far out if we're quiet. And that big oak tree blocks the view of the barn from the front windows." She opened her door and climbed out. They both took care in not shutting their doors all the way.

Ash walked over to Sam's truck. The thing was painted Longhorn orange and had an actual set of longhorns on the front grill. Ash snorted under his breath and whispered, "This thing is decked out. Not a working farm truck, for sure."

"Nope," Kincaid said, keeping her voice low. "He uses the beat-up one by the house for day to day. He keeps this to impress the ladies. When I came over, he wanted to do it in the bed of the truck out in the fields. Like that's romantic. Sex while mosquitoes bite your butt and cows moo in the background. Be still, my beating heart."

As if on cue, somewhere off in the distance, cows mooed. Poor, traumatized cows. God knows what they'd seen.

"I wish I could punch this idiot all over again." Ash lowered the tailgate of Charlie's pickup with care, and they put their hands over their noses in unison. The stench was breath-stealing.

Kincaid tossed him a pair of work gloves from the shopping bag full of supplies she'd grabbed from the truck. "This is both the best and worst idea we've ever had."

"Agreed. It's definitely the shittiest."

She gave him a deadpan look. "Really, Ash?"

He gave her an innocent look. "What? I've been waiting the whole drive to use that one."

"You're ridiculous." She pushed up on her toes and kissed him. "But thank you for this. Feels like old times. Just more dangerous and with kissing."

He tugged on her ponytail, affection humming inside him. "We're living our best life right now."

"We so are. Oprah would be proud." She bounced on her toes and did a quick silent clap. "Let's do this."

Warmth filled him. She looked so alive there in the moonlight. Beautiful in a way he'd forgotten. When he'd left, he'd convinced himself that he'd been seeing her through a teenage crush filter, exaggerating things that weren't there. But in this moment, he'd realized he'd been lying to himself. Kincaid was exactly what she'd always been—the best girl he'd ever known. "I'll do the lifting. You cut the bags open."

She pulled on her gloves and grabbed a pair of heavy-duty shears from the bag, a gleam in her eyes. "Time to get dirty."

Ash started transferring the bags into the back of Sam's truck. Kincaid stood on the bumper and sliced the bags open and dumped them in. He'd wondered if she'd regret the plan once the stench filled the garage. Manure wasn't like the dog food scheme in high school. But she was tough and running high on revenge adrenaline. They worked through all the bags in record time, quiet as thieves. By the time they were done, they were both sweaty and stinky but feeling victorious.

Kincaid looked at her work with delight and then hopped down from the bumper, making the truck bounce. She pulled the gloves off and tossed them into the back of Charlie's truck to dispose of later. "God, I wish I could see his face when he gets out here in the morning."

"He'll smell it way before he sees it."

"Perfect," she said. "Where's the chalk marker?"

Ash pulled it from the shopping bag near his feet and handed it to her. "You do the honors, Ms. Breslin."

Kincaid grabbed the white chalk marker and hustled on quiet feet to the front of Sam's truck. She stepped onto the wheel well, stretched out to reach the windshield, and wrote, SAM CALDONE IS FULL OF SHIT.

Ash choked on his laugh, trying to keep as silent as he could.

She jumped down and sent him a crooked smile. His heart flipped over.

Fuck.

But before he could freak out internally at the feelings bubbling up, a shaft of light shone through the oak tree and into the garage. *Uh-oh.* He jogged to the entrance. The lights had gone on at the main house.

"Oh, crap," she whispered from behind him. "Cowboy's up. Go!"

They broke into a run toward Charlie's truck and hopped in. Ash got the engine started and sent dirt flying as he pulled down the driveway. His gaze flicked to the rearview mirror. The door to the main house opened, and Sam Caldone stepped out onto the porch naked as the day he was born, wearing only his boots.

Ash groaned and focused on the road. "Hell, I could have lived my whole life just fine without seeing that. I guess he's not hiding a shotgun at least."

"Go, go, go!" Kincaid urged, laughing as she turned to stare out the rear window. "Oh my God. He's running. With all his business just bouncing around."

Ash took the turn onto the main road on skidding tires, his heart beating fast and his skin damp with sweat. Slightly rattled. Totally satisfied. Man, that guy was going to be hating life when he saw his truck. "Please tell me he's not going to run down the main road naked."

"He's not that fast." Kincaid had tears streaming down her face by the time they got far enough away to slow down to the speed limit and head toward Wilder. She leaned back in the seat, gasping for air. "Best. Revenge. Ever." She swiped at her eyes. "I bet he had a woman over. He was wearing his favorite outfit. That's just going to make him finding his truck that much better. Explain that one to your date."

Ash realized he had a stupid big smile on his face, his whole system buzzing. He imagined that naked idiot running over and seeing his shit-filled truck, and a giddy, adrenaline-spiked laugh burst out of him—then wouldn't stop. His eyes watered with the force of the laughter, and he had to hold tight to the steering wheel to keep the truck in the lane. Kincaid joined in, letting out a loud, snorting laugh, and all the years that had passed seemed to fade away in that moment. They were teenagers again, running away after the dog-food prank, feeling like they'd won some kind of prize.

When Ash finally got ahold of himself, he swiped at his eyes and smiled her way. "He's definitely going to know who it was."

"Good. Mission accomplished. Now he'll know what it feels like to not be able to prove something you know is the truth." She leaned over and kissed his cheek. "God, I forgot how intense this feels. I kind of want to rip your clothes off right now and ride the high. Too bad we smell like shit."

Ash laughed. "Is this how you felt when we did this stuff in high school? Because I really would've appreciated the benefits of that side effect."

She eyed him.

"What?" he said, still amped up from the escape.

"Nothing," she said, tone careful. "That's just the second time you've alluded to high school Ash wanting high school me."

"Oh."

"So, was that a thing?"

God, he was off his game tonight. He needed to get his filter back in place. "A thing?"

The air in the truck had shifted, the silliness sucked out through the open windows. "Yeah. A thing. Did you want me that way back then?"

He stared ahead at the yellow line in the center of the road, his grip tightening on the wheel. An internal panic was trying to zip his lips shut, but he couldn't bring himself to lie to her. "At points."

"At points? At what point?" she pressed. "We shared a bed a lot, Ash. You always told me I was like a sister to you."

He counted the road signs, trying to get his head together. *One. Two. Three.* "No, I never said I saw you like a sister. You were the one who used to say that. I just didn't correct you."

She inhaled a sharp breath. "What?"

He shifted in his seat, uncomfortable at the direction this was going. "But it wasn't like what you're thinking. The bed thing wasn't some big scheme. We were friends first. I didn't start out wanting you. It was just something that…developed."

She was quiet for a long moment. "How long, Ash?"

"Does it matter?" He wished like hell they could talk about something else, anything else.

"Yes. It matters."

He glanced over at her. "About two years."

"*Two years?*" she asked, a stunned expression on her face. "You liked me for two years and didn't say anything?"

He blew out a breath and looked back to the road. "What would've been the point? I knew you didn't think of me that way. Plus, I didn't want to mess up the friendship. So I waited, thinking maybe one day you'd see me in a different light. But then you got with Graham, and well…" He flexed his hands against the steering wheel. "I saw what you looked like in love. I realized I'd never had a shot."

"Ash…" The word was soft, almost confused.

"It's fine," he said, trying to sound nonchalant. "Stereotypical teenage crush. The geek lusting over the popular girl who sees him like a brother. I was such a cliché, I could've been a character on one of those WB teen shows you used to watch. It's embarrassing."

"But that night we slept together," she said as if not hearing him. "I didn't know. I didn't realize that you felt…"

She let the words trail off. He wasn't going to fill them in with the truth: *that I was in love with you*. "That night was a mistake. We were both out of our heads. It had nothing to do with my silly crush."

She sat back in her seat, looking shell-shocked. "I didn't know you liked me. That night… God, I *used* you. I said Graham's name. And it was your first… Jesus, Ash." She turned to him, a horrified expression on her face. "I'm so sorry."

He reached out and grabbed her hand. "You don't have to apologize. We used each other that night. My feelings were my own problem. We were just two kids dealing with a trauma in a really destructive way."

He released her hand and pulled into her driveway. She pulled a remote from her purse and opened the garage so they could park the truck out of sight. When he shut off the engine, he turned to her and found she was still watching him with a frown.

"It's okay," he said, hating that look of regret on her face. "It was a long time ago."

"All this time I thought you were the one who left. You were the friend who broke my heart." She shook her head. "But that's not true, is it? I was the one who broke yours."

His ribs cinched tight at the words, his throat constricting. "Don't absolve me. You had a right to be angry. I wasn't a good friend to you back then."

I was the worst.

But she wasn't hearing him. She leaned over and kissed him. "Come inside, Ash. We have some lost time to make up for."

"KC—"

She shook her head, and he swallowed his protest.

He'd told Kincaid no once tonight. He wasn't going to do it again.

chapter

NINETEEN

KINCAID'S MIND WAS WHIRLING AS SHE LED ASH THROUGH her house and to the master bathroom. She switched on the double-headed shower to let the water get hot and turned back to him. He'd gone quiet since getting out of the truck and had an unreadable look on his face. She recognized the look. He'd worn it a lot when they were teenagers, this brand of mild indifference that she'd thought was him being chill and aloof. Now she realized the indifference may have been the armor he'd used to keep his feelings hidden.

She'd truly had no idea he'd harbored any kind of crush on her back then, and now she felt stupid for having been so blind. How could she not have seen it? They'd spent every damn day together. She'd curled up next to him in bed on multiple occasions. She'd laid there next to him, telling him about the boys she dated. She'd waxed poetic about Graham and how much she loved him. *Ugh*. She'd been so involved in her own world that she hadn't seen what was going on in Ash's.

She prided herself on knowing what was going on with her friends, sensing when they needed her or when they were going through something tough. She'd always thought of that as one of her gifts. Yet somehow, she'd completely missed that she'd been hurting Ash back then, flaunting her relationships in his face.

Ash leaned against her sink, crossed his arms, and gave her a small smile. "You're freaking out, aren't you?"

She let out a breath and pinched her thumb and forefinger together. "Maybe a little?"

"Don't," he said. "You never led me on or gave me any indication you saw me that way. It wasn't your job to manage my crush. How I felt—that's on me."

"You could've told me."

"And what? Made you feel guilty that you didn't feel the same way and were in love with someone else? Sure, that would've been fun for all," he said drolly. "Our friendship would've been done. The awkwardness alone would've killed it. And even if it didn't, Graham wouldn't have wanted me around you anymore. He would've made you choose between your friendship with me and a relationship with him."

She frowned. "You don't know how he would've felt."

Ash's expression flattened. "No, I really do."

She didn't understand the certainty he had about that, but she wasn't going to argue about it any further. The past was the past. That was what they'd agreed to. Steam started to fill the room. She stepped closer to Ash. "I didn't think about you that way back then."

He unfolded his arms. "Not news."

She reached for the hem of his shirt. "But I can't say the same now."

He arched a brow as she tugged his shirt over his head. "No?"

"Grown-up Kincaid has a newfound appreciation for that boy she used to have sleepovers with." She traced over the compass-rose tattoo on the front of his left shoulder and then pressed her lips to it, loving the salty taste of his skin. "She thinks he's pretty irresistible and would never be able to sleep in a bed next to him now and not get herself in a whole lot of trouble. She'd want to touch and taste all the things."

"That can be arranged." He gave her a look of male promise, that look that said he wanted to completely unravel her and knew which string to pull first. He slipped off his glasses, setting them on the edge of the sink, and moved into her space, forcing her to back up. "Get in the shower, KC. Enough talking."

She kicked off her shoes and walked backward until she could feel the steam rolling over her. He pulled off her shirt, tossing it aside, and then made quick work of her jeans and socks, leaving her standing there in her black lace. She reached for the hook of her bra, but he put a hand on her arm, stopping her.

"Leave it on." He grabbed her waist before pulling her against him. His hand drifted down to her ass, squeezing her flesh. "You look like candy. I want to unwrap you slowly."

A shiver went through her at the feel of his denim-clad erection pressing against her belly. "Can you even see me without your glasses? I'm a mess."

He chuckled, the sound dark and sensual. "I can't see

distance. So that just means I'll need to stay very, very close. Skin to skin, in fact."

"The hardship."

He smacked her butt with a little pop of his hand. "Get in the shower, KC."

She stepped back under the spray, the water pouring over her sweat-sticky skin, and watched as Ash kept his eyes on her and unbuttoned his jeans. He pushed his pants and boxers down and off, and then gripped his impressive erection in his hand, giving himself a slow stroke. Her tongue pressed to the back of her teeth. *Have mercy*. For a quiet guy, Ash was anything but shy in the bedroom. That confidence was even sexier than the body that housed it, and that was saying something.

He stepped inside the shower, crowding her, and shut the glass door behind him. The water cascaded over him, making his dark eyelashes stick together in thick points. She let her gaze follow the rivulets of water as they rippled over the muscles of his chest and belly and then tracked lower, sluicing over his cock and racing down his muscular thighs. Heat and need welled in her like a tidal wave.

She grabbed him by the biceps, steadying herself, and tilted her face to him. He slipped a hand around the back of her neck and kissed her. Slow and exploring, his kiss opened her up and made her muscles liquefy. His naked body pressed against her barely clad one, and the heat thrumming through her burned hotter than the steaming water.

Ash broke the kiss, wiping water off her cheeks, and then reached behind her. He grabbed her shower poof and her favorite vanilla shower gel. He flipped open the cap to pour some on the poof and inhaled deeply. "Mmm. Smells like you." He looked at the label. "Might have to buy some."

She gave him a teasing smile. "Want to smell like a girl?"

He dragged the sudsy poof down her throat and between her breasts, making her skin tingle with awareness and her nipples tighten. "No, but next time I get hard in the shower, guess whose scent I could rub all over me while I imagine being inside her?"

She groaned. The visual of Ash slicking himself up with her shower gel was almost too much. She let her forehead drop to his shoulder. "If you walk into the store smelling like vanilla, I'm officially not going to be able to concentrate."

He dragged the poof lower, painting circles over her belly. "Guess we'll be even then."

She opened her mouth to respond, but her words left her when hot fingers drew a line down the front of her panties. She jolted with the sharp pleasure, her body already on a hairpin trigger.

"Easy there," Ash whispered, his voice its own kind of seduction. He lowered himself to the small bench in the back of the shower, the water splashing onto his shoulders, and kissed her right below her belly button. "Still have lots to get clean before we get to have our fun."

"Right," she said, bracing her hand on the wall and breathing hard. "Because this isn't fun at all."

Ash took his time, dragging the soapy poof along her thighs, down over her calves, and then turning her around and pulling her panties off. He worked his way back up, standing and losing the poof and using his sudsy hands instead. She gasped when his fingers slipped under the cups of her bra and pinched her nipples. Her head tipped back, landing against his shoulder. He unhooked the bra and then kissed the curve of her shoulder, the hard length of him rubbing along her backside in a slippery glide. Every nerve ending sang, her body aching in a way that made it impossible to focus.

She reached behind her and cupped the softest part of him in her palm, relishing the groan that rumbled against her ear. She found her voice. "My turn."

"I'm all yours, gorgeous."

She turned in his hold, soaped up her hands, and then rubbed them down his chest. His gaze incinerated her as she let her hands dip lower and lower. She took her time, liking the way his breath quickened. When his cock was finally in her hands, she slicked him up, watching his pupils dilate and his throat work with restraint. The rush of power that came with seeing how she was affecting him turned her on even more. She'd never had such a strong desire to make someone feel good. She smiled as she stepped back, letting the water wash off the soap bubbles, and then she pushed him against the wall out of the direct spray.

He cursed softly as she got to her knees on the tiles and took him into her mouth. She shuddered with need as her tongue circled around him, the earthy male flavor of him making her thighs squeeze together.

His hand went into her hair and gripped. "KC."

KC. Not *Kincaid*. Not *baby*. But the name only he called her. That simple nickname brought the moment into sharp relief. She could tell herself all she wanted that they were only having fun, but this could never be just a hookup. Even if this was temporary, she and this man had history that went back longer than she'd known most of the people in her life now. He was a part of her, of who she was, of who she became. This was Ash.

The thought should've scared her, that their roots ran so deep. She could already feel her attachment to him growing like vines inside her. But she wasn't going to be a coward. Yes, this would be brief. And yes, it was going to hurt when it was done. But right now, this feeling was worth the price.

Tomorrow was never a guarantee anyway. She was going to live every moment of this time with Ash without her fences in the way. She looked up, letting him catch her gaze, allowing him to see that this was turning her on as much as it was him, and took him deep.

His jaw muscles rippled, and the look on his face was almost pained. His fingers stroked her scalp. "You're so goddamned beautiful."

She closed her eyes, letting herself sink into the moment, into the feel of it all. But before long, Ash was halting her and easing her away. She looked up.

"If I don't stop you now, there will be no stopping." He cupped her chin as if he was hanging on to a lifeline, intensity in every inch of his expression. "I want you up here with me. Let me make you feel good, too."

He helped her to her feet, his breathing heavy, and kissed her as soon as she got there. She could feel his need pouring into the kiss with every stroke of his tongue. It was as if he wanted to absorb her. She grappled for him, her own desire making her feel a little crazed. Their movements became rough, hurried. He

pressed her back against the wall and pulled her leg up,
opening her body to him. He dragged himself against
her sensitive flesh, back and forth, back and forth, until
she was slick with more than water and the ache inside
her was all-consuming.

"Ash, please." She was begging. Kincaid Breslin
didn't beg. But right now, she didn't care.

"Tell me what you want," he ground out, his grip on
her tightening.

"You," she panted. "All of you. Inside me. Please,
Ash."

"With pleasure," he said and shifted his hold on her leg.

She braced herself for the feel of him, but he froze
suddenly.

"What's wrong?" she gasped.

He swore and touched his forehead to hers. "No
condoms. We need to get out."

She nearly screamed at the thwarted pleasure. She
needed him inside her. Right now. She swallowed hard,
her thoughts racing, and words tumbled out. "I haven't
been with anyone for months. I've been tested since and
am on the pill. You?"

He lifted his head, gaze searching. "I got tested as
soon as I found out Melanie had cheated. I'm not on
the pill."

She smiled and touched her lips to his. "I'm okay
going without if you are."

Desire flashed in his eyes, and he dipped his head to
kiss her again, more deeply this time. When he broke
away, they were both gasping for air. He stepped back
and put his hands on her waist, turning her around. "Foot
on the bench. Hands on the bar. This might not take long,

because *fuck* you drive me crazy, but I'm going to make it good for you."

Goose bumps prickled her skin even though the water was still warm. Something about that commanding tone he had did it for her. She followed his instructions and braced her hands on the towel bar.

Ash pressed himself behind her, one hand snaking between her and the wall to touch her where she needed as he entered her. Just the feel of his fingertips stroking her was almost enough to send her over the edge, but when his cock slid inside, bare and hot and thick, she had to fight hard not to fall apart.

He held her in place, pumping into her slow and deep, the water sliding down over them and the scent of vanilla and her own arousal wrapping around them. His lips and teeth went to her neck, kissing and nipping and driving her higher and higher. He growled and his fingers stroked her harder as her body clenched around him.

"Ash, please," she panted. "More. Need…"

His patience broke at her stuttered begging. His thrusts sped up until the sounds of their bodies moving together and the water drumming against the walls were all that was left. Her pleasure was coiling, tighter and tighter, the power to manage her release no longer in her control. She rocked her hips against him, desperate, needy, urging him on. Needing that one little push to set off the bomb inside her. *Please, please, please.* As if hearing her silent words, Ash buried himself to the hilt and stroked his fingers fast and precise against her, hitting just where she needed. Light exploded in her vision, and a cry wrenched out of her.

Ash moaned, a gritty, low sound, and he pulsed inside

her. The distinct heat of his release sent her orgasm even higher, pushing some strange primal button in her psyche. He'd marked her, and she liked it.

She rode the last waves of her orgasm, unashamed of the racket she was making, and then sagged in his hold. Her knees wobbled beneath her. "Ash."

"Shh," he said against her ear. "I've got you, KC. I won't let you fall."

She took a breath, softening in his hold, trusting he would take care of her.

With quiet movements, Ash eased out of her, guided her onto the bench, and turned off the water. He returned with fluffy towels to dry them both, and then he lifted her into his arms.

He carried her to her bed and got them both under the thick comforter. She immediately curled in to him, and he wrapped his arm around her like he used to when they were teenagers. Only this time they were naked. Lovers. Not just friends anymore. Lying in the crook of his arm somehow felt completely familiar and altogether new.

"You okay?" he asked after a quiet minute. "Warm enough?"

"I'm perfect." She tilted her head up to kiss his jaw.

"Perfect, huh?" He let out a put-upon sigh. "The ego on you, Breslin."

She laughed softly. "I have to keep up with yours, right?"

He traced his fingers absently along her arm. "You can try."

"Well, you're already ahead," she said, peering up at him. "You can put a feather in your cap. You just gave me a first time, and I know you did a better job with that for me than I did for you."

He glanced at her, eyes curious. "What do you mean?"

She lowered her head and nestled into his chest. "I've never had a guy go without a condom."

His heartbeat thumped against her ear. "Ever?"

"Nope."

"Not even Graham?"

She closed her eyes. "Not even him."

Ash was quiet for a long moment, and she wondered if he'd dozed off, but then he pressed his lips to the crown of her head. "Thank you for that trust."

Exhaustion was pulling at her, her energy sapped. She slipped her arm over his waist. "I always trusted you, Ash."

His body tensed a little beneath her. But if he said anything in return, she didn't hear it. She was already drifting off.

chapter

TWENTY

ASH SAT BEHIND THE COUNTER OF THE STORE, BUSILY working on his laptop, the sound of the clicking keys like a balm to his writer soul. Over the last couple of weeks, the words had started to come back to him. First, it had been a trickle, just a few whispers of a story idea. But then late one night, lying next to Kincaid in bed and listening to her dream, two characters had walked onto the stage in his brain and had started talking, insistently.

He'd hesitated, the idea not fitting with his other novels and having nothing to do with the proposal he'd sent to his publisher about a thriller set in Mexico, but when the characters wouldn't leave him alone, he'd snuck out of bed and begun writing to get them out of his head. But after a few more sessions like that, the exercise to clear his head became an actual story he was excited about writing. Now he figured *what the hell* — genre be damned. He had nothing to lose at this point anyway. So far, he'd finished six chapters of the book, and his heart was racing with the thrill of creation again.

The chunks of downtime had helped, too. After he and Kincaid had finished cleaning up the shop and rearranging things, he'd volunteered to man the store while a small crew painted the walls a fresh ivory and Kincaid finished the final touches on the decor. They'd put everything on the fast track after Kincaid lost her job since she needed the money from the sale to fund the first round of renovations on the farmhouse. After weeks of hard work, they were just about ready to reopen to the public and hopefully snag a buyer.

Ash leaned back in the chair he'd dragged behind the counter and took it all in. A wash of comfort moved through him. How many times had he stood at this very counter, helping customers, reading, watching Kincaid talk up books to anyone who came inside? This store had been his little corner of happiness in a town he'd never felt a part of, had provided him a family he wasn't born into. This place and the people in it had saved him in a lot of ways.

The store now looked nothing like it did back then, but the soul of it was still there, that welcoming spirit. The air smelled of the fresh paint, but otherwise, the place was perfect. Kincaid and her eye for design had somehow managed to modernize the shop yet keep the cozy feel that so defined it. New overstuffed brown leather chairs were tucked into a few hideaway places. Rosemary plants had been artfully arranged throughout the store, giving the place a rustic feel, and once the paint smell wore off, it'd be a comforting scent. The children's area featured a small canvas tent, homage to the old one that'd been there when Kincaid had first discovered the store. The whole place seemed as if it'd taken a deep, renewing breath.

So had he.

The thrill of travel and living in so many different parts of the world had fueled him for so long. He loved the process of starting brand-new somewhere, being anonymous in a big city, and learning about a new place and the people in it. He'd dreamt of that kind of life from early on. This town had always represented fences to him. Fenced into a location. Into a family. Fenced into labels—the coach's son, the "like a brother" best friend, the school shooting survivor. Out in the world, he didn't have to be any of that. He could change each time he moved if he wanted.

But looking back on how things had gone down with Melanie, he realized he'd played that game so often that he'd lost a piece of himself along the way. Melanie would never have dated Ashton Isaacs, nerdy kid from Long Acre, Texas. She'd fallen for Ashton Stone, traveling thriller writer who had his name splashed across the front of books. Without realizing it, he'd done a bait and switch on her. That was the mask he'd been wearing when they'd met in London, but once they'd settled down in New York for a while, the real version of himself had surfaced. The guy who didn't want to go out for cocktails every night, the guy who didn't want to see and be seen, the guy who just wanted to read, write his books, and plan his next adventure. The guy who couldn't love her fully because his heart already had too many holes in it.

Kincaid had been right. He'd needed time away from the situation. He didn't forgive Melanie for cheating on him. There was no excuse for that. But he understood why her head had been so easily turned. He'd become a stranger to her. And being with her had made him a stranger to himself.

Being with Kincaid these last few weeks had brought that home more than anything. He'd forgotten how it felt to be fully in his own skin and truly seen. He couldn't put on a front with Kincaid because she'd see right through the bullshit. She knew him when. She knew the roots from which he'd grown. She had best-friend intel, and there was no hiding from that.

That feeling was both a relief and terrifying.

A relief because he couldn't remember the last time he'd felt so relaxed and happy.

Terrifying because it was making him consider things that he had no business considering. Things he couldn't have.

The sharp click of shoes heading up the back hallway dragged him from his thoughts, and he turned to find Kincaid hurrying toward him, blond hair blowing back from her face with her swiftness. "Ash."

"Kincaid," he said, matching her urgent tone and smiling. She'd gone upstairs earlier to move a few of her things into his apartment. She'd officially be moving her stuff over to the farmhouse next week and was going to be staying with him for a few days during the transition—not that they hadn't been spending nearly every night together anyway. "What's on fire?"

She slipped behind the counter with him, eyes a little frantic. "It's Charlie and Grace."

His stomach dropped. "What's wrong?"

"No, no," she said, shaking her head. "Sorry, I should've led with 'Everyone is healthy,' but Charlie and Grace are headed over. Like, to see the place. Like, now."

Based on her expression, this was not a good thing. "Okay. They do have the right to do that. They kind of own the place."

She grabbed the front of his shirt. "But it's not ready. And there were still a few touches I wanted to add and they could hate it and—"

He kissed her, cutting off her words and cupping her face. "It's going to be fine. The place looks fantastic. You've done an amazing job."

She let out a breath and wrapped her arms around his neck. "You think?"

"Yes."

"And it's *we*, not *I*. *We've* done a good job," she said adamantly. "This is a *we* thing."

"Right. I like *we* things," he said, pulling her close and touching his nose to hers. "We're good at those things."

"Ashton Isaacs, are you making sexual innuendos at a time like this?" she chided.

"Never." He smirked. He hadn't actually meant any innuendo, but it was better if she took it that way.

She tilted her face toward him and kissed him again. Ash let himself relish the gentle kiss, loving the feeling of ease between them. They were people who kissed now. Just for the hell of it. Not as a prelude to a hookup. Not as a means to an end. Kissing like a couple.

The thought was dangerous as hell, but he couldn't help it. That was how this felt lately. He and Kincaid were acting like a couple.

He eased back from the kiss and smiled at her. "They're going to love it. And even if they hate it, they'll lie because they love us."

She laughed and smacked his shoulder. "Shut up. Don't say that. I want them to be honest."

"The God's honest truth is that it's beautiful," he said. "Just like the woman who designed it."

"Beautiful, huh?" She brushed her fingers along the nape of his neck. "Flattery will get you everywhere, writer boy."

He lifted her up onto the counter, stepping between her legs and nuzzling her neck. "I'm banking on that."

She leaned her head back and let out a little sigh of contentment. "What was I freaking out about again? My memory's suddenly very fuzzy."

He chuckled softly and pressed his nose to her skin, inhaling her scent. "See, you just need me around whenever you get stressed. I've got many means of distraction."

"Be careful," she said, her fingers tunneling into his hair. "Get too good at that, and I won't let you leave this time. I'll lock you in my haunted attic so I can keep you and use you for my wicked purposes."

The words were like pinpricks along his skin and he stilled.

Kincaid, too observant for her own good, let out a breath. Her fingers gripped his hair and she lifted his head, giving him a patient look. "Don't panic, pumpkin. I'm just messing with you."

He frowned. "I'm not panicking. I just—"

"Will leave. I know," she said with an eye roll. "I'm aware. I promise I'm not changing the rules on you or trying to lay a guilt trip. It was just a joke."

He searched her face, trying to get a read on her. "Would you want me to stay?"

She blinked like he'd snapped his fingers in front of her and leaned back a little. "What?"

"If that were an option," he asked carefully, "would you want me to stay?"

She gave him a perplexed smile. "Would I want my best friend to live in the same town as me again?" she asked. "That's a stupid question. Of course I would."

Her best friend. The words rang loud in his ears.

"But I also know that my best friend has dreams of traveling a lot more of the world, and I know he hated living in this town, so I'd tell him he was crazy to stay here just to hang out with me. No matter how awesome I am. But"—she said, touching her forehead to his—"he better damn well visit more going forward."

Ash let out a long breath, absorbing the words. He'd needed to hear them. His mind had spun off down some path tangled with logic-eating vines. He was making the same mistake he'd made last time. He was reading more into something with Kincaid than was there. It didn't matter that they were sleeping together. Kincaid would forever see him as her best friend. Nothing more.

Headlights flashed in the window, and Ash looked toward the front of the store, his stomach tightening. The Lowells were pulling up. Even though the Lowells were selling the place, he didn't want them to be disappointed with the changes.

"They're here," Ash said, helping Kincaid down from the counter.

Ash shut his laptop and grabbed the keys to unlock the front door. Kincaid stayed at his side as they watched Grace help Charlie out of the car. Charlie made a sour face and waved his wife off. Ash shook his head. The guy was too proud for his own good.

"Here we go," Ash said. He leaned down to give Kincaid a good luck kiss, but her hand shot out lightning quick and she gripped his shoulder, halting him. Her gaze held surprise.

"We can't." She shifted her eyes toward the Lowells. "They can't know."

The words weren't a shock, but still, their meaning hit him like an elbow to the gut. *We can't tell. You're a secret. You're just a friend.* He fought back a grimace. If she didn't want the Lowells to know, that was her prerogative. And as she'd reminded him a minute ago, it wasn't as if they were officially dating. What would she even call him? Her lover? Her friend with benefits? But still, he knew that the lack of proper label wasn't the reason. In the Lowells' eyes, she would always be Graham's girl.

Maybe in her eyes, too.

The thought frosted over some of the raw feelings their conversation had exposed. He needed to get his head back in the right place, stop acting like this meant something more than it was. "Got it. No PDA."

Her expression relaxed a little. "Thanks. You get it. It'd be…weird. You know?"

Sure. Yep. Totally get it. He forced a smile and directed it at the Lowells as he held open the door. "Grace, Charlie, welcome to the new Stuffed Shelf!"

Grace was already peering through the main window and clutching Charlie's hand. They had dressed up for the occasion—Grace in a pair of black slacks and a green sweater and Charlie in khakis and a blue dress shirt. "Wow, look at it, honey."

At first Ash couldn't tell if hers was a good reaction or an oh-shit, what-have-they-done one, but when Grace turned toward him and Kincaid, a sunshine smile broke over her face. Ash let out a breath.

Charlie walked up to them, his steps still a little slow, and clapped Ash on the shoulder. "Don't you dare tempt her not to sell the place. I can already feel the sand between my toes on that Bahamas vacation."

Ash laughed. "We'll try to impress but only a little."

"Good man," Charlie said and then leaned over to kiss Kincaid on the cheek. "Lead the way, young lady."

Kincaid guided the couple through the door and flipped on the rest of the main lights. Bright, warm light bathed the new store in its glow, and Grace sucked in a breath. "Oh, my word. It's *stunning*."

Charlie put his fists to his hips and turned in a full circle, taking everything in. "You did all this with the measly budget we gave you?"

Kincaid grinned proudly. "Ash and I know how to stretch a dollar. A big part of it was cleaning things out and paring down some of the stock. We're going for more of a curated look. Like your local bookseller has hand-picked each one with love. The artisanal approach is very in right now. Why not apply it to books?"

Ash's chest filled with affection for Kincaid. She'd worked really hard on getting this place looking just right—modernish but not losing the small-town charm. She'd pulled off a miracle in record time, and her love of the place was evident in every design choice she'd made.

Ash pointed toward the general fiction area. "We've rearranged a lot of the shelves to help with flow. There are still a lot of books in stock, but it gives the illusion of more space and breathing room."

Kincaid grabbed Grace's hand, guiding her and Charlie to follow her to the front aisles. "And this is one of my favorite parts. Ash had the idea to bring in the local flavor with shelf-talkers. Instead of just employees displaying their recommendations, I asked a number of local business owners, high school kids, and just regular people in town to recommend their favorite book and write why on these little cards. That way when tourists come in, they'll get personalized recommendations from the people in town."

Charlie bent to read some of the shelf-talkers they'd set up—books placed cover out with little handwritten recommendation cards beneath them. He grinned. "Of course Dorothy down at the bakery would recommend a mystery about a pie shop."

Grace laughed, and a stray lock of her auburn hair slipped free of her signature twist. She tucked it behind her ear. "And look, Dr. Amanda, the pediatrician, recommended a horror book with zombies. How funny."

"Hardware Store Jim says this book changed his life." Charlie held up a copy of Bruce Springsteen's autobiography and chuckled. "Who knew?"

Grace picked up Ash's first book, which had a shelf-talker in Kincaid's handwriting that read, *A page-turner by a gifted homegrown author that will keep you up all night. Just don't get attached to the bird.*

Grace chuckled and turned to Ash, grabbing his hand and giving it a squeeze. "I love this idea so much. I love that you wanted to bring the local community into the shop." She looked back and forth between him and Kincaid. "I'm so thankful and proud of the both of you."

Warmth filled Ash, and his eyes started to burn. *Hell.* He took a deep breath, trying to get control of his emotions and not cry, but the word *proud* was like a chicken bone lodged in his throat. He couldn't get past it. Had his own parents *ever* said that? "You don't need to thank us. It was our pleasure. You've done so much for us over the years."

His words were croaked like a frog, but he managed not to break down in front of them.

Kincaid shifted to stand next to him as if she could sense he was on shaky emotional ground. "Ash's right. We could never repay you. This is only a drop in a very large bucket, but we're so thrilled you like it."

Charlie wandered away to explore as Grace read more shelf-talkers, but Ash could tell when the man landed in the back of the store. A gruff sound came from that direction, and he called out for his wife. "Gracie, come 'ere."

Kincaid gave Ash a look, slightly wary, and they followed Grace to the back. Charlie was standing with his arms crossed, staring at the black-and-white framed snapshot on the back wall. The second Grace saw her son's photo, tears filled her eyes. She looked to Kincaid and Ash with surprise.

Kincaid wet her lips, looking nervous. "We wanted to honor the person who was supposed to be running this store."

"Oh, sweetheart," Grace said, leaning into Charlie.

In the true crime section, Kincaid had put together a small wall display with a photo of Graham, his smile wide, and a note about the tragedy. Beneath the photo, there were canisters of wooden bookmarks with the words *Love Never Ends* engraved onto them by Hardware Store Jim that people could purchase, all proceeds going to the charity Grace and Charlie would start in Graham's name with the bookstore money.

Grace picked up one of the bookmarks, running her fingers over the thin wood. "Y'all didn't have to do this. You know whoever buys this store will probably get rid of this."

Kincaid nodded. "Yeah, well, until then, this store is Graham's. He has a part in this." She reached out and grabbed Ash's hand. "Plus, the place didn't feel complete without Graham here, too. It was always the three of us hanging out here."

A double-edged pang of sadness moved through Ash.

Kincaid released his hand, and Grace and Charlie hugged them both. Afterward, Charlie dabbed at his eyes with a handkerchief he kept in his back pocket. "This place is going to sell," he said with confidence. "I can feel my son's spirit here, and I can feel the love you two put into this. Someone will see how magical this place is."

Kincaid nodded. "I have no doubt. My friend Ferris already has it up on the website, and it will go on the market tomorrow. He'll fight to get top dollar and to find someone who wants to keep it a bookstore. I have full confidence in him."

Grace frowned. "I'm so sorry about your job, sweetie. I can't believe they just cut staff like that. I wanted you to be the one who got to sell this place."

Kincaid shifted and pushed her hair behind her ears,

looking uncomfortable. "It's okay. I've been managing. Selling the lake house has helped a lot. I'm getting everything moved into the farmhouse this week. As soon as we get the furniture in, I'll be able to sleep there."

"Where are you staying in the meantime?" Charlie asked. "You know our guest room is always open to you."

Kincaid smiled, her gaze briefly alighting on Ash before hopping back to Charlie. "Thank you. I'm staying with a friend. It's not a problem."

Even though Kincaid had barely looked at him, Grace's attention zeroed in on Ash, her eyes narrowing in that way only an observant mother's could. Ash could feel the tips of his ears heating.

"A friend," Grace said, casual as could be. "How nice."

Ash forced a polite smile. "Let me show you the kids' section. We found a great tent to replace the old one."

The tour continued and stayed focused on the store, but at the end, when Kincaid was occupied with showing Charlie the reorganized storeroom, Grace stayed with Ash. She leaned over to smell a rosemary plant on the front counter, and Ash busied himself with packing up his laptop.

"Ashton," she said in that smooth southern lilt, that tone that could hide a death threat in a thick cloud of cotton candy.

"Yes, ma'am." He set his laptop bag on the floor and straightened, trying to keep his expression neutral.

She smoothed her palms on the counter, leaning a little closer, and gave him a pointed look. "You know I'm not one to meddle."

"I—"

"But I also love you and Kincaid like my own and can't hold my tongue when I see the both of you playing out in the road in a busy street."

He stilled. "Pardon?"

"Do you think I'm senile?" she said with a knowing tilt to her lips. "A mother sees things, and I've been one for a long time. You need to take care with her, you hear?"

He swallowed hard. "I don't understand."

She reached out and patted his hand. "You smell like her perfume, dear."

"Grace, I—"

She lifted a palm. "It is not my business. I don't need details. I'm just asking you to take care. Kincaid is a tough young lady. Not many could walk through what she's been through and come out the other end with such grace. That mother of hers..." Grace pursed her lips and shook her head. "But don't mistake toughness for hard-heartedness. Just because her heart has known a lot of hurt doesn't mean it can't be broken again."

The words startled him. "I would never want to hurt her."

She pinned him with a curious look. "Do you love her?"

Ash tensed, the question like a fire alarm screaming in his head. "She's been my best friend for a long time. Of course I do."

She clucked her tongue. "You know that's not what I mean."

"It's not like that," he said quietly. He glanced toward the storeroom to make sure Kincaid wasn't on the way back. "She knows that. And she's not in love with me. Her heart has always been with Graham. This is just…casual."

Ugh. What a disgusting, ridiculous word. *Casual.* What did that even mean? As if their relationship was flip-flops or jeans at the office on a Friday.

Grace gave him a gentle smile. "My Graham had her heart, and she had his, but he's gone." She looked down and took a breath. "A young woman's heart should not be buried with him. That would just be another tragedy."

The easy way Grace relieved Kincaid of the duty of holding a torch for Graham sent a rush of warmth through him at this woman's generosity of spirit, but a wave of resignation quickly followed. He didn't disagree with her, but it didn't mean he could change how Kincaid felt. "We don't get to make that decision for her. You love who you love."

"Of course," she agreed, clasping her hands on top of the counter. "But sometimes safety feels like love. They're not the same thing."

The words stung. "You think she sees me as safe?"

Grace shook her head, an exasperated look on her face. "No, dear. Loving a man who is never coming back is safe. I think you're the dangerous one. Kincaid's put up some tall gates around her castle. They have gotten her through a lot, but I think you could sneak past the guards. A threat with the face of a friend."

Ash stared at her, stunned. "You think I'm using her?"

Grace's kind eyes met his, lines appearing at the corners, reminding him that despite her red hair being the same color and in the same style she'd always worn it, so much time and heartbreak had passed since they'd first met. "Not purposely. Ash, you're a brilliant man with a beautiful heart. Any woman would be lucky to have you love her. But you are also a restless soul. You always felt choked by small-town life. Your dreams are different from hers. Kincaid wants what she never had. She wants roots. She doesn't want to go out in the world and live that adventurous life like you do. She wants to be amazing right here." She sighed. "Why else would she spend all her hard-earned savings on that money trap of a farmhouse? She's planting her own tree, risks be damned."

Ash looked down, the truth landing hard. "Right."

"You both want to be the stars of your own story and deserve to be. Unfortunately, you're in completely different movies."

Ash blew out a breath and ran a hand over the back of his head. "I don't know what movie I'm in anymore. I'm way off script."

Grace considered him as if trying to puzzle him out. "What kind do you want to be in?"

"What do you mean?"

She stepped around the counter and took one of his hands and pressed it between her palms. "I mean, when you close your eyes at night and dream of the future, where are you? What do you see?" She cocked her head. "Who's there with you?"

His eyes narrowed. "Grace, is this some kind of mom trick?"

She squeezed his hand. "All I'm saying is that life is short. Sometimes shorter than we think. It's okay to leave the theater if a movie isn't working for you and to see something else. Maybe an old favorite."

His throat tightened, the feeling she was poking at making him feel a little sick to his stomach. "I can't. That's not what this is between us. She's not…"

"Oh my," she said, deep lines appearing around her mouth and eureka in her voice. "I've read this all wrong, haven't I?"

"Grace."

Awareness was all over her face. "*She's* the one I should be giving this talk to."

He winced.

"Oh, sweetheart," she said, her gaze not leaving his. "You're the one who's in love with her, aren't you?"

The answer was there in his heart like a blinking neon sign. Bright and bold and obnoxious. It didn't feel new. Maybe that feeling had never really gone away but had only been dimmed by the pain of losing her that first time. He closed his eyes, the realization crashing down on him like a landslide. *Fuck*.

"That's not what this is," he repeated, more to himself than to her.

Grace's arms wrapped around him gently, the smell of her flowery perfume winding around him like a warm blanket. Her voice was low against his ear. "I should tell you to end things now before you get even more hurt. That would be the wise advice."

He leaned back, catching her eye, confused.

She gave him a secret smile. "But I say fight."

"Fight?"

"Yes." She patted his shoulder. "Fight like hell for that girl."

He stared at her, shocked. "Grace, I can't. I'm not lying. That's not what this is. No matter what I feel, I can't force what's not there. Kincaid has always seen me as a friend and friend only."

"Oh, don't give me that. You're sleeping together. Which means she's attracted to you." She sniffed. "You know what romantic love is, Ashton?" She didn't wait for him to answer. "It's a long-lasting deep friendship with common ground, respect, and hopefully, lots of really great sex."

"Grace!" His ears went hot again.

She gave him a knowing grin. "Oh, sweetheart, don't look so scandalized. All I'm saying is you two have all the ingredients there already. I just wonder what would happen if you'd stop giving up before you tried and really fought for her? Show her what you got, Ashton."

His face had to be full red now. "Well, she's seen all of that."

Grace snorted. "That's not what I mean. Although, good for you, honey!"

He put a hand over his face, trying not to laugh at the absurdity of discussing his sex life with his surrogate mother.

"I mean…" she said, lowering her voice conspiratorially. "*Woo* the woman. Throw your best effort at her. Bring out all the stops." She shrugged. "At least then if she's still not interested, you know you've given it everything you've got. You can walk away with the kind of peace you get from knowing it truly wasn't meant to be. You can move on."

He stared at Grace. He'd been ready to dismiss her suggestions, but her words rippled through him with a hard shiver of truth. In all his time with Kincaid back then and now, he'd never openly pursued her. He was always careful, always holding his tongue, always staying in the friend role where he knew his place was secure. The most he'd done was the night he'd first slept with her, and even then, he hadn't declared his feelings for her. And walking away, thinking about all the what-ifs had driven him crazy. What if he'd told her about his feelings before she dated Graham? What if she'd known it was him who'd written those love letters and not Graham? What if he'd shared his concerns about Graham early on? What if he'd been one hundred percent honest with her?

He didn't know if it would make a difference. He couldn't force her to feel something for him she didn't. But he'd never given her a chance to make up her own mind on that. He'd told himself *no* long before she had the opportunity to do so.

Maybe Grace was right. Maybe if he stopped editing himself so much, he'd at least be able to get closure when she said she didn't feel the same way. Kincaid had seen so many parts of him, so many sides, but she'd never seen the man he could be when he openly loved someone. *He* wasn't even sure what that looked like.

Maybe it was time to find out.

A slow smile curved his lips. "Grace, I love that you don't like to meddle."

She tipped up her chin and winked. "A true lady knows where not to stick her nose."

"Of course." He gave her a quick hug. "Thanks for this. Even if this blows up in my face, I appreciate the advice."

She gave him a tight squeeze. "I just want to see the two of you happy. Whether that's together or not, it doesn't matter. You both deserve the best life has to give. Plus," she said, releasing him, "I want grandkids and I'm not getting any younger."

He laughed and lifted his palms. "Tap the brakes there, Grace."

She gave him an arch look. "Just sayin'."

She provided him with one last encouraging pat and then headed toward the back to find Charlie, leaving Ash alone with his whirling thoughts and the reality he could no longer ignore.

He loved Kincaid. He *loved* her.

That was enough to knock him on his ass, but now he was actually considering letting himself act on it? Put himself out there with no armor on at all?

Fuck.

This had disaster written all over it. But...

What if it works?

The thought whispered to him like an illicit lover, tempting him with visions of things he hadn't let himself imagine. He gripped the edge of the front counter and leaned forward, breathing in those images and then recognizing them for the insanity that they were. This was nuts.

"Hey, Mr. Broody," Kincaid said, her voice snapping him to attention.

He lifted his head, making himself smile a casual smile. *Casual.* Always so damn casual. "Hey."

"Charlie was tired, so they decided to go out the back door and head home." She walked over to Ash and ducked between the arms he'd braced on the counter. She hooked her arms around his waist. "They really, really loved it. Charlie couldn't stop telling me how great everything looked. He even oohed and aahed over the new stock arrangement. We done good, city boy."

He touched his forehead to hers, inhaling her scent and letting that nervous energy settle a little inside him. He could do this. If he didn't fight it, loving her was as natural as breathing. He just had to let himself show it. "Grace knows about us."

Kincaid lifted her head, worry there. "What?"

"I didn't tell her." He tucked a stray lock of hair behind her ear. "She sensed it with her spidey sense."

"Damn." Kincaid rolled her lips together, a pensive look on her face. "Was she…okay?"

He nodded. "More than okay. She seemed happy about it."

Her brows arched. "Really?"

"You that surprised?" he said, forcing jest into his voice. "She thinks I'm a pretty good catch, you know."

Her lips twitched into a smile, and she rolled her eyes. "Of course you are." She pushed up on her toes and kissed him lightly. "I guess it still feels a little strange for me. Like I'm betraying her son in some way."

"I know," he said, "but you should know that she doesn't see it that way."

She nodded. "Good."

"So what exactly did you tell her?" she asked, her nose wrinkled. "That we were, like…dating, hanging out?"

"I told her you were just using me for my body while I was in town and that you had a thing for shower sex."

She smacked his arm. "Ash."

He laughed. "I told her we were spending time together. She told me I smell like your perfume. I think she figured it out."

Kincaid's cheeks went pink, and she buried her face in his shoulder. "Oh my God. I'm so glad that was you having that conversation and not me."

"I don't mind taking one for the team." He smiled and kissed the crown of her head. "Come on. Let's close up shop, and I'll take you to dinner."

She leaned her weight into him. "We can just order takeout if you want. I know it's been a long day."

"Nope." He gave her a little squeeze. "You look too pretty not to show off. Plus, we can celebrate us moving in together."

She lifted her head and snorted. "For a whole week."

He took her hand and kissed her knuckles. "That's a whole week of waking up with you next to me. I'd say that's worth celebrating."

Her gaze jumped up to his, surprise there, but he didn't flinch. If he was going to do this, he was going to do this. No filter.

A little smile touched her lips. "That's sweet, Ash. I didn't know you had it in you."

He laced his fingers with hers, a buoyant feeling in his chest, and tugged her toward the back of the store.

You don't know the half of it, cupcake.

TWENTY-ONE

THEN—JUNIOR YEAR

ASH WAS GOING TO TELL HER. HE HAD TO. THIS HAD GONE ON too long, and it was getting pathetic. No, it was *already* pathetic. He shifted on a stool behind the checkout counter, his well-worn notebook in front of him, his heart on the goddamned pages. He wanted to shove the whole thing at Kincaid and run like a damn coward. Having her see his words could possibly get him everything he wanted *or*, more likely, would send the best thing in his life up in a ball of friendship-wrecking flames.

Kincaid was singing along to a Kelly Clarkson song from her spot in an armchair near the front of the store. He could see her profile, the afternoon light making her blond hair glow gold as she bopped her head to the music and flipped through another cookbook— something she did when the store was slow. His chest physically ached with all the things he wanted to say to her. But his muscles were locked, gluing him to the spot and making him sweat. The only way his words seemed to come out was on the page.

He looked down at his notebook again. He needed to pull the sheets out and give her the letters now before he missed his chance. He could sense the shift between her and Graham lately. Graham's gaze lingered a little too long. Kincaid's laugh was a little too loud when he made jokes. There was something brewing there, and Ash could feel his sliver of a chance slipping away.

Kincaid had declared that she was taking a break from dating for a while, but Graham wasn't just any rando panting after her. Graham was a friend. A good guy. She might change her mind for Graham.

But would she change her mind for Ash?

He read over his letter again. The notebook was full of them. Page after page of them. He'd write one and then chicken out on giving it to her, then write another the next day, hoping it was better, hoping they were the right words. He would inevitably decide they were not. Then the cycle would start over again.

"What you up to, Isaacs?"

Ash jolted and almost levitated off the stool at the sound of Graham's voice right behind him. "Shit."

Ash's hand splayed across the notebook page to both block and steady himself, and he swiveled toward Graham.

Graham chuckled. "Sorry. Didn't mean to scare you." He nodded toward the notebook. "So who's the sappy letter for?"

"Who's the—" Ash's stomach dropped as the words registered and he stood. "You were reading over my shoulder? What the hell, man?"

Graham crossed his arms and shrugged. "Sorry. I thought you heard me behind you. So who's the lucky girl?"

Ash wanted to shrivel up and die at the prospect of this conversation. His only saving grace was that he hadn't written Kincaid's name on the letter yet. But if Graham flipped a page back, he'd see letter after letter of *Dear Kincaid* and *Dear KC*. He tried to speak past the lump in his throat. "It's, um, an epistolary novel."

Graham frowned. "A what now?"

Ash tried to will his face not to flush fire-engine red. "Just a thing I'm messing around with. It's a novel made up of letters."

"Cool," Graham said. "Come on, let me see it."

Ash breathed deeply through his nose and moved out of the way, trying to act chill but keeping his hand on the edge of the notebook. No way was he letting Graham pick up the thing and turn the pages. Graham's eyes scanned the letter. Certain sentences seemed to glow like neon signs in Ash's vision.

Your laughter is my favorite song.

I want to fall asleep with that song in my ears and your scent on my pillow.

When you're next to me, it feels like the earth stops moving just for us.

Then when I think of kissing you, my world starts spinning too fast.

Graham was going to figure out who it was about. It

was all so obvious. Graham was going to laugh and call Kincaid over, and Ash might as well just die of mortification now and save them all time. He was possibly starting to hyperventilate.

Graham let out a whistling breath. "Wow, man. That's some intense stuff. This guy better win the girl at the end, or this is going to be a seriously depressing book."

"I, uh," Ash stuttered, "haven't figured out how it ends yet."

Graham was still staring down at the page, a line deepening between his brows.

Look away. Look away. Look away. The silent plea repeated in Ash's head.

Graham glanced up and toward Kincaid, a ponderous expression on his face. "Something like this could really make a girl fall for a guy. It's like something out of a movie. Is this guy mailing the letters to the girl?"

Fuck. Ash was going to have to make up a damn novel on the fly. "He, uh, hides the letters where she works so she can find them, like a scavenger hunt, and he just signs them as her secret admirer."

Graham stepped forward, bracing his hands on the counter and still watching Kincaid. "Does she figure out who he is?"

Ash discreetly closed the notebook and shoved it into his backpack beneath the counter. "Yeah, that's part of the story. He wants her to figure it out because then that means she really sees him, you know, like recognizes him in the words. If she does, then he'll know she loves him back."

Ash was rambling now, but the second the words

were out he realized how much he wished that were true. He wished he could send the letters to Kincaid anonymously, and she would instinctively know they were his words, would see that they'd always been meant for each other. She'd see that the love they had in their friendship was only a breath away from a different kind of love, one where he could hold her hand and kiss her and tell her all the things he held inside every time he was around her lately.

"This could be perfect," Graham said, voice so quiet Ash barely registered what he'd said.

"What could be?"

Graham turned to Ash, putting his back to Kincaid and his hand on Ash's shoulder. "Dude, I need your help."

Ash blinked to clear the fogged thoughts he'd been lost in. "Huh?"

"I've been racking my brain, trying to come up with a way to ask Kincaid out. I know she's on her boy ban right now, but God, I'm really, really into her. Like it's kind of been killing me."

Ash's mouth went bone dry.

"And I know I can't just go up to her and tell her she's pretty or whatever. She's shot down every guy who's asked her out in the last few months." He ran a hand through his blond hair. "I need something special. Something that will show her that I'm not just looking to hook up, that I really like her, you know, for her."

"Right," Ash said, the word coming out robotic.

"She's, like, supergreat, you know?" Graham said, gaze serious.

Ash nodded numbly. "I know."

Graham smiled. "Right. Best friends. Of course you know." He squeezed Ash's shoulder. "And you know I'll treat her right. I'm not going to be like those jerk-offs she's dated before. I know she's special."

Ash was going to vomit on Graham's Adidas.

"So will you help me?" he asked, his hand still heavy on Ash's shoulder.

Acid was burning in the back of Ash's throat because somehow, some way, he knew where this was going. "Help you…ask Kincaid out."

"I need your letters," he whispered.

Ash closed his eyes. "Graham…"

"I know they're not my words, but that's totally how I feel about her, and you're so much better at the writing thing than I am," he said, a plea in his voice. "I can hide them in some of the books around the store. Make it like a scavenger hunt for her. She loves romantic stuff. That'd be romantic, right?"

Ridiculously, utterly romantic. He wished he'd thought of putting them in books. He also wished he could scream at Graham to *back the fuck off* and write his own damn letters. He couldn't *steal* Ash's feelings for Kincaid and pass them off as his own. What kind of bullshit was that?

But Graham didn't know they were Ash's feelings. He thought it was fiction, a novel. Nothing real. Not Ash's blood and guts spilled all over the goddamned pages. "Graham, I don't think that's the best idea. KC is—"

"I know you're protective of her. I absolutely respect that, but"—he put a hand to his chest—"it's me. You know I'll be good to her. I already care about her so much."

Ash glanced past Graham's shoulder. Kincaid was

staring out the front window, completely oblivious to the fact that she was the subject of their conversation. Did she like Graham that way? Ash had seen how she looked at him. Was that what she wanted? Some big romantic gesture from Graham? Would that make her happy?

Ash's insides were being pulled and stretched in ten different directions. He didn't want Graham and Kincaid together, but if that was what *she* wanted, who was he to stop it? And if there was a chance that she felt about Ash the way he did about her, could this actually help him find out?

If they hid anonymous letters written in Ash's words and tucked them into her favorite books—favorites Graham couldn't know about—wouldn't she guess who they were really from? Wouldn't it be obvious to her? Ash was the writer. Graham was good at other things, but books and writing were not his forte. Maybe this could be a way to suss out her feelings—like the story he'd made up about the novel. If Kincaid could see Ash in his words, maybe that would mean she loved him back, that she'd been paying as close attention to him as he had to her.

"What do you say, Ash?" Graham asked, trying to catch his eye. "Will you help me out?"

Ash's mouth was a desert, and he was clammy all over at the thought of putting his words out there for Kincaid to read, but maybe it was time to stop being so scared. He took a deep breath and met his friend's gaze. "Let's do it."

Graham's grin went wide and he lifted his arm for a fist bump. "You're the best, Isaacs. This is going to be epic."

Kincaid strolled up just in time to see the fist bump.

She hoisted herself up onto the counter and smiled at them. "What are you two up to?"

Dying, Ash answered silently. "Talking about your appalling love of pop music."

She stuck her tongue out at him. "And also how I'm just the best, most wonderful girl you two have ever known?"

Graham grinned. "Obviously."

"The ego on you, Breslin," Ash said because he was apparently incapable of flirting and could only manage middle-school sarcasm when she was around.

She reached out and messed up his hair. "You're the worst BFF ever."

He sighed. "I know."

———————

Two weeks later, Ash was at the checkout counter again, going through the closing procedures and trying to focus. He'd started the money count three times now and messed up each time. He hadn't been able to think since he and Graham had planted the letters around the store. He knew Kincaid had found some because he'd checked the books after she left at night. But she hadn't said a word. He couldn't concentrate on anything at all when she was near him. He kept waiting for her to look at him and say, *I know*. Or *how could you?* Or in his best fantasies, *I'm totally in love with you, too*.

So when he looked up to find her heading his way with a secretive smile on her face and a sheet of paper clutched in her hand, his heart jumped into his throat and he feared he might pass out. He lost count of the money again.

Kincaid stopped in front of the counter and her smile went wider. "Hey, you."

Her tone was effervescent and filled him up with this fizzy, bubbling rush of hope.

It's happening. It's fucking happening! Breathe. "Hey."

"Almost done with the till?" she asked, eyeing the money.

"Yep. Everything okay?"

She leaned closer as if she was going to tell him a secret. "I think everything is kind of amazing."

Could teenagers have heart attacks? He was worried he was in the midst of one. His ears had started to buzz and he couldn't feel his legs. "Oh yeah?"

"When were you going to tell me?" she said, pressing her hands to the counter, the letter trapped under one palm.

All the air whooshed out of him, and the heavy weight he'd been carrying for so long lifted off him. "God, KC, I've wanted to tell you for so long."

She bounced on her toes. "Ash! I can't believe you kept a secret from me. Graham must've threatened the hell out of you."

The words came crashing down around him like breaking glass, cutting him on the way down. "What?"

She opened the folded letter, showing Ash his own typed words. "Don't pretend you don't know. I know he had to ask you for advice on which books to hide them in. He couldn't have known."

Ash's heart, which had swelled to supernova size when she'd smiled his way with the letter in her hand, collapsed in on itself like a black hole. She'd read his words. *His* words. And she thought they were Graham's.

There was no logical reason why she would think

Graham had written them. Graham wasn't the writer. He wouldn't know the books to hide them in. The only way she could read those words and see Graham's hand penning them was because she *wanted* that to be the case. She'd seen who she wished for.

And it wasn't Ash.

Ash's eyes burned and his throat had narrowed, but he managed to force a smile onto his face. "You got me."

Her face lit up and she hurried around the desk, almost knocking him over with a hug. "Oh my God, Ash. This is the sweetest, most romantic thing anyone has ever done for me. I mean, I thought maybe he liked me, but this… I mean, wow. *Graham Lowell*. I've had the biggest crush on him for the longest time but never imagined he felt like this. Thank you for helping him and not ruining the surprise."

Ash hugged her back, his nose in her hair, his heart in shreds. He closed his eyes, refusing to ruin this moment for her. He'd wanted an answer and now he had it. She wanted Graham.

What else could he do but let her go? She was happy. Of all the people in the world, she deserved that more than anyone. He gave her a tight squeeze. "I'm happy for you, KC."

"Thank you." She leaned back and then kissed him on the cheek. "I love you, Ash. You know that, right?"

He forced his smile to stay on his face and stepped back, touching her suddenly too much to handle. "I know."

"Good."

She loved him.

Just not the way he'd hoped.

That love was meant for someone else.

chapter

TWENTY-TWO

KINCAID LAUGHED AS ASH GROANED AT THE CHOICE OF restaurant. He eyed the door. "I said I'd take you anywhere you want, anywhere at all. We could've gone into the city and picked from like a hundred places that have been featured on TV as the best of Texas."

"But this is where I wanted to go," she declared with a grin. She hadn't felt like driving far and was craving a filling meal after the long day. In Long Acre, that meant Big Willy's BBQ & Dance Hall. The old-school country music was already thumping when they stepped inside, and the smell of smoked meat hung heavy in the air. "What can be bad about BBQ and country dancing?"

"Harboring *Footloose* fantasies?" There was a glint of amusement in his eyes.

"Always." She gave him an air kiss and pulled him along by the hand to get in line. "And don't be such a snob. You know the food is delicious. Plus, the beer is cheap and they have banana pudding. *Not from a box mix.* That is high class, my friend."

Ash laughed. "So your idea of a romantic dinner is eating off butcher paper and watching people line dance. Noted."

She dragged him closer. "Oh, sugar, who said we'd be *watching*?"

A flash of panic flickered through his eyes as he glanced toward the dance floor and then back to her. He gripped her shoulders and gave her a serious look. "KC, I love you, but if you think I'm capable of line dancing, you've far overestimated my abilities."

"But—" Whatever she was going to say dissipated in an instant as his words fully registered. "Wait, what?"

"Huh?" he asked. His gaze had drifted back to the dance floor. "I don't know how to line dance."

"Not that. You said you loved me."

His Adam's apple bobbed, and he waited a beat before turning back to her. "Okay."

"Okay?" she repeated, confused. "Okay, what?"

He gave her an unreadable look. "We used to say that to each other all the time."

She stared at him, some weird sensation rolling around her gut. "Right, but…we were kids. You haven't said that in a long time."

His grip on her shoulders softened, and he rubbed her upper arms. "If it weirds you out, I don't have to say it."

"I—" She clamped her lips shut. Did it freak her out? She said *love you* to her friends all the time. Why should this feel any different? "No, it's fine. I just…don't want us to confuse things."

He gave her an enigmatic half smile. "I'm not confused. Promise."

She nodded and took a breath. "For the record, I love you, too. Even if you don't know how to line dance."

A pleased expression filled his face, and he pulled her to him, leaning down to kiss her. "Thanks."

"Are you two going to order?" a guy behind them asked, his annoyance obvious.

They looked toward the man and his equally annoyed wife, surprised to find anyone there. Ash released her from his hold, and Kincaid offered the guy a bright smile. "Why don't y'all go on ahead of us? I don't know what I want."

Damn, was that ever the truth.

Hearing Ash say *I love you* had poked some anxious part of her. No man had said that to her since Graham. And she knew this was different. Ash was saying it as her friend, but the sleeping-together part was blurring the lines in her head. The man she was sleeping with had said he loved her. She would not, *could not* let that get twisted into something it wasn't in her brain. She and Ash were not meant for that path.

But the wicked part of her mind was putting together a PowerPoint presentation of what-ifs. What if the circumstances were different? What if Ash lived here? Would she still want to keep these lines drawn? Could she see this turning into more?

The thoughts were stupid. The circumstances weren't different. Ash staying here would mean him giving up his dreams. She would never want him to do that. And she wouldn't give up hers to go travel the world with him. Maybe in an alternate universe their paths lined up and they could have something more than friendship, but in this one, they were on decidedly different journeys. They were meant to be friends. Who loved each other.

Ash, who'd turned to look at the chalkboard menu

after the couple had gone in front of them, looked her way again. "You okay?"

She forced nonchalance. "Yep. Just hungry."

For so many things.

They got their order and then headed into the main dining area to find a place to sit. Picnic tables of varying lengths filled the space in a haphazard pattern, and the dance floor stretched out on the left. A few older couples were already two-stepping, and a group of tween girls were trying a line dance.

Kincaid recognized a number of folks at tables as they passed and gave little waves and hellos. For a moment, she thought she saw Sam Caldone, but it ended up being a guy with a similar cowboy hat. *Thank God.* She'd have to see Sam one day. You couldn't escape anyone for long in a town this size, but she was happy that time wasn't tonight.

Along the back wall, a bunch of tables had been pushed together to make one long one, and it was filled with rowdy high-school-age boys. "It's going to be loud at that end," she said as they stopped to fill up their glasses with iced tea at the drink station.

"Not sure there are any other spots," Ash said, holding their tray of food. "And really, with the music, it's going to be loud wherever we sit."

She nodded and followed him toward the raucous boys, but as they squeezed by the table, a woman's voice stopped them in their tracks. "Ashton?"

The bewildered voice somehow cut through the din, and Kincaid almost ran into Ash as he froze. They both turned, and Kincaid's stomach plummeted when she saw the wide-eyed face staring back at her.

Oh shit. Oh *fuck*.

Kincaid's emergency broadcasting system kicked in, pasting a smile on her face and inserting enthusiasm into her voice. "Mrs. Isaacs," she said way too peppily. "How *are* you?"

But Ash's mother's gaze was still locked on her son, her fingers tight around her glass of whatever she'd gotten to drink.

Kincaid glanced toward Ash, who'd gone pale. His gaze jumped from his mother to Kincaid and then back. He cleared his throat. "Hi, Mom."

Mrs. Isaacs put her hand to her chest, and her eyes went shiny. "Ashton."

The weight of the air between them was smothering. Kincaid didn't know the whole story, but she knew Ash didn't talk to his parents, didn't visit. When he came to the Lowells' for the holidays, they were under strict orders not to post photos of him on Facebook.

"What are you doing here?" his mother asked, bewildered.

Ash didn't move. Didn't speak.

"Ash is getting some peace and quiet to write his new book," Kincaid blurted out.

Ash's head swiveled her way and gave her a *really?* look.

She winced inwardly. Dammit. *Shut up, Kincaid*.

"You're staying in town?" The hurt in his mother's voice twisted Kincaid's heart a little. She knew Mrs. Isaacs had let Ash down in so many ways, but Kincaid couldn't help but have some sympathy for her. The grief on her face was raw.

"Not for long," Ash said, his grip tight on the food tray. "Just in between trips."

His mother looked down. "Right."

A boisterous laugh sounded behind them, and Kincaid and Ash turned automatically. Only then did Kincaid realize that the high school boys at the big table weren't alone. Coach Isaacs was at the far end, his arm around one of the kid's shoulders, a big smile on his face. He looked like a father congratulating a son. Her attention shifted back to Ash, her heart splintering for him.

Ash's jaw was locked, expression stony.

As if feeling the chill of his son's hate, Coach Isaacs looked over, his attention zeroing in on Ash. His dumb smile sagged, and he released the kid he'd been embracing. He put his hand on the table and got up from his seat.

Ash set his tray down on a table that hadn't been cleaned off yet and cupped Kincaid's elbow. "Let's go, KC. I'm not hungry anymore."

"Okay," Kincaid said, willing to do whatever he needed.

"Ashton," his mother pleaded. "Don't go. *Please*."

Kincaid could see the push and pull on Ash's face. But before they could make a move, Ash's father was in front of them. He was still a big man, broad and strong, but time had turned his hair gray and his skin lined. Kincaid saw him around town often enough, but he'd learned not to acknowledge her. He knew whose side she was on. The one time he'd greeted her, bringing up something about how she used to be on the dance team, she'd given him an eat-shit-and-die look that cleared up any gray area.

Coach Isaacs looked through the two of them to the woman standing behind them. "Denise."

Ash's mom forced a smile. "Look, honey, Ashton is in town."

Coach Isaacs eyed his son, his expression revealing nothing. "So I see."

"He's here writing a book," his mother added, her upbeat tone like an out-of-tune song.

"Heh." Coach's lip curled. "Which means he's broke. Probably mooching off the Lowells. He can write a book from anywhere."

Ash's fists curled at his sides and his skin flushed. "I'm doing just fine."

"Great actually," Kincaid added. "He's very talented. Gifted, really."

Shut. Up.

Coach Isaacs barely spared her a glance, sniffing derisively. "Denise, did you know about this?"

The words were innocuous on the surface, but Kincaid's skin prickled, some primal part of her picking up the menace in them.

"No," Ash answered, voice firm. "Mom had no idea."

"I didn't," Mrs. Isaacs said. "I would've told you." She looked to Ash. "Ashton, you should come to Thanksgiving. It's been so long…"

Ash's hard expression softened just enough for Kincaid to see how much this was killing him. "Mom, I don't think—"

"He's not invited," his father said brusquely. "Unless he's coming there to apologize, he's not welcome."

His mother's face fell. "But, honey, we haven't seen him in—"

"I said no, Denise," his father snapped. "He knows what he needs to do to get an invitation."

Ash scoffed. "Yeah. Lie. No thanks. I'm good." He stepped over to his mom to lean down and kiss her cheek. "Good seeing you, Mom. I hope you have a nice holiday."

Her eyes filled with tears.

Ash grabbed their tray of food and looked at Kincaid as if she was a lifeline. "Come on, KC. I think there's a better table near the dance floor."

She nodded. She'd been willing to go when he'd suggested it, but now it looked like he'd changed his mind. When Ash turned his back on them, she gave his father a scathing burn-in-hell look before walking away.

Ash sank down into his seat, putting his back to the football players' table. His fists balled beside the tray, and he took a deep breath.

Kincaid placed her hand over his clenched one. "You okay?"

He gave her a helpless look. "Not even a little bit."

Her heart hurt for him. She wanted to scream on his behalf, get in his father's face and just *rage*. How could a family have a son this wonderful and treat him like dirt? How could a man crush a woman's spirit so thoroughly that she wasn't even capable of fighting for her own child? Ash deserved so much better. "We can go. I'll grab takeout boxes."

His gaze flicked up to hers. "No way. I'm not running just because he's here."

She peered over his shoulder, catching his mom looking their way. "Are you sure? This isn't a contest. We don't have to win."

"I'm not leaving," he said resolutely.

"Okay." She gave his hand another squeeze. "We'll

eat then." Kincaid set about getting their food divided up and arranging things on the butcher paper. If he didn't want to talk about it, she would give him his space. "Do you want the fatty brisket, the lean, or the burnt ends?"

Ash let out a breath and closed his eyes, his head resting in his hands for a moment as if gathering himself. "She's going to pay for that."

Kincaid paused at that and set her fork down. "What do you mean?"

He lifted his head, his mouth a grim line. "He's pissed at my mom. I saw how he looked at her. He thinks she knew I was in town. She's not supposed to talk to me."

Kincaid grimaced. "Not supposed to? Like she's under orders?"

Ash's eyes were wary. "Exactly. That's how things work at their house. What he says is law." He sighed. "Only, she's broken that rule a lot. She has an email account he doesn't know about and emails me a few times a year. She isn't lying about not knowing I was in town, but he senses something's up. That's enough to set him off."

Kincaid could feel the worry wafting off him. "You think he's going to hit her?"

"Yes," he said flatly. "He'll punish her."

A chill went through her. "Should we invite her over to your place tonight or something? Get her out of the situation?"

Ash picked up his fork and stabbed a piece of lean brisket. "No. She won't go. I've tried. It's the reason I'm not allowed home anymore." He grabbed a bottle of sauce and poured a puddle onto the butcher paper, his movements stiff. "Before I left for school, I confronted my dad about the abuse and asked my mom to come to New York with me. They both denied everything. Acted shocked. Everything was just peachy in the Isaacs household. Just a little yelling is all. *Why so sensitive, Ashton? Why are you trying to make us look bad? Why are you lying?*"

Kincaid's lips parted in horror. "Are you kidding me?"

"Nope. My own parents tried to gaslight me. I lost my shit and told my mom that I wouldn't come home to that, that I wouldn't stand by and pretend anymore. But I should've known better than to give her an ultimatum. I placed a bet on a losing hand, making her choose between us. Dad kicked me out, and Mom didn't step in when he cut me off, leaving me with only my scholarship to pay for tuition and nothing for room and board."

"*That's* what he wants you to say sorry about? For telling the truth?"

"Yep. And if I'm real nice about it, he'll give me access to the settlement money they got from the Long Acre case," he said with a snide tone. "Isn't my dad just the sweetest?"

"Jesus H. Christ." Kincaid peeked at the coach's table again. "They're holding money over your head?"

"Two hundred thousand dollars could be all mine for the small price of saying I imagined my entire childhood and that I'm *so very sorry* for making up horrible stories about dear old dad." Ash shoveled a bite of food in his mouth.

Her eyes went wide. "Holy shit, Ash. That's a lot of money."

"I wouldn't do it for ten million. Fuck him."

"I don't blame you," she said, fresh admiration for him filling her. She knew how tight things had to have been when he left Long Acre. That money could've changed Ash's life. "I can't believe they're holding your settlement money. *You* were the one who went through the shooting, not them."

"I don't want their money. I just—" He looked down at his food, dragging the tines of his fork through the sauce, his jaw working again. "It guts me to see her, to know what she goes home to. My mom's a grown woman, and I know I can't force her to do something differently. She's made her decisions. But that doesn't make it easier for me. She's still my mom. I want to protect her. That's why I still email her a few times a year. I want her to know she can still ask me for help if she changes her mind, even though I know she won't."

A tender sadness filled her. "I'm sorry."

"It's one reason why I avoid going anywhere local when I come here to visit Grace and Charlie. I don't want to run into my parents. When I see my mom, I want to kill my dad." He looked up. "Like, I scare myself with that feeling. That feeling like I could actually kill someone."

She frowned. "Ash."

"No, I'm serious." He held her stare. "It makes me feel no better than those assholes who put guns in our faces at prom. Something made them that angry. I don't like knowing I'm capable of that kind of violence."

"You're not," she said adamantly. "You have every right to feel rage. Your dad has earned that. But you're nothing like Trevor or Joseph. You just love your mom and want to protect her. That's a natural instinct."

He laced his fingers behind his neck and exhaled.

"But sometimes it's not up to you to save someone else," Kincaid said. "I learned that with my mom. People have to make their own choices, even if they're mistakes. You do what you can, but it's not your job to make that choice for them."

Something changed in Ash's expression, and his Adam's apple bobbed. "Right."

"Because then the person you're trying to save will just blame you for taking their choices away." She sipped her drink. "If you got rid of your dad, your mom would hate you for it."

Ash's skin was paler then she'd ever seen it.

She slid a container of potato salad toward him. "Eat. You look terrible."

Ash stared at her for a moment longer, a haunted look in his eyes, and then he looked down at his plate. He hardly said anything for the rest of the meal.

chapter

TWENTY-THREE

THE LIGHTS IN THE RESTAURANT DIMMED, SIGNALING THE kitchen had shut down. Ash and Kincaid remained at their table as the restaurant transitioned fully into late-night mode. The mason jars of banana pudding sat empty in front of them. He'd lost track of how long they'd been here, but he would not leave before his parents did. He would not run.

That had been Ash's first instinct when he'd seen his dad tonight, the old habit like an automatic reflex. He wanted to run. Out the door. Out of this town. Out of the whole damn state. The only thing that had snapped him out of it was seeing Kincaid's face. Having her there by his side, defending him, had stopped him.

Leaving town meant leaving her.

His father didn't get a say in that. He would not give his father the power to chase him off from someone he cared about, someone who made him happy. He'd always thought of Long Acre as his parents' hometown, but fuck that, it was his, too. Why should he be the one made to feel uncomfortable? Unwanted? He wasn't the one beating his wife. He was here loving someone.

Loving someone he was lying to.

The thought made his stomach hurt. Watching his parents had reminded him of the destructive power of secrets. Secrets were a cancer in his family. His father got to sit and look like the hero to those football players because secrets were kept. His mother was going home to a violent, scary place because she kept her mouth shut.

The woman he was falling in love with deserved better than that. If he wanted any chance of this becoming something more, he had to tell. But her words from earlier were haunting him. *The person you're trying to save will just blame you for taking their choices away...would hate you for it.*

She was going to hate him. He loved her, and there was no way to make it work. If he didn't tell her, whatever they built would have a cancer hiding inside it. If he told her, she'd realize that he'd taken away a choice that should've been hers.

A slow song was playing, the peppy line dances and two-step numbers thankfully over for the night, and Kincaid gave him a little smile. "They're gone now. We can head out."

Ash looked at her, little fractures branching through his heart. "Want to dance?"

A genuine look of pleasure filled her face. "Really? We don't have to. I know it's been a rough night."

He slid off the bench seat and put his hand out to her. "Dance with me, KC."

She put her hand in his and got to her feet. "You sure?"

"I'm sure." He led her to the half-empty dance floor.

A few couples were still out there, the blue-toned lights and slow beat giving it all a dreamlike quality. Ash pulled KC into his arms, cherishing the warm, familiar feel of her. She fell into step with him easily as the current song finished up. They kept swaying as another started. The rich sound of a woman's voice filled the dance floor and Kincaid sighed. "Oh, I love this one."

Ash listened, the lyrics telling a story as so many country songs did, and he spun her closer to the center of the dance floor. "Which one is this?"

"It's the Judds." She put her cheek against his shoulder and closed her eyes. "'Young Love.'"

He pressed his nose to the top of hair, breathing her in and steeling himself for the conversation to come. Would this be the last time he held her like this? The song drifted over them, the women singing about young love being strong love, being true love. They sang about making it through the hard times.

He closed his eyes, letting himself fall fully into the moment. Life had so few of these perfect, sweet seconds that he didn't want to miss them. Like those first few minutes when they'd rushed into prom, all friends, all excited, their lives ahead of them. Everything shiny and fresh and full of possibility. He wished he could've frozen those moments before it all went wrong, remembered what that truly felt like—to be that carefree. To have that much hope.

But time couldn't freeze. Those moments were fleeting.

Right now, he had her. The woman he'd always

wanted. Earlier, he'd told her he loved her, and he'd seen something new in her eyes. Something more. She'd been scared, yes. They'd backpedaled and played like it was about their friendship. But he'd seen the change there, the hope. She'd looked at him with fresh eyes. She wanted him. Not as a friend. Not as a lover. She wanted it all.

He'd been soaring on the way to their table, making plans in his head. Then he'd seen his family, and reality had come crashing down around him. He was a liar.

Kincaid lifted her head and looked up at him, a soft smile on her lips. "You're a good dancer."

"Thanks."

"How did I not know this?" she asked. "Have we never danced together?"

He turned her, guiding her around an older couple. "No. When would we have done that?"

She frowned. "We didn't dance together at prom?"

The word *prom* was like a swift punch to the lung. *Hello, universe. Balancing yourself out again?* He knew then the magical minutes were over. He'd gotten his warning. *You don't deserve this.*

"We didn't," he said as another song started.

Her brow wrinkled. "I feel like I remember we did."

He wet his lips as they drifted toward the edge of the dance floor. "What do you remember?"

She stared up at him, concentrating. "I feel like I have a memory of us like this. Close. You in a tux."

He took a deep breath, his skin prickling with a chill. She remembered him holding her in the hallway, pulling her close. He'd never danced with her. Graham wouldn't have stood for it. "We didn't dance."

She frowned. "Sometimes I hate that I can't remember. I know it's a blessing to not remember the horrible stuff, but I have so many blank spots all through that night. Sometimes I dream and it's like...*right there*, some memory, and then it slips away again."

"Right."

"I know you told me what happened, but big parts of that night are just...lost."

Ash pulled her close, touched his forehead to hers, and grieved for what he was about to lose. "Let's go home, KC. We need to talk."

Ash was leaving. She knew that had to be what this was about. She'd seen his expression tonight when he'd run into his parents. Everything he hated about this town had been thrown in his face tonight. His parents. His father looking like a hero with the football team. His mother turning her back and walking away again. Even the silly restaurant had probably reminded him of why he hated this town.

She'd felt him pulling away, preparing her, even while she was falling head over heels in love with him on the dance floor. God, she was so stupid. She'd known this was going to be the outcome, and she'd let herself love him anyway. Yes, he was supposed to stay longer, but he didn't have to be here anymore. The bookstore was done. He could scrape together enough money to go off somewhere else until the store sold and the money came through from that.

He wanted to talk.

He was leaving.

She forced herself to keep it together. She would not make this a thing. She would not lay guilt on him. She was the one who'd broken the rules. This was her own fault.

Ash unlocked the door to the apartment and let her in. The place was more cluttered with her suitcase and a few boxes, but she'd spent so much time with him here these last few weeks that it had already started to feel a little like home. She took a deep breath and walked over to the bed to sit down.

Ash shut the door and stood in front of her, his face a funeral mask. Already, her eyes burned, tears imminent.

"KC."

"Just tell me, Ash," she said, proud that her voice stayed steady. "I'm a big girl."

He let out a breath and sank onto the bed next to her. He took her hand between his, not looking at her. "First, I need to tell you that I love you."

She swallowed past the hope in her throat. "I know. You told me earlier."

"No." He turned his head to meet her gaze. "I'm in love with you. I was when we were teenagers, and I am now." He shook his head. "Part of me wonders if I ever stopped."

She lost her breath for a moment, the words not what she was expecting. Was this going to be a good talk? Hope bloomed fresh in her chest. "Ash…"

"It was always you," he said softly, almost to himself.

Tears filled her eyes.

He let her hand slip from his. "But you're not supposed to be here with me."

She frowned. "Ash—"

"You were supposed to be with him." His jaw rippled as he pressed his teeth together. "And I took that choice away from you."

Her body went cold. "What are you talking about?"

He lifted his head and turned to her, his eyes shiny. "I lied to you about what happened on prom night. You and Graham weren't even supposed to be in the building. It's my fault he's gone."

She was already shaking her head, the tears spilling over. "No. Don't say that."

He closed his eyes. "You need to know what happened."

chapter
TWENTY-FOUR

THEN—PROM

"Isn't this the best night *ever*?" Kincaid asked dramatically as she stepped up behind Ash and put her chin on his shoulder. "It's so *romantic*. Like right out of a movie. I kind of wish a synchronized dance number would break out. Like in *Footloose*."

"I think that only happened in the eighties," Ash said, turning to face her. Even though he'd seen her a few times tonight, it was still like a gut punch to see her in her low-cut, flowing white dress. She looked like a damn princess. He'd wanted to ask her to dance a thousand times. "I think you're out of luck."

"Boo," she said, taking his hands and spinning him around. "But that's all right. Nothing's going to bring me down tonight. This has been the perfect night already."

Ash resisted the urge to pull her to him, to tell her how amazing she was. He released her hands. "Your perfect night involves bad music and disco lights in the gym? You should raise your standards, KC."

She smiled a secret smile. "No, it involves bad music, disco lights, and…" She leaned forward and lowered her voice. "Graham asking me to marry him."

The dancing people in the background seemed to freeze in Ash's vision, the world halting. "*What?*"

Kincaid bit her lip like she couldn't contain her excitement. "I know it sounds crazy, but he said if we elope this summer when we turn eighteen, we can apply for the married student dorm and I can share in some of his scholarship money. We won't have to live separately, and I can break any ties to my mom for good."

Ash stared at her, his skin going clammy. "You said *yes*?"

She rubbed goose bumps from her arms. "I told him I needed to think about it. I mean, it's a big deal. I wasn't expecting that."

A hard tremor moved through him. "No shit. You're out of your fucking mind to even consider it."

She reared back like he'd slapped her. "Wow, tell me how you really feel, Ash."

"I'm serious, KC. That's nuts."

"Is it really, though?" she asked. "I know we're young, but I mean, it's Graham. I love him. When you know, you know. Soul mates. Why wait?"

Ash's heartbeat was racing like he'd run a marathon. Had he passed out and was now having some nightmare? "You wait because it's dumb not to. Moving in with him would already be a really big deal. You don't need to marry the guy. That's crazy."

His head was spinning. He knew enough to know

that Kincaid couldn't be thinking straight. This was some fucked-up fairy tale she'd conjured up where she got rescued by the prince, had some magical life that would be nothing like how she'd grown up. He wanted to kidnap her until she came to her senses.

Kincaid's eyes narrowed. "Did you just call me crazy?"

"You're acting that way by even considering this," he said without apology. "If you're really that desperate to get away from your mom, come with me."

"*With you?*" she asked as if that were the most preposterous idea ever.

"Why not? We could be roommates. And I don't come with strings like Graham. You don't have to promise me a lifelong commitment and unlimited sex to get access to my bank account."

The ugly words were out before he could stop them.

"Screw you, Ash," she said. "I thought of all people, you would understand."

"KC, you can't—"

But before he could get out his words, Graham stepped up to join them. He threw an arm around Kincaid and smiled a lopsided smile. "They're about to announce prom king and queen. You ready, babe?"

Kincaid, a practiced expert at putting on a happy face, dropped the dagger look she was shooting at Ash and smiled brightly at her boyfriend. "I was born ready."

Graham, who'd been sipping discreetly from a flask since they'd arrived, took another nip from the bottle and tucked it back in his tuxedo jacket. "Where's your date, Isaacs?"

His date. Right. He had one of those. "Not sure." Evie

had disappeared with her friends a few minutes ago. He had a feeling she was leaving the gym in protest over the idea of people being awarded royalty status for popularity. "I think the bathroom."

Graham snorted. "She's going to miss the big show."

"I think she'll survive," Ash said, his gaze on Kincaid, his mind still reeling.

Mrs. McCreedy, the computer science teacher, stepped up to the mic and tapped it repeatedly to get everyone's attention. The obnoxious sound took a few seconds to work, but the crowd eventually quieted down so she could announce the candidates for king and queen. All faces turned toward the stage. Kincaid, ignoring Ash completely, started to bounce a little on her toes and sent Graham an oh-my-God-it's-time look. Ash would've smiled at her unbridled enthusiasm if he hadn't been so freaking pissed at her.

"Thank you for your attention." Mrs. McCreedy went on to list all the candidates in quick succession, only pausing briefly to allow clapping, and then gave a pointed look to the DJ to cue him for the fake drumroll. The school's peppy fight song came on instead, and a soft rumble of laughter went through the crowd. The DJ quickly fixed the mistake, and Mrs. McCreedy opened the envelope. She paused for dramatic effect and then beamed a big smile at the filled gym. "And the Class of 2005 has selected Justin Altemont and Kincaid Breslin as this year's king and queen! Congratulations, Justin and Kincaid!"

Half-hearted applause broke out from some and a few enthusiastic whoops from Justin's friends. A cheesy royal march song came on, but Ash was too busy watching the couple standing next to him to pay attention to anything else. Kincaid's face was all smiles as people turned to congratulate her. She made a little squee of excitement and then pecked Graham on the cheek. "I won!"

Graham's smile was big, but Ash knew him well enough to see that it was forced. Graham was supposed to be king. Not Justin. *Especially* not Justin. Graham leaned down and gave Kincaid a quick kiss. "Congratulations, babe."

"Come on, King and Queen," Mrs. McCreedy called out. "Come accept your crowns and give us a dance!"

Kincaid did a little spin, as though the excitement was too much to contain, and hugged Graham. "I'll be right back."

Graham didn't release her immediately. He put a hand on her forearm. "Don't dance with him," he said, his voice hard. "You know how he is with you."

Kincaid rolled her eyes and shoved him playfully in the shoulder. "Oh, come on, don't be silly. It's tradition. It'll be quick. Love you!"

Kincaid slipped out of Graham's hold and hurried off, completely oblivious to the stewing man she'd left behind. Normally, Ash would've put a hand on Graham's shoulder and talked him down, but after what Kincaid had shared with him, he suddenly didn't want to intervene. He wanted to see what would happen. *Needed* to see.

Ash shoved his hands in his pockets and stood next to Graham while Kincaid stepped onto the stage and accepted her crown. He wet his lips and glanced at Graham. "She looks beautiful up there. Every dude's going to be jealous she's not with them."

Graham's fist flexed at his side. "Not Justin. Fucker gets to put his hands all over my girl. Look at that shit-eating grin on his face."

Ash looked toward the stage. Justin had wrapped his arm around Kincaid's waist and was mugging for the photographer who was snapping photos from every angle. Justin looked more concerned about the camera than Kincaid, though. "They're just old friends."

Graham didn't look Ash's way. "Yeah, old friends who've seen each other naked. Look how flirty she's being. She doesn't even see what she does."

Mrs. McCreedy announced that it was time for the royal dance, and "She Will Be Loved" by Maroon 5 started up. Justin took Kincaid's hand, bowed dramatically, and kissed her knuckles. Ash could feel Graham tense next to him. Kincaid, oblivious to anything at the moment but the high of winning prom queen, laughed and gave Justin a quick kiss on the cheek before they walked hand in hand to the dance floor. The crowd parted, and Justin pulled Kincaid closer than he needed to and danced while everyone watched.

Ash couldn't help but notice how breathtaking she looked under the lights. She was having such a good time, glowing with happiness, and a pit settled in his stomach because he could feel the anger wafting off Graham like a cloud of poison. The combo of alcohol and jealousy was swirling into a dangerous mix Ash was all too used to recognizing. A rope coiling tighter and tighter.

The song seemed endless, but as soon as the final bars finished, Graham was striding forward. He reached Kincaid, a razor-sharp smile on his face, and took her by the elbow, extracting her from Justin's hold. Kincaid looked up at Graham, clearly startled, but then an easy smile touched her lips, and she let him lead her away. Another song immediately started up, but Ash didn't move from the dance floor. His eyes were glued to his two friends.

They walked toward him, Kincaid beaming and Graham on edge. Kincaid adjusted her tiara when she reached Ash. "Hello, loyal subject. Your queen has arrived."

Ash bowed slightly, trying to play along. "Your Majesty."

"We're going to get out of here," Graham said abruptly.

Ash straightened at the harsh tone.

"What?" Kincaid frowned over at Graham. "But there's still an hour left. I'm supposed to take more pictures with Justin."

"Justin," Graham bit out, "can take pictures without my girlfriend draped all over him."

Kincaid rolled her eyes. "Not this again. I'm not into Justin. Stop freaking out about it."

"I'm not freaking out. I just want to be alone with my girl," Graham said, his tone softening, words slurring a little, a smile breaking through the tense line of his lips. "Is that too much to ask?"

Kincaid looked at him, obviously deliberating, and then sighed. "Fine. I guess we don't have to stay to the end. My feet are killing me anyway."

"Come on, let's go," Graham said, taking her hand. "I've got to call the limo driver and tell him we're ready early."

"Wait." Ash panicked, his hand shooting out to grab Graham's arm. "Hey, why don't you go and take care of that? I need to borrow Kincaid for minute. I'll walk her out after."

"For what?" Graham asked.

"Borrow? I'm not a library book, Ash," she said, still clearly mad at him. "What do you need?"

Ash scrambled, trying to come up with something that would make sense. "I have a... Evie needs something."

She gave him a look that said she was going to call him on his bullshit.

"Like a girl something," he hedged. "Please. She texted me from the bathroom."

"Oh." Kincaid sighed, and her expression turned sympathetic. "Damn, poor girl. Period on prom night is epic suckage, and they never stock those damn bathrooms. Yeah, I can help her out. Walk me to my locker."

"Can't she get that from someone else?" Graham asked.

Kincaid patted his shoulder. "I'll just be a minute, baby. Girls need to help out other girls. I'm sure the limo guy will take a few minutes anyway."

Graham sighed. "Five minutes, all right? Don't get distracted. I'm ready to get out of here."

"Got it." Kincaid gave him a quick kiss and started to walk toward the side door.

Before Ash could follow her, Graham grabbed his tuxedo sleeve. "Keep Justin away from her, okay? I don't want to have to beat his ass on prom night."

"No problem," Ash said, his neck muscles so tight he could barely nod.

Graham released him and headed for the main doors,

his gait a little off-kilter from whatever he was drinking. Ash strode after Kincaid to catch up. She glanced his way when he fell into step beside her. "I don't want to fight with you. Can we drop it?"

"I don't want to fight either."

She took that as meaning he was done talking to her about it, even though that wasn't what he'd said. She made a sour face. "I can't believe Graham wants to leave early. I'm supposed to be in the pictures. I'm supposed to dance around with my tiara. This is our last high school dance ever. Why the rush?"

"He's pissed about Justin," Ash said carefully. "Like really, really pissed. You should've seen him when you were dancing."

"Oh my God," she said with a dramatic groan as her heels clicked along the gym floor. "He needs to get over that shit. I already dated Justin. I have no desire to do that again. How could he propose to me and then suspect I'm, like, interested in someone else?"

"Because he's got major jealousy issues." They pushed the metal bar that opened the side door and stepped into the hallway, the music dulling when the door clicked shut. Kincaid turned as if to go toward the main hall and her locker, but Ash touched her shoulder, halting her. "Hey, hold up."

She turned, distracted, her mind probably already three steps ahead of where she needed to be. "What's wrong?"

Ash glanced down the hallway to make sure they were alone. "I don't want you to go home with Graham tonight."

Her brows dipped in confusion. "What are you talking about? I know he's been drinking, but we have a limo."

Ash squared off with her, putting her back to the end of the hallway that opened into the main part of the school. Her tiara had slipped a little sideways and her lipstick was long gone, but Ash had never seen her look more innocent. She had no idea, and he didn't want to hurt her with what he knew deep down was the truth. But he couldn't keep his mouth shut any longer. "It's not just that he's drinking. He's crossed the line from being the loving boyfriend to being the possessive, suspicious asshole. Graham is my friend, but he's going down a scary path, and I'm not going to let him take you down that path with him. I know where it leads. I live in the house at the end of that path. It's not safe to go home with him tonight. And it's sure as hell not safe to move in with him or marry him."

Kincaid's eyes widened. "Have you lost your mind? You think Graham would *hit* me? Ash, that's crazy. He would never."

"Why do you think he proposed, KC?" he said, a pleading note in his voice.

She gave him an affronted look. "Because he *loves* me. Oh my God, what is wrong with you?"

"No, it's because he's insecure," Ash said, talking fast. "He wants to lock you down."

"Jesus. This is ridiculous." She stared at him as if he needed to be put in a white padded room. "Graham isn't violent."

"He's ready to hit Justin. He told me before he walked out. Justin who didn't do a damn thing."

She threw her hands out to her sides. "It's just because he's drinking and because I didn't say yes to the proposal yet. His caveman gene has been poked."

"It's more than that," Ash said, in too deep to turn back now. "I've been worried for a while with some of the stuff he's asked me about you. It's only a matter of time before that anger is triggered and directed at you. When you're living in some apartment with him away from everyone you know, when there's a legally binding ring around your finger and he's all you have. No one will be there to help you then. And his parents will be paying your bills. You'll be stuck."

She made a frustrated sound. "You're totally overreacting. Graham is not like your dad. You're seeing things that aren't there. Look, I've got to get going. He's waiting."

"Make him wait," Ash said, his own frustration boiling over. "You don't have to do any of this, KC. If you want to get away from your mom, come with me to New York. There are community colleges there. Get loans. We can get part-time jobs together. Earn our own way. Not be dependent on anyone."

She stared at him, incredulous. "Ash…what is all this? I don't understand."

Footsteps sounded somewhere down the hall behind her. Ash's gaze jumped that way, monitoring. He could feel the clock ticking down. "Stay here. Enjoy the rest of prom. If he wants you to go home, he can come and drag you out. Then you'll see."

"See what?"

"That he's dangerous."

Graham appeared at the end of the hallway, far enough away not to hear but close enough for Ash to see his annoyed stance. Kincaid must've noticed where Ash was looking because she started to turn, but Ash gripped her shoulders before she could, pulled her to him, and kissed her.

He felt her body jolt at the contact, and a sound squeaked past her lips, but Ash wasn't going back now. This was his last chance to convince her. He let one of his hands slide up from her shoulder to the back of her neck under the curtain of her hair. He expected to have about one point two seconds before she shoved him away or kneed him in the balls, but to his shock, she didn't move away. Instead, her lips parted, maybe on surprise, but it deepened the kiss, and he felt fire race through his veins.

The footsteps in the background quickened. Ash made a sound in the back of his throat that he would've liked to say was for the show he was putting on for Graham but was completely involuntary. He was kissing Kincaid. *Finally.* And she was kissing him back...

But one moment he had that thought, the next, Kincaid was being yanked back from him. Kincaid yelped and Graham glowered at Ash. "What. The. Fuck?"

Ash had never seen such absolute rage in Graham's eyes, but he saw it now. His survival instincts said to run, but he'd started this. He needed to finish it. He forced his voice not to shake. "Sorry you had to see that, man. We've been trying to find a way to tell you."

"Ash!" Kincaid gasped, horrified, her cheeks flushed beet red. "What—"

"I told her we should tell you," Ash plowed ahead, trying to sound casual. "But things just happened. You can only sleep in your best friend's bed so many times before lines get crossed, you know."

"That's not true!" Kincaid protested, looking

frantically back and forth between the two of them. "Oh my God, Graham, don't believe him."

Graham sent a hateful look her way, his grip on her upper arm harsh. "How long?"

"Never," Kincaid said, tears flooding her eyes. "Ouch, you're hurting me."

The sight of her so upset broke Ash into pieces, and he wanted to rip Graham's hand off her, but he had to do this. "It only happened a few times. We were going to tell you after prom."

Kincaid turned to him with a devastated look on her face. "Ash…"

Ash's heart broke. She would hate him after this. He would lose her. But she would be safe.

There was a ruckus somewhere out of sight down the hall, but neither Kincaid nor Graham turned around to look.

"You fuck her?" Graham said, trembling with volcanic anger.

Ash's gaze met Kincaid's, a silent sorry, and then he shrugged. Graham charged forward, and Ash tried to duck but it was too late. Graham's fist smashed into his jaw. Ash fell backward, skidding across the slick floor, pain radiating through his face and ear.

"Stop it!" Kincaid yelled. "Both of you!"

But Graham had lost all ability to control himself, exactly what Ash had wanted to show her. That almost made the kick Graham delivered to Ash's ribs worth it.

Kincaid grabbed at Graham. "Stop! You're going to really hurt him."

"That's the idea." He kicked Ash again, making him curl into the fetal position.

Kincaid sobbed and yanked at Graham's jacket. "Stop. Please."

Graham whirled around. "Why? Don't want me beating up your best buddy? I always knew you two were too close. I should've known."

"What?" she pleaded. "Graham, I would *never*. I love you. I don't know why he's saying this."

Graham grabbed her roughly by the bicep and hustled her away, one of her heels falling off in the hallway as he guided her into an alcove farther down the hall. Ash could hear him yelling and tried to roll to his feet. Pain was shooting through his side where Graham had kicked him, every move making him gasp. This wasn't part of the plan. He wasn't going to let him hurt Kincaid.

But right as Ash climbed to his feet, a loud noise like a firecracker sounded from somewhere down the other end of the hall, out of sight. Someone screamed, and there was another bang.

No.

Not a firecracker.

Ash remembered the sound from when his dad had made him go to the range.

A gunshot. An icy sense of dread filled him.

A figure dressed in black appeared at the end of the hallway. Ash's whole world zeroed down to that one sight, and panic bolted through him. "Oh fuck."

Ash took off in the opposite direction, running toward Kincaid and Graham, even though it was a dead end. A new kind of fear filled him, one that had his muscles wanting to seize up. When he turned the corner into the alcove, Graham had caged Kincaid in with his arms. He was sobbing and asking her why, why had she hurt him like this. Mascara-black tears streaked her face as she pleaded with him to believe her.

"Stop," Ash cried. "We've got to run. Someone's—"

"Get the hell away, Isaacs," Graham seethed. "Or I will fucking end you."

Kincaid's eyes went wide.

Ash forced himself between them, pushing Graham away from her, but Graham shoved him hard, knocking him backward into Kincaid. Ash felt her body collide against his back, heard her hit the cinder-block wall.

He spun around right as she slumped to the floor. Her eyes closed, knocked out cold.

"No. No, no, *no*," Ash said, terror overtaking him.

"Oh God." Graham rushed to Kincaid. He cradled her head in his hands, all traces of anger gone. "Baby…" He looked to Ash. "She's hurt. I didn't mean to. I swear…oh God."

Ash's heart was going to beat out of his chest. "Listen to me. We need to pick her up and get out of here," he said, his voice shaking. "Someone has a gun."

Graham blinked. Ash could hear screams now coming from the gym, a steady *pop, pop, pop* sound. It was like being in a nightmare, everything moving too slow and too fast at once.

"*A gun?*" Graham asked as if coming out of a fog.

Ash needed him to move and stop asking questions. "We have to—"

"Yeah, a gun," said a cold voice.

Ash's and Graham's attention whirled to the entrance of the alcove. The barrel of a black gun was aimed right at them, Trevor Lockwood's eyes looking deadly serious as he glanced down at Kincaid's slumped form on the floor. Graham jumped to his feet, hands going upward.

Ash shifted in front of Kincaid, blocking her with his body, his limbs shaking with adrenaline.

Graham took a slow step to the side, distracting Trevor from his aim at Kincaid and Ash. "Whoa, dude, put that away. That's not funny."

Trevor swung his aim toward Graham. "Oh, it's not funny? Good observation, Lowell."

Ash's throat had gone so narrow he didn't know if he could force out words. "Trevor, please. Don't do this."

Trevor cocked his head to the left. "Get out of here, Isaacs. You're not on the list." He peered down at Kincaid. "But these two are."

Ash wet his lips, his body numb with fear. "I'm not leaving her."

"Oh, but her boyfriend's expendable, huh?" Trevor asked, the gun trained on Graham.

Ash froze, no words coming out of his mouth.

Trevor's gaze went hard. "Good call."

"No!" Ash cried out.

Graham lunged to tackle Trevor, but Trevor was too quick. He pulled the trigger twice, hitting Graham right in the chest. Ash screamed, the sound lost to the deafening shots exploding in the small space, and his vision dotted with black. No...*red*.

Trevor looked at Ash after Graham slumped to the floor. Ash lay across Kincaid, his whole body racked with tremors. They were going to die.

"She's all yours now." Trevor smirked, his eyes cold and empty. "You're welcome."

And then he was gone, jogging down the hallway

and toward the sounds of chaos in the gym. Ash gasped for breath and was shaking all over as he crawled to Graham's side. Graham was breathing but barely. "Graham, it's going to be okay. I'm going to get help. Just hang on, man. Please."

Graham didn't open his eyes, but his lips moved as he struggled to whisper something.

Ash didn't understand. "Graham."

"Get her out," he whispered, voice strained. "Go."

Tears fell down Ash's face. "I'll send help. I'm sorry, man. I'm so fucking sorry. She loves you, okay. I lied. I made it all up."

Graham didn't say anything after that, and Ash couldn't wait around. He had no idea how many shooters were in the school. All he knew was that Trevor wasn't alone. He had no guarantee that the next one who found them would spare them. He hustled back to Kincaid and lifted her off the floor, cradling her against him. With one more look at Graham, Ash checked to make sure the hallway was empty and then ran for their lives.

On the way, he tried not to look at the blood on the floor, tried to block out the screams. Kincaid moaned in his arms, coming to, as he pushed through a doorway and into the side parking lot where they stored the buses.

"What's going on?" she mumbled, confused.

"Shh," he said, glancing over his shoulder, making sure no one was behind them as he weaved around a bus. "Quiet, KC."

"Ash?" she repeated. "My head…"

His arms were quivering, his legs burning, and his lungs screaming from the hard run and the kick to the ribs. He was going to drop her if he didn't put her down soon. He needed to find a place for them to hide. Police sirens wailed in the distance. *Too far*.

Ash got to the far side of the parking lot and hurried behind a fenced-off dumpster. He lowered Kincaid to the ground as gently as he could, propping her up against the fence. His entire body was shaking so hard he could barely control his movements. He knelt next to her, pushing her hair away from her face. "KC, listen to me. We need to be quiet."

"Why?" Her eyes squinted as she tried to focus on him. She reached up and touched his cheek, which he knew had to be wet with more than tears. Fear entered her expression when she realized it was blood. "Oh God. You're bleeding. What's happening?"

His heart broke open. He didn't want to tell her. He didn't want this to be real. *Please don't let this be real*. But there was no waking up. He swallowed past the fear trapped in his throat. "Someone brought guns to prom. They opened fire. You were knocked out."

Awareness widened her eyes, and she sat up straighter, reaching out to grab his arm as though she was dizzy. "Where's Graham?"

Ash closed his eyes.

"Ash," she said, an urgent whisper. "*Where is he?*"

Tears dripped off his chin. "He was shot, KC. Trevor Lockwood shot him. As soon as the cops get here, I'll tell them where to find him so they can help him."

She stared at him as if she hadn't heard the words right. "Graham's alive?"

Ash couldn't breathe. "He was…struggling."

She tried to scramble to her feet, her balance off. "We need to go back in. We need to get him out!"

Ash jumped up and grabbed her arm. "KC, we can't. The shooters are still in there. You can't go back in."

She looked at him like he was crazy. "Graham is *in there*. I'm not leaving him."

She tried to push past him, but Ash wrapped his arms around her from behind, some reserve of strength coming from a deep place of fear. "You can't."

"Let me go, Ash," she said, near hysterical, struggling in his grip.

More screams came from the school, a few people probably running out.

Ash wished it were different. He wished there was a way to go in and save Graham, save anyone in there who needed help, but he knew if they went back in, they wouldn't be coming out. Kincaid was on whatever sick list Trevor had. So even as Kincaid started to sob and curse at him, he held tight, his bruised ribs screaming in protest, his eyes closed, and grief like he never experienced filling him.

"You can't go," he said in a whisper. "I won't let you."

Kincaid fought for a few seconds longer, but the sirens got closer, and her strength wore out. They both slumped back to the ground, Ash still bear-hugging her from behind. He wasn't sure his arms would've released even if he'd wanted them to.

By the time the cops and paramedics were able to get into the building, Graham had stopped breathing. He was gone. Ash had drawn his friend back into the school to prove a point, and Graham had never walked out again. He'd given a killer an opening. And when he'd been asked if Graham was expendable, he hadn't shouted his protest.

Graham was dead because of him.

chapter

TWENTY-FIVE

ASH FINISHED HIS STORY, HIS SKIN HOT ALL OVER, HIS CHEST aching, and his eyes damp with tears. He stared at his hands, afraid to look at Kincaid. He already knew she was crying. He could hear the hitch in her breath, see the tears that had fallen onto her hands, which she'd braced on her thighs. "I'm so sorry."

She was quiet for a few long moments, her breathing audible in the quiet apartment. "You're sorry."

He closed his eyes, hearing the knife edge in her voice. "I know that's not enough. I don't know what else to say. There aren't words for this."

She took a shaky inhale next to him, and her hands curled in her lap. "Ash, do you know how many times I've had to sit down with my friends and tell them that what happened at the shooting was not their fault?"

He pressed his lips together and ventured a glance over at her.

Her eyes were red and puffy but her gaze was resolute. "From day one, I have believed and still believe that no one in the school that night was responsible for deaths besides the two people who had the guns." She licked her dry lips. "You are *not* responsible for Graham's death. We could've been shot in the parking lot. Or stopping by the bathrooms. If you hadn't been there, they would've shot me, too. You had no idea any of that was going to happen when you asked me to stay behind. Don't put that on yourself."

Hope rushed through him like clear, cool water. "KC—"

"But—" she said, cutting him off. "*How could you?*"

He winced at the betrayal in her voice.

"How could you lie to me all this time?" She pressed her fingers to her lips to stave off a sob, her eyes glittering with tears. It was a few seconds before she spoke again. "You let me think Graham was a hero. You let everyone think he was a *hero*."

"He was," Ash said emphatically. "In the worst moment of danger, he jumped for the gun. He put himself between the gun and us. He was trying to stop Trevor."

She squeezed her eyes shut. "He knocked me out, Ash."

He looked down. "That was an accident. I've gone over and over it in my head. Maybe I was seeing things that weren't there because of how my family was or because I wanted you so badly for myself. I wanted him to be flawed. When I found you two, I thought he'd hit you, but he was crying, devastated. He hadn't hurt you. He just wanted to punch me. He was panicked when you fell. His last words were telling me to get you out safely. He loved you. Everything else aside, I know that without a doubt."

A choked sound escaped her as the tears kept flowing. "You *lied*, Ash. You let me go on believing this myth." She winced as if in physical pain. "This myth that I had this great love in my life. That I'd had this soul mate who'd saved me."

"Kincaid—"

"When the truth is, he was just going to be another guy to let me down. Another bad choice." She looked up at him. "I'm real good at falling for guys who hurt me. And ones who lie to me."

The knife landed solid. "KC—"

She stilled suddenly and then looked at him with fresh horror. "When you came over to my house, *you knew all this*. You let me cry about Graham, and you climbed in my bed." She pressed her hand to her forehead. "Jesus. After all that, you got what you wanted. Graham was out of the picture, and you could look like the one to save me."

"No, *God*, it wasn't like that," he pleaded. "I was so messed up in the head that night I went to your house. I swear it wasn't calculated. When things started to cross the line, I thought maybe you had feelings for me. You'd kissed me back at prom. I was grieving and confused. But then you said Graham's name, and I knew I'd made a huge mistake."

She looked away.

"Afterward, I knew I had to leave town for good. I didn't deserve you, but I also knew I couldn't stay away. If you left the door open for me, I'd walk in. I didn't want to benefit from Graham's death." He raked his hands through his hair. "It makes me sick to think I'd get any benefit. Every time Charlie and Grace do something nice for me, every time they've welcomed me as their own, I feel that gut-wrenching guilt. And I swore I'd stay away from you. I tried to forget about you, tried to write my feelings off as a misguided high school crush. But…"

"But what?" she asked, not looking at him, tone unreadable.

He stared at nothing, feeling empty and scraped out from the inside. "But you're you. You were my best friend and the only girl I've ever loved like that. I loved you before him and after him and I love you now. I've accepted that the feeling is never going to go away. It's part of who I am. In my bones." He looked her way. "I'm the guy who's in love with Kincaid Breslin."

She stared at him for a long moment, her hazel eyes glistening. "Someone who loved me that much wouldn't have lied to me."

His breath sagged out of him, inevitability washing through him. He hadn't expected her to react any differently. He'd known what it would mean to tell her. This was his penance for what he'd done. He was destined to love the woman who could never love him back.

He rubbed his sweaty palms on his jeans and took a steadying breath. "I'm going to go."

She stiffened next to him. "What? Now?"

He stood, the bed squeaking. "I don't think there's anything left to say. The Lowells will let me use their guest room. You can have this place as long as you need."

Her jaw flexed. "You're just going to go?"

"KC…"

She looked away. "Fine. Go."

He moved quickly around the apartment on numb autopilot, dropping toiletries and clothes in a bag and grabbing his laptop and backpack. Kincaid stayed where she was on the bed, not saying a word.

When he grabbed the doorknob to leave, he looked back at her one last time, trying to memorize her face. "Goodbye, KC."

She didn't look his way. She didn't say goodbye.

He lifted his bag over his shoulder and walked out.

Kincaid lay in Ash's bed for hours, staring at the ceiling and letting the grief wash over her in a flood. She didn't know where to start with processing everything he'd told her. For all her adult life, she'd believed one story about what had happened to her the night of the Long Acre shooting. She'd used that story as a touchstone, a formative moment in her life, and then had painted myth and magic around it to give it meaning and purpose. She'd canonized Graham, had used him as proof that true love existed, that soul mates were real. She'd used her and Graham's relationship as a yardstick by which to judge all others. She'd believed that he'd been The One, that she'd lost The One.

But all this time, it'd been a lie. She'd just been fooling herself with some ridiculous fairy tale. There was no soul mate, no The One. The man she thought loved her had been possessive, manipulative, and insecure. The best friend she thought she could count on had lied to her face.

Men couldn't be trusted. Period. Full stop.

Maybe her mother had been right.

The early-morning sun started to turn the room pink, the ceiling she'd been staring at shifting shades. She took a deep breath. Her throat was raw, her eyes burning, and her body sapped. Part of her wanted to lie here all day. Be miserable. Feel sorry for herself. Wallow with a capital *W*. But another part of her, the outspoken part of her, was wagging a finger at her. This was not who she was.

She would not be this person.

With all the effort she could muster, she rolled over and felt around for her purse on the floor. When she found it, she dug inside and pulled out her phone.

Screw this crying-alone bullshit. She called the people in her life she could actually count on.

Liv answered on the third ring with a groggy "Hello?"

She cleared her throat, trying to find her voice after all the crying. "I need brunch."

"Kincaid?" Liv asked, sounding more awake. "It's barely seven. And it's not Sunday."

"An emergency brunch. I—" She choked on a sob. *Dammit.*

"Are you crying? Shit. What's going on? Where are you?" Liv's voice was sharp now, concerned. "Are you okay?"

"I'm in the apartment above the bookstore." She sniffed. "Ash and I... He left."

"Give me thirty minutes," Liv said over the sound of rustling sheets. "I'll call Bec and Taryn."

A wave of relief went through Kincaid. "Thank you."

"Of course," Liv said, her tone tender. "We've got you, girlie. We've always got you."

Kincaid closed her eyes, quiet tears tracking down her face. "That's all I need."

And it was. If life was trying to teach her a lesson, that was it. She ended the call and inhaled a deep breath, letting it fill her with resolve. She grabbed the bedsheet and wiped the tears from her cheeks. *Enough*. She'd survived far worse. She would get through this.

So she'd been lied to. So she'd been hurt. So she'd fallen in love and, for one brief moment, thought she would finally get her own love story and the romantic fairy tale.

But she didn't need that manufactured dream anymore.

She already had a family. She had her friends. Three strong, amazing, wonderful women who loved her and always, *always* had her back.

That was enough. That was everything.

Kincaid Breslin was *not* going to lose it over a guy.

She would get her happy ending—all on her own.

chapter
TWENTY-SIX

LIV PUSHED A STACK OF BOXES INTO A CORNER OF THE kitchen, making sure they weren't going to topple over, and then stretched her arms above her head. Her back popped in three places and she groaned, the physical exhaustion complete.

She, Kincaid, and the guys had spent the entire day carrying boxes out of the moving truck and into the farmhouse. Finn, Wes, and Shaw had handled the furniture, and Liv and Kincaid had focused on the boxes. Taryn and Rebecca had been under strict orders not to lift anything, so they'd taken on other tasks—unpacking a few of the boxes, cleaning windows, and keeping everyone hydrated. They all looked as if they'd been through a long day at the gym.

"Is that the last of them?" Taryn asked as she loaded dishes into the kitchen cabinets.

"Yes, thank God," Liv said and went to the sink to rinse her hands. "The guys headed out. Shaw said to give him a call before bed and not to lift anything heavy."

Taryn rolled her eyes, but a little smile played around her lips. "I think he told me that approximately a hundred thousand times today. I'm pregnant, not an invalid. I actually feel great."

Liv smiled. "I think it's cute, how beside themselves Shaw and Wes are around you two. Just imagine how they're going to be once the babies are here."

Taryn snorted. "Picture padded rooms and no sharp corners in the entire place. Shaw may try to wrap the kid in bubble wrap."

Liv laughed.

"Don't laugh, lady," Rebecca said, stepping into the kitchen, her auburn hair in a messy ponytail and cleaning supplies in her hands. "Finn will be worse whenever y'all have kids."

Liv took the cleaning supplies from her and tossed her a hand towel. "I think we're going to stick with being a fantastic aunt and uncle for now, maybe forever. We're talking about getting a puppy, though. I think that's more our speed."

"Ooh," Rebecca said. "You should talk to Marco. He works with a great shelter. Knight can have a cousin!"

Liv grinned at the idea of Rebecca's big floppy dog trying to play with a puppy. The cuteness would probably kill them all. "Sounds like a plan."

"Speaking of which," Taryn said, turning around and leaning back against the counter. "What's our plan for tonight?"

"I'm not sure." Her friends' grim expressions probably matched her own. They'd been spending time with Kincaid since the morning of the emergency brunch, but none of them felt like they'd gotten a handle on what exactly was going on with her. After the early-morning phone call a few days ago, Liv had expected a sobbing, heartbroken Kincaid. But when she'd picked her up for brunch, she'd been dressed to the nines, makeup perfectly applied despite the puffy eyes, and a determined smile on her face.

All she'd told them was that Ash had to leave and their "little tryst" was done, but that she was going to be *fine, just fine. No big deal*. Liv knew that mode. She'd been a regular practitioner of the never-let-them-see-you-cry method for years before she met Finn. Her mask was a badass bitch face—the I'm-tough, nothing-gets-to-me, I-don't-need-anyone face. Kincaid's mask was the everything's-just-peachy-keen smile and a relentlessly positive attitude.

Rebecca nibbled at her thumbnail, a line appearing between her brows. "I'm really worried about her. I don't know why she feels like she has to hide whatever is going on from us. I mean, she's seen us at our worst. She doesn't always have to be the cheerleader. We can be that for her when she needs it."

Taryn sighed. "I don't think she's hiding from us. At least not purposely. Whatever went down with Ash was a big deal." She crossed her arms, her pondering psychologist face on. "She's selling this *happy, happy, joy, joy* thing to herself so she doesn't have to deal with whatever she's feeling. But if we call her on it, she'll just get defensive and retreat further into denial."

Liv frowned. "So there's nothing we can do?"

Taryn shrugged. "All we can do is be here for her, show her that she has our support, and when she's ready to talk, hopefully she will."

"I think getting this place in livable order will help," Rebecca said. "I know when I'm upset about something, having a big project to focus on can do wonders."

"Well," Liv said with a yawn. "I'm done with *this* project for today. I'm thinking our intervention for tonight should be finding the lady in question to make her stop working and then ordering pizza and settling in for a night of Netflix."

"I vote for that," Taryn agreed. "That is, if the Wi-Fi that got installed this afternoon actually works. The cable guy looked perplexed by the farmhouse's wiring. It's never a good sign when a technician leaves and wishes you good luck."

Rebecca smirked. "Guess if that doesn't work, we'll be down to telling slumber-party ghost stories."

"Oh, hell no," Liv said, opening the fridge to grab a few bottles of water. "We are not telling creepy-ass stories in this big, old house. That's how horror movies start out."

Her friends laughed, and they all went in search of Kincaid to declare quitting time. Liv called out Kincaid's name, and her voice echoed down the hallway and up the stairs. Even with the furniture and boxes moved in, this place swallowed Kincaid's stuff. The house had to be three times the size of the lake house.

When Kincaid didn't answer, they peeked into a few of the rooms on the ground floor and then headed upstairs. "Kincaid," Liv called out in a singsong voice. "Where are you?"

There was a creaking sound from one of the rooms.

Liv groaned. "Girl, if you jump out at me from the dark, I cannot be held responsible for what I do to you. My husband has taught me FBI moves."

Taryn made clucking chicken sounds behind her, and Rebecca snickered.

"Shut up, you two," Liv said, her skin prickling even though she knew there was nothing to be afraid of. She walked over to the one closed door on the second floor and turned the knob. For a moment, she was bracing for a jump scare from her friend. But instead, she found Kincaid sitting on the floor of a guest bedroom, legs pulled up to her chest with her forehead resting on her knees. Under the high ceiling and in the mostly empty room, she looked like a sad Alice who'd just tumbled into the rabbit hole.

"Kincaid?" Liv stepped into the bedroom, her heart sinking. "You okay, *chica?*"

Kincaid lifted her head. Where Liv had expected to see that fake smile Kincaid had been wielding for days, she saw tears instead. They'd tracked lines down the smudged dust on her face.

Taryn and Rebecca stepped up behind Liv. "Oh, honey," Taryn said, empathy heavy in her voice.

Kincaid gave them a terse smile. "I'm fine."

"Yeah, you totally look it." Liv walked over and crouched in front of her. "I curl into the fetal position and cry when I'm fine, too."

Kincaid sniffled. "I'm just overtired."

"Uh-huh." Liv sat next to her, a ripple of relief going through her. She hated to see her friend sad, but that was better than seeing her pretend everything was fine when it so obviously wasn't. "What's going on?"

"Nothing." She swiped at her face. "It's stupid."

"I love stupid," Liv assured her. "Tell me."

Kincaid exhaled and pointed to an open box a few feet away. "That."

The box was labeled *Random Shit*. That made Liv smile. Throughout the day she'd been amused by Kincaid's creative use of labeling. *Kitchen Junk. Stuff I Should Get Rid of But Won't. Photos to Blackmail Friends With. The Body.*

That last one had given Liv pause, especially since the box had been so heavy. But when she'd opened it, it'd been filled with fitness equipment. Kincaid had laughed. *"You were supposed to bury that one. What kind of friend are you?"*

Rebecca walked over to the box and opened the flaps. Liv got to her feet and joined her. She pulled out a stack of business cards wrapped with a rubber band. The name of Kincaid's food blog was on it. She dropped those back inside. There were books about flipping houses. A legal pad with what looked to be a menu scribbled on it in Kincaid's looping handwriting. Real estate books. Yarn. Some kind of machine to make jewelry.

Liv turned to her, confused. She'd thought this had something to do with Ash. "I don't get it."

Kincaid leaned against the wall, arms still wrapped around her knees. "I should've labeled that box *Half-Finished Projects*. Or maybe *Failures*. Or *Impulsive Things I Bought But Never Followed Through On*." Her eyes welled again. "I'm a real pro at starting things."

"So," Liv said, coming back to her side of the room and sitting in front of Kincaid cross-legged. "That means you're creative, that you have a lot of ideas."

Kincaid shook her head. "That's just it, though. I'm full of ideas and dreams and plans, but I go off half-cocked all the time. I curl my lip at my mom's gambling addiction, but who am I to judge? I'm addicted to the ideas of things.

To the fantasy images of a happy life. What's the point of having grand visions if I don't have what it takes to make them come true? That box is filled with things I was so excited about." She leaned her head back against the wall and closed her eyes. "Just like this house."

"Kincaid—" Taryn said from somewhere behind Liv.

"Look at this place." Kincaid spread out her hands. "You know how much it needs to turn it into a retreat where people would actually want to stay? To turn it into a business?"

Liv gave her a sympathetic look. "Babe, it's okay to feel overwhelmed. Yes, this is going to be a huge project, but it's not an impossible one. It's like me trying to imagine an art show before I've taken one photograph or created one piece. That feels daunting and impossible every time. You have to start with one little step forward. Eventually you get to the end."

"I don't have the money." Quiet tears trailed down her cheeks. "I thought maybe I could make it work. But this is too big. Too grand." She pressed the spot between her eyes. "When am I going to stop hoping for the fairy tale? What is wrong with me?"

"The fairy tale?" Liv asked, pushing a stray hair away from Kincaid's face, her heart hurting for her friend.

Kincaid looked down. "Yes. I think it's the lie I had to tell myself when I was little. If things were as bad as they were, then I must be Cinderella, right? I was paying some penance that was going to get rewarded down the line."

A little fissure went through Liv's heart at the earnestness in her friend's voice. She knew what that felt like. "Kincaid."

"One day, I would get to be happy. I wouldn't be the girl ignored by her mom or deemed not worth the trouble by her dad. I'd have my pretty house and a job I loved and maybe my very own prince. Friends who loved me. A family." Her voice caught. "I thought I was on my way senior year. That life was falling into place. I had plans for school. I had a boyfriend I loved. A best friend who meant everything to me."

Liv nodded, listening, knowing how that story ended.

"And then the shooting happened," she continued. "I lost Graham. Everything fell apart. And I thought, *surely*, this is the ultimate penance. I get to the good part now. I get to the part that doesn't hurt so much. Right?"

Liv's ribs contracted. "Oh, sweetie."

Kincaid lifted her gaze. "I've tried so hard to be happy," she said, voice fervent. "I've been determined not to give my parents' failings a say in my life, not to give the shooters a say. I've tried to give them all the finger and declare, *Just you wait. Look at me. I'm going to show all of you how deliriously happy my life can be*." She started crying audibly, her breath hitching. "And I am sometimes. I really am. I have Grace and Charlie. I have you guys. Y'all are my heart." She pressed her hand to her chest. "I'm so lucky in so many ways. But right now, sitting in this house that I know isn't going to become anything, this house that will one day be labeled *Kincaid's Random Shit*, I just feel like I never got out of that crappy house on Pine Street. This place is bigger, but there are still holes in the floor and empty rooms with no one home but me."

Liv's heart broke for her friend, and she slid into the spot next to her to put her arm around her. Taryn and

Rebecca lowered to the floor with them, surrounding Kincaid and putting their hands on her.

Liv squeezed her friend tight as Kincaid cried softly. "You are not alone, *chica*. You will always have us, and even if it takes a few years, you can make this project happen. We'll help you with whatever you need."

"She's right," Rebecca said in a gentle voice. "I know this feels overwhelming right now, but if I had any doubt at all that you could turn this place into that dream you see in your head, I would tell you. You're looking in that box and seeing the things you've quit, but I can look at your life and see the things you haven't." She squeezed Kincaid's knee. "You came from less than nothing. You had so much working against you. Do you know how many people actually make it out of that kind of situation?"

Kincaid was curled into Liv's shoulder, but Liv could sense she was listening.

"You had no one giving you a hand. You had a mother who probably should've been locked up for negligence. An absentee father. *You survived a goddamned massacre*," Liv said. "Yet you walked away from those things and built a career. You saved your money and bought a house. You brought us back together and have been such an amazing friend to each of us that none of us would be where we are right now without you in our corner. Now, you're starting your own business." She brushed a hand over her friend's hair. "You, Kincaid Breslin, are astounding."

"And amazing," Taryn added.

"And adored," Rebecca said with a smile.

"And absolutely not alone," Liv finished.

Kincaid sniveled against Liv's shoulder. "Yeah?"

Liv smiled. "One hundred percent. You are stuck with us, cookie. Get used to it."

Kincaid lifted her head and looked at all of them, a quivery little smile breaking through. "Hey. You can't steal my baked-goods terms of endearment. They're trademarked."

"I apologize." Liv said with a grin. "But seriously, close your eyes for a second."

Kincaid lifted a brow but obliged.

Liv looked to Rebecca and Taryn and then back to Kincaid. "I want you to imagine it's two years from now. You've saved some money and found a few investors. You've made the bed-and-breakfast into the place you imagined when we first stepped inside the farmhouse. It's now your opening weekend. You're standing on the porch, you're humming with excitement, and your hand is on the doorknob. You open the door to go inside. What do you see?"

Kincaid kept her eyes closed and took a deep breath before wetting her lips. "I see a big arrangement of wildflowers on the table by the door, and I hear people talking. I walk in, and the hardwood floors are buffed to a shine and creak just enough to be comforting. There's music playing, someone tinkering on the piano in the room off to the left. In the main living room, it's afternoon snack time. The smell of fresh baked cookies and brewed coffee is in the air. Two kids are sitting in front of the fireplace playing a board game. Adults are chatting. The whole room is done in whites and earthy greens. It's almost Christmas, and a giant tree has been put up in front of the main windows. Each guest gets to make and add their own ornament."

Liv nodded, trying to imagine it along with her. "And what are you doing?"

"I'm circulating the room, passing around cookies I made, talking with everyone, making them feel at home. I feel energized by all the chatter, but then I sneak off into the kitchen to refill the plate. The kitchen is shiny and new, the counters gleaming. The whole room smells like browned butter. I want to sneak a cookie myself, so I take a plate into the main bedroom, which is done in pale blues with a big, fluffy white bed. I think I'm alone, but then a hand reaches out and takes me by the elbow and…"

Liv nudged her. "And what?"

Kincaid opened her eyes and ducked her head, not meeting her friends' gazes. "Never mind. I get your point."

Liv searched her face. "Who took you by the elbow?"

Kincaid shifted away. "Doesn't matter. Y'all are going to let me get carried away with the fantasies, and we'll starve to death. Thank you for the pep talk. Let's get cleaned up and order some pizza."

"Hey," Taryn said, catching Kincaid's eye. "Was it Graham who took your elbow?"

Kincaid winced. "No. I don't need a guy in this fantasy. This is going to be my business."

Liv could tell she was spooked, but maybe they were finally getting somewhere. "Kincaid, was it *Ash*?"

Kincaid stood and dusted off the back of her jeans. "You think they deliver pizza all the way out here? Maybe we should drive into town and eat out."

Liv got to her feet, a pang of compassion filling her. "Oh, *chica*, why didn't you tell us?"

Kincaid crossed her arms. "Tell you what?"

Rebecca smiled sadly. "That you fell in love."

———

Kincaid looked around at her friends' empathetic faces, panic welling in her. She shook her head, not wanting to cry anymore. "I don't want to talk about it."

Liv smirked. "Uh-huh."

Her friend's knowing look had her defenses crumbling like a gingerbread house. They knew her too well. When did she ever *not* want to talk? She let out a defeated sigh. "Let's order pizza first and then I'll tell y'all everything."

Rebecca smiled and reached out to give Kincaid's hand a squeeze. "It's about time."

"Yeah," Taryn said, stepping up next to them. "You've been there for us. Now it's our turn to repay the favor."

"Falling in love sucks," Kincaid declared.

"Ha," Liv said, joining them. "Girl, preach."

"Amen," Rebecca said.

"And hallelujah," Taryn finished.

They walked downstairs together, ordered pizza, and settled in for a long night.

chapter
TWENTY-SEVEN

ASH SAT DOWN AT THE BUSY RESTAURANT IN CHELSEA, THE noise and compactness of the restaurant almost too much after his time in Long Acre. He'd already forgotten how frenetic the pace was in New York City. He adjusted the collar of his shirt and tried to settle his nerves.

"What's your poison?" Alice, his editor, asked as she took her seat across from him and picked up the menu.

"Club soda with lime." He didn't think his stomach could handle much more than that. He'd barely been able to choke down a meal since he'd left Kincaid in that apartment. Everything he ate tasted like dust.

Alice smiled at the waiter. "Make that two."

The waiter hurried off, and Alice folded her hands on the table, her short blond hair glinting in the bright light of the restaurant. "It's great to see you, Ash. I didn't realize you were back in New York already."

"Just got back," he said, trying to sound upbeat and failing miserably. "Thanks for being willing to meet with me on such short notice."

"Not a problem. We've got lots to discuss." She pulled out a Moleskine notebook from her bag. "Did you enjoy your visit back home?"

"It was fine." If *fine* was getting your heart thoroughly broken and your guts dug out with a rusty spoon. "Visited family. Got some writing done."

She nodded, warmth there, and he settled some. He could do this. He could pretend to act like a normal, functioning human for a little while. He and Alice had always had a great working relationship. Just because his last book hadn't sold as well as they'd hoped didn't mean she didn't want to ever work with him again. Publishing was a business. They both had the same goal—sell a lot of great books. "So I hear. Your agent sent me your most recent pages. It's quite a shift from your previous books."

He sat up straighter in his chair, worried the hammer of a big, fat *no* was about to come down on him. "I know it's pretty different from what I've written before, but—"

"I loved them," she said, saving him from his rambling.

Ash let out a breath of relief. "Really?"

"Truly," she said with a nod. "I've always been impressed with your fast-moving plots, and I never see your twists coming, which is why I bought your first series in the first place." She accepted her drink from the waiter. "But these new pages… The characters really leap off the page, especially"—she checked her notes—"Katherine. She's a really strong partner for Gideon, challenges him. I'm rooting for her. Readers will, too."

His neck muscles seemed to be unlocking one by one,

his shoulders sinking down from their tight position by his ears. He couldn't get his life right, but at least he could still write a story. He'd try to ignore the fact that Katherine was one hundred percent inspired by Kincaid. "Thank you."

"And I understand why you set it in a small town," she went on. "I'm sure you picked up a lot of the local flavor back home, but..." She tipped her head slightly side to side as if weighing her thoughts. "I think that location may be too big of a jump from what your readers will be looking for. Your audience loves to travel with you, explore a setting they're not familiar with. That's what makes you stand out."

"Right," he said, unsurprised at her reaction.

"Do you think you could set it in a close-knit town that's in a more exotic location?" She flipped a page in her notebook. "The other proposal you'd sent me a while back was set in an ex-pat community in Mexico. Maybe that could work in this book instead?"

He considered her suggestion, the idea not at all what he'd planned for the story but not impossible to pull off. "I could adjust that without changing the heart of the story."

"And you'll need to amp up the thriller element a bit more. Right now, you're a little too focused on the relationship subplot. I *love* that part, but it needs to play a supporting role and not take over the main story." She gave him a playful smirk. "Can't have Ashton Stone writing a romance, you know?"

"Right. Of course not." God knows he shouldn't be trusted to write one. He couldn't manage one in real life for damn sure. "Whatever you think is best."

She smiled, pleased. "I think this could be the start of a great series for you. These two characters could go on a lot of adventures together." She considered him. "Do you think you could live with writing them for a while? I know you haven't done an ongoing series before."

An ongoing series meant thinking about Kincaid every single time he wrote Katherine. Leave it to him to find new ways to torture himself. But it also meant steady work, a steadyish income. That was what he needed most right now—to stay busy and earn some money. He could get lost in the writing and forget that he felt broken and numb inside, that his heart was never going to be the same, that he'd ruined everything with the woman he loved…again. He cleared his throat. "A series sounds awesome."

"Excellent." Alice clapped her hands together as though she was crossing that item off her mental list. "Then I'd love to make an offer on a three-book series. I'll get with your agent to work out numbers, but I'll make sure there's a travel stipend added to give you some research time in Mexico. I want the setting to be authentic. That's your writer superpower. Lean into that."

Ash breathed in that good news. A deal. Guaranteed money. An escape. He should feel more excited, but he just felt…blank. Tired. "Thanks, Alice. I can't wait to get started on all of it."

She tilted her head, a bemused expression on her face. "You sure? You kind of look like I just told you your puppy died."

He forced a smile and ran a hand over the back of his head. "No, I'm sorry. I think I'm just a little worn out from my trip. This is amazing news. I'm excited."

She lifted her drink. "Then cheers for the next Ashton Stone adventure."

He raised his drink and clinked her glass. "Cheers."

He tried to feel happy about it, tried to find some place inside him that could still feel excitement. This was what he had wanted when he'd left New York. He'd saved up money, had found time to write, and had gotten another book deal. He could continue his life as Ashton Stone, thriller writer extraordinaire.

He could travel the world.

Get a nice place.

Move on.

Move on. Right. Two out of three would have to be good enough.

"So when do you think you'll head down to Mexico?" she asked, looking down at her menu.

Ash peeked at his phone and its absence of messages. Not that he'd expected Kincaid to call. She didn't owe him a damn thing. But he'd let a little bit of hope burn for the first few days afterward. Maybe she could forgive him. Maybe she loved him back, and they could work through it. That candle of hope had officially burned out.

He'd lost her. As a friend. And as more.

He squinted toward the bright window, watching people hustle by on the street, wondering what they were rushing off to, wondering if he'd ever have anything to rush toward again. "As soon as possible."

TWENTY-EIGHT

KINCAID STOOD IN FRONT OF THE NEWLY BUILT PEN ON HER property and grinned down at Barry and Beula, who were currently nosing around everything and exploring. "What do you think of the new digs, kids?"

Beula bleated, the obnoxious goaty sound growing on Kincaid, and nudged Barry out of the way so she could climb up on a big tractor tire that had been half buried in the ground. Beula looked mighty pleased that she could get higher up than her mate.

Marco laughed and leaned on the railing. "I think the company you used to build the pen did a great job. They have their own little obstacle course. That will keep them stimulated. They look happy to be back home."

Kincaid sighed. "I think their place is nicer than mine right now."

Marco glanced back at the main house. "Well, yours is a little bit bigger project. You'll get there, though. Just take it one step at a time. Once you get everything unpacked, it'll start to feel more like home. Boxes have a way of making everything feel unfinished."

Kincaid groaned. "There are *a lot* of unpacked boxes in my life right now."

His dimple appeared, reminding her how handsome the guy was. A wistful feeling went through her. Why couldn't she have fallen for Marco instead? That would've been so much easier, would've made much more sense.

"How are you feeling about being a goat mama?" he asked, shifting his attention back to the animals, his dark hair ruffling in the breeze.

"Excited. I've never had pets before. My mom was staunchly anti-animal." Which had probably been a blessing to the animals. Her mom had barely remembered to feed *her*. "I really appreciate all the notes and stuff you sent me and for bringing over some supplies. I owe you a home-cooked meal."

"Ah, lucky me," he said, looking over at her. "Ms. Kincaid Breslin's cooking is the stuff of legend."

She propped her arms on the railing next to him. "And I'm sorry about taking a while to get back to you when you called after our date. I didn't mean to ghost you."

He shrugged. "No worries. I'm pretty good at taking a hint." He bumped her in the shoulder. "Plus, my brother gave me a heads-up. Bec told him you were seeing someone else."

Kincaid looked down, putting her foot on the bottom rail and letting the familiar sadness weigh her down. "Yeah. Long story."

"It's fine," he said affably. "If it's not meant to be, it's not meant to be, right? In fact, I actually met someone a few weeks ago. If you had taken me up on the second date, I may have never asked her out."

Kincaid turned her head toward him. "Really?"

He got this adorably affectionate look on his face, and for a moment, Kincaid forgot that she'd given up on being a romantic. "Yeah. Ilsa."

Kincaid couldn't help but smile. "Tell me about her."

Marco looked toward Barry, who was climbing onto one of the elevated wooden platforms. "She came in to the clinic late one night after rescuing a litter of kittens. She was horribly allergic and sneezing her head off, but they were climbing all over her sweater and she was beside herself that someone had abandoned them." He smirked. "I could hardly tell what she looked like with her eyes so swollen, but she had this way about her that, I don't know. I just knew I needed to see her again."

Kincaid watched him, saw the adoration play across his features. A tight feeling clamped over her chest. "So you did."

He glanced her way, warmth in his eyes. "I did. And we've seen each other almost every night since. I've never felt like this before. Where you can't get enough of talking to a person, where you can't wait to discover every little thing about them. It's freaking me out a little to be honest." He shook his head, chagrined. "Like fate just stuck its fingers into my life, and now I'm powerless to resist it."

Fate. Kincaid didn't believe in that concept anymore. But she wasn't going to rain her stormy self all over Marco's happiness. "That's great, Marco. I'm really happy for you."

"Thanks." He nodded toward her. "And your guy?"

She wrinkled her nose. "Kind of broke my heart into a million pieces."

"Aw, hell," he said, his face falling. "I'm sorry. I shouldn't have asked."

She waved him off. "No, it's fine. I'm a big girl. I've got too much going on right now to worry about dating anyway. Bigger priorities. I've got goats to feed, for heaven's sakes."

Marco gave her a kind look. "Even so, I'm sorry it didn't work out."

"Thanks."

"And for what it's worth, any guy who'd walk away from you is a dumb-ass." He leaned closer as though he was going to tell her a secret. "I mean, have you met you?"

She laughed and gave him a friendly side hug. "Oh, Marco. I hope your girlfriend isn't the jealous type."

"Why's that?"

"Because you just got yourself adopted as a friend of Kincaid." She hooked her arm in his. "That's a lifelong contract, so she's going to have to get used to me."

He chuckled. "I think we can both live with that."

"Good. Now let's head up to the house." She tugged him toward the main path. "I have a batch of cookies I can send home for you and your lady as a goat thank-you."

"I'll never turn down cookies."

After Marco left, cookie tin in hand, Kincaid looked around the disorganized farmhouse and tried to decide where to even start. There was still a ton of boxes to unpack, and she needed to sit down and figure out some kind of budgeting plan. There was no way she could start renovations anytime soon. The money just wasn't there. If the bookstore ever sold, she'd have something to get the house at least looking like a home, if not bed-and-breakfast ready. That would be something. The B and B portion of the plan would just have to wait a couple of years. She'd already put in for a meeting with a smaller realty company in Wilder. She'd get back into real estate and go on a hard-core savings plan.

She stared at the endless stacks of boxes in the living room. But before she could pick a pile to start with, there was a knock at the door. She checked the peephole and then swung open the door. Taryn greeted her with a broad smile, a backpack, and a bag of takeout from the Thai restaurant in town. "Shaw has a big event at the gym tonight that's going to keep him out late. Can I be the first overnight guest at the B and B?"

Something loosened in Kincaid's chest. Sometimes her friends had radar for when she needed them most. The lonely night of unpacking faded into the background. "That would be amazing."

"Yay! Slumber party." Taryn stepped past her and into the house, her smile falling as she took in the state of things. "*Girl*."

Kincaid lifted her hands. "I know, I know. It looks worse than when y'all left. I was trying to come up with a system to organize everything but…so many boxes." She shut the door. "I think they have sex at night and make box babies. The more I unpack, the more show up."

Taryn snorted as she set down her backpack. "All right. New plan. We eat our takeout, and then we're going to power through some of these boxes. You need some space to breathe, my friend."

"God, do I."

An hour later, they were in the middle of the living room, sorting. Taryn had tied her hair back with a bandanna and was in full mission mode—talking to Kincaid in her authoritative professor voice. "Box of craft supplies, mostly unopened."

"Add it to the pile for bedroom three," Kincaid said, setting a box of knickknacks in a different pile.

"If you're not going to use something, you should just donate it," Taryn said. "Remember what the last box of unfinished project stuff did to you. Fresh start, girl. Fresh start."

Kincaid narrowed her eyes. "I like crafts. Bedroom three."

Taryn shrugged, shoved the box over to Kincaid for her to move and then opened another. She lifted her gaze from the box and gave Kincaid a you've-got-to-be-kidding look. "A crap ton of CDs."

"Bedroom—"

"Not so fast, sister. Do you even own a CD player anymore?"

"It took so long to collect those," Kincaid complained.

Taryn gave her a no-mercy look, all pursed lips and attitude.

Kincaid stuck out her tongue. "Fine, Ms. Bossypants. Donation pile."

"Good choice." Taryn shifted the box to the side and clapped her hands together. "Making progress." She walked over to another box, which was unlabeled, and leaned over to rifle through it. "Uh…high school stuff?"

Kincaid frowned. "Like what kind of high school

stuff? I thought I already put what I had away in the guest closet."

Taryn crouched down. "Hmm, let's see. Notebooks. Graduation cap. Yearbooks."

"Yearbooks?" Kincaid walked over. "Now I *know* I put those away."

She'd put them deep into the back of a closet, in fact, not wanting to stumble upon high school reminders by accident.

Taryn pulled one from the box and handed it to her. "Senior yearbook."

Kincaid stared down at the beat-up cover, not remembering hers being in such rough shape. "Weird." She opened it to look at the messages inside, but the liner pages only had a few signatures. Her brow wrinkled. Hers had been filled to the edges with well wishes and *have a great summer* declarations. Silly notes scribbled before everything had gone so wrong. "This isn't mine."

Taryn put her fist to her hip. "What?"

"It's not mine." She turned a page and let out a breath when she saw her own handwriting filling a page and staring back at her. A note from her. *To Ash.* "Shit. This is Ash's stuff."

Taryn cocked her head. "Why would you have his?"

Kincaid tucked a lock of hair that had fallen out of her bun behind her ear, her eyes scanning over the note she'd written him. "I must've grabbed this box from his place thinking it was mine when I moved my stuff out. Damn."

Taryn groaned. "Which means you need to give it back. Do you want me to take care of it? I know you're not exactly in the mood to talk to him."

Kincaid flipped through the pages absently. "No, it's

all right. He's staying with the Lowells. I can bring it by when he's not there."

She reached out to hand the book back to Taryn, but sheets of folded notebook paper fell out and fluttered to the floor. Kincaid bent to pick them up. She didn't plan to look at them, but when she saw her name, she couldn't help it. She gathered them up and walked over to the couch.

"What are those?" Taryn asked.

"Not sure." She unfolded one of the pages and her breath caught.

Dear Kincaid,

You are the most beautiful girl I've ever seen. When you're in a room, it's like there's no one else there because you're all I can focus on. I wish I could tell you all the things I think and feel about you to your face, but I'm not sure I'm the guy you'd want to hear them from. Even so, I want you to know that there's someone in the world who realizes how special you are. Not because you're pretty. Not because you're funny. Not because you're smart. Though you are all those things. But because you are full of a light that outshines everyone else I've ever met. You, Kincaid Breslin, are singular. You are everything.

> *Always,*
> *Your secret admirer*

She blinked at the words, ones so familiar, ones she'd read over and over when she was a teenager and in the years since. She had a copy of this very letter tucked in that box she'd hidden in the closet. A whole stack of them. But…

Hers were typed.

She stared down at the page, the handwritten words swimming in her head, nothing making sense.

"What is it?" Taryn asked, coming to sit next to her. She leaned over, reading the letter. "Whoa. That's…"

"It's a letter from Graham," Kincaid said softly.

"From Graham?" Taryn asked, picking up another of the ragged-edged pages. "Why would Ash have them?"

Kincaid stared down at the letter, at the neat, slanted handwriting. Something about it was making her heart beat faster. The way the *g*'s looped was so unique and familiar. The handwriting was…*the same handwriting that was currently on the shelf-talkers at the bookstore*. The blood drained out of her fingertips. "Oh my God."

A wave of nausea filled her, her stomach flipping inside out and a loud buzzing filling her ears.

"What?" Taryn asked, looking from her to the letter. "What's wrong?"

"Not from Graham," Kincaid whispered more to herself than Taryn. "Oh God. *Oh God*." Her throat stung with acid. "*Ash* wrote these."

"Ash?"

Kincaid put her hand to her mouth and leaned back on the couch, afraid she may vomit on the nice pregnant lady. The romantic words were burned into her brain. She'd always wondered how Graham could be so effusive and poetic on the page but rarely said such things in person. She'd cherished these letters. They were imprinted onto her heart. But God, she'd been so *stupid*. How had she not seen it? Graham wasn't the writer. Ash was. The books they'd been hidden in were favorites only Ash would've known. "The letters I got from Graham were typed. Either Ash wrote these and Graham took credit for them. Or Ash wrote them *for* Graham."

Taryn's eyes widened, and she looked at the page in her hand. "So all these romantic declarations?"

Kincaid closed her eyes. "Ash."

"*Girl*," Taryn said softly. "Wow. This guy...has loved you for a long time."

Frustration rushed through Kincaid, chasing away the sick feeling, and she stared up at the ceiling. "Why didn't he just *tell* me how he felt? Why help Graham? Why not take credit for these letters? He knew I loved them. I talked about them all the time. They made me *fall for Graham*."

Taryn reached out and grabbed her hand in sympathy. "He says right here why. 'I wish I could tell you all the things I think and feel about you to your face, but I'm not sure I'm the guy you'd want to hear them from,'" she read aloud. "For some reason, he didn't believe you were capable of feeling that way about him."

"He's an idiot," Kincaid declared.

Taryn laughed without humor. "Most teenage boys are. But," she asked gently, "would you have returned these feelings back then? Would you have wanted him to be the guy?"

Kincaid looked at her friend, at the questioning brown eyes, and the truth came to her with harsh clarity. "No. I wouldn't have. I already had a crush on someone else."

Taryn gave her a sad smile. "And Ash gave that guy to you. Complete with a stack of love letters to seal the deal."

Kincaid put a hand over her face, the reality of it all crashing over her. Ash had known who she wanted, and he'd made it happen for her, even when it meant he got left out in the process. She groaned aloud. "*Fuuuuuuuck.*"

Taryn made a sympathetic sound and sank back next to her, still holding her hand. "Welcome to your fairy tale, Kincaid Breslin. I think you were missing a few pages of the book."

Kincaid shook her head, feelings warring inside her. "He lied to me, Taryn. He lied to me about the shooting."

She put her head on Kincaid's shoulder. "Yes. In one way, that was really shitty. In another, he was trying to protect you."

"*Protect* me?" she said with a scoff. "He was trying to protect himself."

"I don't know. He gave you and the Lowells the story y'all wanted to hear. It's easier to process the grief when the person is labeled a hero. It gives a death some kind of meaning." She was quiet for a second. "Believe me, I know. I've given my sister all kinds of hero labels. I don't know what she did during the shooting, but I want to believe she helped others, protected them."

Kincaid squeezed Taryn's hand.

"Don't you think it's better that the Lowells think their son saved you and Ash instead of knowing that he punched Ash right before and that he was arguing with you? What good would the truth do for them?" she asked. "It'd only make the pain that much worse."

Kincaid's chest was burning. Her head hurt. A lie was a lie. There was no excuse for that, right?

Gah. She didn't know anymore. Everything black and white had merged into a murky gray.

"I don't know what to do with all this," she admitted.

Taryn lifted her head and turned toward Kincaid. She set the letter in Kincaid's lap. "Do you love him?"

Kincaid stared at her friend, a bone-deep exhaustion settling in like a flu. "I feel like my guts have been ripped out."

Taryn smirked. "Hello, love. There you are."

"But it's so much more complicated than do I love him," she said, frustration building again. "Even if I forgive him. I live here. He's a traveling writer. He hates this town. His parents live here, and they're awful. Whether we love each other or not, whether he still feels the same about me, I would never make him live here. And I'm not leaving."

Taryn picked up one of the letters. "'Dear Kincaid, You were sad today, and it physically hurts me to see you upset. I wish I could hold you and tell you that everything's going to be okay, that you're amazing and that you're loved. I wish I had the power to show you what I feel inside when I see you. You would never doubt yourself again. You shine light into all the shadows. You are my light on the tough days. I would do anything to see you smile because when you smile, all feels right in my world.'"

Kincaid didn't realize she was crying until she felt the tear drip off her chin. "*Lord*. How am I supposed to stop loving him when he writes shit like that?"

Taryn shook her head and pressed a finger to the corner of her eye. "This boy's got me tearing up." She handed Kincaid the letter. "This sounds like a guy who would do just about anything to be with you. Maybe instead of deciding that he can't live here, you should give him the chance to make his own choice. Maybe he just needs the chance to say yes."

Kincaid held the letter in her shaking hands, staring down at the deliberate handwriting, picturing a teen Ash pouring his heart onto the page and then letting Graham take credit for it, giving her the guy she thought would make her happy.

Kincaid carefully folded the letter and set it aside. "I'm going to need a big-ass glass of wine and a ride to the Lowells'."

Taryn lifted her hands above her head and cheered. "Woo-hoo! Field trip!"

Twenty minutes later, Kincaid's heartbeat was in her throat as she walked up the sidewalk to the Lowells' front door. The glass of wine had done nothing to quell her nerves. She had no idea what she was going to say, which was a completely foreign feeling. She always had something to say.

She looked toward the driveway, and Taryn gave her a thumbs-up from the car. Kincaid shook her head and forced her feet up the sidewalk.

After a long pause at the door, she rang the doorbell. Grace answered almost immediately and smiled broadly when she saw Kincaid. "Oh, honey, what a nice surprise."

"Hi, Grace," she said, smoothing her lipstick and trying to quiet the tremors working their way through her body. "Can I talk to Ash?"

Grace frowned. "Ash? Well, honey, he left over a week ago."

Kincaid blinked. "What?"

Her brows dipped. "I thought you knew. He said something came through for his book, and he was going back to New York to meet with his editor."

"New York," Kincaid repeated dumbly.

"He said you knew," she said, looking confused. "Oh, and he left something for you. Hold on. Let me see where I put it."

Kincaid stood there, feeling stupid and lost. He'd left. Of course he had. The bookstore was done. They were done. What did he have to stay for?

Grace came back with a manila envelope. "Sorry. I was supposed to get this to you a few days ago, but with taking care of Charlie, I just hadn't had the chance to drive out to your place. Ash said you'd know what to do with it."

Kincaid had no idea what it could be. Another letter? An apology? No. Probably a goodbye. She didn't want to open it. "Thanks, Grace."

Deep lines bracketed her mouth. "You okay, sweetheart?"

Kincaid tried to look upbeat. "I'm fine. Just a little tired. I've been working long days, getting everything moved in."

"You want to come inside?" She opened the door a little wider. "I have leftovers I can heat up."

Kincaid shook her head. "No, thank you. I have a few errands to run. I'll stop by soon and we'll have dinner, okay?"

Grace gave her a quick hug. "Sounds good. And we'll makes plans for who's bringing what for the holidays."

Kincaid perked up. "Is Ash coming back for that?"

Grace sighed. "No. He said he wouldn't be able to make it this year. I think he's going to be headed to his next adventure. You know that boy. Can't stay in one place too long."

Kincaid's heart sank lower. "Right. Well, thanks again. I'll see you."

"Good night, hon."

Grace shut the door, and Kincaid walked on wooden legs down the sidewalk. Taryn was frowning at her from the car.

Kincaid fiddled with the envelope in her hand. Part of her wanted to toss it into the trash and not look. He'd left. What else did she need to know? Whatever was inside would only make it hurt worse. But after a few seconds, she couldn't help it. She needed to know what he had to say. She pushed her finger under the flap and opened it. There was no letter inside, only a slip of paper. She pulled it out and stared down at it, the moonlight giving her just enough illumination to see what it was.

Her hands began to shake.

A cashier's check with her name on it.

For two hundred thousand dollars.

Her body went hot all over. She flipped the check over. The sticky note on the back simply read in that familiar slanted handwriting: *For the Breslin B and B*.

She sank down, her legs giving out on her, and plopped onto the lawn. She heard the car door slam and saw Taryn approaching, but her vision blurred with tears. Her head was spinning. Her one glass of wine now felt like ten. She lay back in the grass, the stars winking above her.

Two hundred thousand dollars. The exact amount

that had been sitting in his parents' account for over a decade.

She closed her eyes, clutching the check to her chest, letting the reality of what this meant sink in.

Ash had apologized to his father. Ash had done the one thing he'd sworn he'd never do.

For her.

So she could have her dream.

Hot tears tracked down from her eyes and to her ears. The thing that bloomed inside her heart was unprecedented. She'd never felt such a powerful force before, such an all-knowing assuredness that finally…finally…

She had found her soul mate.

He'd been there all along.

And she'd let him go.

She'd hurt him and had no idea where to find him or how to get him back.

This wasn't supposed to be how her story ended.

chapter
TWENTY-NINE

Tuesday—1:15 a.m.

> **Kincaid**: Hey, Ash. Not sure where you are right now, but I got the money you left with Grace. We need to talk.

11:17 a.m.

> **Kincaid**: This is not about the money.

11:59 a.m.

> **Kincaid**: Call me. *GIF of a dog making a phone call*

Wednesday—9:01 a.m.

> **Kincaid**: You're really going to ignore me? Did you miss the part about me being relentless? We need to talk.

9:05 a.m.

> **Kincaid**: Where are you? We can do this
> face-to-face. I'll come to you.

11:59 p.m.

> **Kincaid**: Ash, please. Don't shut me out.

Thursday—2:17 a.m.

> **Kincaid**: You're making me look like a crazy
> ex-girlfriend.

2:19 a.m.

> **Kincaid**: Is your new girlfriend going to
> answer and pretend you're in bed together?
> I heard you're not above that. :P

Friday—7:05 a.m.

> **Kincaid**: I'm not using this money.
> **Kincaid**: We have to talk.

KINCAID EYED THE SCREEN OF HER PHONE, HER DESPERATE messages from the last two weeks both embarrassing and enormously frustrating. She'd verified with Grace that Ash's number hadn't changed. Grace had said he was doing some research in Mexico, but she didn't know which part and that his phone signal could be spotty. Kincaid didn't think this was a phone coverage issue.

Ash was ignoring her messages. She'd gotten a *dot dot dot* once, and her heart had leapt with hope, but then it'd just disappeared. Ash was reading the messages. He just wasn't responding.

Or maybe he was too busy drinking excellent tequila and sleeping with beautiful women he met on the beach.

Kincaid collapsed back onto her bed with a groan. Fate was being a total bitch. How could it finally show her who she was meant to be with and then not give her access to him? Was this her punishment for not realizing what Ash meant to her from the start? *Ugh.* Probably. She'd made the guy pine for years. Now she got to pine.

Pining sucked.

Pining made her want to eat all the Christmas cookies she'd baked for her friends.

Pining made her want to throw things.

She picked up her phone, tempted to toss it, but it vibrated in her hand and made her yelp. She sat up and flipped it over, hope sparking through her, but she sighed when she saw the name on the screen.

She put the phone to her ear and tried to sound more pleasant than petulant. "Hi, Grace."

"Hi, sweetie," Grace said, her tone as cheerful as a Christmas elf. "You busy?"

Yes. Pining. "Not really. What's up?"

"I have great news."

"Oh yeah?" Kincaid perked up a little.

"The Stuffed Shelf has sold!" she announced with glee. "And it's going to stay a bookstore."

"Oh, Grace, that's fantastic," she said, genuinely happy for the Lowells but a pang of loss going through her. The bookstore would be in someone else's hands. It was like losing her version of her family home. "I'm so glad it worked out. Did a local buy it?"

"No," she said, sounding distracted. "Someone moving here from out of town. But it will be in good hands. They loved the look of the store. You did a great job with the holiday decorations."

Kincaid had spent the weekend getting the place gussied up for the Christmas season, making it look magical and inviting. "That's great. And it was really no problem. I enjoy decorating."

"I appreciate it regardless, but I was hoping I could ask you for one more quick favor," she said a little tentatively.

"Sure." Kincaid swung her legs over the side of the bed. "Whatever you need."

"The new owner needs someone to walk him through the inventory system and the order of the storeroom. He's going to be stopping by there around lunchtime," she explained. "Do you think you could let him in and give him a little rundown? I would, but I'm volunteering at a church event today and—"

"No problem," Kincaid said, interrupting her. "I've got nothing going on today besides a few errands. I don't mind helping out. Plus, I need to eyeball this new owner, make sure he understands not to screw up your store."

Grace laughed. "It's not going to be mine anymore, but I appreciate the sentiment. I'll tell him you'll meet him there and let him in."

"Sounds good," she said. "Oh, what's his name?"

There was a shuffling of papers on her end. "Um, Robert Jones. I think he goes by Bob."

"Well, that will be easy to remember." Kincaid hung

up, was tempted to text Ash about the store being sold, but she resisted. Ash had waited over a decade for her. If he needed space now, he had the right to it. Maybe he didn't want to talk because there was nothing to say. He was back to his traveling life. He didn't want to have to tell her the obvious—they lived different lives in very different places. Falling in love didn't fix that.

The thought made her chest ache, but she forced herself out of bed. She would not wallow today. Grace needed her, and the store selling was good news. That meant Kincaid would have money to start some renovations because she hadn't cashed Ash's check. She couldn't take that money in good conscience. That was Ash's money.

She grabbed her favorite sweater dress and a pair of knee-high boots. She'd been schlepping around in grungy clothes for the last few weeks, always getting dirty with house stuff, but it was time to feel pretty again. Sometimes the outside gloss could help the inside glumness. At least she hoped it could.

The store was closed as she pulled up in front of it. The window shades had been drawn and a sign had been taped to the door. *Under new ownership. Reopening on New Year's Day.* Her eyes misted a little, but she stanched the tears. Everything had to come to an end at some point. This was just another chapter closing in her life.

She parked in the back of the building and dug her keys out of her purse. She'd have to turn those over, too. With a sigh, she climbed out of the car and headed to the building. She checked the time on her phone. The new owner would be here in fifteen minutes or so. She could go in and turn on all the Christmas twinkle lights and have the store looking nice for him.

She opened the back door, glanced wistfully at the stairs that led up to the apartment, and then shook her head. None of that. She unlocked the door to the store and slipped inside. All the lights had been turned off except for the red safety one in the hallway. She flicked on the hall light and dropped the keys back into her purse.

The familiar smell of books mixed with the fresh scent of the rosemary plants she'd added. She inhaled deeply, trying to imprint it on her memory. Her boots echoed on the wooden floor as she headed to the front of The Stuffed Shelf. She halted when she saw that the white twinkle lights that she'd twined with the dark-green pine garland decorating the store were on. Their subtle glow gave the darkened store a magical quality, as if she'd entered a secret chamber. But it gave her pause. Had Grace left these lights on all night? That was a fire hazard with all these books.

She headed toward the main light-switch panel, but a sound off to her left made her freeze. She turned her head, but she couldn't see more than the shelf in front of her, the main desk area obscured. She strained her ears. A footstep.

Her throat tightened, and her hand reached out for a thick Stephen King hardback. She lifted it, ready to take aim, and backed up a step, trying to return to the hallway and the exit.

More footsteps. Closer now.

Shit. She gave up the stealth and darted toward the hallway, but a large shadow intercepted her, grabbing her. "K—"

She screamed and swung the book at her assailant.

"Ow!" The hands released her. "What the—"

She lunged toward the hallway, the book falling to the floor with a heavy thump.

"Dammit, KC," the guy said, a grimace in his voice.

Her hand gripped the doorjamb, and something fluttered in her chest. *KC*. She flipped on the hallway light and spun. Ash was standing there with his hand pressed to the side of his face and a what-the-hell look.

Her lips parted in shock. "Ash."

He smirked, his cheek already turning red from where she'd hit him. "You know, for someone who claims to carry pepper spray, you're really into projectiles."

Kincaid couldn't move. Ash, whom she'd been blatantly stalking for the last two weeks, was standing there as if he'd never left. Dark-rimmed glasses, skinny jeans, and T-shirt that read *They used to laugh and call me names* with a picture of Rudolph in front of a wall of mounted antlers.

She couldn't absorb this as reality. "What are you doing here? How did you get in?"

He pulled a set of keys from his pocket. "I never turned in my set."

She stared. "I sent you, like, a thousand text messages."

He lifted a brow. "Did you?"

"Ash," she said, stepping forward and holding her hands out at her sides. "Why are you here?"

He gave her a small smile. "Because you sent me a thousand text messages. I got the impression you wanted to talk."

"You think?" She wrinkled her nose. "But we can't."

He frowned. "We can't?"

"Not right now." She took a breath, trying to calm herself, trying not to lay everything she'd been wanting to say to him out in one big run-on sentence. *I love you and you're amazing and I'm sorry and you were stupid and I was stupid and we're both so stupid and tell me you love me back and hey, I love that T-shirt.* She bit back the verbal flood before it poured out. "The new owner is going to be here soon. The store is sold. I'm supposed to show him around."

"Ah," he said.

"Are you back for the holidays?"

He nodded. "I am."

She filed away that information. He was here visiting. It didn't mean he was here to discuss their relationship—or lack thereof. "I'm glad."

He stepped a little closer, his gaze tracking over her, reading her. "Yeah?"

"Did you miss the thousand messages? I was ready to hire a private detective to find you in Mexico. Of course I'm glad."

He stopped an arm's length from her and tucked his hands in his back pockets, making his silly T-shirt stretch across his chest. "What did you want to tell me, KC? If it's about the money, I'm not taking it back, so you can save yourself that argument."

She shook her head. "I can't believe you gave in to your dad. I would never have asked you to do that."

"I know." He shrugged, as though giving someone two hundred grand was no big thing. "But that money was doing no one any good sitting there. What does it matter if I tell him what he wants to hear? He gets to feel like the big man, like he won? Okay. Fine. He wins. That doesn't make the truth not the truth. He knows what he does. He knows I know. This way, I get to visit my mom without her getting in a fight with him, and I get to put the money to the best use possible. That money was meant for the victims. Now one will make her dream come true with it."

Kincaid wanted to reach out and hug him, touch him, but she kept her hands at her sides. "Ash, you could use that money. You have dreams, too."

He smiled. "I do. But I'm good. I got a bigger advance than I was expecting for my new series. I have what I need to get what I want."

"A beach house in Mexico?" she guessed.

He laughed. "What did you want to talk to me about?"

She glanced toward the clock on the wall. The new owner would be here any minute. She needed time with Ash, but part of her was afraid if she let him walk out, he'd slip away again. She pushed past her nerves and met his eyes. "I found your letters."

His brow wrinkled. "What?"

"The letters you wrote to me. The ones I thought were from Graham."

Ash's eyes widened and a breath whooshed out of him. "Oh."

She ventured a little closer. "Ash."

"I'm sorry, KC," he said, regret on his face. "God, you must think I'm the biggest liar. I—"

She lifted her hand, pressed it over his lips to halt him. "Ash."

He blinked down at her.

"I know you're just here for the holidays. I know I've

said hurtful things to you. I know you have to travel and write your books and live your life, but I can't let you go on thinking I hate you." She lowered her hand. "I'm not upset that you lied about the letters."

His gaze searched hers. "You're not?"

"No. I'm upset that I never saw it."

A line formed between his brows. "Saw what?"

She looked into those beautiful blue eyes of his, her throat tight with emotion. "That the boy I fell in love with when I was seventeen years old was *you*."

He stared down at her, confusion on his face. "What?"

"The letters are what made me fall, Ash. Those words were tattooed on my heart." She pressed a hand to her chest. "And I knew that the boy who wrote them was the one I was meant to be with for always." Her eyes stung with the beginning of tears. "I always loved you, Ash. You were my best friend. Not because you weren't hot enough to date. Not because you weren't boyfriend material. You were both, but you were so much more than that. I never let myself go there because I didn't want to risk what we had. You were everything to me."

His throat worked.

"But if I had known these words were yours, if I had known you felt that way…I would've risked it all." She pressed her palm over his heart, feeling the quick beat beneath her hand. "Because you, Ashton Isaacs, are my soul mate."

Ash's eyes glittered in the twinkle lights, his expression full of wonder. "KC…"

"And I'm not telling you all this to try to make you stay. You deserve your dream. I know this town doesn't mean good things for you. But I don't want you leaving again without knowing that I'm in love with you." She took a deep breath. "Like, really, really in love with you."

Ash stared at her in awe for a long moment, and then the biggest, most beautiful smile broke out on his face. He lifted his hands and cupped her jaw. "Well, it's about damn time, Breslin."

She choked, some combination of a laugh and a sob trying to come out at the same time, and tears spilled over. But before she could say anything back, he bent and kissed her.

The moment his lips touched hers, everything that had been knocked out of alignment for so long seemed to click into place, the universe giving its nod of approval. She looped her arms around his neck, and he picked her up off her feet—or maybe she floated there. She hooked her legs around his waist, and they kissed until they were breathless.

Ash broke for air first and smiled at her with the most tender look. "God, I missed you."

"Of course you did," she said playfully. "Beautiful beaches in Mexico and the jet-setting life have nothing on me."

He gave her a serious look. "You're right. They don't."

"No beach bunnies turned your head?" she teased.

"Of course not. Don't you get it?" He touched his forehead to hers, his voice soft. "You've never had any real competition. It's always been you, KC. Always."

She closed her eyes. The buoyant joy that filled her made her feel like she'd float to the ceiling. "We can figure this out, right?" she asked, hope making her voice crack. "I can travel with you sometimes. Do the long-distance thing if we have to. I'm awesome at phone sex."

Ash laughed and lifted his head. "Have you lost your damn mind? The girl I've loved my whole life just told me I'm her soul mate. You think I'm setting up shop in some villa in Mexico?"

She frowned and shook her head. "I'm not making you give up anything for me. That's not what I'm asking for."

He carried her over to the counter and sat her atop it. "Hush, gorgeous."

"Ash." He leaned down to kiss her again, but she put a hand to his chest. "We need to discuss this. And we can't make out right now. The new guy is going to be here any second. This isn't exactly the kind of welcome party he's expecting."

"Oh, the new guy will love this." He kissed her again, his hand sliding along her thigh.

"Ash," she said on a laugh. "I'm serious."

"So am I." He braced his hands on either side of her and put his mouth next to her ear. "Hey, KC, I've got a secret."

"A secret?"

"Yes." He kissed the spot behind her ear. "Meet the new guy. He's about to christen his new store by showing the girl he loves just how much he missed her."

She stiffened and dipped her head to catch his eye. "Hold up. *What?*"

Ash gave her a smug look of satisfaction. "Surprise."

Her brain couldn't put the pieces together. They didn't make sense. "You? But Grace said there's a Bob Jones."

He laughed. "Bob Jones? Wow, she came up with a real original alias there. Is his business partner John Smith?"

Goose bumps broke out over her skin. "*Ash*."

He tipped his head to the side, indicating the store around them. "It's all mine, KC."

Her lips closed, opened again. "How? You didn't even know what I wanted to say to you. How could you know?"

"I didn't. I had hope when you texted me, but I didn't know how you felt. Maybe you just wanted to tell me not to give you the money and send me on my way." He pushed her hair behind her ears and gave her a tender look. "But I realized soon after I left that even if things weren't going to work out with us, I couldn't go back to how I was living. I love seeing new places and exploring, and I still want to write. I have a contract for a new book series I'm excited about.

"But after being here with you, with Grace and Charlie, with your friends, I could finally pinpoint what that restless, itchy part inside me was, what has kept me from really touching any kind of real contentment or happiness." He exhaled. "I missed having a home—*this* home. All this time, I thought I was chasing a dream, but I've only been running. Long Acre holds my most painful memories, but it also holds many of my happiest ones. I love this store. I want to spend time with Grace and Charlie. I want to have long-lasting friends. I want to build a life."

She smiled through her tears. "Oh, cupcake."

He swiped away her tears with his thumbs. "I want to build a life with you. Here."

She stared at him in amazement. How had she ever looked at him and not seen what was in his heart? Not recognized what was buried deep in hers? Nothing had ever felt so right. Her whole life, her biggest joy had been her friends. Of course she was meant to fall in love with one.

This one.

The one who'd brought so much light into her life growing up. The one she'd always thought of first when she wanted to share something great or cry about something sad. The one who'd held her and promised her that she never had to be anyone but herself, that she was just right exactly as she was.

"You sure you're not going to get tired of me?" She poked him in the shoulder. "I've heard I'm best in small doses."

He cupped her face and kissed her forehead. "I've never been more sure of anything in my life. You, my love, are best in really big, superintense, lifelong doses."

The words rolled over her like a song, one that filled her up and turned into the sweetest melody she'd ever heard. That song had been playing between them for a long time. Finally, she could hear it. "Baby-fox coffee."

"The best the world has to offer," he said softly. "And she's all mine."

"Forever," she said, any doubts she'd ever had about happy endings melting away.

Ash's gaze went shiny in the twinkle lights. "I'm counting on it."

chapter

THIRTY

ASH KISSED KINCAID, HOLDING HER AGAINST HIM AND riding high on a feeling he didn't know he was capable of—pure, unadulterated joy. The feeling was so strong, he feared he might crack open and all the energy would just spill out and blind them both with all its white light. He'd taken a risk, ignoring Kincaid's texts and surprising her like this. Things could've gone so wrong. On the way back from Mexico, he'd imagined all the millions of ways it could go badly.

She didn't owe him forgiveness. She didn't owe him anything. But when he'd gotten that first text as he unpacked his bags in Mexico, he'd felt a surge of fight rise in him that had nearly knocked him off his feet. So many times over the years, he'd had similar urges to go after what he wanted and had talked himself down. *Don't make a fool of yourself. Don't be pathetic. Don't make a scene.* But in that moment in the hotel room, he'd realized that could've been a speech his father gave to him or his mother. Words that told Ash he wasn't worthy or good enough. That he was a bother. That keeping the peace and saving face were worth more than feeling what he was feeling or fighting for what he wanted.

That script had been running underneath so many events in his life, guiding him like a director he hadn't hired in a movie he didn't want to be in. He'd run from Kincaid the first time when she'd sent him away because of that script, and it'd been a mistake. She'd been angry and heartbroken back then, not because they'd slept together but because he hadn't stayed to work it out, to fight for their friendship. In Mexico, he'd realized he was doing it again. He was leaving before he got left. The coward's way. The you're-not-good-enough-so-why-bother way.

Fuck. That. Those were the two words that started screaming in his head and building this inner fire that he didn't want to put out.

Kincaid deserved a guy who would fight for her, who wouldn't run scared to protect his own heart. That was what Grace had been trying to tell him. Kincaid had been left so many times and in so many ways by the important people in her life that she now expected it. She had a theory that would get proven again. Ash would just be another person she was too much for. Another person who could easily be pushed away and not fight for her.

He'd always known she was the one for him.

The problem was he'd never truly believed that *he* was the one for *her*.

Not until she'd looked at him on the dance floor that night at the restaurant had he seen the truth. She didn't see him as a second choice. As someone to settle for.

The feelings he felt for her had been shining in her own eyes. Yearning. Attraction. *Love*.

More than friendship. More than history. He was the one she'd been looking for. He was the one who could give her the kind of love she deserved. And she wanted to give that kind of love back to him.

She was looking at him that way now, and he knew that finally, *finally*, he'd won the fight. Not with her. Not with Graham. Not with the shooters. But with himself.

He could be happy. He could be loved. He could spend his life with this amazing, smart, beautiful woman and not run anymore.

He could come home.

"Ash, please." Kincaid gasped as he kissed his way down her neck and nipped at her collarbone. Her skin was salty sweet beneath his mouth, her heartbeat visible at her throat. She grappled for his hair as though she wanted to both keep him there and push him lower. "I need you."

He would never get enough of hearing her breathless sounds, his name on her lips. He didn't want to wake up another morning without her there next to him. "I need you right back, baby," he said between kisses. "Do you still have the key for upstairs?"

She let out a sound of frustration. "No."

Ash stared down at her parted lips, the wanting in her gaze, as fire raced through his blood. He wanted this woman in so many ways. To love her. To make her happy. And to have her like this, hot and needy and looking for him to make it better.

"Mmm," he said, sliding his hand along her thigh and relishing the way she shivered as his touch moved higher and higher. "No bed to take you to upstairs? What shall we do?"

She gasped when his thumb traced over the front of her panties. His arousal spiked at the feel of the clinging fabric, at how ready she was for him. He put pressure where he knew she needed it most. She whimpered and her hand flew back to brace herself, knocking a stack of books to the floor. She tried to correct the movement but ended up taking out a canister of pencils instead. The pencils clattered against the hardwood. "I'm going to destroy your store like this. Or get impaled by a writing implement."

He laughed softly and kissed the curve of her neck, his thumb still lazily stroking her, heat building behind the fly of his jeans. "Can't have that. Guess we'll have to improvise."

"Storeroom?" she suggested, her head tipping back as he slipped her sweater dress off her shoulder.

"I've got a better idea." Before she could say anything else, he lifted her up from the counter and carried her away from it.

"Where are we going?"

"I have just the place." He carried her through the aisles, careful not to knock her into anything, and headed toward a very familiar corner. The canvas tent glowed beneath the white Christmas lights like a mirage, like it'd been waiting just for them. He kicked open the flap with his foot. Fat cushions filled the inside, padding the floor for the perfect reading spot, and a small battery-operated lantern was tucked into the corner.

There would be no reading tonight.

Ash bent down to set Kincaid inside the tent and then turned on the lantern to the lowest setting. Her blond hair fanned out over the dark-green cushions as she looked around. When she realized where they were, she grinned. She lifted a copy of *Where the Wild Things Are*. "The children's section? You are a dirty, dirty man."

He took the book from her, tossed it outside the tent, and then climbed in with her. He braced himself over her, taking in the softly lit woman beneath him and the love in her eyes. "Guilty. You know how many times I would lie in this spot after hours, reading racy books and thinking of you? Imagining you climbing in here with me just like this?"

Heat flared in her hazel eyes, and she slipped her hands beneath the hem of his T-shirt, dragging her fingertips over his abdomen and making him hard and hot. "Tell me what you imagined, Ash."

He reached down and helped her slip her dress over her head, leaving her in a dark-red bra and pair of panties. "Whatever novel I was reading, you were the heroine. The sharp-tongued lady in Regency England spoke with a southern accent. The sexy demon hunter called the vampires she slayed *sugar* and *cupcake*." He ran a fingertip over the curve of her breast. "The hooker with a heart of gold..."

Kincaid smirked. "Yes?"

"Well," he admitted, "I was seventeen. She looked like you and, you know, did really obscene things with me for money."

She laughed and rolled her eyes. "And could only be satisfied by one particular man who maybe wore glasses and liked to write stories?"

He traced the edge of her bra, loving the way goose bumps rose on her skin at his touch. "Of course."

"You know," she said, her fingers teasing at the button of his jeans. "For future reference, since we have a future now…"

"Yes?"

She gave him a saucy look. "Role-playing kind of does it for me."

His eyebrow lifted, another electric current of desire moving through him. "Does it now?"

She gave him an innocent little shrug as she undid the button of his jeans. "Have you ever known me to turn down the opportunity to wear a costume?"

He laughed. "Truth. Seeing you in that vampire-slayer costume that one Halloween nearly killed me. All that clingy fabric? I'm still not sure I've recovered from that night."

"Hmm," she said, pondering. "I bet I still have that one somewhere."

He groaned as his mind went to all the possibilities. "God, KC. Loving you is going to be so much fun."

She gave him a pleased look. "You bet it will be, cupcake. Now, get undressed. Too many clothes. Not enough Ash to ogle."

He grinned and shucked his clothes, heat building hard and fast at the base of his spine, and then stripped her of her bra and panties. The clothes were tossed out of the tent, and then it was just the two of them. Skin to skin. She was so damn beautiful he could barely believe the moment was real, that she was his. He cupped her breast, circling his thumb over the sensitive point, and dragged his erection over the hot, slick part of her. Her moan was the most erotic sound he'd ever heard, and the feel of her against him nearly did him in. "I love it when you call me cupcake."

She arched her back, a pink flush of heat along her neck, and rocked her hips against him. "I love it when you do that."

He pulled her knee up and opened her body to him more, dragging his cock over her, angling where he knew it would feel best for her. The sensation of her slippery heat against him was going to melt his brain, but he refused to end this too quickly. He wanted to see his woman come apart in his arms. "I love when you moan like that. I love how much noise you make."

She writhed beneath him and reached for him. "Ash, please. Need you."

He grabbed her wrist and pinned it over her head. He wanted to be inside her more than he wanted to draw air, but he wanted her pleasure first, wanted to see her melt. "Not yet, gorgeous."

"I love it when you boss me in bed," she said, her voice whisper soft. "Don't try it anywhere else."

"Wouldn't dream of it." He slipped two fingers inside her, still rocking his body against her, and groaned when her muscles clenched around him.

Kincaid stopped talking, which let him know he was doing his job. He curled his fingers inside her and picked up the pace, stroking her until she was gasping. He watched as a sheen broke out on her skin and the pleasure hit her like lightning. She arched and cried out, cutting through the quiet in the bookstore and sending a wave of heat through him that nearly sent him over the edge.

She called out his name and reached for him blindly with her free hand. He didn't deny her this time. He shifted his position and pushed inside her, shuddering when her body enveloped them and they joined. Her arms wrapped around him, her nails digging into his back. She pressed her face into the curve of his neck, letting his skin absorb the sharp cries of her orgasm.

She wrapped her legs around him, and he let himself go, drowning in the scent of her, the feel of her, losing himself in the knowledge that she was now his and he was hers, and this, this was real. This was love.

Kincaid started murmuring *I love you I love you* like a desperate mantra, like a prayer, and that was all it took. He cried out in pleasure and held her against him as they peaked together and went to the place that had no words. Where it was just the two of them. No pretending. No rules. No more secrets.

Together. Finally.

The store was quiet as she and Ash lay next to each other in the tent, cuddled close under a blanket he'd stolen from the storeroom, heartbeats slowing after a second round of lovemaking. The twinkle lights looked like stars through the canvas of the tent, and the world around them had faded completely.

Kincaid felt as if they were in a dream. Had she fallen asleep? Time seemed to shift back and forth in her mind. She could picture the store around them, could see their younger selves moving through the aisles, laughing with each other, teasing. With new eyes, she could see things she hadn't before, could see her and Ash's love story unfolding. The way a teenage Ash looked at her during the in-between moments, when her eyes were squinted with laughter and he didn't think she was looking. The way he pulled books off the shelves that he knew she would like and made a monthly stack for her. Could recognize it in the times she'd work late just to hang out with him longer, felt it that first night when she'd crawled into his bed after the bad date and he'd held her with no other intention but to make her feel protected. Could see it in the pain she'd felt when she'd heard his father hurting his mom, the way her heart had ached for Ash.

She'd labeled it as friendship back then, and it was, but now she could see the layers beneath it, the foundation that had been built brick by brick. She'd always thought of love as a rush, a lightning bolt. When you knew, you knew. She'd been so wrong.

She'd been falling in love with Ash for a very long time. Maybe from the first day she'd met him in grade school. She just hadn't understood what that feeling had been.

Images of their time together flitted through her thoughts as she lay there next to him. The night of prom, always so hazy in her mind, drifted back to her in wisps. Her insisting that Ash go to the dance because she couldn't imagine prom without him. How she'd felt when she'd seen him in his tux. She could feel it again, that little nudge of awareness when he'd gotten into the limo and sat next to her. She could feel Graham's hand on her knee, feel the squeeze he'd given it, as if he'd sensed that, for a second, she'd thought something she shouldn't about her best friend.

A memory hit her suddenly, and she let out a gasping breath.

"You okay, baby?" Ash asked, voice sleepy.

The pictures in her mind sharpened, turned into high definition. "I asked you to dance."

Ash, who'd been lying quietly next to her, eyes closed, turned his head and looked at her. "What?"

She wet her lips, staring at the canvas but seeing the night in the gym more clearly than she ever had. The lights from the cheesy disco ball, the crowded gym, the corsage on her wrist. Graham had asked her to marry him, and she'd felt giddy and scared at the same time. She'd wanted to tell Ash, get his opinion, but then she'd seen him standing there in his tux without his date, hands in his pockets, eyes on her. She'd felt his stare as if it'd been a touch, and a wave of longing had gone through her. One that had flat-out terrified her because she wasn't supposed to feel things like that for her best friend. She was in love with someone else. But she'd walked across the room anyway. "At prom, a slow song came on, one we both liked, and I asked you to dance."

His arm tightened around her. "I remember."

She could see the moment like a movie. The way Ash had looked at her, the flash of pain in his eyes, the way his gaze had shifted away. "You said no."

He took a moment to respond. "I know."

"Why?"

He let out a breath. "So many reasons. I didn't trust myself not to reveal how I felt about you. I was good at hiding it, but that night, the wall I'd put up was crumbling. If we danced, if I held you against me, I was going to ruin prom for you. Make a scene."

She closed her eyes, the realization hitting her like a gut punch. "I wanted you to say yes."

"What?" He shifted onto his side and propped his head on his hand to look down at her.

She met his gaze, her heartbeat thumping hard. "I'm remembering, Ash. I can see prom. Pieces of it."

Concern creased his face, and he pushed a stray hair away from her eyes. "KC…"

"I wanted you to say yes because that was the first night I was having doubts," she said, speaking in a rush now.

"Doubts?"

"Yes. Graham had asked me to marry him, and I think it triggered something. I knew saying yes meant saying no to every other future possibility." She pressed her hand to her forehead. "I realized I wanted you to be a possibility."

Ash's gaze searched hers, a line between his brows. "What do you mean?"

She closed her eyes, inhaled, the full memory rushing back at her. The moment in the hall, the argument, the confusion. Ash pleading with her not to go home with Graham.

Then the kiss. That *kiss*. The shock of being grabbed by her best friend and feeling his lips on hers, feeling his feelings for her pouring into it. The panic fading, the warmth building.

The devastation when they broke apart and Ash had started lying to Graham, when she'd thought it hadn't been real, that Ash had just been proving a point.

Tears burned beneath her lids and she opened her eyes, Ash hazy in her watery vision but a shot of awareness going through her that filled in gaps that had been empty so long.

Ash was frowning in confusion. "KC, what is it?"

She shook her head in wonder, feeling as if a piece of herself had been put back in place. "I kissed you back."

Ash gave her a half smile. "I know. I think you forgot it was me for a second."

"No, I didn't," she said. "I kissed you back because I felt it. Because I wanted it to be true."

His eyebrows lifted in question.

"I wanted it to be real. I wanted it to be *you*."

Awareness dawned on Ash's face. "KC…"

"The moment you kissed me changed everything. If all three of us had walked out of prom, I wouldn't have been able to go back, to unfeel what was there between us." She looked at him, the reality of it locking into place. "It would've been you. It was always going to be you."

His eyes shone with tears.

A long moment passed as a pang of sadness went through her. "I'm sorry I didn't remember," she said softly. "All these years…"

He pressed his fingers over her lips and shook his head. "We weren't ready for each other then. We wouldn't be the people we are now if we had gotten together so young. We would have messed it up." He touched his nose to hers. "You needed to get idiot cowboys out of your system to realize bookish dorks are totally where it's at."

She laughed. "Bookish dorks are my favorite."

"You're my favorite," he said, no jest in his voice.

She looked up at him, at his handsome face, at the love in his eyes, her heart feeling too big for her chest. "Is it time for our happily-ever-after yet?"

He pressed a kiss to her cheek and then whispered against her ear, "Once upon a time, there was a feisty little girl named Kincaid who met this awkward little boy when she was out walking one day. She adopted him as her friend on sight, and he knew his life would never be the same…"

Yes. It was just about time.

epilogue

ONE YEAR LATER

"We should've gotten fireworks." Kincaid frowned at the wreath she'd hung on the door of the B and B. "Or maybe a marching band. I bet the high school band would work for a small donation. They could do Christmas carols and the fight song." She turned to her husband. "Or maybe..."

Ash, who was on a ladder hanging the last of the Christmas lights, peeked at her over his shoulder. "I think Barry and Beula would veto fireworks and the band. We might give them little goat heart attacks."

Kincaid peered out at the two goats munching on a nearby bush, their little tails twitching happily. "Yeah, you're right. Don't want to scare the kids."

He chuckled as he climbed down from the ladder. "You never get tired of that joke. I don't think they're technically kids anymore."

"They'll always be kids to me." She walked over and

wrapped her arms around Ash's waist. "So you don't think I need more flash and sparkle this weekend?"

Ash smiled, his jaw shadowed with sexy winter scruff, and kissed her. "I think you're all the sparkle the grand opening is going to need. You've invited the whole town, your friends have tapped into all their networks, and I confirmed that two travel-and-leisure reporters from Austin are coming. You're going to wow them with the menu, the accommodations, and your charm."

She sighed, her nerves still hopping in her belly. "You really think so?"

He kissed the tip of her nose. "How could they not be wowed? You're completely irresistible."

She grinned. "I think you may be a little biased, cupcake. I sleep with you."

"Nope. It's a scientific fact," he declared. "We're already booked up for Valentine's weekend. I have a feeling after the opening celebration, word is going to get out and we're going to have a packed house all the time."

"Mmm," she said, picturing the B and B filled with happy guests. "A packed house. No more sex on the living room floor."

He laughed. "This is why we're closed one week each month. That's living-room sex week."

"Ah." She nodded. "I'll mark that down on the calendar."

He kissed her again, but they were interrupted by the sound of a car coming up the drive. She lifted her head and smiled at the parade of vehicles making its way to the farmhouse.

Ash released her. "Looks like we're officially open for business."

Kincaid clapped her hands together and let out a little squeal of delight. She was looking forward to the official grand opening this weekend, but she was even more excited about this very unofficial one. She hurried down the steps as the cars parked in the spaces at the side of the house.

Liv and Finn were the first out. Finn had his arm around Liv's waist as they walked over, but Liv's wide-eyed gaze was on the freshly painted farmhouse and all its holiday decorations. "Oh my God, Kincaid. This looks amazing!"

Kincaid bounced on her toes. "*Right?*" She'd banned her friends from coming by the house for the last month as the final renovations were completed. She wasn't about to miss an opportunity for a big reveal. She felt like she was on one of those home improvement shows. She was just missing the big sign or tarp blocking the house to do the voilà. "No more haunted house."

Liv came over and gave her a tight hug. "This is unbelievable, *chica*. I'm so freaking proud of you."

Kincaid's throat tightened, but she was not going to cry right now. This was a happy moment. She didn't want to give the house tour with Alice Cooper mascara streaks down her face. "Thanks, sugar."

More arms went around them as Taryn joined in and made it a group hug. "You did it, girl!"

The two women released Kincaid, and Rebecca and Wes walked up. Rebecca gave Kincaid a quick hug and then leaned back and shook her head. "This looks fantastic. Wow."

Kincaid curtsied and smiled. "Thank you very much."

Liv leaned into Finn, grinning her way. "We never had any doubt, you know?"

Kincaid snort-laughed. "Oh, hush your mouth, Olivia Arias. You thought I'd bought a demon portal."

Liv lifted a finger. "But I knew if you survived the hell beasts, you would totally make this place gorgeous. Full confidence, I tell ya. Full confidence."

Kincaid rolled her eyes, and affection welled up for her friends. Despite the teasing, she knew that they'd believed in her. Even if they thought she'd made a crazy decision, they'd rallied behind her. That was what friends did. They supported you in your crazy and held out their arms to catch you if it didn't work out.

Shaw took Taryn's hands and smiled Kincaid's way. "The place really does look great. I've handed out flyers to everyone at the gym. I'll be sending some people your way."

"And we've been tucking those coupons for a discounted stay in with the meals at the food truck," Wes added as he wrapped his arms around Rebecca from behind.

Kincaid pressed a hand over her heart. "You guys. You don't have to—"

"We do." Taryn reached out and squeezed her hand. "That's what family does. We want to watch your dream come true."

Ash stepped up behind Kincaid and put his hands on her shoulders. She leaned back in to him and smiled at all her friends. "It already has."

A few years ago, she'd agreed to participate in a documentary about the shooting because she thought the victims' stories deserved to be told, to be heard. She had no idea that night when she'd sat at a table with these women—seeing them for the first time in twelve years and reading the time-capsule letters they'd written—that her life was going to change in the best way possible.

They'd all needed healing. They'd all needed hope. But none of them had realized what they needed most of all—each other. Kincaid had spent the last year enjoying every moment in the newest part of her fairy tale, loving and being loved by Ash. But that wasn't the only love story in her life. Without these women, she never would've been able to break out of the cycle she'd been in.

These women had taught her what real love felt like, had shown her the kind of love she deserved. That was why she'd been able to finally recognize it when Ash came back into her life. Her heart couldn't be fuller, and she had the people in front of her to thank.

She hoped they liked her gift.

"So," she said, choking back the emotion so she didn't turn into a blubbering mess. "Ready to see the place?"

Taryn pressed her hands together and grinned. "Bring it on."

Ash took Kincaid's hand, and they led the group up the front stairs and onto the porch. The boards still squeaked a little, but that only made Kincaid smile. Silent boards had no personality, no stories to tell. A line of white rocking chairs had been added and they swayed in the slight breeze.

Kincaid turned the knob on the front door, the little bells on the Christmas wreath tinkling as she opened the door. Inside, the air was warm from the fire in the hearth and smelled of the cinnamon rolls she'd baked for her VIP guests' arrival. A large Christmas tree filled a corner of the living room, the white lights dancing in time to the instrumental holiday music she had playing.

Her friends filed in behind her into the foyer, and Kincaid reveled in their gasps and sounds of delight like it was the most delicious cake. She knew the place was beautiful. She'd worked hard over the last year to get every detail just right. The vision from her dream was spread out before her like a postcard. She barely resisted pinching herself to make sure she was awake.

Her friends oohed and aahed and roamed around, taking in all the little differences and upgrades, and Ash stayed at her side, his fingers intertwined with hers. "You doing okay, gorgeous?"

She leaned her head against his shoulder. "I'm perfect."

He kissed the top of her head. "Truth."

She smiled, and they headed into the living room. After her friends had explored the kitchen and dining area, she gathered them up at the bottom of the stairs. "Ready for me to show you to your rooms?"

Liv swept her arm toward the stairs. "Lead the way, lady of the house."

Kincaid and Ash led them upstairs, her heartbeat picking up speed. Her friends would be her first guests. The most important ones of all. She guided the group to the far end of the hall, and Ash handed her a bag he'd stashed in a corner.

Kincaid stood in front of the group and cleared her throat, her fingers worrying the handles of the bag.

"When I bought this place, it was on impulse. I think I was looking for something I thought I'd never really have. All my life, I've lived alone. Even when my mom was under the same roof, I was by myself. There were no family dinners. There were no movie nights curled up on the couch. There was no place that felt welcome and safe."

Rebecca's eyes softened with empathy.

"So all my life, I've worked hard to surround myself with people. To be the center of attention, the life of the party, the popular girl. If people were talking to me, I wasn't alone. If I was helping someone or meddling in their love lives as I've been known to do…"

Liv smirked.

"I was part of something. I had a scrap to hold onto." She blinked, her tears trying to spill.

Ash's hand slipped around her waist, giving her hip a squeeze.

"But as I put this place back together, as I built the dream I thought I couldn't have, I realized I already had it." She looked at the faces of her friends. "This place is just walls and pretty decorations. The night you three ladies came back into my life is when I got the map." She smiled, her tears sneaking out. "You helped me find my way home."

Her friends stared at her, and then Liv pressed her fingers to her lips, her dark eyes going shiny. "Dammit, woman. Are you trying to kill us?"

Taryn smiled, a tear slipping down her cheek. "She is." She swiped at her face. "And you know you did that for us, too, right?"

Kincaid shook her head.

Rebecca wasn't letting her get away with the denial. "She's right. You helped us find our dreams first. We may have had a map, but you were the compass. You pointed us in the right direction."

"Or kicked our asses when we didn't go the right way," Liv added.

"You even kicked my ass once," Finn said with a smirk. "And I kick ass for a living."

Kincaid laughed, the sound coming out choked.

"We love you, girl," Taryn said. "You know that."

Kincaid nodded, the power of that filling her. "I know. I really do." She dabbed at her eyes. "And that's why I wanted to give y'all this." She reached into the bag, her hand trembling a little, and pulled out the three engraved plaques.

"What are those?" Liv asked, eyeing the plaques.

Kincaid stepped away from Ash and opened the door to the first guest room. "It's to hang outside the room." She handed Liv the plaque with her name engraved on it. "This room is the Olivia."

Liv looked down at the little sign and then peeked into the room. Kincaid had decorated the space with mostly white decor and just a hint of green. She hadn't wanted to distract from the real showpiece of the room. Liv's gorgeous photography hung on every wall. Liv gasped. "Oh my God."

"Anytime someone rents the room, they'll have the option to buy your art," Kincaid said. "And a portion of the revenue from renting the room will go to the Long Acre fund in your name. Plus, it's free for you and Finn whenever."

Liv's eyes widened. "Oh, *chica*."

Kincaid left Liv to take a closer look at the room and continued down the hall. She gave Rebecca her plaque and opened another door. "This is the Rebecca." She had done this room in warm and cozy colors and added a bookshelf filled with Rebecca's favorite books. "A portion of the proceeds from this room will go to you and Wes's teen program. And of course, the room is always open to the two of you and the kiddo for free. I'll even let Knight come over if he promises not to chase my goats."

Wes laughed. "No promises on that last one."

"And if you need someone to watch baby Simone while you're here, you know Aunt Kincaid is down for the job," she added.

Wes got to Kincaid before Rebecca and gave her a bear hug. "You're amazing."

Rebecca joined in on the hug. "What he said."

Finally, Kincaid led Taryn down to her room. She opened the door to a room done in cool blues and grays. An acoustic guitar sat on a stand in the corner. "And the Taryn," Kincaid said. "A portion of the proceeds from this room goes to your school program. And of course, I'm stealing baby Nathaniel when you visit because I won't be able to resist his cuteness while he's in the same house."

"Oh wow," Taryn breathed. "I love it so much. And I think my kid loves you more than me, so he'll be totally down with that plan."

Kincaid snorted. That was definitely not true. Taryn and Shaw's son was the happiest and most energetic baby she'd ever been around. And when he looked at his momma, it was like he believed angels existed.

Kincaid looked down the hall at her friends standing in front of each of their respective rooms. They'd all turned toward her, their husbands at their sides.

"So," she said, smiling, "all this to say, you are my family. There is always room here for you. You are my home. Now you can go and christen your rooms."

Her friends gathered around her, hugging her and telling her they loved her. As soon as they released each other, the excited chatter started up again, and the women dragged their guys into their rooms to explore.

Kincaid took a deep breath, feeling high on friendship love.

A delighted laugh came from down the hall in Liv's room, doors shut, and the squeak of a bed sounded from another. Ash turned to her. "I think they like them."

"You think? I'm not done yet, though."

"What?"

Kincaid took his hand, leading him to the last room. "Just one more room."

"What are we going to call this one?" he asked, peering in.

She stepped inside the room and grabbed what she'd stashed behind the door. She handed him the last plaque. He gave her a startled look. "The Ashton? I don't need my own room, KC. I plan to spend every night in *the Kincaid*."

She snorted. "Never with that joke again. That was your one allowance and now it's used up."

He chuckled. "No promises."

She pressed her hand over the plaque. "I wanted to give this room your name. A percentage of proceeds from this room are going to the local women's shelter."

He blinked at her, and then the meaning dawned on him. His features softened. "KC."

She looped her arms around his neck and gave him a serious look. "I know it hurts you that you can't help your mother like you want, but that doesn't mean we can't help at all. The money you got from your parents built this place, but I want it to do more. I want it to help people like your mom."

He gave her a tender look that nearly broke her in two. He cupped her face and kissed her gently. "Did anyone ever tell you that you are the most wonderful woman in the whole world?"

She smiled. "All the time. Every day. I was thinking of getting a name tag with that on it."

"You should," he said and kissed her again. "Because it's absolutely true. I love you, Kincaid Breslin Isaacs."

She pressed her cheek against his chest as he embraced her. "I love you back, writer boy. Forever."

—◆◆◆—

Hours later, the farmhouse was dark and quiet except for the wind rustling the trees outside. The scent of the roast Kincaid had made for dinner hung in the air, and moonlight shone through the windows. Ash was sleeping soundly at her side, the covers thrown off him and his chest rising and falling in the silver light. She leaned over and gave him a barely there kiss on his shoulder. He stirred a little but didn't wake up.

Kincaid peeked at the clock. One in the morning. It was time.

She climbed out of the plush four-poster bed and tugged on pajama pants and wool-lined booties. She grabbed a bag from the closet where she'd stored what she needed and then quietly exited the room. The hallway was dimly lit and empty.

As part of the remodel, they'd sectioned off the owners' suite and a few rooms of their own on the first floor for privacy. She padded down the hall in silence and stepped into the main part of the house. The lights still glowed on the Christmas tree, and a few electric candles were flickering.

She looked out the window and saw the lick of real flames. She smiled, grabbed her coat, and slipped out the front door. The night sky was crystal clear, filled with stars, and a full moon shone down on them. She could remember a night so much like this fifteen years ago when she and her friends had written those letters, shoved them in a jar, and buried their hopes.

Of course the universe would give them another night like this. She made her way down the porch stairs, and Rebecca lifted a hand in greeting from the far side of the firepit. Four Adirondack chairs surrounded the newly built firepit and only one was left open.

Kincaid hurried over. "Am I late?"

Liv, who was dressed in candy-cane Christmas pajamas, shook her head. "Nah, we're early. I heard Taryn sneaking down the hall, and we all ended up coming down together."

"Stealth is not my forte," Taryn said with a sleepy smile.

Kincaid set down her bags and took her seat. "I brought the supplies."

Taryn dug inside one of the bags. "Ooh, marshmallows. But more importantly"—she pulled a bottle out of the bag—"Kincaid's famous homemade spiked eggnog."

"Score," Rebecca said, lifting a fist in the air.

Kincaid passed around red Solo cups, and they poured their drinks. The firelight flickered over her friends' faces, making them look alive and almost magical. "Did everybody bring the most important thing?"

"Yep." Liv pulled a folded square of paper out of her pocket. Rebecca grabbed one from the inside pocket of her robe. And Taryn had hers tucked under her thigh.

Kincaid pulled her crinkly sheet of paper from her pajama pocket. "All right. I think it's time."

She stared down at the letter in her hand. She'd written the words on that page over a decade ago. At the time, she'd put on a brave face. *We're going to take the universe by storm. We're going to make something of our lives. We're going to honor those we lost.* The time-capsule letters had been her idea. But she'd never felt so lost and alone as when she had written hers. Her boyfriend had been murdered. Her best friend had left her. And her whole world was burning down around her.

But still, impulsive as she was, she'd made promises she didn't truly believe she could keep. Her letter was filled with declarations of future success and happiness and love. She wasn't going to let those shooters change her. She wasn't going to let the fingerprints of tragedy mar her life. She was going to live every day as if it were her last. She was going to win.

She didn't believe it then.

But sometimes her brash, impulsive self knew what it was doing. She and her friends had put a call out to the universe, and it had answered.

She had a home. She had her friends. And now, she had her soul mate.

Love. It all came back to love.

She looked around at her friends' faces—Liv, Rebecca, Taryn. "You ready, ladies?"

The three of them smiled victorious smiles.

"Let's do this," Liv said.

At the same time, they all leaned forward, holding their brittle loose-leaf pages over the fire, and watched as the flames licked up and caught the paper in its fingers. The edges of the paper blackened, and Kincaid dropped her letter into the fire.

All four letters caught fire in front of them. The words disappearing. Promises made. Promises kept.

On this day, I, Olivia Arias…

I, Rebecca Lindt…

I, Taryn Landry…

I, Kincaid Breslin…

Promise the Class of 2005 that I will not waste the second chance that I have been given, that I will honor all the people we lost by living my life to the fullest…

That we will not give in. That we will not give up. That we will love.

Taryn lifted her cup of eggnog. "To the next chapter."

They all raised their glasses. "To us."

The letters turned to ash, and they drank and laughed and told stories until the first rays of sunlight peeked over the horizon. When they couldn't keep their eyes open any longer, one by one, they rose from their chairs, went inside to the warmth of the house, and crawled into bed with the men they loved.

Happy.

Strong.

Survivors.

THE END

acknowledgments

First, thank you, dear reader, for going on this journey with me. I hope you've enjoyed spending time with these characters as much as I've enjoyed writing about them. This series has been a special one to me, and I'll be sad to leave these four ladies behind, but I hope you'll join me on the next bookish adventure. There are more happily-ever-afters to come.

To Donnie and Marsh, my personal rock stars, who keep me from taking life or myself too seriously. You make me laugh, you play awesome music for me, and you both make me proud. I couldn't ask for a better family.

To my parents, who I'd want to hang out with even if we weren't related.

To Dawn, who I could ask "What would Kincaid do?" in a scene, and she would always know. I'm glad I have my own Kincaid in my life. ;)

To Genny, for your dry sense of humor and your no-nonsense advice.

To my agent, Sara Megibow, who has championed my books for a decade now. Thanks for always being in my corner.

To my editor, Cat Clyne, who helps makes these books the best they can be. Thank you not just for your expertise but for your enthusiastic comments in the edits. They never fail to make me grin.

And finally, to the whole Sourcebooks team, thank you for being fully behind these books. This series wouldn't be what it is without y'all.